THE RELUCTANT DUKE'S DILEMMA

Book 1 of The Hope Clinic

TRISHA MESSMER

DEDICATION

For all those who have defied convention for the sake of love.

CONTENTS

ACKNOWLEDGMENTS

As with any creative process, I have many people to thank.

First and foremost to my family, whose love and support have gotten me through many rough days.

To my online critique group at Critique Circle, whose encouragement and occasional slap alongside my head kept me on track and going. To Ellie for hounding me about adverbs and prodding me to use comparisons specific to the character's personality. To Felicity my lovely British critique partner who slapped me upside the head when I said something too modern or "gasp" too American. To Vanessa for reminding me to dig deep into the character's feelings and thoughts. To Clarissa for pushing me to use fragments when necessary. To Jessica, for understanding the psyche of Margaret and for being my cheerleader. When I started this story, I didn't even have the confidence I could write a historical romance and do it justice. Thanks for the push to keep at it, giving me the courage to try something new.

And a special shout out to Brad Jenson, my one faithful male critique partner, who always let me know if I did something stupid with Harry. You kept Harry "real," and for that I'll be forever grateful. He's a better hero because of you, my friend.

Thank you all for making this book better, and for making me a better writer.

CHAPTER 1—UNEXPECTED FREEDOM

KENT, ENGLAND, JULY 1822

Margaret grabbed the balustrade and stared down at her husband, George Alistair Radcliffe, the Duke of Ashton. He lay face down, motionless, at the foot of the long staircase.

Candles from the wall sconces flickered in the late-night darkness, casting dancing shadows across his body and playing cruel tricks on her eyes. The smell of burnt cotton from a single extinguished wick swirled in the air. But no breeze stirred.

She blinked, clearing her vision. *Did his hand move?* Instinct overruled reason, and she primed herself to run if he rose, knowing full well he would come after her and there was nowhere to hide. He had keys to every room.

"Your Grace?" she called, her voice barely more than a whisper. Nothing.

Her grip relaxed—but only minimally. Breath still trapped in her lungs, she exhaled and forced out the name he forbade her to use. "George?"

Nothing.

The tension in her muscles eased, replaced first by a warmth, which spread through her body, then a giddiness as though a flock of birds had taken flight in her chest.

One by one, her fingers released their grip, and she compelled her feet to move. Reluctant to remove her gaze from the figure below, she backed up, one step at a time, across the hallway to the nearest room until she reached the bell pull to summon the servants. After giving it a strong tug with a shaking hand, she prayed her loyal butler, Burrows, would answer the call.

An eerie silence filled the massive house, the only sound her telltale heart pounding a rapid tattoo in her chest. She jumped as the clock in the entrance tolled two-o'clock, the noise reverberating its hollow echo.

All moisture seemed to have been pulled from her mouth, and she licked her lips, tasting the saltiness of her own perspiration. It beaded her forehead and trickled down her neck as she resumed her position at the balustrade and waited.

The clock chimed the quarter hour as long minutes passed until Burrows appeared. Remarkably put together for this ungodly hour, only his disheveled white hair betrayed his disrupted slumber. He shuffled toward the staircase, then jolted to a halt and lowered the candle he held to better illuminate the floor. After a quick glance up to Margaret, he bent down to the prostrate duke.

Margaret clutched the pale-blue satin wrapper tightly to her slight frame and moved unbidden down the steps. Her breath once again remained trapped and unwilling to release, as her heart continued its unrelenting pounding.

She met Burrows' eyes, grateful he didn't give voice to the questions they held.

He placed a wrinkled hand on the duke's shoulder and nudged his employer. "Your Grace?" After laying his candle down, he rolled the body over. Cold, lifeless eyes stared up at the ceiling.

Her knees buckled, and she reached for the banister to steady herself.

"Is he . . ." Unable to utter the word, she waited for Burrows' confirmation.

"Dead, Your Grace." The butler's words were liberating.

Hope expanded in her chest as it broke out of its prison. Tears of relief streaked down her cheeks, and a shaky laugh from deep within begged for escape. She was free.

CHAPTER 2—UNEXPECTED NEWS

BOSTON, AMERICA, APRIL 1823

Exhaustion threatened to overtake Dr. Harrison Radcliffe as he lumbered into his spartan office at the Boston Dispensary. Barely large enough to hold a desk and a chair, the room served as a respite when he wasn't treating patients. He splashed his face with water from a bowl on a table, then collapsed into the chair at his desk, satisfied with a job well done.

An explosion on the docks the day before had required every available physician and surgeon to tend the wounded. Mr. Lampley had been the last of Harry's patients from the disaster. The delicate operation shouldn't have been difficult, but Harry had been awake for eighteen hours when it began. Lack of sleep adversely affected his concentration, and he had stilled his shaking hands more than once as he cut through the flesh.

Now, two hours later, he could rest.

He'd barely closed his eyes when a cacophony of voices erupted from outside his inner sanctuary.

"You can't go in there!" Sister Ursula's formidable voice rang through the air. "He's resting."

"I've got urgent news," a man said. "I'm supposed to deliver it personally."

"Give it to me, I'll see he gets it." Sister Ursula's overly large frame blocked the office entrance.

"It's fine, Sister," Harry said, his voice calm, belying his annoyance at the interruption. He straightened to receive his visitor.

Sister Ursula swiveled to face him. "I tried to tell him, Doctor. You need your rest."

Harry waved the overbearing, but lovable, nun out of the way. "Let the man in, Sister."

Sister Ursula moved aside, her fists resting firmly on her hips, poised to hoist the man out at a moment's notice.

The rail-thin man's clothes were in tatters. He reeked from the smell of alcohol mingled with the pungent odor of urine. Harry observed the slow-healing scrapes on the man's hands—scabbed but still red and swollen—and his sallow skin and instinctively diagnosed malnutrition.

"What's your name?" Harry asked.

As the man shuffled forward, the odor grew stronger, and Harry had the urge to spit out the foul taste the stench created.

"Jeremiah, sir." He held out an envelope with an unsteady hand. "The postmaster told me to wait, said you may need to reply."

The words *Urgent, deliver immediately* were scrawled on the envelope. Fingers breaking the seal, Harry opened the missive, and his eyes scanned the contents. The date at the top read July 16, 1822, the news—devastating.

The salutation alone caused him to stiffen and his heart to plummet.

My Lord Duke,
*   It is with utmost regret I inform you of the death of your brother, George Radcliffe, Duke of Ashton.*

Harry raked a hand through his hair and slumped in his chair. His mind struggled to comprehend the remaining words as the correspondence dropped to the desk. *Nine months. Nine months to get a letter.*

He sighed and removed a sheet of foolscap from his desk drawer. After writing his response, he folded the letter, addressed it, withdrew a half dollar coin from his pocket, and handed everything to Jeremiah. "Use what they need for the postage and keep the rest."

Jeremiah's eyes bulged at the amount. "Thank you, sir, thank you."

Harry grimaced at Jeremiah's toothless grin. The man would most likely visit the nearest tavern rather than purchase a nourishing meal. "And Jeremiah, don't spend it on drink. Buy some food."

Sister Ursula scowled at the man before she turned her glare on Harry. "You need to go home and get some rest, Doctor."

A heaviness borne from more than exhaustion weighed him down. His heart beat a slow, dull thud in his chest. All his hopes and dreams shattered in one cruel twist of fate. With nine months already passed, he could hardly delay the inevitable.

Harry dragged his body from the chair and rose. "I *am* going home, Sister."

Satisfied, she crossed her arms over her vast bosom. "And don't you be sneaking back here to check on Mr. Lampley. I'll keep an eye on him."

"I know you will, Sister."

Grabbing his medical bag, he moved away from his desk.

"Doctor," Sister Ursula said, her expression softening. "The letter, was it bad news?"

"The worst, Sister."

Hands back on her hips, she stood blocking the door again. "Well, are you going to tell me?"

Harry ran a hand down his face; exhaustion had displaced his usual exemplary manners.

"Forgive me, Sister. I'll send word to Dr. Michaels to take over my patients, but I won't be returning. When I said I'm going home, I meant to England. I'm the new Duke of Ashton."

CHAPTER 3—HOME

The sea churned, thrashing the ship back and forth—Harry's stomach with it. Salty spray dotted his face, the tang adding to his nausea as he leaned over the railing and lost his meager breakfast. The evacuation of his stomach's contents did little to ease his queasiness. Cold sweat beaded his forehead, and his mouth, fouled from retching, remained clammy.

One week had passed since he'd left Boston harbor, and, according to the captain, six more remained. When he had made the voyage from England seven years ago, he had hoped never to repeat it. Yet, here he was, going home.

A foreign word, home. In truth, he missed England, even the dreary weather. Life in America had proven hard but rewarding, leaving little time to reminisce over the past. He didn't miss the self-important *ton* with its rules and arrogance. Now, as duke, he would be mired in it, knee deep, with no escape except death.

Yet duty compelled him to return, to fulfill a promise made—what seemed—so long ago.

His stomach roiled, and he leaned over the railing again and heaved, but nothing remained to provide the hungry, angry sea.

"Doctor," someone called.

Harry's head snapped up and around, finding the captain's solemn gaze.

"I have an injured man who requires attention. Come with me, if you please."

Harry followed the captain through the bowels of the ship, stumbling and reaching for purchase each time it pitched and lurched. He envied the captain's grace as he navigated the vessel's corridors to the seamen's quarters.

"Where's the ship's surgeon?"

"He's who's wounded. Jack, one of my crew, broke his leg when he fell off the rigging. He was drunk. When Dr. Somersby set his leg, Jack knifed him. He's a mean drunk."

Harry's eyes widened. "Is Jack confined?"

The captain nodded. "In the brig."

Screams preceded the sight of the injured doctor surrounded by his shipmates. The men parted upon their captain's approach.

The stench of unwashed bodies assaulted Harry's nostrils.

He fought back the resurgent nausea and pulled the surgeon's blood-stained shirt aside to assess the wound. The deep laceration located low in his abdomen oozed blood.

The captain stepped closer. "Can you help him?"

Unsure if the foul odor in the confined room could be isolated to the patient or to the conditions in general, Harry shook his head and turned grave eyes on the captain. "I'll try. If the knife lacerated his bowel . . ."

"Do what you can."

OBDURATE WORDS TAUNTED HIM. NO MATTER HOW MANY TIMES Harry read the missive, the message remained unchanged. He lowered the letter—resisting the urge to crumple it—when his patient groaned.

Harry placed his hand on the man's forehead. Warm, but not hot. Mercifully, it had appeared the bowel remained intact, so Harry had simply stitched and dressed the wound.

"Water," his patient croaked.

Harry lifted a cup to the surgeon's parched lips. "Just a sip."

"How bad?" he asked, his voice still cracking from dryness.

"Better than it could have been. A deep laceration, mainly tissue and muscle damage, but thankfully it missed your organs and intestines. So barring infection, you should make a full recovery, Dr. Somersby."

"Oliver, please. You have me at a disadvantage, sir."

"Harrison Radcliffe—Harry."

Harry lifted the cup, allowing Oliver another sip.

"You're . . . English?" Oliver said. "Going home?"

"Save your strength." Harry placed the cup down and sat next to his patient. "Yes."

Oliver's eyes flitted toward the letter as Harry folded and tucked it into his pocket, then rose again to meet Harry's. "You appear upset. Does the letter contain distressing news?"

Harry flinched at the question, his eyes darting away from Oliver's gaze.

"My apologies. I've no right to pry. Shall we speak of the weather instead?"

Compassion flowed from understanding as Harry realized Oliver wished for a distraction from the pain. Discussion of the weather simply would not suffice. He removed the letter from his coat and unfolded it for the eighth time, the idea of sharing his news somehow comforting.

"Yes, bad news, I'm afraid, and the reason for my return home. My brother has died."

"Terrible news, indeed, sir. My condolences."

Harry nodded. "Unfortunately, that's not the worst of it."

Oliver lifted an eyebrow, waiting for Harry to continue.

"George, my brother, was the Duke of Ashton. I'm his heir."

Oliver's raised brow nearly reached his scalp, and he tried to rise in deference until Harry pushed him back onto the bed. "Pardon? Is the estate in dire straits?" Oliver winced. "I'm not sure I understand, Your Grace."

Harry gave a derisive chuckle. "I've no idea of the financial status of my inheritance. It's the 'Your Grace' part that distresses me."

He pulled a flask from his pocket and handed it to Oliver. "Just a sip." After retrieving the flask, Harry took his own small sip, the whiskey providing the courage he sought to continue his tale. "I left England when my father died. My brother, George, assumed the responsibilities of duke leaving me free to pursue my passion, something my father discouraged."

"To be a physician?"

Harry nodded and took another sip of whiskey. "Father frowned upon his sons working. George agreed, so he turned a blind eye when I left home, washing his hands of me."

"You weren't close?"

Another derisive chuckle. "It depends on your definition of close. But if you mean was there affection, no, at least none on his part."

"And yours?"

A shoulder lifted in a quick shrug. "At first, but George had a talent for killing any affection anyone had for him."

"So you were the spare? He had no wife or sons?"

Harry glanced at the letter. "A wife. To be precise, I'm the heir presumptive as there were no sons at the time of his death. By the time I arrive home, I should know for certain."

Oliver motioned toward the flask. "May I?"

"One more sip," Harry said handing Oliver the whiskey. "Then try to sleep."

BLESSEDLY, THANKS TO CALMER SEAS, THE SHIP ARRIVED IN London's port three days earlier than predicted. After exchanging goodbyes with Oliver, who had recovered fully, Harry spent a restful night at a London inn, before leaving for Kent the next morning. Grateful to be on dry land, his shaking legs would never have permitted the day's trip on horseback. No matter, he was in no hurry.

Although the presumed Duke of Ashton, he concealed his identity and hired a coach requesting to be its sole passenger. Prior to boarding, his intention was waylaid when a young couple approached the coachman, pleading for passage.

"Be off with you! The gentleman here has asked to be the only passenger and has paid me handsomely for the privilege," the coachman said.

The young woman sagged against the man who wrapped an arm around her waist and said, "Dinna worry, we'll find a way home."

Harry's chest constricted, and his skin prickled with guilt upon witnessing the disappointment on the couple's faces. "Let's make an exception for them, shall we?"

George would have frowned over his gesture which made it even more satisfying.

Gratitude brightened the young man's face and warmed Harry's heart. "Thank ye, sir, thank ye." The young man reached into his pocket to pay the coachman, and Harry observed the man's carefully patched waistcoat and scuffed boots.

Harry met the coachman's gaze. "My payment covers their fare, does it not, sir?"

The coachman nodded his agreement. "Indeed, it does, sir."

Once settled inside the coach, they made their introductions. "Owen MacDougall," the man held out his hand. "And this is my wife, Lily." Owen's other arm wrapped around his wife's waist and gave her an affectionate tug, pulling her close to his side.

"I thought I detected a Scottish burr. Harry Radcliffe. Pleased to meet you." Harry offered a warm smile, shook Owen's hand, and tipped his hat to Mrs. MacDougall. The girl looked no older than eighteen, her husband barely older. "Are you newly wed?"

The couple beamed at each other. "Is it that obvious?" Owen asked, his eyes never leaving his wife's blushing face.

"Simply that you appear so in love."

"Aye, that we are," Owen said, the smile on his face stretching from ear to ear. He pivoted toward Harry. "Although I fear our love will be tested when we inform my wife's family."

Harry's eyes widened. "They don't know?"

Owen shook his head. "No, they dinna approve of me, so we eloped tae Gretna Green."

"Your family lives in Kent?" Harry asked Mrs. MacDougall.

"Yes. Is Kent home for you as well, sir?"

"It is. May I ask your family's name?"

"Morrison, sir." Lily paused, her head cocked as if studying Harry. "You said your name is Radcliffe? Are you related to the Duke of Ashton?"

Twisting in his seat, Harry evaded the question. "In a manner of speaking." The name Morrison sounded familiar. "Did you know the duke?"

Lily's frown abated quickly, but her reaction gave her away. "I knew of him, although I never met him. My father is a tenant on his estate. The duke rarely visited, and when he did, my father sent us out."

Ah, that's where he remembered the name. She would have been a mere child when he left for America. "How did a lad from Scotland meet a young woman from Kent?"

Owen grinned. "God above had His hand in it, he did. I traveled down with my brother from Edinburgh by boat tae Ramsgate. We go down once a year in the summer tae sell our goods. My brother makes the finest whiskey ye'd ever drink. Lily was in the shop looking so pretty, I couldn't help but buy her the trinket she was admiring. I think she stole my heart that verra day."

Harry smiled at the tale. "So, are you returning to tell your family of your marriage?"

"Aye," Owen said, Lily's hand clasped in his own, "and it breaks my heart tae think she will have tae choose between us."

"I will always choose you, Owen." Lily's eyes shimmered with emotion, and Harry resolved to meet with the Morrisons as his first order of business. Perhaps a word from the new duke would help the young couple.

Envious of their freedom to marry for love, Harry had hoped for the same, but that hope died the moment he received the letter summoning him home.

If his memory remained true, finding a love match with an intelligent, spirited, and honest woman among the *ton* seemed unlikely. The Marriage Mart offered one thing, women seeking a title or wealth, women who would do whatever necessary to secure it.

His thoughts turned to his brother's widow. The words of the letter now burned in his mind, he no longer needed to read them. *Her Grace, the duchess, resides at Briarfield until your return.* The duchess. Though he'd never met her, in his mind's eye he imagined her. Cold, haughty, condescending, and heartless. Physically beautiful, no doubt—George would demand physical beauty—with an aristocratic countenance, fashionably blonde hair, and blue eyes. Eyes as cold as ice, revealing a soul as black as night. A perfect bride for his brother. He prayed his brother's will would provide a dower house for her many miles from his own. In the meantime, he would make himself scarce.

Harry had instructed the coachman to first deliver the MacDougalls to the Morrisons' doorstep, wishing them well as they departed. The coach jerked to a stop at Briarfield. A deep intake of breath fortified him as he stepped out and made his way to the front door of his childhood home. Tan and russet stone soared before him, turrets no longer used for defense had been useful hiding places for a boy. A strange mixture of nostalgia and trepidation swirled in his mind.

The door cracked open, and an elderly man waited to greet him. The man's eyes widened briefly before regaining his composure and bowing deeply. *Had no one informed him of my exact relationship to George?*

"Your Grace, welcome home." He stepped aside allowing Harry to enter. "I'm Burrows, sir, the butler."

"It's good to meet you, Burrows." *Where is Walters?*

Burrows took Harry's hat. "I hope you had a pleasant journey, Your Grace." Burrows motioned for two footmen to bring in Harry's trunks.

"I'd hesitate to call it pleasant, but I suppose it could have been worse."

Little had changed in his boyhood home, at least regarding the furnishings and ornamentation. Dark colors, heavy pieces of furniture, and gilded sconces exuded a sense of not only wealth, but gloom. Harry exhaled a deep sigh.

"Should I gather the staff, Your Grace?"

"That can wait, Burrows."

"Perhaps some tea after you refresh from your journey? I'll have the footmen take your belongings up to the main bedroom. I trust you know where to find it."

"Yes, thank you, Burrows."

Alone, Harry wandered the halls, contemplating how to adjust to his new life. A noise of something shattering, followed by an expletive caught his attention, especially considering it was a woman who uttered it. Harry traced the sounds to the library and entered to find a woman straining to reach the top shelf of books. She balanced precariously on the ladder, the broken remains of something glass on the floor beneath. As she placed a small object behind the books, Harry stepped closer, coughing to announce his presence, and she jerked around toward him removing one hand from the ladder. That had been her undoing. One look at him, and her face turned deathly white before she proceeded to fall in a dead faint.

He ran forward, hoping to catch her before she hit the floor.

CHAPTER 4—THE NEW DUKE

Margaret fidgeted while her lady's maid, Jane, dressed her hair. She had little patience for the perfect coiffure today. Besides, a simple hairstyle would support her planned excuse.

"Jane, that's fine. I'm not feeling well. The pins will make it worse. I'll remain in my room to rest."

"Another megrim, Your Grace?"

"Yes." A lie, but it proved effective to keep Jane from hovering. Although the recurring, debilitating pains in her head had become less frequent since George's death—now only occurring during her courses—she found the condition to be a useful diversion.

In the past eleven months, Margaret had increased her secret visits to Ramsgate, limiting them to once a month in order to avoid Jane's suspicion. When word had arrived late yesterday that, after a restful night in London, the new duke would be traveling to Briarfield posthaste, Margaret planned one final excursion.

Once Jane left, Margaret waited for the signaling tap—tap, tap—tap, tap, tap on her door, then hurried downstairs. Burrows stood in the foyer, holding her pelisse.

"The carriage is waiting, Your Grace. I have seen to it that Jane is occupied."

Margaret nodded and, after slipping on the pelisse, boarded the carriage, relieved as it pulled away from the house and out of sight.

She settled back on the plush seat, the early morning light streaming through the windows lifted her spirits while she contemplated her fate. With the contents of the will yet unknown, per George's instructions, worry plagued her. Had George provided the customary living for her, and if not, would the new duke show compassion?

Due to the uncertainty of her future, she hesitated replacing Jane with a more agreeable maid. She resisted hiring someone only to let them go should she be unable to afford them. In contrast, she would take great pleasure in giving Jane her leave.

Her thoughts returned to the new duke. Rumor had it he had died, but George had never mentioned him—not once, a fact Margaret found curious. *Had they had a falling out? Had his brother done something disgraceful?* The latter seemed unlikely, considering George's behavior and the ability of the *ton* to turn a blind eye to transgressions of males of the Peerage. Through the solicitor she learned his name was Harrison, but little else.

Would he raise questions concerning George's death? And most importantly, was his temperament similar to George's?

The new duke's arrival would provide answers, but in the meantime, these same questions prompted her discreet visit to a pawn shop in Ramsgate.

An hour later, a tinkling bell announced her entry into the shop, and the pawnbroker, busy with a customer, nodded his silent greeting.

"It's all I can offer, sir," the pawnbroker said to the man before him.

Shelves and tables displayed an assortment of items. Margaret sighed over the personal treasures relinquished for a few coins. She turned her back to the men on the pretext of examining a mantle clock. A small wooden doll propped next to it caught her attention. The cracked paint on its face gave a strange impression of tears, and Margaret pushed the fleeting nostalgia of girlhood from her mind. Her fingers traced the curve of the clock. It emphasized the need for expediency, and she prayed the customer would accept the offered price and move along.

She tipped her head away, keeping her back turned as the customer grumbled over the settled amount and left.

"Mr. Darrow," she said, turning to the pawnbroker.

"Your Grace, may I help you?"

She removed the jewelry from her reticule and placed them on the table before him. "I have these."

He examined them using his magnifier. "These are very fine, Your Grace. Are you sure you wish to part with them?"

She had refrained from selling these particular pieces until the last moment, worried Jane would notice them missing. Except for one item, they held little sentimental value. Her finger brushed the gold locket—a gift from her father.

"Perhaps not this one." She pulled it back and tucked it inside her reticule.

Mr. Darrow's eyes lifted. "The others are worth far more, madam. Do you not wish to keep at least one?"

She shook her head. George had given her each piece after— what he called—a loss of temper. She would say it was to assuage his guilty conscience, but she didn't believe he'd ever had one. No, it had been more to convince their acquaintances he was a generous husband. She was glad to be rid of them, and it seemed fitting the proceeds would aid her independence.

After returning from her trip to the pawnbroker, Margaret hurried to the library to hide her funds. The hiding place for the small box nestled behind a book on the top shelf had served her well over the course of her marriage. She hoped the service would continue at least while she stayed in the house.

As she stood on her toes and reached to find the hidden box, a vase blocked her way. A momentary loss of balance caused her hand to brush the vase and knock it to the floor with a resounding crash. The involuntary curse escaped her lips seconds later. Habit trapped the breath in her lungs as she waited for George's reprimand and punishment. The breath released upon remembering he could no longer harm her. Quickly finding the box, she deposited her new funds within, and slid it back into its hiding place.

Someone coughed, and she pivoted, foolishly removing her hand from the ladder. Terror gripped her, and her blood froze as she stared at the face of her husband, risen from the grave.

AN ACRID ODOR HIT HER NOSTRILS, RESULTING IN A COUGHING FIT, and her eyes flew open. Her head spun, her thoughts muddled. The figure looming before her coalesced in her foggy mind. Her gaze swung wildly, scouring the room, then traveled back to the man and the vial in his hand. She recoiled, wrapping her arms around herself.

"Take a deep breath," he said, his voice soothing. "You fainted. Almost hit the floor before I caught you."

He stood, alleviating some of her fear, only to return holding a glass of liquid. "Here, have a sip." He held the glass to her lips, his other hand lifting her head.

His position above her thwarted the overpowering urge to run. She blinked to clear her vision.

A nightmare? Nails digging into her palm, the pain confirmed she was awake.

Impossible.

He's dead. She witnessed the interment of his coffin in the family mausoleum.

Yet . . . here he was. Same blond hair, same handsome face often distorted by cruelty, same hazel eyes—cold and . . . no, not cold . . . warm, kind, concerned. Confusion filled her, her mind a morass of thoughts. She stared at the glass in his hand, her eyes narrowed in wariness. "What is it?"

His lips tugged in a small smile. "Just brandy. Sip, it will help."

This couldn't be George. He'd never allowed her to imbibe strong spirits—no matter how much she might want them, need them. Warmth spread through her as she took a tentative sip of the sweet liquid. Realization dawned. *The new duke, George's brother.*

She straightened, pulling herself upright. "Your Grace. I apologize for not greeting you." With shaking hands she smoothed her skirts and unconsciously shifted away from him on the settee. *The settee.* Her brow creased as she glanced down where she sat. "How did I . . .?"

"As I said, you fainted, dead away. The settee seemed preferable to laying you on the floor."

"You . . . caught me?"

"Yes." He removed the glass from her hand, setting it on a nearby table. "You seem . . . surprised by my arrival. Didn't you receive my letter?"

She forced down the lump in her throat. "We did. Your appearance . . . startled me."

His eyebrow arched in question. "You didn't know George and I were identical twins?"

IT SEEMED A SIMPLE QUESTION TO HARRY, BUT THE DUCHESS appeared unable to answer, her mouth opening and closing soundlessly. A rustling sound behind him caught his attention.

Burrows stood at the entrance to the library, eyes narrowed and wary. "Your Grace, may I be of assistance?"

"No thank you," Harry answered, but when Burrows' gaze moved from the broken vase on the floor to remain fixedly on the duchess, Harry realized his error, deriving new meaning from the concern on the butler's face.

"Some tea would be lovely, Burrows," the duchess said. Her trembling hands belied the calmness of her voice.

Burrows' gaze returned to the broken vase and then landed squarely on Harry. "Has His Grace had the opportunity to freshen in his chambers?"

"Unfortunately, I haven't. A noise pulled me here to discover the duchess had a small accident. Would you mind cleaning the broken glass before someone gets injured?"

Burrows' eyes widened, and Harry cringed. The man probably

expected a barked order rather than a polite request. Regardless of his position, Harry refused to treat people like slaves.

"Of course, Your Grace. I'll see to it straightaway." After a momentary hesitation, Burrows gestured toward the hall. "Would Your Grace care to follow me? I will direct you to your room so you may refresh from your journey."

Burrows was clearly trying to remove him from the library. *Why?*

"Pray excuse me, madam." Harry rose and followed Burrows to his rooms.

Once Burrows left, Harry stripped out of his coat, rolled up his shirtsleeves, and washed his face and hands in the bowl of warm water on the washstand. Admittedly, washing the dust from the road did his soul good. While the night's rest in the inn had done wonders, he was still bone tired from his journey.

The dark, dreary room added to his weariness. Although as a boy he knew the location of his father's quarters, he and George were never permitted entrance. Once, when his father was in London for Parliament during the Season, George suggested they sneak a look, and at ten years old, it seemed a deliciously defiant thing to do. No one would have been the wiser had George not pilfered a pipe from their father's dressing table. Lord, what a beating they received. Twenty years later, the room remained unchanged—the memory with it.

Harry stretched out on the bed, booted feet dangling off the edge. A few moments rest would surely help. His eyes closed, and the face of his brother's widow surfaced, reality eradicating his initial mental picture.

Raven hair, not blonde, thick and lustrous, the kind a man wished to thread his hands through. Eyes so blue they appeared violet, not cold, but warm, soft—haunted. Her countenance, though charming, didn't reflect the aristocratic haughtiness he expected, but instead conveyed a whimsical air with her pert, upturned button of a nose. Full and impossibly sensual lips had riveted him, his gaze inexplicably and repeatedly drawn to them. Taller than the average woman but light as a feather when he caught her in his arms.

The only part of his preconceived image that remained was her beauty. Yet even that was off. Her beauty defied his imagination. She was exquisite—alluring. An unease rooted in him trying to reconcile his image to reality, and he reminded himself as George's wife, he shouldn't trust her, regardless of his attraction to her. Wouldn't George have chosen a bride as deceitful and cruel as himself?

The quick tap on the door roused him from his meandering thoughts. "Come," he answered, sitting up.

A tall, thin man about forty entered and bowed. "Your Grace, I'm Hastings. Burrows informed me you arrived without a valet. Might I provide my services?"

Harry bit back the groan threatening to escape his lips. For eight years, he'd managed to dress himself. He motioned the man forward. "I'm afraid I'm out of practice, Hastings. Please indulge me with your patience as I become reacquainted with life in the *ton.*"

Hastings didn't bat an eye. "Of course, Your Grace."

God, how Harry was growing to hate the salutation. "And if you would indulge me one other thing. A simple *sir* will do nicely. No need to 'Your Grace' me for everything."

Hastings' mouth twitched with a restrained smile. "Yes, Your . . . sir. Will you be joining Her Grace in the library for tea?"

Violet-like eyes and sensual lips beckoned him. "Certainly." He rose, reluctantly allowing Hastings to assist with his coat.

Apparently, his cravat wasn't up to snuff because the valet uttered a quiet "tsk, tsk" and made some adjustments. After brushing off the road's dust from Harry's coat, Hastings nodded his satisfaction. "I shall unpack your clothing and have it thoroughly cleaned and pressed." Hastings' gaze traveled to Harry's feet. "I'll have your boots polished tonight."

Harry resisted rolling his eyes and delivered a curt, "Thank you, Hastings."

"I shall return at seven sharp to dress you for supper."

Once outside and away from Hastings' watchful eye, Harry's suppressed groan broke free. Good Lord, how would he ever survive this madness?

CHAPTER 5—IDENTICAL?

Twins. *Identical.* The words coalesced in Margaret's mind, and with it terror returned. Were they identical in more than appearance? Her earlier question regarding the new duke's temperament took precedence.

Yet, his actions thus far suggested a kinder, gentler disposition. Had he really caught her as she fell in a faint from the ladder? Now alone, she rose from the settee and moved her limbs, testing for the familiar discomfort. She found none. The glass of brandy remained on the table, and, glancing toward the door, she lifted it, drained its contents, and placed the cool crystal next to her cheek.

Warmth from the brandy spread through her, easing the shock of witnessing a face from the grave. How could a visage so handsome strike such terror in her? Indeed, George's appearance initially had drawn her to him not knowing the ugliness hidden beneath. When he made his true nature known, it had been too late. She'd been a foolish girl, believing George's smiles and attentiveness, so quick to dismiss the flash of anger the first time she disagreed with him, so unbelieving of the treachery he employed to marry her. That girl died on their wedding night the first time George struck her, leaving only fatalistic resignation and a will to survive.

Did the same ugliness lurk behind Harrison's handsome features, crouched and waiting for her to make a misstep? *I must be on guard.*

Flora arrived to sweep away the broken vase, her concerned eyes darting toward her mistress. "Did you cut yourself, Your Grace? Mr. Burrows was worried."

Dear Burrows, of course he's concerned. "No, Flora, I'm fine. In my clumsiness, I knocked the vase from the shelf."

Flora's gaze darted to the top shelf where the vase typically resided. "Way up there?"

Margaret nodded and, clearing her dry throat, diverted Flora's attention. "Flora, the duke has arrived. Have you seen him?"

"No, Your Grace. Do you need me to fetch him?"

Margaret sucked in a breath, Flora had misinterpreted her question. "No, Flora. It's just . . . when you see him, don't be alarmed."

"Alarmed?"

Goodness, she was making a muck of this. "He is my husband's identical twin."

Flora's wide eyes communicated her comprehension. She swung toward the entrance of the room, broken glass rattling within the dustpan.

Margaret's heart went out to the young parlor maid, understanding well her reaction. "His Grace retired to his rooms to refresh from his journey. I simply wished to prepare you."

Flora nodded. "Will there be anything else, Your Grace?"

Margaret forced a smile and shook her head. "No, that will be all, Flora. Thank you."

After a quick and clumsy curtsy, Flora exited the room, glancing both ways at the doorway before stepping out.

Margaret stared at the empty glass in her hand then the brandy decanter on the sideboard. Her bottom lip pulled reflexively between her teeth as her body moved toward the beckoning beverage. One step. Two steps. Her hand outstretched to grasp the container as she approached.

"Your tea, Your Grace."

Her arm snapped back to her side, and she pivoted toward Burrows, realizing she still held the empty glass. Quickly placing it on the sideboard next to the decanter, she returned to her seat on the settee.

"Thank you, Burrows. Will His Grace be joining me?"

"I'm not certain, madam. Hastings is seeing to his toilette now."

He settled the tea tray on the table by the settee and straightened, his direct gaze somber. "Your Grace, if I may speak frankly."

"Of course, Burrows. Continue."

He nodded. "The duke's appearance, it's most—unsettling, is it not?"

Tears threatened, and Margaret inhaled and exhaled slow, even breaths, regaining her composure. She must remain calm. She lifted the teapot with a trembling hand and poured the hot beverage into a cup. "I'm certain everyone will adjust quickly. This is his home now, and we must welcome him."

He stepped closer and lowered his voice. "Your Grace, if there's anything I can do, anything at all, you've only to ask."

Burrows had already proven his loyalty on numerous occasions, but his offer still warmed her heart and lifted her spirits. A lump threatened to form in her throat at his concern. "Thank you, Burrows. That will be all."

A voice startled her. "I understand there's tea."

The teacup in Margaret's hand rattled, and her head jerked toward the entrance of the library. The duke stood just inside the room, his body looming in the frame of the doorway. *Must he be so large?* After placing the teacup on the table, she rose in greeting. "Please join me, Your Grace."

Burrows made a hasty retreat, leaving her alone with the duke.

After the duke seated himself, Margaret poured his tea, the cup tinkling against the saucer when she passed it to him. His eyes lifted to hers and narrowed. She released her grasp on the saucer, averted her gaze, and folded her shaking hands in her lap, hoping to still them.

Uncomfortable silence filled the room, and she resisted reaching for her teacup until her nerves settled. Her heart pounded as if a wild animal struggled to break free, and she searched for a safe topic of conversation.

"How do you find the weather, Your Grace?"

A soft chuckle caused her to blink. She chanced a quick glance in his direction; his upturned lips confirmed his reaction. "You find the weather—amusing?"

He shook his head and laid his teacup on the nearby table. "Please forgive me. It's not the weather, but your question I found humorous. As I mentioned to Hastings, I'm sorely out of practice for interactions within society. I beg your indulgence." He paused, meeting her eyes, the smile since faded from his lips. "Discussion of the weather was not a pressing topic in America, at least not in my typical, daily routine."

A sensation like a boiling pot of water bubbled within her, arousing her curiosity. "What was it like? America?" The question left her lips before she could withdraw it. She braced for his censure.

"Different. Oh, they still have their societal hierarchies, but there is a wildness, a freedom there that's invigorating. I had a purpose there."

As she listened, her hand, no longer shaking, drifted to pick up her teacup. The image her mind painted fascinated her. *Freedom.* What it must have been like! A pang of envy ripped through her as she studied his face. *Calm, intelligent—compassionate?* Confusion eddied.

"You will have a purpose here, Your Grace, in the House of Lords and running the estate."

A smile traced his lips as he picked up his cup, sipping slowly before addressing her again. "Harry, my name is Harry."

"I . . . I beg your pardon?"

"Call me Harry. This 'Your Grace' thing is most disconcerting and tedious. I have a name."

She simply stared, her lips parted. Five years of George's insistence of the address, even from his own wife, was so ingrained in her it had become an unconscious habit.

He sighed and continued. "I realize I will have to bear the title and salutation in public, but I thought at least in private you might call me by my Christian name."

Ashton perhaps, but his Christian name? It simply isn't done. She blinked. *Could I?* An ember from a fire, long ago quenched but still smoldering, reignited deep within her. After taking a fortifying breath, she reformed her statement. "Surely your duties in the House of Lords and managing the estate will provide a purpose . . . Harry." Her body tensed as she forced the name out, and she waited.

His head swiveled, gazing around the room. "Amazing, the world didn't end." After a sip of tea, he continued. "I suppose serving in Parliament has an appeal to most, but until I can effect real change, I would prefer to be useful elsewhere."

She cocked her head. "The estate, then?"

"Perhaps. At least I will have marginally more control here than I might have in London."

Unable to stop herself, the question tumbled out. "What changes would you hope to make?"

He picked up a biscuit from the tray, took a bite, and examined it. "Larger biscuits?"

A laugh burst from her, uncontrolled, foreign—and absolutely glorious. Her hand flew to cover her mouth, realizing in horror what he must think. "I apologize, Your Grace."

The familiar frown covered his face, and she braced herself for the inevitable ridicule and subsequent punishment. Relief flooded her with his next words.

"Harry, remember?" He took another bite of biscuit, chewing slowly, his eyes trained on her. "What are you afraid of . . ." He shook his head. "I don't know your name."

"My name?"

"Yes, I'm Harry and you're . . ." His hand extended toward her.

"M-M-Margaret." Mortified at her stammer, she dropped her eyes and focused on the hands in her lap. He remained quiet, and she ventured a quick glance in his direction. No amusement shone in his eyes.

"Margaret. It suits you. What are you afraid of, Margaret?"

HARRY REGRETTED THE QUESTION IMMEDIATELY WHEN HE WITNESSED the color drain from her face. *What is she hiding?*

When she didn't answer, he moved to another topic. "Margaret, may I ask, how long were you and George married?" Harry delivered his question in a deliberately gentle voice, hoping to soothe her.

She lifted her gaze from her lap and met his. "Five years when he . . . died."

"I don't remember you." How could he forget those eyes? "When did you and George meet?"

"We met in 1817 when I was nineteen. I missed my first two Seasons. My mother had consumption, and my father remained by her side until her death. He sent me to live with my elderly aunt in the country, and she refused to travel to London." She took a tiny sip of tea, her movements methodical.

"Your father very well may have saved your life. Missing two Seasons seems a minor price to pay."

Pink flushed her cheeks, confirming his gibe found its mark, the cut most ungentlemanly and unlike him. Remorse rose swiftly and powerfully, and the tea churned in his stomach. "I apologize. I'm certain a young woman's coming out is of utmost importance."

"No, sir, you are correct. I suppose I never thought of it that way."

"George never told you we were identical twins?"

She shook her head. "No, he never mentioned you."

Tea would not suffice for this conversation. He rose, poured himself a glass of brandy, and took a slow drink. "I'm not surprised. George disowned me when Father died. He most likely forbade anyone who knew of me to speak my name."

A reprehensible action for anyone, and for George—predictable. Not that he minded at the time. It gave him the freedom to pursue his dreams, leave the pressures of society behind, and hope for the opportunity to find a woman to love. He had achieved all but the last. Work as a physician had kept him too busy, and often too exhausted, to seek someone to share his life, his love. Now, fate had ripped everything away. He lifted the glass to his lips and took another long swallow.

"Is that why you went to America?"

Her question jolted him back to the present. "Yes," he answered, refusing to elaborate. What would discussing impossible dreams accomplish?

As he took his seat, he focused on her, studying her. *Nervous or frightened?*

Her eyes followed his movement when he reached for another biscuit.

He held the plate out to her, surprised her face paled as she shook her head. "You don't like biscuits?"

With eyes the size of the saucer holding his cup, she stared at him. "I . . . I do."

"But?"

"You don't mind?"

What on earth? "Why the deuce would I mind?" He moved the plate closer, and she gingerly reached for a biscuit, broke off a tiny piece and nibbled, eyes on him the entire time as if he would snatch it away. *How can she nibble something already so small?*.

"If you met George in 1817 and were married five years, you must have had a short courtship."

"Yes. Two months." Her eyes darted away, nervous, anxious.

"You had no children?"

Sadness in her eyes answered his question before her response. "No."

His last hope eradicated, his fate sealed.

Silence, heavy and uncomfortable, settled around them. The clock on the mantle chimed a six count, and her body jerked, producing another series of rattles of the teacup against the saucer.

As he lifted his own cup to his lips, he peered over the rim at her, his medical mind assessing, diagnosing. *A nervous condition?* He didn't espouse the theory of female hysteria—in fact, he thought it was hogwash—but her behavior gave it credence. He searched for an alternate explanation, and he returned to Occam's Razor, the simpler explanation is the better. Something in the room made her anxious. Or someone. *Aha!*

"Margaret, do I cause you distress?"

Her eyes darted up to his, the truth of his question clearly written in their depths. "Forgive me," she answered. "It's most disconcerting to look upon the face of someone whom you believed was dead."

"George *is* dead, Margaret. I'm not George."

CHAPTER 6—THE DINING DILEMMA

Margaret's anxiety remained, along with the disturbing sensation of George haunting her from beyond the grave. True, he wasn't George. But concern that identical meant more than likeness of appearance exacerbated her distress.

Initially, George, too, had been charming, lavishing attention and compliments, and she had trusted what he presented. She was no longer that foolish girl; she would not trust so easily.

"I beg your indulgence, sir. The shock lingers, and I'm certain with time I shall adjust."

"Of course," he said, his tone less than convincing. He reached for another biscuit.

"We should be dining in an hour." She hoped she conveyed the warning in a non-accusatory manner.

An impish grin spread across his face, drawing her eyes to his lips.

He removed his hand from the plate. "I apologize, I'm like a small boy when it comes to biscuits. I cannot resist them." He gave a deferential nod toward her. "Consider me thoroughly chastised."

Oh, dear.

Heat rose to her cheeks. "I only meant to alert you. I instructed Cook to prepare a large meal as I feared you would be famished."

As if sensing her discomfort, Burrows appeared in the entryway of the library and bowed toward Harry. "Pardon the interruption, Your Grace. Hastings has a question regarding your formal attire."

"Thank you, Burrows." Turning his attention to Margaret, he added, "Please excuse me. I suspect Hastings will deliver another chastisement."

Confused, she tilted her head, her brow creased. "Your meaning, Your Grace?"

Unsure if the heavy sigh he emitted indicated his annoyance with her, her confusion, or the expected but unknown chastisement, she waited for an explanation.

"Harry, Margaret. Harry. I expect a good scolding for my lack of clothing." He turned and exited the room, leaving Margaret to puzzle over his statement.

He doesn't have—clothing?

HARRY TRUDGED UP THE STAIRS, STEELING HIMSELF FOR THE VALET'S questioning. The innumerable changes of clothes yet another reminder of the fastidiousness of the *ton*. *Hell and damnation!* It was his home now, was it not? If he wanted to dine buck naked, he would. The image conjured in his mind produced a guffaw of laughter at the precise moment he entered his chambers.

Hastings waited, raising a brow at his master's amusement. "Your Grace, we have a slight problem."

"Hastings, stop with the *Your Grace*."

Hastings gave a quick nod and proceeded. "I've unpacked your trunks, and your evening wear is missing."

"No, it's not."

Hastings circled back to the trunks, opening them as if the missing clothing would magically appear.

Taking pity on the man, Harry put him out of his misery. "Hastings, the evening wear isn't missing. I don't own any."

Hastings' head snapped up like a marionette pulled by a string, eyes wide and disbelieving. "Pardon?"

"When I departed for America, I left the trappings of the *ton* behind."

Hastings turned a putrid shade of green, and Harry expected him to be sick on the spot. In spite of it, Harry suppressed a ripple of laughter. After a brief pause, Hastings jumped into action, his face brightening. "Perhaps His Grace's clothing. You are identical, so they should fit nicely. I shall return shortly." Hastings bowed and made a quick exit.

A shiver ran up Harry's spine at the thought of wearing George's clothes. A visit to a tailor would be in order for his new role. In the interim, eager to provide a smooth transition for the staff, he would acquiesce.

Minutes later, Hastings returned, arms loaded with the appropriate attire. "Let's try the coat first." Arms outstretched, Hastings held the coat open.

Harry slipped out of his day coat and slid his arms into the tail coat. "It feels tight."

Hastings scowled. "It should fit snug, Your Grace . . . err, sir." He fiddled with the coat, tugging at the shoulders. "Although I will admit it is a mite too snug in the shoulders and arms." He buttoned it. "And too loose in the waist. A bit of tailoring should address those issues." He leaned in conspiratorially, his voice a mere whisper. "The padding in the shoulders and arms can be removed."

Harry bit back a snort of laughter. George notoriously avoided physical activity that would strengthen his musculature; no wonder they padded the coat.

Shirt, stockings, trousers, waistcoat, cravat, and shoes followed, with only the trousers and waistcoat slightly ill fitting. Once Hastings slipped the snug coat back on Harry, he stepped back and nodded his approval, proud of his ingenuity.

"Now, your hair." Hastings reached for the comb, but paused as he assessed the imposing figure before him. Instead, he reached up and gave a quick tousle to a forelock, causing it to dangle carelessly across Harry's forehead.

Harry felt like a complete fool.

⚜

SINCE GEORGE'S DEATH, CHANGING HER ATTIRE FOR EVENING seemed pointless, one black dress the same as the other. However, tonight Jane's choice appeared too plain.

"Not that one, Jane. I'd prefer the one with the embroidery on the sleeves."

Jane's eyebrows raised, but she remained silent and complied.

"And Jane, my megrim is much better. Style my hair as well."

Later, while she waited in the drawing room, her mind raced with curious thoughts. Why was she concerned about her appearance? Was she trying to impress Harry? Would he care what she wore? She twisted her hands in her lap, and she drifted back to her brother-in-law's statement. *Lack of clothing?* A brief image flitted through her mind, and she pushed it away, her cheeks heating.

A strange mix of fear and attraction warred within her, filling her with confusion. Shocked by the unexpected direction of her thoughts, she focused on her nails, hoping to eradicate the picture her mind evoked. In an attempt to calm herself, she repeated her newly created mantra.

He is not George. He is not George.

Footsteps echoed down the hall, and she smoothed her skirts, inhaling several deep breaths in preparation for his arrival. Her efforts proved lacking.

He is not George. He is not George.

Oh my! A sudden whoosh of air left her lungs when she gazed on him standing rigidly in the entry. Handsomely dressed in evening wear, the starched cravat intricately folded, his blond hair tousled, a lock playfully falling over his high brow, he was every inch the Duke of Ashton.

Instinctively, she rose in greeting and executed a perfect curtsy. "Your Grace."

His heavy sigh drew her attention to his face, and he rolled his eyes, effectively defusing her terror.

"I look like a dandy," he said, strolling over to a wingback chair and taking a seat.

The beginning of a giggle bubbled dangerously close to her lips. She bit it back. "You look perfectly presentable, Ha—" She corrected herself when Burrows appeared at the entrance of the drawing room. "Your Grace."

"Supper is served, Your Grace."

Margaret waited, prepared to follow Harry to the dining room. He rose and offered his arm, leaning in to whisper, "I will forgive you this once for not calling me Harry since Burrows was in earshot."

The soft chuckle he emitted, although pleasant, was foreign to her ears. She rested her hand on his arm, surprised at the warmth emanating from him. She cast a cursory glance in his direction. His superfine coat, somehow familiar, bulged at the upper arms and chest. He cut a striking figure.

"Your concern regarding your wardrobe seems to have been unfounded, sir. It is most becoming."

"You don't recognize it?"

She assessed him more thoroughly, her gaze more focused on the fine details of the waistcoat, the pattern unmistakable. Her eyes widened. "They're . . ."

"George's, yes. Hastings' remedy to my faux pas of utter disregard for convention."

His muscled arm flexed under her hand, pushing against the fabric and sending an odd fluttering within her chest.

"They're damned uncomfortable. I fear if I move too suddenly or too strenuously, the seams will burst."

"Perhaps some tailoring would help?"

His lips quirked upward, causing her to wonder what was so amusing about tailoring.

Once seated in the dining room, the footman brought the first course. Margaret dipped her spoon in the consommé, the warm liquid welcome in her empty stomach.

"I plan to meet with the steward tomorrow to familiarize myself with the needs of the estate. Any words of wisdom or warning you care to impart?" he asked

She studied his face, attempting to discern if he baited her, then chose the path of caution and shook her head. "His Grace handled all matters concerning the estate. I was never privy to them."

"No unruly tenants? Are you acquainted with the Morrisons?"

Her throat tightened. What did he know of the Morrisons? Had someone informed him of her assistance? "Do you have reason to believe the Morrisons are problematic, Your Grace?"

"No, no. nothing like that. I met their daughter on my trip from London. A lovely girl. I plan to visit her family. She and her new husband shared my coach on the journey. Apparently they eloped when her parents didn't approve of the match. I'd hoped, as duke, I could smooth things over for them. They appeared very much in love."

Her mind sifted through his words. *Concern over a young couple? Love?* George's only concern was working his tenants to the bone. He cared little for their happiness. And the word love certainly never crossed his lips.

She remained silent, but he seemed unconcerned by her lack of response.

The footman removed their bowls, preparing for the next course. She'd eaten little of the fish course, hoping the main course offered a dish with more flavor. The smell assaulted her as the footmen entered the room with the chafing dish. When he lifted the lid, Margaret's heart fell at the sight of Brussels sprouts. The cook must have decided to make George's favorite dishes, anticipating his brother would enjoy them as well. Either that or she delighted in torturing her mistress, something Margaret had often speculated.

It had been a glorious eleven months enjoying the foods she loved and avoiding those she detested. However, if she had learned nothing else in the five years of her marriage, it was to be cautious. She would return to the prescribed practices while in the new duke's presence.

Carefully breathing through her mouth, out of habit, she

selected the mandatory ten sprouts from where they taunted her and placed them on her plate.

The footman leaned down and offered the vile vegetable to Harry, who hesitated before serving himself two.

The next two dishes proved more welcome, and although she would have liked to take more of the roast potatoes and lamb with mint sauce, she lifted but one thin slice of lamb and three potatoes and placed them on her plate. Harry helped himself to four slices of lamb and a large serving of potatoes. She cast a coveting gaze at his plate.

Long ago, Margaret learned to force herself to eat the most vile portion of the meal first while hunger pains remained sharp. She held the piece of sprout to her lips and prepared herself. After placing the despicable morsel in her mouth, the inevitable gag followed. *Swallow, swallow.* But it was too late. The horrible retching sound escaped without warning.

Harry leaped to his feet. "Raise your arms over your head," he said as he delivered a forceful swat to her back. His voice was authoritative, but calm. The sprout flew from her mouth to rest aside its companions on her plate.

He lifted the glass of wine to her lips. "Sip, slowly."

Mortified, after sipping the wine, she delicately wiped her mouth with her napkin. "I beg your pardon, Your Grace."

He studied her and, taking his fork, moved the offending piece of vegetable around on her plate as he examined it. "It doesn't appear to be overly large. Perhaps you were over zealous in your fondness for them and swallowed too quickly."

Her fondness—for Brussels sprouts? "I'm not fond of them, Your Grace." She flinched. Her confession, although honest, would invariably lead to retribution.

"If you're not fond of them, why the deuce would you take so many? Personally, I cannot abide the blasted things, but I didn't want to offend you." He paused, staring at her face. "You weren't choking?" He peered at the tiny piece of food. "You were gagging."

Relief replaced the fear growing inside her when he turned to a footman. "Remove these at once and bring Her Grace a clean plate." He lifted her plate, handing it to the footman. "And tell the cook, I never want to see these horrible green blobs on my table again."

Unable to speak, she stared at him, her mouth agape as he returned to his seat.

When the footman provided a clean plate, Harry asked, "What about the lamb and potatoes? Are those to your liking?"

"Yes, Your Grace."

He gestured to the footman. "Please serve Her Grace again."

As she lifted another small portion of lamb, she glanced over to him, and bravely took another slice. She placed more than three potatoes on her plate, surprised at his approving nod.

"I find it curious that you took such a large amount of the item you don't like and so little of the items you do. Why is that?"

In an attempt to stall and form an appropriate response, she deliberately chewed the tender lamb longer than necessary. What could she say that would not enrage him yet remain truthful? The piece of lamb masticated to mush, she swallowed. "It was expected of me, Your Grace."

"Expected of you?" His eyebrows drew down, forming a deep V, drawing her eyes to his. Anger flashed, hot, raw, and she braced herself. "By whom?"

❦

THE WOMAN MADE NO SENSE. UNLESS—THE FLASH OF understanding struck. *George!* "Did my brother insist on this peculiar dining practice?"

An almost imperceptible nod confirmed his conclusion. *Damnation!* As a child, George derived much glee watching Harry and their younger sister, Emmeline, struggle to eat their least liked vegetables, always tattling to their nanny when they refused to eat them.

Once, George admitted to Harry that he also disliked Brussels sprouts, but lied to Nanny stating he loved them. To please the heir apparent, Brussels sprouts were served regularly, and George would giggle in devilish amusement at his siblings distress when faced with them on their plates. *Emmeline.* Other painful memories surfaced, but he pushed them aside and returned to the present.

"Such nonsense is intolerable," he said. "Although a healthy serving of vegetables is important, no one should require you to eat anything you find repulsive."

When the footmen cleared the plates, Harry waited, eager for his favorite part of the meal—sweets. The footman placed a generous portion of syllabub in front of him. Not his favorite, but still enjoyable. He waited for Margaret to be served, puzzled when the footman simply took his place at the sideboard.

"Have you forgotten Her Grace's syllabub?"

The footman shifted nervously, his eyes darting from Harry to Margaret and back again.

"Please, Your Grace," Margaret said, "don't blame Peter. I'm not customarily served sweets."

"Not because you don't like them?"

A pink blush crossed her cheeks. "His Grace was concerned I would become overly large with the consumption of sweets."

Harry snorted in disgust. "I see no immediate danger of that. You're thin as a rail." After pushing his untouched dessert toward Margaret, he addressed the footman. "Place this in front of Her Grace. I trust there is more syllabub in the kitchen?"

"Yes, Your Grace." The footman placed the dish in front of Margaret and left in haste to fetch another serving.

Still uncertain what type of woman his brother had married, Harry *was* certain of one thing, George treated her like he had so many others—abominably. *His own wife!*

As he tasted the sweet cream, his gaze traveled to Margaret. The spoon held daintily in her hand remained in her mouth for an inordinately long period of time as she savored the treat. Her eyes momentarily closed in delight. *Wouldn't George want to witness such pleasure?*

"Tell me, Your Grace," Harry said, careful to use the proper address in front of the footmen, "did my brother often deny you little pleasures such as sweets?"

The spoon remained poised above her dish. Her face paled, and her eyes darted away. "I'm sure he meant well."

"Perhaps." Harry's discomfort grew. "Was my brother a good husband? Was he kind and generous to you?"

Her reaction answered his question. Fear. The blanched color of her skin, the reflexive move of her hand covering her mouth, the retraction of her arms making herself smaller, the haunted look in her near violet eyes before she averted them. Harry had witnessed the emotion all too often when he walked the back streets of Boston assisting those in need. Children discarded or orphaned, women beaten by their husbands or lovers—*dear God!* His own spoon clattered to his plate.

CHAPTER 7—THE ESTATE

After a fitful night, Harry rose early and, with Hastings' fussing, dressed. Harry repressed a groan as the valet added each piece of clothing. Buckskin breeches, a little snug in the thigh and loose in the waist, a soft linen shirt, a delicately embroidered cream waistcoat, an overly starched cravat which Hastings arranged in unending folds, and a superfine brown tailcoat completed his ensemble. Polished two-tone top boots now replaced his worn, comfortable ones. All thanks to George.

Hastings had managed to remove the padding in the coat, greatly improving the fit, but Harry's skin crawled. A bitter tang settled in his mouth, but not from the lingering odor of cigar smoke that clung to the fabric. Harry instructed Hastings to make an appointment with a tailor in London to take measurements. If the estate's coffers permitted, Harry would order a new wardrobe, if not, although not desirable, tailoring George's would suffice.

Anxious to meet his steward and later tour the estate, Harry hurried downstairs, eager for a brisk walk outdoors prior to breakfast. There, lined up at the foot of the staircase, the staff stood at attention.

"Your Grace," Burrows said, "I've assembled everyone in the

house to meet you."

Harry bristled at the delay to his plans, but he forced a smile, hoping to keep it brief. Apart from Hastings and Burrows, whom he'd already met, each member introduced was an unfamiliar face. Nervous eyes flitted toward him as he worked his way along the line. Only Jane, Margaret's lady's maid, held his gaze a moment longer before casting her eyes downward.

Her stance, ramrod straight, and her serious expression reminded Harry of a soldier preparing for inspection. Dull brown hair pulled back from her gaunt face only made her appearance more stern. Her thin lips puckered as if she had swallowed an unusually large dose of castor oil.

"If I may be of any use to you, Your Grace, you have only to ask." Her words, a secretive whisper, confused Harry.

"Use to *me*?"

"Yes, sir. Any information you may require about . . . the estate."

The footman next to her shifted, his eyes darting to Harry then back to focus ahead of him.

What on earth does she mean? What information? Harry ignored her strange proposition, deciding to question her at a later time, and moved to meet the remainder of the staff.

Once Harry dismissed them, he turned to Burrows. "Not one of my father's staff remains?"

"I'm afraid not, Your Grace. After your father's death, His Grace, your brother, replaced them." Burrows hesitated. "If I may be so bold to ask, will you be making changes?"

"No, Burrows. Not unless it's warranted."

"Very well, sir. If that is all?"

"One other thing, Burrows. How long has Jane served as Her Grace's lady's maid?"

"I believe His Grace selected her specifically upon his marriage."

Harry stepped outside to the brisk morning air and made a mental note to speak to Jane as soon as time permitted.

He loved this hour of the day, the first light, the peaceful sounds of birds singing in the trees, the dew on the grass. He breathed in the fresh air, contemplating how much he had missed it in the bustling city of Boston. This would be his sanctuary when everything closed in on him.

He strolled the grounds, coming upon a fenced paddock. A beautiful black horse, about sixteen hands high, romped in the enclosure, and Harry stopped to admire him.

A short, thin man in his twenties approached carrying grooming brushes, a saddle, and bridle. After a momentary falter in his steps, he bowed. "Good morning, Your Grace. I'm James, the groom."

"Good morning." Harry nodded toward the horse. "He's a beautiful specimen."

"Yes, sir, he is." He lifted the saddle a bit. "I'm going to exercise him."

Harry straightened from where he leaned against the railing. "May I? I had little opportunity to ride in Boston, and I've missed it."

James tilted his head, his lips pursed before speaking. "I'm not certain that's wise, Your Grace."

"Why not? Are you still breaking him?"

"Well, no, sir. He's broken, but there was an incident with His Grace, and so far I've been the only one permitted to ride him."

"What happened?"

"Satan, that's his name, sir, reared and threw His Grace off. Before His Grace could get out of the way, Satan gave him a good kick. His Grace wasn't pleased."

Harry stifled a laugh, picturing the scene. "What a horrible name for a horse so beautiful."

"Yes, sir. His Grace said he expected to ride him to hell and back."

Harry snorted and rolled his eyes. Just like George to be dramatic. "I'd like to try, if I may?"

Harry and James entered the paddock, but as Harry grew closer, Satan stamped the ground and gave his tail a strong swish. Harry backed up and removed his coat, draping it over the fence.

"James, do you have anything to feed him? Any carrots or apples?"

James left to get something to tempt Satan, and Harry sat on the railing calling to the horse, his voice soothing and calm. Several times, Satan moved a bit closer but then trotted away. Once James returned, Harry held out a carrot and called again.

"Careful, Your Grace, he may take off your hand," James said as he stood at the ready to help.

"He wouldn't do that, would you Satan? Here you go." Seated on the railing, Harry waited, patiently calling, and each time Satan moved a little closer, gradually approaching enough to snatch the carrot from Harry's hand before turning away to chomp his treat.

The sun rose higher in the sky, and after two more carrots, Harry held out an apple. "I'll bet you like apples, don't you, Satan?"

As Satan munched the apple, he stayed close, his ears flickering as he eyed Harry. Harry eased off the railing, his movement slow, and reached out his hand to touch Satan's muzzle and up to stroke his forehead. "Good boy."

With gentle strokes, Harry brushed Satan's coat, then turned to James, "Let's see if I can saddle him. After several attempts, Harry slipped on the headcollar and led Satan around the paddock, much to James' astonishment.

With Satan saddled, Harry tugged his coat back on and placed his foot in the stirrup to mount.

James called out, "Take care, Your Grace."

Harry grinned at the groom. "Worried you'll have to find yet another duke?"

He mounted Satan, but Satan reared and threw him off. Quickly rolling out of the way, he bounded up and moved to grab the reins. Satan snorted and backed away.

George's scent! After removing the coat, Harry tried again. Several attempts later, sweaty and grass-stained, Harry remained seated on the horse and trotted around the paddock.

"Well done, Your Grace," James said as Harry dismounted.

"I'd like to take him out today when I make my rounds to the tenants."

"Yes, sir. I'll brush him down and have him ready."

Having worked up a sufficient appetite, Harry returned to the house. After calling Hastings, he changed into a fresh shirt and pair of breeches, but insisted on wearing his own coat.

"Air out my brother's coats until I can have new ones made, Hastings."

Now freshened, he headed downstairs to breakfast. As he helped himself to several rashers of bacon, two boiled eggs, and a slice of toast, footsteps sounded behind him.

"Good morning, Your Grace."

Harry turned, surprised to find Margaret. His mother had always taken breakfast in her room and never rose before ten.

"Good morning, Margaret." As she approached, he moved aside allowing her access to the food. "You don't take breakfast in your room?"

"No."

Of course she doesn't. Another of George's expectations no doubt. Presumably to watch every morsel she put into her mouth. "If you wish to do so, you may."

The tiniest of smiles flitted across her lips. "Thank you, Your Grace. However, I find the practice of eating in one's bed at least awkward if not indolent."

Both her smile and remark amused him. "Don't like crumbs in your bed?"

A pink blush covered her cheeks, his question perhaps a bit too familiar.

About to take his plate to the table, he stopped when her hand hovered over the bacon, then moved aside and took one egg and one slice of toast. "Wouldn't you care for more, Margaret?"

He placed two rashers of bacon and another slice of toast on her plate.

Deep blue eyes, wide with surprise stared at him, then drifted down to her plate.

"If you don't eat all of that, I will," he said with a low chuckle and took his seat.

"Are you meeting with the steward this morning?" she asked as she seated herself.

"Yes, I've sent word for him to join me at the stables. After visiting the tenants, we will discuss the financial health of the estate."

She nodded but didn't offer additional information, and they ate the rest of their meal in silence. She finished every bite.

A footman approached, holding a silver tray in front of Harry, a letter lay in the center.

Written in an uneven hand, the words "His Grace the Duke of Ashton" were scrawled across the foolscap. Hoping it wasn't an invitation to visit a neighboring peer, Harry ran his finger along the seal and opened the missive. As he skimmed the message, he imagined a resounding thwack from the last nail pounded into his coffin.

He delivered the news to Margaret. "Mr. Jenkins, George's solicitor, will be arriving tomorrow to read the will."

"Do you require my presence?"

"Of course. It affects you as well."

"Then I shall be present, Your Grace," she said, her voice flat and unemotional. Her normally perfect posture faltered as her shoulders dipped slightly.

Wasn't she curious as to George's bequeathal to her, a dower house, a stipend? Still young, he expected her to have more interest in what may very well determine her future. Perhaps she'd already planned to remarry once the period of mourning ended.

As Harry made his way to meet the steward, Margaret's reaction to his announcement nagged at him.

He pushed concerns regarding Margaret from his mind when he approached the stables where a wiry man stood at the entrance.

The man executed a deep bow and introduced himself. "Chester Archer, Your Grace, at your service." Obviously forewarned, he seemed unaffected by Harry's similarity to his brother.

Harry extended his hand and gave Mr. Archer's a firm shake. "Pleased to meet you, Archer. I had hoped we could ride across the estate and visit the tenants before going over the books."

Mr. Archer nodded and called for the stable boy to bring two horses. The boy approached with a gray gelding, about fifteen hands high, and the groom led out Satan.

Archer's brow furrowed. "Is that Satan?"

"Yes, sir. His Grace requested him after riding him this morning," the groom said.

Archer grinned. "Well, I'll be damned."

As Archer guided Harry across the estate in an efficient route, Harry enjoyed the ride much more than what greeted him upon meeting the tenants.

Initially, many were cautious, eyeing him suspiciously and stopping just short of rudeness. When Harry inquired about their well-being and what he could do to help, they warmed, some inviting him in for tea and biscuits, which he graciously accepted.

When he visited the Whitcombs, the condition of their home and surroundings appalled him. Wind whipped through cracks in the walls, pots scattered across floors to catch dripping water from leaking roofs, and privies not fit for wild animals turned his stomach.

"You're in need of extensive repairs, Mr. Whitcomb," Harry said.

The elderly man dropped his gaze. "I do what I can, Your Grace, but my rheumatism gets the best of me."

Harry observed the man's gnarled hands. "I have some medicine that will help with the pain and stiffness. I'll bring it next time."

The man's eyes lit up. "Thank you, Your Grace. That is most kind."

"And perhaps we can find someone to assist with the repairs, another tenant perhaps?"

Mrs. Whitcomb handed Harry a cup of tea. "We would be even worse off if it wasn't for the Angel."

The Angel? Harry's curiosity piqued. "To whom are you referring, madam?"

Mr. Whitcomb gave a slight shake of his head toward his wife. "My wife is superstitious, Your Grace. She believes heavenly spirits keep us from perishing."

Throughout his visits, Harry had heard the "Angel" mentioned several other times from tenants whose properties suffered disrepair, enough to cause him to doubt Mr. Whitcomb's explanation.

As he and Archer rode on, Harry said, "Perhaps I should have reviewed the accounts first. I had no idea the estate was in such financial straits."

Archer twisted in his saddle, head turned away from his employer's gaze.

"Archer? What is it, man?"

"There's money enough, Your Grace. It's just . . ."

"Say no more, Archer. George!" Harry spit the vile name from his lips, anything to clear the distaste spreading through him. "We shall remedy this immediately. Do you have a record of the tenants' needs? Been making notes regarding the required repairs?"

Archer's brows lifted as he stared at Harry a long moment. "Aye, sir. It's not something easily forgotten."

As they rode to the outermost part of the estate, Harry recognized the Morrisons' home where the coach had deposited Lily and Owen. A burly man busied himself chopping wood, while a lad around fifteen helped stack it neatly in a pile. Both glanced up from their labors as the riders approached. The older man called to someone inside the home, and two women appeared. One Harry identified as Lily, the other most likely her mother.

"Mr. Radcliffe!" Lily exclaimed, her face bright with pleasant surprise. "How good of you to visit."

The older man scowled and admonished her. "Hush, girl. Don't address His Grace in such a manner."

Harry dismounted and offered his hand to the older man. "Mr. Morrison, I presume?"

The man gave a brief nod, staring at Harry's hand incredulously. As if made of lead, he lifted his own hand and placed it in Harry's, a broad grin spreading across his face when Harry gave it a firm shake.

"A pleasure to meet you, sir. Please don't chastise your daughter. I met her and her husband during my journey from London. I'm afraid I concealed my identity."

Harry turned his attention to Lily. "How is Owen, is he nearby? I should like to say hello."

Mr. Morrison spat on the ground. "I sent him back home. Ran off with my daughter, he did, the Scottish scoundrel."

Harry's gaze darted to Lily, her eyes pleading, hopeful, and he remembered his vow to assist the young couple. "Perhaps, we could have a chat, man to man, Morrison," Harry said, "but first, would you mind showing me around?"

Pleased to find the Morrison home in better condition than others, Harry listened to the man's account of his crops as they strolled outside to the fields. "You've done well, Morrison, better than other tenants I've seen today. Perhaps sharing your secrets would allow them to succeed as well."

Mr. Morrison snorted. "Nothing more money wouldn't help. My wife takes in sewing, and the lad there has a talent carving trinkets. We take them to Ramsgate to sell at market. Doesn't bring in much, but it helps."

"Very resourceful, Morrison. I'm impressed."

"If you don't mind me saying, it's eerie, Your Grace. Your resemblance. But I remember you both as boys, and I could always tell you apart."

"Oh?" Although Harry remembered the name Morrison, he didn't remember this man.

Morrison grew quiet as he stared fixedly ahead, his fingers tapping an uneven rhythm on his thigh. "You both sneaked out here and swam in my pond—your pond," he corrected. "It wasn't a difference in appearance, but how you behaved, especially with others. I was a lad myself, older than you, mind you, but still a boy. You invited me to join you in the pond. Your brother . . . well, he wasn't quite so welcoming."

Harry's eyes grew wide with recognition. "Clive?"

A grin spread across the man's lips, exposing his missing tooth. "You remember?"

"How could I forget? Your pond was the clearest, coolest piece of water on the property, a welcome respite on a hot summer day."

"That's generous of you, sir, to call it my pond when by rights it's yours."

Clive paused as if considering something. "We heard a rumor you were killed at Waterloo, Your Grace. I'm pleased to know it was false."

Harry shifted uneasily at the memory of his brother's deception. "Yes, my service during the war is something best forgotten."

"You wanted to talk to me about Lily?"

Grateful for the change in subject, Harry nodded. "Yes. Why don't you approve?"

Clive snorted. "He's a Scot."

Harry quirked an eyebrow. "Clive," Harry paused, "may I call you Clive?"

"You're the duke, you can call me Beelzebub if it suits you."

Harry barked a laugh. "One minion from hell is enough for one day."

Clive cocked his head.

"The horse is Satan." Harry pointed to the horse enjoying some tender grass.

Clive shook his head. A lopsided grin covered his face. "You might consider changing his name. Satan doesn't suit him."

Archer stood nearby and overheard the conversation. "It suited him perfectly before His Grace tamed him. Wild as storms at sea, that one. Only the groom rode him."

Harry turned to Morrison. "Now back to your son-in-law."

Morrison grimaced at the term.

"Clive, my best friend is Scots. They're not the villains we English make them out to be. Angus is one of the finest people I know. I don't hold his heritage against him. Nor should you do so with Owen. He loves your daughter, that much was clear to me when they shared my coach."

Clive rubbed the back of his neck and emitted a low grumble. "Are you telling me to accept the lad?"

"I'm asking you to give him a chance. It's a blessing to marry for love. Would you rather see her leg-shackled to someone who uses her, mistreats her? I've seen what happens to women in bad marriages, the toll it takes. You love her, don't you want her to be happy?" Unbidden, Harry's mind turned to Margaret.

"With respect, Your Grace, the man's got no living. Love won't feed them, clothe them, take care of any babies that might come along."

"Archer," Harry called to his steward. "Do we have any property available for a new tenant?"

Archer pursed his lips, his brows scrunched together. "There's old man Turner's place. Turner's still there, but he's older than Methuselah and unable to care for the place properly."

"I wouldn't say no to a cup of tea, Clive, if you'd offer. We can ask Lily where her husband might be, and if he'd be interested in farming. I'm sure Mr. Turner would appreciate the help."

While he enjoyed the refreshments, Clive's son Tom showed Harry some of his carvings, a menagerie composed of lifelike figures of birds and woodland creatures.

"These are remarkable, Tom. How much for this fox?"

"It's yours, Your Grace," Clive offered.

"I insist." Harry took a coin out of his pocket and handed it to Tom.

"The Angel helps us take them to market sometimes," the boy said.

Angel again? Who is this mysterious benefactor?

Harry sent a questioning glance toward Clive.

"Pay no heed to the boy, Your Grace. He has a vivid imagination."

Harry left the Morrisons' pleased to have helped the young couple, but as he and Archer rode back to Briarfield, he puzzled over the enigmatic angel. "Archer, who is this Angel the tenants mentioned?"

Archer's eyes darted away, his smile vanishing. "Not sure, Your Grace. These folks are a superstitious lot. No telling what their imaginations conjured."

"No, no. They spoke as if this was an actual person. Tom Morrison said the Angel helped him sell his carvings. A disembodied spirit can't sell at market."

MARGARET PACED THE LIBRARY, GLANCING AT THE AREA OF THE bookshelves that hid her meager funds. *What will the tenants say? Will*

they keep the secret, or will Harry embolden them to confess? Her ears strained for the sounds of the opening front door, her eyes continually darting to the entrance of the room, her hands red from twisting them mercilessly.

Footsteps sounded from the entryway, Burrows' greeting following. "I trust you had a successful day, Your Grace?"

She moved closer to the entrance of the room to listen.

"It was most enlightening, Burrows. Thank you. Where is Her Grace?"

She tensed, her heart beating a furious tattoo. Quickly smoothing her skirts, she steeled herself for his appearance.

The smile that greeted her did little to alleviate her anxiety. Charming smiles often hid darker intentions. Yet, she curtsied and forced a smile to her own lips. "Your Grace. How did you find the estate?" The breath she pulled into her lungs at her last words stalled, trapped, waiting for his answer.

He strode to the sideboard and poured himself a small glass of brandy. "Unfortunately, disappointing."

She swallowed, forcing the lump in her throat down to her empty stomach. "How so?"

He sat in the large wingback next to the fireplace, and she took a seat on the settee. "In some cases, the conditions of the tenants' homes are deplorable. Extensive repairs are necessary. Luckily, after reviewing the books with Archer, funds aren't the issue."

Such news did not surprise her. Her own visits to the tenants confirmed his statement regarding their condition. On the other hand, George never confided in her about the financial condition of the estate. She presumed that George's proclivity for gambling and other more unsavory activities depleted the estate's coffers for the necessary repairs. Still, she waited for Harry to continue.

"Archer and I have developed a plan to begin repairs to the homes in the worst conditions." He took a long swallow of his brandy and examined the glass in his hand. "It would appear my brother preferred spending funds on expensive liquor rather than the well-being of his tenants."

Among other things.

His finger tapped against the crystal. "Of course we need to wait for the full details of the will before proceeding. I wouldn't want to spend any money allotted for your stipend."

She studied him for the sneer of narrowed eyes and curling lips often accompanying George's sarcasm, but found neither.

He peered up at her over the rim of the glass. "I do have some other good news. I met with the Morrisons, and they have agreed to give their daughter's marriage a chance. Archer and I will offer young Owen MacDougall the Turner farm."

Margaret's spine straightened further, any more rigid and she would snap in two. "Isn't Mr. Turner still living there?" *Surely, Harry wouldn't remove the man from his home? He is a dear old man, albeit somewhat senile.*

"He is. Archer and I met with him. MacDougall will help him with repairs and learn how to work the fields until . . ." Harry trailed off.

"Until Mr. Turner passes?"

"Yes. After some convincing, Turner agreed. The first order of business will be to build a new house, one the MacDougalls will occupy once finished. When Turner passes, we can either tear the old place down, or repurpose it."

Words failed her—almost. "Why, that's a brilliant idea." Hope bubbled to the surface of Margaret's heart that, finally, the tenants on her husband's estate would have a master worthy of them.

Harry's lips tugged upward in a small, satisfied smile, and Margaret admired the genuineness of it. "It seems, Your Grace, you have already found a purpose back home in Kent."

"Tea, Your Grace," Burrows announced as he entered the library. "I took the liberty of asking Cook to add more biscuits as I understand His Grace enjoys them."

Harry placed his hand on his stomach, drawing Margaret's eyes to his striking figure. "Although I appreciate your attention, Burrows, for once in my life, I cannot imagine having room for another biscuit. I've gorged on them all day."

Warmth spread through Margaret. "They served you biscuits?"

George shared little regarding his rare visits with the tenants, but she was positive biscuits were never included.

"And tea," Harry answered, viewing the teapot with trepidation.

"Shall I remove it, sir?" Burrows asked, glancing over at Margaret.

"No, no, I wouldn't dream of depriving Her Grace her afternoon tea. As long as she doesn't mind if I don't join her."

After placing the tray on the table by Margaret, Burrows exited the room. Harry's eyes followed him, then turned toward Margaret. "That leaves more biscuits for you, Margaret."

Her head turned in his direction at her Christian name, and although not unpleasant, its use remained foreign to her ears. A smile, unforced, found its way to her lips, and she placed two biscuits on a plate, then poured herself tea.

Harry rose and, after stretching, strolled around the room. Margaret peered at him over her cup, admiring the snug fit of his buckskin breeches and how the tapered tailcoat emphasized his trim waist. The arms of the coat bulged at the biceps as he rubbed the back of his neck. He wore the coat he had arrived in, its fit more becoming than George's.

"This is interesting." He lifted and examined a small wooden carving of a doe. One of Margaret's favorites. Hidden until after George's death, the tiny figure so lifelike she decided to display it in her favorite room. Harry turned toward her. "Where did this come from?"

A splash of tea spilled over the rim of her cup onto the saucer. "If memory serves, a little shop in Ramsgate sells those carvings." *There, not a lie, simply a half-truth.*

His narrowed eyes remained fixed on her, the silence interminable. At last, he returned the carving to its place. "The Morrisons' son carves figures like this. They mentioned someone called the Angel who assists in taking them to market at Ramsgate." A dramatic pause followed. "Might you know to whom they're referring?"

The question, more direct, proved harder to avoid answering truthfully. "A benevolent person, I would presume." Lifting her cup, she sipped, desperately searching for a way out of her dilemma. "The Morrisons are good, hard-working people, many would happily assist them." Another sip of tea. "Your solution for the young couple is a prime example."

Harry's mouth opened, and she expected him to accuse her of avoiding the question. A crash sounded outside the room, drawing Harry's attention away from his inquisition.

"What the deuce?" He strode to the doorway and peered into the hallway.

Margaret followed him, hoping to make her escape.

In the hallway, Flora stared at a broken pitcher at her feet as water pooled on the floor and runner.

"What happened?" Harry asked.

Flora twisted her hands in her apron, her eyes large as saucers as she stared at her master. "I'm so very sorry, Your Grace. My foot caught on the runner, and I lost control. Please forgive me, it was an accident."

Margaret searched the girl's face. Her terrified expression no doubt the result of more than dropping the pitcher. Before she could reassure the girl, Harry stepped forward.

"It's only a piece of pottery, it can be replaced. Are you injured?" he asked, his voice calm, reassuring. Margaret suspected deliberately so, unlike George. Flora continued to stare, her mouth opening and closing soundlessly. "What's your name?"

"Flora, sir." She executed a clumsy curtsy.

"There's no need for that, Flora. Now, why don't you find something to sop up the water and sweep up the broken pieces of"
—Harry waved his hand at the shattered pottery—"whatever that once was."

"Yes, Your Grace." Flora executed another awkward curtsy and hurried away.

As Harry turned to re-enter the room, Margaret quickly slid into the hall, announcing as she did, "I shall see you at supper, Your Grace."

She continued to walk, her steps brisk, even when he called out to her, "You didn't answer my question."

HARRY STARED AT MARGARET'S RETREATING BACK. INSTINCT TOLD him she knew more than she admitted about the carving, about the Angel. Why was she so evasive? He would drop it—for now.

He made his way to the room that had served as his father's study, anxious to begin reviewing the ledgers. The sweet fragrance of a floral arrangement within the room evoked the memory of his mother's scent.

He paused at the portrait of his mother hanging in the study, pleased George hadn't removed it. Such a gentle creature, and although she had appeared delicate, Harry remembered her strength and her belief in duty and adhering to society's rules. Duty that had brought him home. He stared at his mother's likeness, his mind drifting back.

He'd held his mother's hand, so frail in his, as she pulled him close.

"I must confess. You are and always have been my favorite son. I wish you had been born first, Harry. You would make such a wonderful duke."

"Mother, save your strength." Harry brushed his lips to his mother's forehead and cursed his father. Called home from university, he and George had returned to find their mother dying from childbed fever, his infant brother stillborn.

"Promise me if anything happens to George, you will fulfill your duty as duke. Marry a refined girl with a noble lineage and raise a family to carry on the line."

"Hush, Mother, you should rest."

"Please, Harry."

He couldn't refuse her. "I promise."

Harry shook the memory away, drowning it with a large swallow of brandy. At that moment, he decided not to pursue questioning Margaret about the carving or the Angel. Tomorrow the reading of the will would settle both their futures.

CHAPTER 8—THE WILL

Harry's skull pounded, and he squinted against the sun streaming bright through his window. At the memory of his promise to his mother, he had imbibed more than his usual quantity of brandy the night before. His throbbing head now paid the price, overshadowing the prospect of a sunny day.

After the ritual of Hastings fussing, Harry descended the stairs, dressed, groomed, and polished. As he stood at the foot of the staircase, he pivoted at the rustling of skirts. Margaret paused several steps above him, turning such a deathly shade of white, for a moment he worried she might faint. Though he steeled himself to catch her, color returned to her face, and the tension in his chest eased.

Her day gown, the same dreadful black as her gowns from the previous days, draped softly over her body. The surprisingly lower neckline drew his eyes like magnets. Had she forgotten her fichu?

He held out his arm when she joined him. "Good morning."

"Good morning, Your Grace." A momentary halt to her hand before she placed it on his arm reminded him of their conversation the previous evening and her hasty retreat from his questioning.

He decided to put her mind at ease. Today would be difficult enough without adding to it unnecessarily. He leaned in closer to whisper in her ear, and her fingers tensed. He pulled back, still keeping his voice low.

"Is it me, or is the sun exceedingly bright this morning? The throbbing in my head has robbed me of all intelligent thought."

She turned and concern shone in her eyes. "Are you ill?"

He chuckled, hoping to allay her anxiety. "Nothing reducing my intake of brandy won't cure. It seems to have dampened my memories of our conversation yesterday afternoon. I do hope you'll forgive me if I said anything ill-advised."

"Certainly, Your Grace. But rest assured, you were, at all times, a gentleman."

Margaret excused herself to take advantage of the sunny day and stroll in the garden. Tempted to join her, he remembered his duties as duke required him to focus on less pleasant activities, so he made himself comfortable in, what was now, his study to continue examining the ledgers he'd received from Archer. He had done more drinking than reviewing the night before.

Surprised at the surplus of funds, he suspected withholding repairs and other necessities for the tenants accounted for the profit. His fingers raked through his hair, mussing the effects of Hastings' ministrations. If he funneled money into repairs, would he be able to keep the estate afloat? He would need to examine the ledger more thoroughly to identify any wasteful spending. Brandy alone wouldn't offset the cost needed, there must be other luxuries he could eliminate. Although his remark was an intended cut, the truth remained that Margaret's stipend may affect the estate's finances—if George was overly generous.

Harry leaned back in the chair. What had their marriage been like? Did George love her? Did she ever love him, or did he kill any affection she might have had? And why did that matter?

Harry flipped through the pages of the ledger, scanning for very specific items. Large purchases of cigars, liquor—ah, there—clothing. Unfamiliar with modistes, either local or in London, Harry would ask Archer. His finger slid down the column of entries and stopped short. £350 for Miscellaneous. He fell back against the chair. A hefty sum for a trifle, enough to rent a carriage, a pair of matched horses, and a coachman for a year in London. Harry jotted down a note, marking the place on the ledger.

A soft knock brought his attention to Burrows at the doorway. "Your Grace, Mr. Jenkins has arrived. Shall I show him to the parlor or would you prefer to meet him in here?"

"The parlor would be more comfortable for Her Grace, Burrows. Have you informed her?"

"I sent Flora to find her, sir. She should only be a moment."

"Very good. Offer Jenkins some tea if you haven't already done so. I'll join him momentarily."

Harry closed the ledger and placed it along with the others in the desk, carefully locking the drawer.

When Harry entered the parlor, Jenkins rose and bowed in greeting. "Your Grace."

Harry bit back a groan at the address. Tall and gangly, with a large bulbous nose, Jenkins reminded Harry of a pelican. Sparse strands of hair were ridiculously combed from approximately two inches above his right ear over to the left side of his head. The effort to cover his balding pate lacking, Harry forced himself not to laugh.

"Jenkins." Harry offered his hand. The man's handshake was weaker than his attempt to conceal his baldness. "Her Grace should join us in a moment."

No sooner had Harry spoken, Margaret appeared in the doorway.

Jenkins straightened his shoulders and puffed out his scrawny chest before executing a woefully inadequate bow. "Your Grace." Color rose to the man's cheeks causing Harry's gaze to travel from Jenkins to Margaret and back again. *The man is smitten.* Harry could hardly blame him.

"Mr. Jenkins," she said before turning her attention to Harry. "Shall we sit?"

Margaret took a seat on a small settee, and Jenkins settled in a large wingback. There was another chair unoccupied, but Harry sat next to Margaret, noticing when he did, she shifted away from him.

"First, let me offer my condolences, Your Grace," Jenkins said to

Harry. "It was unfortunate you were abroad and missed your brother's funeral. It was a difficult task tracking you down. Your cousin Elinor alerted us you were alive and proved to be extremely helpful in locating you."

For once, Harry almost regretted his correspondence with his cousin. They'd exchanged letters sporadically during his time in America. "Indeed. It took over nine months for your letter to reach me."

Jenkins emitted an uncomfortable cough. "Yes, my apologies, Your Grace. Now, with your permission, shall we begin?"

"By all means." Harry extended his hand, waving Jenkins to proceed.

Jenkins pulled several sheets of parchment from his satchel and held them in his shaking hands. After a series of unpleasant attempts to clear his throat, he began.

"I, George Alistair Radcliffe, Sixth Duke of Ashton, being of sound mind and body—"

"I hate to appear callous, Jenkins, but could you skip the formalities and cut to the heart of it?"

"Of course, of course, Your Grace. A thousand apologies."

Harry rolled his eyes and out of the corner of them, caught Margaret attempting to stifle a laugh.

"Upon my death, the estate shall be left to my heir." Jenkins raised his eyes. "A mere formality, Your Grace, since that would be the case regardless of your brother's wishes. However, I do believe it was a nice touch."

Harry waved his hand for Jenkins to continue.

"Should I not produce any male issue, my brother, Harrison Malcolm Radcliffe shall receive the title and all that entails." Jenkins paused again. "There's more in the event you predecease him, but that seems to be a moot point. Should I continue past those entries?"

"Please."

"To my wife, Margaret Elizabeth Farnsworth Radcliffe"— Jenkins peered up over the paper, his face assuming an oddly motherly affectation—"I leave a stipend of ten pounds per annum."

Harry straightened, unsure he heard correctly. "I'm sorry, Jenkins, could you repeat that?"

"To my wife—"

"Not that part, man, the amount."

"Ten pounds per annum, Your Grace."

Harry's body rose unbidden from the settee. "Are you saying my brother left his widow a measly ten pounds a year to live on? What about a dower house?"

Jenkins turned an unattractive shade of pink. "There is no mention of a dower house, Your Grace. If I may continue?" He cleared his throat again. "All jewelry and priceless articles are to remain in the estate. She may keep her clothing." Jenkins' eyes darted toward Harry, his face now a ghastly red. "Must I read the next part, Your Grace?" Jenkins' gaze avoided Margaret entirely.

"Yes, unless it's some formality."

Jenkins' finger made a circuit around his cravat, and he finished in a voice no more than a whisper. "It is more than she deserves."

Harry stared incredulously at the solicitor. If George weren't already dead, he'd take great satisfaction beating him bloody.

Suddenly remembering the person affected most by this bequeathal, he turned toward Margaret. Other than her wide eyes and blanched complexion, she remained stoic, her posture straight, her hands folded in her lap. A perfect example of decorum. The *ton* would be so proud.

Her voice gave her away, cracking slightly. "Is that all, Mr. Jenkins?"

Harry returned to his seat next to her, resisting the urge to comfort her. She had to be devastated. "Margaret?" He kept his voice low, soothing. Now was not the time for propriety. If the solicitor found fault with his familiarity, so be it.

She turned toward him, the evidence of the humiliation in her eyes brimming with unshed tears. She gave him a weak smile. "I'm fine, Your Grace."

She definitely was not fine, but Harry admired her courage and fortitude. "Is there more, Jenkins?" Harry asked, anxious to finish this unpleasant business, if not for himself, for Margaret.

"Yes, Your Grace." Jenkins returned his gaze to the will. "To Madam Bertha Morley, I leave the sum of £1,000 so she may continue her establishment."

Harry's brow furrowed in confusion as he searched his memory. "Who is Bertha Morley? I don't remember any relative by that name. And what is her establishment?"

Jenkins appeared to be on the verge of apoplexy, his eyes darting around the room, refusing to make contact with either Harry or Margaret. "Your Grace, perhaps it is a matter best discussed without Her Grace present."

Harry glanced toward Margaret. *George's mistress? Does Margaret know?* "Would you prefer to leave, Your Grace?" She deserved the dignity of her title, and he chastised himself for using her Christian name earlier.

"It's not necessary. I'm well aware who Madam Morley is and her occupation." Her hands, held in her lap, shook as she tried to still them.

Jenkins lowered his voice as if conveying a state secret. "Your Grace, Madam Morley runs the establishment The Wild Boar." He leaned in closer, perched so precariously on his chair it appeared he might tumble off. "A bawdy house, Your Grace."

£1,000 for a brothel? Was George mad? Perhaps this explained the large sum for Miscellaneous. "Please, Jenkins, continue with the next item."

"That's essentially it, Your Grace. A paragraph regarding the settlement of his debts, and oh, wait"—Jenkins turned a horrid shade of puce. The man had exhibited multiple shades of the color spectrum in one morning. "It states that the horse named Satan should be shot."

At this, Margaret sprang from her seat. "Absolutely not! It is unthinkable."

Harry stared in amazement. She had no objection to her measly ten pounds per annum stipend, little reaction to George's bequest to a whorehouse, yet she leaped to the defense of an animal. Harry's esteem grew ten-fold.

"Her Grace is correct. Why I rode Satan yesterday, and with the right touch, he's a fine specimen."

Margaret spun on her heel toward him. "You rode Satan?"

Harry's chest expanded, proud he had impressed her. "It was nothing. Patience and a few apples and carrots."

The smile that etched her face communicated her awareness of the true extent of his feat.

"Well, it doesn't say you have to kill him." Jenkins offered.

"This is absurd." Margaret said. "We must devise a solution, something that satisfies the stipulation but protects the horse from harm." Her hands fisted at her sides as she marched the length of the room and back again. She looked like a warrior ready for battle, and Harry admired the determination on her face.

She continued to pace before him, muttering, "Shot, shot, is there another meaning to the word?"

Harry's head snapped up, and his body followed, resisting the urge to pick Margaret up and spin her around. "Margaret, you're brilliant. What if we send a cricket shot his way? Jenkins, would that suffice?"

"You intend to hit the horse with a cricket ball?" The man's voice rose in pitch, ending on a squeak.

"It's decidedly preferable to a bullet, wouldn't you say?"

"It is indeed, Your Grace, but won't it hurt the horse?"

"Not if it doesn't hit him, and even if it does, no one has to whack the ball with full strength, do they?"

Jenkins made a great show of studying the document. "Nothing specifies the force of the shot. I believe you have your solution." Jenkins returned the will to his satchel. "Your Grace," he said, directing his attention to Harry, "might I have a word in private?"

"Of course."

"Mr. Jenkins," Margaret said, "thank you for your time in this matter. If you will excuse me, I'll allow you gentlemen to finish your conversation." She exited, closing the door to the parlor behind her.

Jenkins' finger repeated its circuitous route around his cravat. "Your Grace, about Her Grace's stipend."

Awareness dawned. "Jenkins, did you purposely delay relaying the contents of the will to provide Her Grace more time at Briarfield?"

"Well . . . I . . . err. It did stipulate the heir should be present."

"It's fine, Jenkins. You did the right thing. How could my brother be so callous? It's disgusting."

"I'm glad . . . err, not about the stipend, about your sentiment, Your Grace. When your brother passed, I suggested she consider marrying again. She's young and attractive, many men would be proud to have such a refined woman as their wife."

"It sounds like a reasonable solution, however something tells me Her Grace did not receive it well."

"Exactly, sir. She rejected it entirely. I would even offer for her myself if I thought she'd have me." The man's cheeks pinked, and he glanced at Harry sheepishly.

"She must have her reasons." Harry could think of several and restrained the laugh bubbling to the surface.

"Perhaps you might help convince her. Ten pounds a year is barely enough for a servant's living, much less a duchess."

"I'll see what I can do. She scarcely knows me, I doubt I would hold any sway with her, but I'll try."

Jenkins removed a handkerchief from his pocket and wiped his forehead. "Your Grace has been most kind. To be honest, I did not anticipate this meeting with pleasure."

"You've just done your job, no one can blame you for that." Harry walked Jenkins to the door of the parlor. "Isn't there anything we can do about the bequest to Madam Morley?"

"I'm afraid not, Your Grace. One of the witnesses to the will was Lord Nash, your brother's closest friend. I fear he would object."

"I know Nash, and you're correct. He's a scoundrel of the first order." Harry sighed. "Thank you for your service, Jenkins. Burrows will see you out."

After Jenkins left, Harry debated having another glass of brandy. He decided against it, his head already pounded.

He returned to his study and examined the ledgers for more miscellaneous entries. Fingers drummed against the desk as Harry searched for a solution to Margaret's pitiful plight. Marriage, as Jenkins suggested, seemed the best possibility. With her breeding, youth, and appearance, a marriageable earl or marquess would suit. Perhaps she rejected not the idea of marriage in general, but Jenkins in particular. Who could blame her?

He'd been away too long, he needed more information. He rose from the desk, tugged the bell pull, and Burrows appeared.

"Your Grace?"

"Burrows, I wish to speak with Jane, Her Grace's lady's maid."

Several minutes later, a knock sounded on the open door, and Harry raised his head from the ledgers to find Jane.

"You wished to speak with me, Your Grace." A strange restrained smirk played at her lips.

"Yes, Jane, please take a seat."

She moved to close the door.

"Leave the door open. For propriety, you understand."

She nodded and took a seat at the desk across from him.

"Jane, you mentioned you may be able to provide information about the estate. I had the distinct impression you wished to tell me something in particular. Anything you may have said to my brother, feel free to say to me."

She no longer contained the smirk as she leaned forward, a strange, manic glint in her eyes. "Well, Your Grace, I've noticed some jewelry missing."

Not what he expected. "Indeed? Jewelry of Her Grace's you mean?"

"Yes, sir."

"Perhaps it's misplaced?"

"I don't believe so, sir. I believe someone stole it."

She had his attention.

"Whom do you suspect?"

She hesitated. "Her Grace."

Harry bit back a laugh. Yet, what did Jane imply? Did George confide the details of his will to her? It seemed unlikely. "It's her jewelry, you can't steal what you own."

If anything, Harry admired Margaret's resourcefulness, and he would be the last person to demand the jewelry's return. It would be a small recompense for George's insulting bequeathal.

Jane squirmed in her seat. "I realize it sounds odd, Your Grace, but there have been items missing before this, and when I questioned her she said she misplaced them."

"But you don't believe that's the case?"

"No sir." Jane's eyes darted away, then met his. "There's more."

"More missing items?" Harry grew more annoyed and prepared to sack her on the spot.

"No, sir. I'm convinced His Grace's death wasn't an accident."

Harry's mind froze. "They informed me he fell and broke his neck. From what I learned yesterday, I presumed he fell from his horse."

"No, sir. He fell down the staircase. I believe he was pushed."

Harry jerked back in his seat as if struck. His blood chilled, his mind drifting, but he forced himself to remain in the present. Although anticipating her answer, he asked anyway. "Your suspect?"

"Her Grace."

A disquiet settled upon Harry. "And your reason for this conclusion?"

"She hated him, Your Grace. He didn't trust her and instructed me to advise him of any odd behavior. She would disappear for hours. They think I don't notice, Your Grace, but I do."

"They?"

"Burrows and Her Grace. They're thick as thieves, those two."

"Well, this is startling news. I appreciate your candor. That will be all."

Jane rose, a wicked grin appearing on her face.

"Jane, one more thing."

She turned, her eyes wide.

"I'm curious. If what you say is true, Her Grace could be imprisoned or hanged. You would lose your position." Little did she know that would be the case regardless unless Margaret found a way to pay her.

"Well . . . I . . . His Grace rewarded me for my loyalty."

"To him, not to Her Grace."

"Well, yes, sir. He paid my salary."

"And you expect the same reward for this information now?"

She adopted a demure manner Harry found so ludicrous as to be comical. "If Your Grace is generous, I would be most appreciative."

"Don't worry, Jane, I'll see that you get everything you deserve."

Harry turned back to the ledgers, but his mind spun. *Could Margaret have pushed George?* From the little he had witnessed, Jane's accusation that Margaret hated his brother was most likely true, but kill him? Part of him couldn't blame her if she did. Truth or not, Jane would find herself without a position in short order.

He slammed the ledger shut and searched the house for Margaret. Unable to locate her, he stopped the little parlor maid, dusting the knickknacks in the hallway. "Flora?"

The girl turned, and the duster poised in mid-air trembled. "Your Grace," she said, executing a somewhat less clumsy curtsy.

"Have you seen Her Grace?"

"I believe she's out in the gardens. Should I fetch her?"

"No, no. Don't trouble yourself. I'll find her. Continue with your work."

She curtsied again and resumed her dusting.

"And Flora," Harry added. "You needn't fear me. I'm not my brother."

Harry wondered how many times he would have to remind his staff of that simple fact. It grew tiresome. He missed America where people only knew him, not his despicable twin. *Damn you to hell, George.* Ironically, that was most likely George's current location. Harry focused on more immediate things, leaving the house to find Margaret in the gardens.

CHAPTER 9—LOVELY BUT DEADLY

W hy should she be surprised? Margaret's intention to calm herself with a walk in the gardens became waylaid when her feet led her toward the family mausoleum. Hatred swelled in her breast. Even from beyond the grave, George tormented her. She imagined him laughing at her from hell.

Picking up the nearest rock, she hurled it with all her might at the massive doors that waited—chained and locked—until it received another resident.

"Damn you, George. Damn you to bloody hell!" Her words became unintelligible as she screamed in frustration at the locked doors. Her throat now raw, she hung her head and cursed her future. The sprig of lily-of-the-valley she'd plucked fell to the ground at her feet.

"Margaret." Her blood froze with the whisper of her name.

"George?" she whispered with a trembling voice. The chains on the mausoleum's door remained secure, and Margaret exhaled a relieved breath.

The call came again. "Margaret."

Not from the tomb, but behind her.

She spun around, expecting to see either a ghost or the

decomposing body of her husband. She blinked, her mind slowly registering not a specter, but Harry. Her hammering heart slowed to a normal rhythm.

"Your Grace, I didn't hear you approach."

He took a tentative step toward her. "I didn't mean to startle you."

Sudden heat flashed across her cheeks, remembering her outburst. "How long have you been standing there?"

"Long enough." The toe of his boot nudged a small rock on the ground. Then he stooped, picked it up, and flung it at the mausoleum, landing a direct hit on the doors. "Damn, that felt good." He lifted another and held it out to her in his open palm.

Her gaze traveled to the offering, then to his hazel eyes, sparkling with mischief as they crinkled at the corners. A sharp contrast to those that had displayed only cruelty. He moved his hand forward in encouragement. With four hesitant steps, she stood before him and plucked the stone from his palm.

As she pulled back to hurl the stone, he laid his hand on her arm to stop her, and picked up another rock. "Together. On the count of three, ready? One, two, three."

They each hurled their stones at the oppressive doors of the mausoleum, resulting in two mighty bangs.

"Remind me not to allow you to pitch the cricket ball toward me when we fulfill the request about Satan," he said. "With that force, we might injure him."

"That was a stroke of genius, Your Grace."

He gave a sheepish grin, and his already tall stature straightened. "Harry, Margaret. Harry. We're alone now."

His eyes traveled down, landing on the sprig of lily-of-the-valley. He stooped to retrieve it. "What's this doing out here?"

In her anger, she had forgotten the tiny flowers. "I must have dropped it. I picked it to place at the doors." Her head gestured toward the mausoleum.

"For George?" His low baritone rose in pitch.

"No. A child is buried in there. I brought it for her."

"George told you about Emmeline?"

"No. At George's interment, I saw her marker. I . . . I'd only heard her name once." Her mouth grew so parched, she struggled to swallow. "She was so young. No one spoke of her. Who was she?"

"Our sister."

An odd sense of clarity formed in her mind knowing the identity of the girl who bore the name. "What happened? Did she become ill?"

"No. There was an accident."

Without hesitation, Margaret reached out, touching Harry's sleeve. The sadness etched on his face so deep and troubling she wished to comfort him. "I'm so very sorry."

"It was a long time ago." Harry jerked his head to the side and swiped a shaking hand over his eyes. "Margaret, how did George die?" The sudden softness of his voice soothed her and encouraged her trust.

"He fell."

"Yes, but how, where? Jenkins wasn't clear in his letter, and I'd like to confirm what someone else said. You must know."

What has he been told? She forced out the words. "Down the stairs."

"Were you there when it happened?"

Tears welled in her eyes. Perhaps she need not worry about her future if there was to be none.

"Yes."

"Tell me what happened, Margaret."

"It was an accident, truly." *Will he believe me?* The truth so strange she hardly believed it herself. She hadn't even told Burrows. She took a breath. "I fear you will think I'm mad."

"Margaret, it's clear my brother mistreated you. Did you push him? If you were defending yourself . . ."

No longer able to withhold her tears, they seeped from the corners of her eyes. "It was late, he had been drinking . . . again. He hadn't . . . demanded his . . . rights . . . for some time. When I refused, he insisted."

She said a prayer to give her courage as she fought the memory.

"I tried to run, but he came after me. We struggled at the top of the stairs. I . . . struck him, and he stumbled back."

"Go on, Margaret. It's all right. Did he fall then?" He leaned toward her, his gaze direct and steady, but comforting. His voice, reassuring and calm, encouraged her to continue.

"No, he started to come at me again, and I backed up, prepared to run, but he had stopped. He stood frozen, as if he stared at someone, something. His face drained of color, and he began shaking and mumbling, making little sense. George never showed fear, but it's the only way I can describe it. Something terrified him."

"What did he say?"

She would never forget his words. "He said, 'You. Get back, stay away from me,' and he shouted a name I had never heard before that night. Then, as if someone pushed him, he stumbled and fell down the stairs."

"Whose name, Margaret?"

"Emmeline."

Harry staggered, the sprig of lily-of-the-valley dropping from his fingers when his hands grasped the back of his head as if in pain.

"No, it can't be." He shook his head and stared straight ahead, eyes glazed. "Impossible."

His eyes narrowed in distrust as they bore through her, and a vision of George flashed through her mind.

She forced down the bile rising in her throat. Determined, she fought the blackness threatening to take her with it and held his gaze.

"Why are you doing this, Margaret? You're as cruel as George."

Doing what? Tears streamed freely down her face. "I . . . I . . . it's what happened. It's as if he saw someone, I swear."

Harry paced in a circle, muttering to himself.

Torn between the urge to run and to comfort him, she settled for a compromise and waited until he stilled.

"You're lying about your knowledge of Emmeline. Admit it, Margaret." He spat the words at her.

She shook her head, her throat constricting from the wild look in his eyes. Panic rose as she fought the memory of George that

Harry's angered face resurrected. Had she been a fool to trust him? "No, I didn't know who she was until you told me."

The muscle in his jaw pulsed. "And what did *you* see, Margaret?"

"Nothing, there was no one there."

Harry stared at the ground before him, then picked up the flower he'd dropped. His gaze swept between her and the tiny blossoms. He turned his back on her and faced the mausoleum.

The silence became ominous as she puzzled over his visceral reaction. She expected disbelief, but not this vitriol.

A question arose in her mind, and although she feared asking, she could not withhold it.

"Harry, what type of accident?"

His head snapped up, and he turned toward her. "What?"

"Emmeline. You said it was an accident."

"She fell down the stairs."

HARRY STARED AT MARGARET. PREPOSTEROUS. THERE WERE NO such things as ghosts. A man of science, Harry trusted in reason and logic. But why would she lie? He had practically handed her a legitimate explanation. Why didn't she say George had fallen as he stumbled back when she struck him? Why would she concoct such a fanciful tale? Why not say he fell in a drunken stupor? Occam's Razor failed him . . . or did it?

No, Emmeline's specter didn't appear and push George in retribution, he couldn't accept that. But a guilty conscience can play strange tricks on the mind.

His eyes searched Margaret's. Even frightened, she stood her ground, facing him. Ludicrous as her account sounded, she clearly believed it. Could he?

She touched his arm. "Tell me about Emmeline; what was she like? Would it help to talk about it?"

Would it? After her death, his father forbade them to speak her name.

He took a deep breath and released it, the air burning his throat as it escaped his lungs. "Emmeline was eight and George and I were fourteen when it happened. She was such a pretty thing with her blonde curls and bright blue eyes like our mother. A beam of sunshine, she was all smiles and laughter, filled with wonder for everything around her."

He fought the heaviness weighing on him. "We were home from school for the holidays. Her chattering and fussing delighted me, but annoyed George."

A strange grip compressed his chest, squeezing—painful, yet oddly not.

"She loved animals and begged our father for a pet. A cat kept in the stables for mousing had given birth to kittens, and Emmeline brought one home. She was my father's one weakness. He doted on her, so he allowed her to keep it. It angered George because Father had denied him a pet."

"I can't imagine George wanting an animal to love."

"You would be correct. Father said pets were women's folly, but I suspect he didn't trust George to care for an animal properly and believed he had more nefarious reasons for his request."

The ache in his chest grew more painful now, and he instinctively rubbed a hand over it. "The kitten died a week later."

"What happened?"

He shook his head. "No one knew. The kitten started acting strangely, becoming lethargic and wouldn't eat. I found it on the floor in front of Emmeline's bedroom where it had vomited. I tried to help, but . . . it was too late."

"Poor Emmeline." Margaret's hand traveled to his sleeve, her touch comforting. Her eyes met his, waiting for him to continue.

"That night, sounds of arguing woke me, and a scream followed. I ran out of my room and found Emmeline lying at the foot of the staircase."

"And George?"

"At the top, staring down at her. He said she'd slipped."

Color drained from Margaret's face, becoming so pale he feared she might faint, and he slid an arm around her waist to steady her. "Margaret?"

She shivered. "Do you suspect . . . George . . ."

Her color returned and he removed his arm. "I had no proof. My parents were heartbroken. How could I tell them? They buried the kitten with her, in her arms."

"I'm so sorry, Harry." Fresh tears welled in her eyes.

Harry twirled the flower sprig in his fingers. Emmeline had loved the bell-like blooms and their sweet fragrance. "Were you aware these are poisonous?"

"Yes. It's hard to believe a flower so lovely could be so deadly."

Her words teased something in his mind as he remembered Jane's accusation and his reason for searching for her.

"Margaret, tell me the truth. Did you push George? I would understand if you did."

"No, I swear." Her gaze met his—direct and unwavering. "But I wanted to."

As with Satan, he wanted—no, needed—to gain her trust. He'd won a minor victory in the battle when they each hurled their stones at George's tomb.

"Then we'll speak of it no more."

He held out the sprig. "Let's put them on the doors for Emmeline. Together, as we did the stones for George."

As they approached, she hesitated, so Harry took her hand and placed the flowers in her fingers. With her hand clasped in his, he moved them both to the crack in the door to place their offering.

"She loved them," he said.

Margaret stared at the doors. "I hate to think of her in there with him." A negative comment, but honest. Perhaps the small victory was greater than he supposed.

"It's only their bodies. I'm sure their spirits are in entirely different locations."

She gave an almost imperceptible nod, and her lips twitched upward.

"Margaret, are you fond of Jane, your lady's maid?"

Her eyes widened. "No, but it seems a moot point. I won't be able to pay her wage."

"Margaret, about the stipend."

Immediately her demeanor changed. The softness in her face he witnessed a moment ago vanished. She squared her shoulders and lifted her chin. "What about it, Your Grace? Mr. Jenkins was perfectly clear."

Aware he'd raised her defenses, he proceeded with caution. "You can't live on that paltry amount, Margaret. Do you have family who can assist you?"

Her posture changed yet again, her shoulders relaxed, then slumped as she shook her head. "No. As I mentioned, my mother died before George and I met, and my father passed a month after we married."

"You have no siblings? Brothers who would take you in?"

"No. I was an only child. Upon my father's death, my inheritance transferred to Geo . . ."—her eyes darted to his, and her skin first blanched then pinked—"Forgive me, to His Grace."

"You can use his name with me, Margaret." Harry considered his next question carefully. "How much, perhaps I could—"

"Absolutely not. The sum would cripple the estate."

Harry jerked, unsure he understood. "I beg your pardon? How much, Margaret?"

"Fifteen thousand."

Dear God! Harry's mind churned at the amount, and words failed him. George's cruelty knew no bounds. He searched for some comfort to offer.

"Margaret, Jane approached me to discuss . . . some matters." He refused to mention the jewelry.

She stiffened. "Oh, was she concerned about her position?"

"No. But I found her message distasteful, and I intend to sack her. Might one of the other servants provide assistance? Flora, perhaps?" She began to speak, but he stopped her. "I'll pay her wage."

She blinked rapidly. "That's most generous, but I'm capable of taking care of myself."

"If you would indulge me, at least until . . ."

"Until I leave?"

Heat burned his ears, and he struggled for a way to recover. "Have you considered remarrying?" Why did that idea disturb him?

"Your concern about my future is most kind. I assure you, it is foremost on my mind, and I shall seek a solution expeditiously and remove myself from your presence. Now, if you will excuse me, Your Grace, I should like to return to the house. I feel a sudden chill."

The chill she spoke of flowed over him, yet the air was warm. Her shift in how she addressed him jarred, his small victory in winning her trust somehow diminished. Harry mumbled a short, "Of course," as his eyes met hers, catching the mistiness that threatened them. She turned, and he watched her back straighten, her head lifted high as she walked toward the house.

One more rock found its way to the mausoleum doors.

CHAPTER 10—LATE NIGHT DISCOVERIES

Margaret paced the length of her room, her footsteps creating a pattern in the rug. *What to do?* Her fingers drifted to her mouth, but she resisted chewing at her nails. Ten pounds. Although George's complete lack of decency didn't surprise her, the amount was a pittance. Thank goodness for her secret funds. Would the sum be sufficient to provide transportation and lodging in London? Perhaps reputable employment would be available within the bustling city.

Her mind whirled with questions and possibilities. *I must develop a plan of action.*

A soft knock interrupted her strategizing, and Flora poked her head around the half-open door.

"His Grace requests you join him in the parlor, Your Grace."

Margaret nodded. Something had changed between them when they shared their troubling memories that morning. She no longer feared him, but until she could find a solution to her situation, she relied on his generosity for the very roof over her head. It would not be prudent to ignore his summons.

She halted at the open doors to the parlor, unsure if she should interrupt. Jane stood before Harry, her expression smug. Harry's head turned, and he motioned for her to enter.

"Ah, Your Grace. Thank you for joining us. I thought you might like to deliver the news to Jane."

"I beg your pardon, Your Grace?" Jane sputtered her question, and her perplexity appeared rather comical, although Margaret found herself as confused.

"Her Grace has information regarding your position."

Power surged through Margaret upon grasping the meaning of Harry's summons. With slow steps she moved to stand next to Harry and faced Jane, warmth flowing through her body at her vindication.

Jane shifted, refusing to meet her gaze.

"Jane." Margaret waited until Jane raised her head. She needed to look into her eyes. A wicked sense of satisfaction thrilled her, and she wet her lips. "I no longer have need of your services."

Jane blinked, then turned toward Harry. "I don't understand, sir."

"Why are you addressing me, Jane? Her Grace has made it clear." He faced Margaret, his eyes glinting with mischief. "Perhaps rephrase in simpler terms? I've found gossips to be a bit dense."

Like a cat who had trapped a mouse, Margaret executed the final blow. "You're sacked, Jane."

Jane persisted in her appeal to Harry. "But you pay my wage, Your Grace. I can be of use."

"I have no need for a lady's maid."

"But our agreement."

"What agreement?" Harry said. "I promised you would receive what you deserve, and that has been delivered. If you continue to argue about this matter, you will find your references lacking."

Jane's head dropped as her body seemed to collapse on itself, her smug appearance wiped away. "When do you wish me to leave?"

Margaret hesitated, but Harry turned toward her and whispered. "It's up to you."

"As soon as possible, Jane. Pack your trunks now. You're dismissed."

Harry touched Margaret on the arm. "Before you go, Jane. If I hear a whiff of gossip regarding Her Grace, you will find yourself unable to secure a position even as a scullery maid. I can and will rescind my recommendation. Am I clear?"

Head held low, Jane only nodded.

"I'll have a carriage brought around to take you to the nearest posting inn. After that, you're on your own."

When they were alone, Harry faced Margaret. "How did that feel?"

She gave him a genuine smile. "Iniquitous, but most gratifying."

He squeezed her arm, then released it. "You were kinder than I would have been. She deserved much worse."

"She mentioned an agreement. I presume to continue the arrangement she had with George."

"Yes, she expected payment for information. You should have sacked her immediately after George died."

Margaret sighed. "I'd thought about it, but with the uncertainty of my future, it seemed unfair to employ another maid I couldn't pay."

"My offer holds, Margaret. Choose someone from the staff, or hire a new one. It's the least I can do."

His kindness—for more than his offer—overwhelmed her as she fought back tears of gratitude and the impulse to throw her arms around him. "I refuse to be a burden. Nothing keeps me here. I must make do on my own."

"There's no rush for that. If you prefer someone already on staff, I will increase their wage commensurate with the position. In fact, I intend to raise Burrows' wages as well."

His comment surprised her. "Burrows?"

"Yes. I respect those who do the right thing, especially when it isn't self-serving."

Her mind whirled. What did he know? What did Jane tell him?

"Besides, I'm not above bribery to keep a good servant. I fear, should your fortunes change, he would leave me in an instant."

The twinkle in his eye gave him an attractive boyish appearance, and an odd fluttering arose in her stomach. She searched his eyes, getting the impression he wanted to say more but held back. With emotions threatening to overtake her, she needed distance from him.

"If you will excuse me, there's much to contemplate."

After retreating to her room, Margaret spent the rest of the day in solitude, examining her options. They were few, and as she stared at her list, a position as a governess seemed the most promising. Since the Season hadn't ended, perhaps if she made it to London, she could contact some of her old acquaintances and make inquiries. She moved London to the top of her list.

As Margaret prepared to change for supper, Flora knocked softly and entered.

"Your Grace, I'm here to help you dress."

"Did His Grace send you?" she asked, her tone a little too sharp.

Flora's cheeks pinked as she ducked her head. "Yes, Your Grace. I'm sorry, I didn't say it right. He instructed me to ask if you would like my assistance."

Margaret struggled with her pride in accepting Harry's charity. Her tension eased as she stopped to consider the difference it would make to Flora if she learned to be a lady's maid, not to mention the increase in her wage.

She smiled warmly, "I would be most grateful for your help, Flora. I was about to select my gown for this evening."

As she looked through her depressing assortment of black gowns, her fingers paused on the soft lavender muslin embroidered with white flowers.

"That gown is lovely, Your Grace."

She turned to Flora. "Yes, I'll wear this one."

It was a risk wearing something colorful, but the power she experienced sacking Jane swelled in her, giving her courage.

Once dressed, Margaret's mind wandered while Flora attempted to style her hair.

". . . isn't he, Your Grace?"

What had the girl asked? "I'm sorry?"

Flora twisted another lock of hair in an attempt to pin it to

Margaret's head. "I said he's different from his brother. The new duke, he's very kind. He even told me not to fear him, that he isn't his brother."

No, he isn't. "Do you like him, Flora?"

"I do, Your Grace. I just wish he looked different, although he is very handsome."

Yes, he is.

Flora struggled to manage the elaborate arrangements Jane had accomplished, so they settled on a simpler style with soft, wispy tendrils falling at the nape of her neck and in front of her ears.

Completed, Margaret stood before her. "How do I look?"

Flora gave an approving nod. "Beautiful, if I do say so."

Margaret patted Flora's arm. "You did well, Flora. We'll work on your hairstyling skills."

As Flora left, a pang squeezed Margaret's heart causing her breath to hitch. Flora deserved more than false promises. If only she could afford her. It would be a comfort to have someone kind as a companion, a far cry from Jane. However, having a servant of her own would be out of the question if she found employment as a governess.

As Margaret entered the parlor, Harry rose in greeting. Her heart raced as he stared, his lips slightly parted, and she regretted her choice of evening dress. Did he disapprove?

"That gown is most becoming, Margaret. It's good to see you wearing something other than black."

Lightness flowed through her like the sunshine of earlier that morning, and the tension in her shoulders eased.

"Thank you, Harry. After the events of the day, I felt rather rebellious."

He chuckled, the sound pleasant and comforting.

"Thank you for sending Flora to assist me. Although, I fear I've encouraged unreasonable hopes. When I leave, I won't be able to take her with me."

When Harry opened his mouth to speak, Burrows entered announcing supper.

As they enjoyed their meal, free of Brussels sprouts, Harry provided a solution to at least one of her dilemmas.

"I'll be leaving for London on Thursday. I must present myself to Lords in Parliament while it's still in session."

He sipped his wine, then met her gaze. "I would appreciate your company."

She strained to contain her exuberance over his suggestion and kept her countenance passive.

His eyes drifted from hers. "I'm woefully out of practice with the *ton*, and your guidance would be most welcome. In addition, perhaps interactions with others might lift your spirits."

She stared wide-eyed, stunned that he not only sought her assistance but considered her well-being. Words failed her, and he seemed to sense her shock.

His hand lifted covering his mouth as he stifled a cough to clear his throat. "It can't have been easy being isolated in this gloomy house for the past year."

"It's not yet a year. I'm still in mourning."

The laugh he snorted caused her fork to rattle against her plate and her eyes to meet his.

"I apologize, I meant no disrespect. It's not precisely your statement I found humorous, but simply that anyone would mourn George at all, much less for an entire year. It's been eleven months, has it not? Surely an appearance in society wouldn't raise too many eyebrows. It would be easier if I had a friend to shield me from the onslaught of fortune seeking females."

He considered her a friend? "Do you not have former friends and acquaintances with whom you could reconnect?"

"Possibly, but I won't know until I've arrived."

His imploring gaze reminded her of Jasper, the sad-eyed beagle her elderly aunt had owned. She never could resist that dog.

"Then it shall be an honor to accompany you to London, sir. However, I'm not certain how much protection I will provide against status seeking debutantes or their mamas. You realize they will consider you a remarkable catch."

"My title, you mean."

Not precisely. Although a duke with a thriving estate would be the primary impetus in most cases, Harry's intelligence, kindness, and sense of humor would be enough to place any man high on a young woman's list of desirable suitors, no matter what his social status. Not to mention his undeniable handsome appearance. Marriageable women of the *ton* would devour him. Why did her heart sink at the idea?

"You have many fine qualities."

His eyebrow quirked at her remark, but she refused to elaborate. Did he not realize his appeal?

"I will admit," she deflected, "I would love to see my friend, Camilla again. We were very close before my marriage."

"Then it's settled. We'll leave first thing Thursday as soon as our trunks are packed."

Margaret turned to Burrows, standing at attention by the sideboard. "That's only two days, Burrows."

"With His Grace's permission, I shall travel ahead with several others to prepare the residence. Hastings will stand in my stead during my absence."

"Of course, Burrows, whatever is necessary. Is it still the house in Mayfair on Grosvenor Square?"

"It is, Your Grace."

Harry's lips curved in an enigmatic smile. "I do hope there will be time to walk through Hyde Park. It was one of my favorite pastimes as a lad."

Margaret envisioned him scampering through the park as a child, perhaps attempting to fly a kite, the image flooding her chest with warmth. George detested the park and only visited when he wanted to show off new horse flesh—and he always rode alone.

"If you require me to accompany you, I shall be happy to oblige." She cast a quick sideways glance through her lashes to gauge his reaction.

A provocative curl of his lips assuaged her concern. She breathed easier with his reply. "It's settled then. It will be one thing to look forward to during our stay."

Margaret excused herself after supper and returned to her

room, a spark of hope now flickering in her chest. To proceed with her plan, she needed to retrieve the hidden funds from the library.

WHEN THE CLOCK CHIMED ONE, MARGARET ROSE FROM HER BED. Plans racing through her mind proved sufficient to keep her from drifting into slumber. She threaded her arms through her wrapper, cinched the belt, and tucked her feet into her slippers.

Careful to avoid each squeaky floorboard, she tiptoed downstairs, a solitary candle held in her hand to light her way.

She paused only for a second at the foot of the staircase, sending a quick glance upward, then pushed the haunting memory aside before she continued toward the library.

A soft beam of light emanated from between the double doors —curiously ajar—causing her brow to furrow. *Has someone left a candle burning?* Her hand placed on the less squeaky door, she eased it open further and slipped inside, rebuffing the ghostly fingers creeping up her spine and neck. Dying embers glowed in the large fireplace, and a candle burned on the mantle, its wax a mere stub. As she replaced it with her own, a shadow cast by moonlight streaming in from the window moved abruptly. She gasped and spun toward it.

Harry stepped from the shadows into the dim light of the room. "Margaret?"

Instinctively, she clutched the wrapper, pulling it tight to her throat. "Y-Your Grace. I didn't expect anyone to be here." She breathed easier at his smile, her pounding heart slowing to a more steady pace.

In his shirtsleeves, legs still encased in snug-fitting breeches and boots, he looked magnificent, and her breath hitched at the sight. With no cravat around his neck, the shirt hung loose and open, revealing his throat and broad chest. Her pulse picked up speed again.

He lifted a glass in display. "Couldn't sleep. You?"

"Yes . . . I mean, no." Unable to pull her eyes from him, she struggled to respond coherently. His disheveled hair—an errant spike rising from the side, forelocks falling loosely over his brow—looked adorably like a small boy's. She ached to run her fingers through it and straighten it. *Would it be as soft as it appeared?*

"Care to join me?" He lifted the glass again and motioned toward the settee.

"I . . . just a little."

He poured a minuscule amount of brandy into a glass and joined her on the settee.

After taking a sip of the liquor, she remembered the purpose of her late-night visit. She glanced up to the shelf of the bookcase that hid her treasure and frowned as she noticed several books moved from her hiding spot.

"Looking for this?" Harry held the small wooden box in his hand.

Her eyes jerked toward the box and then to meet Harry's gaze. Heat flooded her. He had found her out. His eyes penetrated hers so fiercely, she averted her gaze from his face, landing on his bare chest where a dusting of soft blond hair poked through the opening of his shirt. The lump in her throat threatened to choke her as she forced it down then opened her mouth, searching for the air her lungs required. "Harry, I can explain." Could she?

He placed the box in her hand and closed her fingers over it. As his hand wrapped around hers, exuding a warmth that—surprisingly—made her shiver, her eyes widened at their gentleness. Acquainted with the strength residing in those hands as well as their ability to inflict pain, her mind struggled to make sense of the situation.

"No need to explain, Margaret. I only regret you couldn't confide in me."

As her gaze moved from the box to meet his eyes, she found no flash of anger, no contempt, only kindness and compassion. "How did you know?"

"Our first meeting, remember?" He removed his hand from where it encased hers, taking his warmth with it. "I apologize for removing it from your hiding place. My curiosity has been with me since childhood, at times leading to unfortunate consequences."

She held the container securing her future out to him. "Everything in this house is your property. You had every right to remove it."

He shook his head and pushed the box back toward her. "No, Margaret, not everything."

Her hand toyed with the clasp of the box, hesitant to open it in his presence. Her eyes darted toward his.

"It's all there, I assure you, a sum of £147 and a few shillings by my count. If I may ask, what were your plans for such a fortune?" His eyes crinkled at the corners.

"I . . . I . . ." She struggled with her explanation and opted for a lie. "I hoped to purchase a reticule I admired."

His eyebrow quirked, and one corner of his mouth lifted. "An expensive reticule, perhaps encrusted with jewels?"

Her shoulders sagged, her instinct to protect herself warred against her urge to trust him.

Warmth from his hand found hers again as he gave it a gentle squeeze. "Forgive me, Margaret. Your money is yours to do with as you see fit. No need to make account to me."

Candlelight reflected from his eyes cast a golden hue, and warmth spread through her body. But unlike the heat of shame, it proved welcome, pleasant.

She dropped her gaze away from his searching gaze. "In truth, I planned to use it to start a new life."

She chanced a quick glance up and seeing his understanding, she continued. "At first I used the box to hold funds for the tenants, or the money I obtained by selling Tom Morrison's carvings at Ramsgate."

"You're the Angel. I suspected as much."

She blushed at the name and hoped he didn't notice in the dim light. "I'm not an angel. I've done horrible things, lying, keeping things from George. But I wanted to help. I was able to fetch a better price than Tom." She met his eyes. "A title gives one power, even as a woman. Other times I saved from the allowance George provided."

She sighed, remembering the deceit. "I wasn't always successful in secreting or distributing the funds."

Harry remained silent, but he gave her hand a reassuring squeeze.

"When George died, I expected he wouldn't be generous, so I began selling my jewelry."

"Jane mentioned missing jewelry to me." He held up his hand to stop her from speaking. "I told her you can't steal what you own."

She nodded. "Part of this goes to the Morrisons for Tom's carvings and another I planned to give the Whitcombs. Mr. Whitcomb needs to see a physician in Ramsgate."

Harry smiled. "I can help with that."

"You'll pay the physician's charge?" The strange fluttery sensation in her stomach returned.

"No. I will see to him myself."

"You? I don't understand."

"I'm a physician."

Margaret's lips parted, but she struggled to form a response.

"You disapprove?"

She shook her head. "I . . . I think it's wonderful."

His shoulders straightened, drawing her eyes to the opening of his shirt as it gaped wider. "Father turned a blind eye when I studied medicine at University then purchased a commission in the army as a medical officer, but I embarrassed George."

It seemed ludicrous, but then again, it was George. "But such service is noble."

She sighed as she pictured him in dress uniform. He would have been even more dashing. Her mind whirled. A physician. He could do so much good.

For the first time since his arrival, her gaze upon his face was more than a glance, and she noticed the thin, pale scar that traveled from his temple down to his left cheek. As she focused on the scar, George disappeared, and Harry remained. Her resulting smile was wan but genuine.

"This isn't about me, Margaret, we were speaking of the plans for your funds."

She nodded, her mind returning to their discussion. "I hope to find employment in London. Perhaps as a governess. Your offer to accompany you has helped immensely. The remaining amount should be sufficient to obtain lodging until I can find a position."

His lips pursed, attracting her attention. "Margaret, a governess is barely a step above a servant. Won't you consider the possibility of remarriage? Perhaps a widowed marquess or earl."

Pressure swelled in her skull, her blood pounding. She pulled her hand from his. "I'm not afraid of honest work, and I have no desire to remarry."

"I've offended you, I apologize. But there's no reason to rush. You're welcome to stay here and at the townhouse for as long as you wish."

A pang of guilt that she had taken affront soured her stomach. "That's very generous. Thank you, Your Grace. However, as we discussed at supper, you will be seeking your own wife, and I'm sure she would not be pleased to have me underfoot."

He reminded her again, his voice gentle, reassuring, "Harry, Margaret. Harry. I'd hoped we were finally past the formalities."

His hand reached up toward her face, but hesitated then drew back.

Oddly, she didn't flinch. Instead her skin tingled in anticipation of his touch, the sensation of birds taking flight rose in her stomach, but plummeted when he failed to follow through.

"I don't expect to find a bride during my first trip to London as duke. Please consider staying with me this time."

The fluttering in her stomach resumed, and her heart raced.

"Thank you, Harry."

He patted her hand. "Now, why don't you try to get some sleep?"

A odd blend of emotions brewed within her. Relief she no longer had to hide her funds eased her conscience. Gratitude for Harry's understanding and willingness to assist the tenants mixed with admiration of his former profession as a physician.

Determination and desperation battled against each other regarding her future, with a burgeoning shred of hope reaching out with tentative fingers. But the most troubling emotion was the attraction slamming into her at Harry's touch. As she returned to her room, she remained unconvinced she would find respite in sleep.

CHAPTER 11—FULFILLING PROMISES

A heavy sigh escaped Harry's lungs as Margaret walked from the library, his gaze drawn to the sway of her dressing gown as it swished at her hips and against her limbs. Her raven hair flowed down her back, loose and wild, and he ached to thread his hands through it.

Even in the candlelight, he had noticed the circles under her eyes, stark against her porcelain skin. Were they testament to her worry about her secret funds or simply lack of sleep?

Regardless of the cause, they did nothing to mar her beauty. Those soulful, almost violet eyes, framed with dark, thick lashes pierced his when confronted with his discovery. Her enticing lavender scent had filled his nostrils, encouraging him to breathe deeply. When her lips had parted slightly as she tried to form her explanation, the urge to press his own to them had startled him.

The small wooden box had provided the answer to his overpowering need to touch her. As he'd placed it in her hand, he'd allowed his fingers to embrace hers, and a shiver had passed through him, despite the warmth of her skin.

Now alone in the dim light, his analytical mind sifted through the evidence and came to one conclusion. He found his brother's widow extremely attractive. God help him, he'd almost cupped her cheek and brought his lips to hers. Sitting with her bathed in candlelight during the wee hours of the morning had not been advisable.

Harry slouched onto the settee and dragged his hand down his face, suppressing a laugh at the irony of it all. He didn't believe in ghosts or superstition, but a small part of him swore George had cursed him from hell. Who would have thought that returning home to fulfill his dying mother's wish he would meet the woman capable of winning his heart and his mother's approval? Well-bred, intelligent, resourceful, and compassionate, Margaret was everything he would ever want—barring one thing. She was the one woman he couldn't have—his sister by marriage.

She had the right of it, though. His future wife would not be pleased to have Margaret in the same household, especially when the master of the house was so thoroughly smitten. In addition, her effect on any warm blooded male would diminish her chance of securing employment as a governess.

Picking up his drink, he downed the remaining brandy in one gulp, the sweet liquid burning his throat, and he questioned his request that she accompany him to London. True, he wished to assist her, but he admitted a less altruistic motive lurked within his offer. Could he keep his passions in check?

He was no saint, but a mere mortal man. The irony of the situation enraged him, leaving him powerless. He flung the glass against the fireplace, the resounding crash shattering the crystal into tiny shards that reflected the dying light of the fire.

THE NEXT MORNING, HARRY SET OUT TO FIND WHAT HE NEEDED TO prepare some medicine for Mr. Whitcomb's pain. He found the perfect white willow, still young enough to have good potency, and scraped a large amount of bark from the trunk.

When he returned to the house, he searched for Margaret and located her reading a book in the parlor. As he entered, she raised her head and gave him a welcoming smile, and his heart thumped so hard in his chest he decided to save some willow bark for himself.

"Margaret, I'm going to see Mr. Whitcomb this morning. Would you care to join me? We'll also stop by the Morrisons to give young Tom his profits from the carvings and see if Lily has located Owen."

"I would love that. How soon will you be leaving?"

"I have to prepare the willow bark first, but it shouldn't be long."

"Willow bark?"

"Yes, medicine for Mr. Whitcomb."

"The doctor in Ramsgate gives him laudanum."

Harry frowned, he'd seen the effects of the opioid. "This is much safer yet effective, and it doesn't cost anything."

"That sounds fascinating." She paused, pursing her lips as if in thought.

"What is it? You'd like to say something?"

"May I watch you prepare it if I'm not in your way?"

Air filled his lungs with lightness at her interest. "Of course. Follow me."

He led her to his room where he extracted the mortar and pestle from his medical bag. After pushing aside the books on the escritoire, he placed the bark into the mortar and began shredding it.

"Do you have to eat it?" She moved closer, craning her neck.

He smiled. "No, you make tea from it. It's an effective pain reliever."

Margaret stared wide-eyed, and he suddenly felt much taller than six foot two.

"What kind of pain?"

"Many kinds. It should be especially helpful for Mr. Whitcomb. From the appearance of his hands, I believe the pain is located in his joints."

"Oh," she said, her voice tinged with disappointment.

"It helps with other types of pain, not just joints."

"Would it be effective for megrims?"

He lifted his head up from his focus on his task. "Do you get them?"

"Yes, at times."

"Would you allow me to examine you? If I can identify the cause, I may be able to alleviate your pain."

Her cheeks pinked. His exuberance in practicing again, albeit limited, blinded him to what she no doubt interpreted as a familiarity. He rushed to clarify. "I would only examine your eyes, head, and neck. Nothing improper, I assure you."

"Why don't you concentrate on Mr. Whitcomb. My troubles are of no importance."

He nodded, but her troubles mattered to him, more than he cared to admit.

Once he finished preparing the bark, he wrapped the shredded bark in packets using thin paper he retrieved from his medical bag.

After instructing Burrows to have the carriage brought around, he gathered his bag and escorted Margaret downstairs.

Their first stop was the Whitcombs. Mrs. Whitcomb's eyes widened upon seeing Margaret with Harry, her head turning from them to her husband. Her frail body attempted a curtsy, and as she stumbled forward, Harry reached out and steadied her.

"Careful, Mrs. Whitcomb, or you'll also be needing my services today."

He turned to Mr. Whitcomb. "I have some medicine for the pain in your hands and, I suspect, your other joints."

Mrs. Whitcomb began bustling about in a frantic pace, clearing her mending from a chair and wiping down a table. Her eyes darted between Harry and Margaret throughout the process.

"Mrs. Whitcomb, if you could put the kettle on for some tea, His Grace and I would be most appreciative," Margaret said.

Harry smiled at Margaret's good sense to occupy the nervous woman while he tended to her husband. "Indeed. In fact, prepare Mr. Whitcomb's tea from the medicine I've brought." Harry reached into his medical bag, pulled out one of the packets of willow bark, and handed it to Mrs. Whitcomb. "Steep a teaspoon's worth for ten minutes in boiling water."

"It's not laudanum?" Mr. Whitcomb asked.

"No, and unless the pain is unbearable, I suggest you avoid using laudanum. It will be difficult if you've used it for some time, but try to avoid it. This,"—he nodded toward the packet he provided Mrs. Whitcomb—"is willow bark and is effective in reducing pain and inflammation of the joints without the addictive properties."

Mr. Whitcomb's eyebrows lifted. "Willow bark? You want me to drink tea from a tree?" His nervous gaze darted toward Margaret.

Margaret touched Mr. Whitcomb's sleeve. "His Grace is a physician. Trust him."

Those simple two words impacted Harry more than he cared to admit, and for a moment, he remained speechless. As his patient relaxed, he apologized. "Of course, I forgot to mention that. I served as an army medical officer and later as a doctor in America."

"Were you at Waterloo?" Mr. Whitcomb's eyes searched Harry's. "We lost our only son in that battle."

Without warning, the mere mention of the name threatened to pull Harry under as he fought the memory. He would never forget the bloodied and maimed bodies of those men. Other than Emmeline's death, he had never felt so helpless. Screams of agony pierced the quiet of the small cottage as the gruesome images flashed in his mind. His throat constricted, and he lost focus on the couple before him. His palms and forehead grew damp with sweat.

"Ashton."

A hand on his arm snapped him back, and his eyes refocused on Margaret's concerned face.

"Are you ill?" she asked.

No bloody bodies surrounded him, no stench of gunpowder and death filled the air, only Margaret's soft scent and the comforting smell of baking bread.

He coughed, clearing the obstacle in his throat and gathering his wits. "I apologize, sir. Yes, I was. I'm so sorry about your son. Many a good man sacrificed his life during that battle."

After discreetly wiping his hands on his trousers, he removed his stethoscope from his bag. "May I listen to your heart, sir?"

Upon Mr. Whitcomb's agreement, Harry placed the wooden trumpet-like device against the man's chest and listened. "You have a good strong heart, sir."

Both Mr. and Mrs. Whitcomb chanced glances at Margaret, the concern evident on their faces.

"Her Grace told me of her assistance to you as well as the other tenants. Please accept my apologies that she had to go behind my brother's back to extend such kindness. From now on, I hope you will come to me with your concerns."

The kettle screeched its whistling call to action, and as Mrs. Whitcomb rose to make the tea, Margaret joined her.

While the women busied themselves, Harry examined Mr. Whitcomb's hands and tested for stiffness in his knees and shoulders. "Let me know if the tea helps. Drink three to four cups a day. If necessary, increase the amount you steep to two teaspoons, but no more or it may upset your stomach."

The old man grinned at him. "The question is, Your Grace, will I *want* three or four cups a day?"

Harry chuckled and patted the man's shoulder. "I'm not promising it will taste good, but if it helps, you will. You may add a touch of honey to sweeten it."

Mr. Whitcomb turned his head toward the women bustling in the kitchen, then back toward Harry. "So you know Her Grace is our angel, and you're not angry?"

"Why would I be angry about someone's kindness?" Harry looked up toward the women, affection flowing through him. "I find her bravery admirable."

"Forgive me, Your Grace, but it seems your brother finally did something good."

Harry's attention returned to Mr. Whitcomb, catching the glint in his eyes and the quirk of a smile.

After sharing tea with the couple, and providing Mr. Whitcomb with several more packets of willow bark and instructions to message him should he need more, Harry escorted Margaret to the waiting carriage.

As they rode to their next stop at the Morrisons, Harry reflected on Mr. Whitcomb's statement. Could good come from George's death? Certainly not for Margaret. Whether fulfilling his promise to be a good duke would bring him contentment remained to be seen. Goodness didn't necessarily guarantee happiness.

As if reading his mind, Margaret pulled him from his dark thoughts. "The tenants are fortunate to have you, Harry. I have faith you will be able to accomplish so much here."

"As you have. I hope to continue your legacy."

A blush spread over her cheeks, giving her face an attractive, innocent appearance, and Harry fought the urge to touch it, to feel its softness.

How would he manage with her so close in the carriage all the way to London when he couldn't take his eyes off her during the short ride across the estate? Perhaps, to put her out of his mind, he should seek a bride expeditiously, but if he did, where would that leave Margaret? No matter what he did, his thoughts returned to her. He turned toward the window and forced her from his mind as the scenery breezed by.

"You were at Waterloo?"

Margaret's words jolted him.

"Pardon?"

"You told Mr. Whitcomb you were at Waterloo?"

"Yes."

The tension in his shoulders released when the carriage came to rest at the Morrisons' home, preventing him from adding to his reply. Waterloo was a subject he avoided if at all possible, and he dreaded a repeat of the episode he had experienced at the Whitcombs.

Exiting the carriage first, Harry held out his hand to Margaret, though the coachman stood prepared to offer assistance. Even through her glove, the heat of her touch radiated up his arm, and he held onto her hand longer than he should.

Mr. Morrison strode toward them from the fields, Tom and Owen accompanying him, while Mrs. Morrison and Lily emerged from the house, each face bearing a look of unease upon seeing Harry and Margaret together.

Clive addressed them first. "Your Grace, this is . . . unexpected."

Harry scrambled for a way to explain their visit, but especially the reason Margaret accompanied him.

"Mr. Morrison, please forgive our unannounced arrival," Margaret said. "I wished to deliver the money from the sale of Tom's carvings before I travel to London. His Grace kindly offered to accompany me as he wanted to stop and say hello and see if you were able to locate Lily's husband." She turned to the young man standing next to Clive. "I presume this gentleman is he?"

Harry couldn't help but stare. His doubts about traveling with Margaret floated away with her effective and graceful handling of what might have been an uncomfortable situation for the Morrisons. In a few words, she had let them know he not only was aware of her assistance, but that he approved, putting everyone at ease. Any man in his right mind would be proud to call her his wife.

Lily's giggle shook him from his musings. "He is, Your Grace. Papa has been teaching him how to work the fields."

Clive grunted, and Harry chuckled. "Still not completely sure of him, Mr. Morrison?"

"He's tolerable, I suppose," Clive groused, his face squeezing into a pained expression. "He loves my girl, I'll give him that."

Harry nodded toward the fields. "You're busy, so we won't keep you, but I wondered if I might borrow Mr. MacDougall for a bit? Her Grace and I planned to visit Mr. Turner next. We can discuss the arrangements for Owen and Lily's assistance and eventual ownership of his property."

"Oh, please do come in for a few minutes, Your Grace," Mrs. Morrison said. "I just pulled some sweet cakes from the oven."

The corners of Margaret's lips twitched upward, Harry presumed as she stifled a laugh.

"Well, as Margaret knows, I can't resist sweet cakes."

From the look of horror on everyone's faces Harry realized his error, and his eyes shot to Margaret, pleading for her forgiveness.

She remained calm and smiled sweetly. "His Grace has taken to calling me by my Christian name in an effort to make me feel more comfortable during his transition. I've found it quite refreshing."

Clive cocked his head, his eyes squinting even though the sky was overcast with clouds, pausing only for a moment before motioning them all toward the house.

As they entered, Harry leaned in toward Margaret and whispered, "Thank you."

She gave a small nod, her expression neutral, causing him to wonder if he truly had offended her.

When they'd settled in, and Mrs. Morrison had provided tea and cake, Margaret pulled the proceeds for Tom's carvings from her reticule.

"The deer seem to be the shopkeeper's favorite, Tom. I would recommend you carve a few more of those. They fetched a good price."

She turned to Harry. "Would you be able to assist Tom in selling them at Ramsgate, Your Grace?"

Before Harry could answer, Tom piped up, his face contorted with worry. "You can't do it anymore? I like when you do it."

Clive shot his son a quelling glance.

"I'm sorry, Tom, but I might not be returning to Briarfield after our trip to London. His Grace has graciously allowed me to stay until I find a new home, but eventually he will be bringing his own wife to live here."

"But I like *you*," Tom whined.

Harry cleared his throat, struggling for a way to save the conversation. "Tom, I'm not as pretty as Her Grace, but I promise I'll do my best to negotiate a good price for your carvings. In fact, may I commission one for myself? I admired the doe Her Grace kept. It's fine craftmanship. Would you carve a stag for me?"

The boy's face lit up. "I would be proud to, Your Grace."

Something brushed his arm, and he glanced down to see Margaret's hand nearby. Although she stared straight ahead, the slight curve of her lips and glint in her eyes told him she approved. He sat straighter in his chair.

After departing from the Morrisons with Owen following on horseback, Harry settled against the plush seat of the carriage.

"Margaret, thank you again for saving me from my egregious slip. I hope it hasn't damaged your reputation."

Her smile eased the tension in his chest, replacing it with a feeling of warm sunshine. God, how he loved her smile.

"I doubt my reputation has suffered. In fact, I understand that being a widow provides certain freedom from maintaining a reputation."

"Still, it wouldn't help your search for employment as a governess if people believed you had become . . . familiar with the master of the house."

Her blush indicated she understood his implication. "The Morrisons hardly travel in the same circles as those who would employ me, but your concern is touching."

"I promise to be careful while we're in London."

"Even there, they would forgive you. I am, by law, your sister. It would be a perfectly acceptable reason to use my given name."

A brief sting shot through him at the word *sister*, reminding him of her status, yet he grinned at her. "Why, Margaret, you sound practically rebellious."

"Perhaps you're a bad influence on me. However, I would advise you to consider finding a bride as soon as possible to silence any wagging tongues. I would hate to see you find a suitable woman, only to have malicious and unfounded gossip hurt her."

"You're more concerned about me and my future wife than yourself? It's your reputation that concerns me."

Perhaps it was the light streaming in from the windows of the carriage, but a shimmer appeared in Margaret's eyes.

"Then, as we're both concerned with the other's reputation, there should be no problem in maintaining decorum. Besides, I've dealt with the gossip mongers before."

The carriage jerked to a stop at Mr. Turner's as Harry opened his mouth to pursue her statement.

After exiting the carriage, they joined Owen at the entrance to Mr. Turner's home, and Harry gave two sharp raps against the door.

Once again, Harry witnessed the shock on his tenant's face upon seeing him with Margaret, and he prepared himself to explain.

Mr. Turner didn't give him the chance, He raised the cane held in his gnarled hand and took a feeble swing, barely missing Harry's head as he ducked.

"You bastard," the old man bellowed. "I thought the devil dragged you to hell! What are you doing here with her! I don't care who you are."

Margaret stepped between the old man and Harry while Owen wrestled the cane from Mr. Turner's hand.

"Mr. Turner," Margaret's voice shook, although it was clear she tried to remain calm. "This isn't my husband. This is his brother, remember? He visited you the other day. We've come to check on you and discuss what assistance Mr. McDougall may provide."

Mr. Turner eyed Harry, then turned to Margaret. "He's not here to cause trouble?"

"No, not at all. We're here to help," Harry said.

"I want to hear it from Her Grace," the old man said, his eyes narrowed in suspicion.

"His Grace is correct, Mr. Turner. May we come in?"

Grateful for Margaret's soothing effect on the man, Harry followed her into the house.

"Give me my cane," he snapped at Owen, and Harry took several steps back once Mr. Turner had the makeshift weapon in his grip.

Harry pulled in a deep breath. "Mr. Turner, I'm sorry I alarmed you. Remember we discussed young Mr. McDougall and his wife helping with some repairs to your home and learning to work the land?"

"Is this him?" Turner pointed at Owen with a gnarled finger.

"Aye, it's me, sir."

Mr. Turner's eyebrows raised, and Harry worried Owen might be the next victim of the cane-wielding septuagenarian. Apparently Owen had the same fear, and he tensed and backed up a single step. Curiously, Margaret's smile grew wider.

"My late wife was Scottish. You would never find a finer woman."

Harry and Owen released a collective sigh of relief.

"I thought you and Owen could discuss what repairs to start first and where he and his wife might build their home. He's married to Mr. Morrison's daughter, Lily."

The old man nodded. "I know them. Can she cook?"

"Aye, she's a fine cook, sir," Owen said. "However, she cannae make haggis to save her."

The old man slapped his knee and chortled. "Son, I've had enough haggis to last me the rest of my days. You'll be hearing no complaints from me at its absence."

Harry turned to Margaret, "Like our Brussels sprouts."

Margaret laughed, the sound like the tinkling of crystal to Harry's ears.

"Before I leave you and Owen to discuss things, Mr. Turner, I wondered if you would allow me to examine you?"

Mr. Turner's eyebrow quirked again.

"I'm a physician, sir. I promise you it will be quick and painless."

Mr. Turner nodded but turned toward Margaret. "If I'll be having to undress, you might want to step outside, Your Grace."

Margaret excused herself, and Harry proceeded with his examination.

Once finished, he placed his stethoscope and instruments back in his bag. He provided several packets of the prepared willow bark to Mr. Turner with instructions how to prepare the tea.

"That should help with some of the chest pain you're experiencing, Mr. Turner. I'll be traveling to London tomorrow, but if you need anything, please have one of my remaining staff send word to me."

He turned to Owen. "Before you discuss the repairs with Mr. Turner, might you accompany me to my carriage?"

Harry picked up his bag to leave.

"Your Grace," Mr. Turner said, "I'm sorry I almost took your head off." The twinkle in his eyes implied the statement was a partial truth.

Harry chuckled. "It's understandable. There were times, sir, I wanted to take a swing at my brother myself."

Once outside, Harry pulled Owen aside. "Owen, do what you can for him. If you and Lily can make him comfortable, please do so. His heart is weak and its rhythm erratic. I'm concerned about him. If something happens . . . send word and I'll provide funds necessary for a nice service."

Owen nodded and shook Harry's hand. "Thank you, Your Grace, for everything."

Harry climbed into the carriage where Margaret waited. He smirked. "Well, that went well."

Her tinkling laugh sent gooseflesh up his arms. Her eyes sparkled, and she looked even more beautiful when she laughed. "That was quite a pugilistic move avoiding Mr. Turner's cane."

"I've had my share of dodging upset patients."

She grew serious. "How is his health? The color of his skin seemed gray."

Her observant eye impressed him. "His heart is failing. I gave him some willow bark for his pain, but . . ." He shook his head.

Seated across from him, Margaret reached over and took his hand, sending his pulse racing. "You did what you could for him. Is he in much pain?"

"It's hard to tell. He's a tough old codger and probably wouldn't admit it if he was. I asked Owen to look after him."

She nodded and slipped her fingers from his. He fought the urge to hold on as her warmth left him.

"He really is a dear. When his wife passed, I worried he would waste away, he mourned her so grievously." She sighed, a wistful expression in her eyes. "It's quite romantic how they met, something like Shakespeare's *Romeo and Juliet*, but of course, less tragic."

Like a child awaiting a bedtime story, he leaned forward. "You must tell me."

"I don't know it all, you understand, but they had both gone to pay tribute to their fathers who had lost their lives at the Battle of Culloden."

He anticipated the next. "Fighting for different sides, I imagine?"

She nodded.

"Wouldn't that make him close to eighty if not older?"

"The way he told the tale, he was a toddler when his father left for the war, and Katie, his wife was still in her mother's womb. Neither remembered their fathers, nor fully understood the reason for the animosity between their countrymen. According to him, it was love at first sight, and he lied to win her over."

Harry couldn't restrain the laugh. "I can imagine that. What did he lie about?"

"That his father was actually a Jacobite."

"And she couldn't tell he was lying from the way he spoke?"

Margaret joined him in laughter. "Oh, she could, but the fact he would lie to woo her won her over."

"Did you visit him often?"

"Whenever possible, usually when George traveled to London."

"He didn't take you with him?"

"At times." She shifted on the carriage seat. "At the beginning of our marriage I accompanied him, but in the last few years, I rarely went."

"Did you miss it?"

She tilted her head as if in thought, and he admired the delicate curve of her neck.

"I missed seeing my friends, but staying here also provided a respite of sorts."

From George.

"Are you looking forward to going tomorrow?"

Her serious expression lightened, pleasing him that he had made her smile again.

"I am. Thank you, again."

"My pleasure." *And it is.* "Your diplomacy and grace today confirmed how much I will need your assistance navigating the protocols of society. It's clear the tenants love you, especially young Tom. He's smitten."

She shook her head, but her cheeks pinked. "He's just a boy, Harry."

"Perhaps, but old enough to appreciate and be enamored with a lovely woman."

Her blush deepened, and she turned toward the window. Harry's stomach knotted, and he berated himself for making her uncomfortable. He missed her smile already and searched for another topic to return it.

Upon arriving back at the house, Harry announced, "We have one more promise to fulfill before we leave for London tomorrow."

"Oh?"

"Satan. Will you assist me?"

"If you like. You won't hurt him?"

"Do you trust me?"

His heart thumped when she graced him with another smile.

"Yes."

Harry instructed the coachman to have the groom bring Satan to the fenced field where he first discovered him and requested a footman to find a cricket bat and ball.

He then offered his arm to Margaret as he led her to the enclosed pasture.

Once everything was in place, Harry removed his jacket and took his stance. "Now remember, Margaret, bowl the ball gently toward me."

Her first two attempts didn't even make it to Harry, bouncing and rolling to a stop several feet in front of him.

"A little harder, Margaret. I promise I won't hurt him."

She threw, and he connected with the cricket bat, aiming the shot low to the ground. The ball rolled toward Satan as the groom held him still, landing against his rear hoof, the bump so gentle all Satan did was neigh and move out of the way.

Margaret had turned to watch, then spun around, her expression jubilant.

"Well done, Harry."

He grinned and strode toward her. "I might have failed to mention I was one of the top batsmen on our cricket team at Eton."

Her smile lit up his world as she threw her head back and laughed. Could another woman cause his chest to ache so gloriously?

"Let's go apologize." He grabbed her hand and led her to Satan.

He pulled a sugar cube from his pocket and offered it to

Margaret. "Would you care to do the honors of rewarding his bravery in the face of being shot?"

"You should do it. It was your idea and skill that resulted in such a wonderful outcome."

He nodded and held the sugar in the palm of his hand for Satan. "I thought we could give him a new name for the occasion, to christen his rebirth."

"What did you have in mind?"

"Satin."

"It's perfect."

His only thought, *as are you.*

CHAPTER 12—LONDON

The night before they were to leave for London, Margaret's mind raced as she tried to sleep. Each time she closed her eyes, Harry appeared, smiling, lightly touching her hand, tending to Mr. Whitcomb and Mr. Turner, holding the cricket bat while she bowled him the ball.

His words implied he thought her pretty, he even used the word lovely. Was he being kind, and why did it matter? She stared at the dimly lit ceiling. *If only he didn't look exactly like George.* She focused on the scar. *Did he get that at Waterloo?* The picture of him in uniform coalesced in her imagination, and a foreign sensation fluttered low in her abdomen.

An image floated in her mind of him at Almack's while dozens of giddy debutantes surrounded him, vying for his attention. She frowned and pushed it away. Perhaps he would hold a soiree or even a ball at the townhouse. Would he request she be the hostess? She imagined herself on his arm, greeting their guests, the picture much more pleasing.

She sighed heavily and turned onto her side. *Stop deluding yourself.* She squeezed her eyes shut, attempting to force aside the lovely thought.

The tumultuous feelings warring inside puzzled her. She remembered something similar years ago upon dancing with Laurence Townsend during her coming out. The racing heart, the breathlessness, the fluttering stomach, the tightening in her bosom, the tingling sensations low in her body didn't frighten her then. But now they terrified her.

She mentally ticked through the items on her list of options for employment until her eyelids became heavy and her mind fuzzy.

Harry appeared at the doorway to her bedroom. His shirt, open as it had been the night she encountered him in the library, exposing his skin. She sat upright in bed, her breath catching in her throat at the sight of him.

He said nothing but walked toward her, his steps slow but deliberate, and took a seat on the bed next to her. His hazel eyes were intense, dusky, the brown overpowering the specks of blue and green. He lifted a hand to her cheek and caressed her, his touch warm and gentle. Her lips parted as she exhaled a sigh, and he bent to capture them with his own.

Margaret melted into the kiss, so sweet, so tender. She closed her eyes and savored it.

Harry reached for the strings on her night-rail, and she pulled away and shook her head. Would sex be as painful as it was with George?

Before her eyes, he changed—his expression no longer caring, his eyes cold and hateful. She searched for the thin scar and found none, and her heart beat a frantic rhythm. Terror seized her, recalling memories of brutal assaults.

Grabbing the neckline, he ripped the night-rail away from her body. He threw his head back and laughed, harsh, wicked, then slapped her hard across the face, the signet ring on his hand breaking the skin on her cheek. As he grasped her shoulders in his steel grip and pushed her down on the bed, she struggled against him.

The sound of her screams woke her. Sweat covered her palms, chest, and neck, her heart hammered, and her breath came in quick gasps. The adjoining door flew open, and a familiar silhouette, cast by the dim candlelight, filled the doorway.

She screamed again, clutching the covers tight against her throat, and scrambled back against the headboard of the bed.

"Stay away, George! Don't come near me!"

"Margaret, it's me. Harry."

A foul taste rose in her mouth as she stared at him and tried to still her shaking body.

He stepped into the room, and she tensed.

She lifted a hand to her cheek, testing for the pain and blood, confused when she found none.

He continued, chancing another step further into the room. "Margaret, I'm Harry, not George."

"Harry?" Her breathing eased as her mind cleared. "A dream?"

"A nightmare, I'd say. One moment." He disappeared back into his bedroom then reappeared moments later with a glass in his hand. "May I come closer?"

Still clutching the bedding to her chest, she nodded.

With slow, deliberate steps, he approached the bed and held out the glass. "I keep some in my room to help with my nightmares. Sip."

She sipped, the liquid burning her throat but sending a pleasant warmth through her. "You have bad dreams?"

He nodded. "Occasionally."

She searched for the scar, but the darkness in the room cast his face in shadow. *Is it there? Let it be there.* She squinted, willing her eyes to adjust to the dim light.

"May I sit? I'd like to take your pulse."

She nodded and moved to make room on the bed.

As he sat, the scar became visible, and she breathed a sigh of relief.

He gently lifted her wrist in his fingers and pulled out his pocket watch. "A little fast, but steady. The brandy should help."

He reached cautiously toward her and cupped her face, his voice low and soothing. "You rubbed your cheek, does it hurt?"

Her gaze shot to his face and double checked for the scar, confirming it was still there.

"I . . . no. I should have known it was a dream. He never hit me where it would show."

His eyebrows drew together. "George?"

Her face heated from shame. "Yes."

"Would it help to talk about it? The dream?"

The heat rose to the level of an inferno as she remembered the beginning of her dream. She could never tell him that. What would he think of her? She forced her eyes to meet his, so calm and patient, the color more blue than brown.

"You turned into George and then hit me."

"I would never hit you, Margaret. I'm so sorry George did, but he can't hurt you any longer."

She gave a sharp nod, not sure she believed him.

A smile played at his lips. "You were dreaming of me? What happened that changed me into George?"

Oh, dear. She forced down the lump that had lodged in her throat. "I . . . you . . ." She pulled at the neckline of her night-rail and blushed when his eyebrows rose.

THE INITIAL ELATION THAT FILLED HARRY UPON HEARING MARGARET had dreamed of him soured. His stomach lurched. *She dreamed I attacked her? No, George attacked her.* The fact didn't lessen his disgust.

"It's all right. Don't upset yourself. You don't have to tell me."

Fresh tears slid down her cheeks. He reached up to brush them gently away, relishing in the silky softness of her skin.

"Would you like me to stay with you until you go back to sleep? We can talk about other things." He had no desire to leave her for the isolation of his room.

"You said you have nightmares. What about?"

He drew a fortifying breath, praying the flashes wouldn't surface. "Waterloo."

"Is that where you got your scar?"

Tempted to ignore her question, his intention to soothe her overrode his own demons. Instinct nudged him onward, coaxing, prodding. *Trust her.* Perhaps it was sharing with a kindred spirit. Or perhaps something more. "Which scar?"

"The one on your face."

Of course. She wouldn't have seen the others. "No, George gave me that one."

"What happened? Will you tell me?"

"We were ten, wrestling and playing outside as boys do. But George didn't like to lose. I had him pinned to the ground, and he managed to grab a rock and hit me in the head."

"Oh, Harry." Her delicate fingers traced a line down the scar, sending tingles up his spine, and at that moment, he thanked George. He resisted the urge to cup her hand with his and bring it to his lips.

"You asked which scar. You have more? From Waterloo? You said you had nightmares about it."

Perhaps he should take his own advice. He'd only confided his hellish memories to the bottle and found its comfort fleeting.

"It's difficult to speak of," he mumbled as he turned his gaze away.

Her hand slid into his, as if it had always belonged there, giving him strength, and he looked up and met her waiting eyes.

"It's as if I'm there in the midst of it all again. The endless onslaught of wounded, limbs blown off, sometimes faces obliterated, maimed beyond recognition, men dying in my arms as they ask for their sweethearts, wives, and mothers. The stench of blood, bile, and death. Screams of agony, cannons and gunfire roaring around me causing my hands to shake as I try futilely to patch up one man before moving on to the next. I'll never know how many men lost their lives because of me."

Words poured from him like vomit, harsh, bitter memories he had tried in vain to forget, purging him from its sickness. "There's no glory, no nobility in war. Only blood and death."

Fresh tears flowed down her face. "Harry," she whispered. "I'm so sorry. I shouldn't have asked."

He forced a weak smile. "No, I'm glad you did, Margaret. I've held it in so long, it's been eating me alive. It's good to get it out."

"My own problems seem so foolish."

"You lived through your own hell, but it's over for both of us. Let's make a pact, starting tomorrow, when we go to London, we'll start fresh."

Her hand remained in his, so he lifted it and said. "Shall we shake on it as friends do?"

She hesitated, and his stomach knotted. He prepared to apologize for offending her when a tiny smile crossed her lips.

She grasped his hand firmer and gave it a hearty shake. "Yes, as friends."

"Now, perhaps we both should try to get some sleep. We have a long journey ahead of us tomorrow."

"To start our new lives."

He forced another smile and nodded. When he returned to his room, his smile faded, and his heart sank that her new life would take her out of his.

HARRY ROSE EARLY THE NEXT MORNING TO FIND THE HOUSE bustling with activity. Hastings finished packing his trunks as Harry made his way downstairs. The maids curtsied in greeting as they tidied the rooms and covered the furniture.

Although patches of gray clouds littered the sky, he decided on a brisk ride to clear his mind before the journey to London. With Satin saddled, Harry galloped down the road only to be met with an abrupt downpour thirty minutes later. Rain beat against him as he rode back to the house.

Water dripped from his clothes and hair as he entered the house to find Margaret descending the stairs.

The lightness of her laughter lifted his spirits. "I would ask about the weather, but your appearance answers my question."

He raked a hand through his drenched hair and grinned. "I'm sure rats are more presentable."

Hastings ran up, tsk, tsking. "Sir, give me a moment to remove some fresh garments from the trunks." He removed Harry's soaked coat and waistcoat, muttering something about having sense to come out of the rain.

Harry chuckled to himself and prepared to follow him upstairs for a dry change of clothing. He halted when his eyes caught Margaret's as she stared at his wet linen shirt and buckskin breeches clinging to his body. "Forgive me, Margaret. In his haste to remove the coat and waistcoat, I'm afraid Hastings failed to think things through." As he bounded up the stairs, warm satisfaction rushed through him at Margaret's expression and the definite interest in her eyes. He barely restrained the grin that threatened to stretch across his face.

Once Harry changed and Hastings repacked his clothing, footmen loaded the trunks on top of the carriages for their trip to London. He settled in the seat, Margaret across from him, as the rain steadily beat a soothing rhythm against the carriage roof.

Hastings, Flora, and most of the remaining servants who hadn't left for London with Burrows followed in separate carriages.

"You seem especially cheerful. Is it in anticipation of the excitement waiting in the House of Lords, or does the gloomy weather often have this effect on your disposition?"

Harry turned his gaze from the window toward Margaret, her eyes glinting with laughter.

His laugh filled the interior of the carriage. "Margaret, I do believe you're being facetious. I doubt long debates about the proper way to tie a cravat or drink a cup of tea could engender anything but boredom. As for the weather, rain typically makes me reflect on the past, but since we vowed to start anew, I have no wish to look back on what was or might have been."

"You have no regrets?"

He fought the sadness that crept up and tapped at his heart, and he sighed. "Two perhaps, but there's no sense dwelling on them."

His admission flowed naturally, stemming from the bond they had formed the night before. Still, he held his breath as she pursed her lips as if she considered pursuing what those regrets might be. He turned his attention to the carriage window.

After a brief moment of silence she said, "When I was a girl, I made all kinds of plans. My father was a viscount, and he often spoke of the plight of the poor. I had lofty dreams of helping the less fortunate."

"A most unusual goal for a young lady."

"It wasn't altruistic, I assure you. I was certain I would become famous, and people all over would sing my praises. I'm ashamed to admit I was quite the attention seeker as a child."

He imagined her, full of spirit and confidence, her black curls bobbing behind her as she wrapped her father around her tiny finger. "And would they have proclaimed you Saint Margaret?"

"Well, of course," she laughed, the tinkling crystal sound he loved to hear. She paused and stared out the window, her cheerful tone becoming despondent. "I did hope to do some good when I married George, but my efforts proved lackluster."

"You did what you could have given the circumstances, and without the acclaim you sought as a child."

A blush crept over her cheeks as she turned back toward him. "Tell me about your dreams as a boy. Did you always wish to be a physician?"

"Not at first. I wanted to be a head groom. I loved the horses and spent the majority of my time at the stables."

"That explains your success with Satin."

He chuckled. "I doubt it. Although the stable master welcomed me, I fear I became more of a hindrance than a help. But I'll admit, being around the animals, I developed an interest in their physical well-being."

A pleasant memory drifted into his mind. "I especially loved assisting with the foaling, watching new life appear before my eyes. There's nothing like it."

Her eyes trained on him, never leaving his face. "I stole down to the stables once when a mare was foaling. Papa was not pleased, but my mother told him it would prepare me for . . ." She cast her gaze down, and her smile disappeared.

"Did you want children, Margaret?"

"At first, yes. I thought it would be wonderful having a child to cherish. Having someone to love and who would love me in return. But then I was grateful. Children aren't perfect, and George demanded perfection. I shudder to think what he would have done to a child."

The sadness radiating from her squeezed his heart, and he ached to comfort her, but he found no adequate words.

They fell into a silence that lasted hours as each stared out their respective carriage windows. The comfortable camaraderie had slipped through their fingers like dust.

After stopping several times to change the horses and refresh themselves, they arrived in the outskirts of London early that evening.

"I had forgotten the stench," Margaret said as she held a handkerchief over her mouth.

Harry peered out the window at hopeless faces as the ducal carriage wound up the road. His stomach twisted in the knowledge that the only thing separating him and the unfortunate poor was to whom he was born. Perhaps Margaret was right, he could make a difference here.

They arrived at the house in Mayfair to find Burrows had everything in order. He bowed as they entered, "Your Grace. I trust your journey went well."

"Yes, thank you, Burrows," Harry answered.

"Would Your Graces care for refreshments?"

After their close confinement in the carriage for hours upon end, he needed a diversion and some distance from his ever increasing feelings.

"Actually, if Her Grace doesn't mind me deserting her, I'd like to go for a stroll to White's, stretching my legs."

"I would love some tea, Burrows," Margaret said before turning to Harry. "Enjoy your walk, Your Grace."

The rain had cleared on the trip to London, and Harry strode down the street admiring the lovely buildings—such a contrast to the crowded rookeries they passed as they arrived in the bustling city.

He entered the stately building and deposited his hat with the doorman. The smell of cigar smoke and hushed echo of male voices reverberating through the hall greeted him as he entered one of the main rooms.

Curious eyes turned in his direction. Hands holding crystal glasses containing amber liquid stopped midpoint to their destinations with Harry's entrance.

He searched each face, hoping to find a familiar one. A grin broke across his face at one such astonished member. There was no mistaking the owner of that shock of red hair. "Weatherby!" With long strides, Harry maneuvered through the crowded room to his boyhood friend.

"Harry?" Andrew Weatherby whispered. "Is it really you?"

"It is! So good to see you, old friend." Harry clasped Andrew's hand, giving it a firm shake, then patted him on the back.

"Your brother said you were killed at Waterloo. Then a rumor spread that you were alive and had returned to assume the title. I could scarcely believe it, but here you are." He shuffled, a red tinge coloring the tips of his ears. "Forgive me, Ashton, I've forgotten my manners."

"I'll always be Harry to you, Andrew, but I suppose we should stand on formality here."

Andrew shook his head, a lopsided grin spreading across his freckled face. Mischief shone in his clear blue eyes. "It's been no fun around here without you. Let's make trouble in the card room."

Harry laughed, remembering their escapades. "Your only trouble was over betting on a poor hand. But yes, a game of cards sounds like the ticket."

Quiet concentration greeted them in the smoke-filled room. They made their way to a table with some open seats. Once again, heads turned, pausing to stare momentarily as Harry approached.

"Ashton, Weatherby," an older man nodded as Harry and Andrew took seats, joining him.

"Harcourt," Harry acknowledged back, trying to remember something about the baron. Scarcely over twenty-one when he purchased his commission as an officer in the army, Harry's priorities at the time hadn't included learning about members of the peerage.

As they enjoyed the game of Speculation, Harry glanced over when another man took a seat at the table. As with Andrew, there was no mistaking the slightly hooked nose, dark hair, and equally dark eyes of Lord Nash, George's best friend.

"When did you arrive, Ashton?" Nash asked.

"In the country or in London?"

Nash's dark eyes met his. "Either," he said, carelessly tossing his ante in the center of the table as the next hand was dealt.

"I arrived back in England a week ago." The pleasure of the game waned even though Harry's winnings had increased.

"Shame about your brother. That fall seemed very convenient."

Harry tensed. "What are you suggesting, Nash?"

Nash looked up from his hand, challenge in his eyes. "Not a thing, Ashton. Simply that George had confided in me that his little wife was, well, let's say, not very cooperative."

Andrew touched Harry's arm, leaning over to whisper, "Let's go, Harry."

Nash quirked a brow. "Still associating with this blunderbuss Weatherby, Ashton? Now that you're duke, you should raise your standards."

"Now see here," Andrew started to rise from his seat and Harry tugged on his coat sleeve, keeping him in place.

Harry scooped up his winnings. "I believe you're right, Weatherby. This table has begun to reek. I find myself growing nauseous from the odor. Let's move elsewhere."

Nash's eyes narrowed, defiant, challenging. "Oh, now, don't be a spoil sport, Ashton. The fun's just starting."

"I have no quarrel with you, Nash . . . yet. But if you continue to disparage my friends or speak ill of my brother's widow, you will answer to me."

As Harry and Andrew rose to leave, Nash leaned back in his seat, an arrogant smirk creeping across his face. "I shall look forward to it."

After moving to a quieter room, Andrew poured a drink for

himself and Harry. "Where Nash goes, trouble follows," Andrew said, settling into a comfortable wingback chair next to Harry.

Harry nodded. "Indeed, but let's not ruin our reunion speaking of him. What have you been up to?"

"I've gone and got myself leg-shackled." Andrew's broad smile conveyed he wasn't at all sorry about the fact.

Harry chuckled. "And how, pray tell, did you manage to convince someone to marry you? Did you compromise the poor unsuspecting woman?"

Andrew threw his head back with laughter, eliciting angry glares from several occupants of the room. "No. You may find this hard to believe, but the lady loves me."

"And you her, I can see. Tell me about her."

Harry sat back and listened as his friend extolled the beauty and virtues of his wife, Alice. A strange mix of happiness for his friend and envy of his good fortune weighed him down and squeezed his ribs like a plaster of Paris cast.

"You must bring Alice around to the townhouse to meet us. I insist on seeing this flaxen-haired goddess myself before I'm convinced she's not a figment of your vivid imagination."

Andrew leaned forward in his chair. "Us? Ashton, have you married?"

Harry cringed. "No, no. My brother's widow has accompanied me."

"Is that wise?" Andrew dropped his voice to a whisper. "Not to give credence to Nash, but some ugly rumors circulated regarding your brother's death."

"Unfounded, I assure you." The temperature in the room quickly became uncomfortable, and Harry searched for another subject of conversation.

Lips drawn in a tight line, Andrew lowered his head, his brow furrowed as he studied Harry. "You're withholding something, Ashton, and I intend to discover it."

Nash's assessment of him was bluster. Andrew's perception and intelligence was legendary. Harry would be unable to hide his deepening attraction for Margaret much longer.

CHAPTER 13—HYDE PARK

The silence in the townhouse should have been welcome to Margaret, but she yearned for Harry's laugh resonating through the empty parlor.

After supper, she busied herself writing letters to her friends, inquiring about any open positions for a governess or companion. As she sealed the final letter and rang for Burrows, she sighed, wondering how society would view her disgrace. That would not deter her, though. She meant what she said to Harry. She was not afraid of honest work, and the possible humiliation of working seemed preferable to the marital bed.

The image of him, drenched to the bone as he stood in the foyer at Briarfield that morning resurfaced, and she smiled. How her breath had hitched at the sight of him as the wet clothing hugged his body!

Her cheeks flamed at the memory, and she questioned if all relations between spouses were violent and painful. Could they be— pleasant? Perhaps if she summoned the courage to ask Camilla, Harry's suggestion of remarriage might not be so distasteful. However, the only man who appealed was Harry, and marriage to him was out of the question for multiple reasons.

She ticked off the problems in her mind.

Could she give herself to another man after her experience with George?

As duke, Harry needed an heir, and she had remained childless.

Even if she could bear children, if someone contested the union, as her brother by law, their marriage could be voided, and their children would be declared illegitimate and lose their inheritance.

If those weren't reasons enough, Harry deserved to find a woman he loved, not be saddled with his brother's widow. Surely, he would never risk his children's future for her?

She pushed aside the idea, acknowledging the insurmountable obstacles, and prayed that a position as a governess would be forthcoming.

Yet, Harry remained foremost in her thoughts. All evening she waited for him to return from White's, but by midnight, she accepted the fact he might not arrive home until morning. Such was George's habit when she accompanied him to London. However, she hoped Harry was indeed at White's and not one of the other establishments George frequented.

THE NEXT MORNING, MARGARET SAT READING IN THE PARLOR WHEN Harry entered. If he had been carousing, he bore none of the effects. His change of clothing indicated he had at least returned prior to her rising. Impeccably dressed in a silver waistcoat, charcoal gray trousers, and black coat, he appeared rested and relaxed.

"The rain has stopped, and it's a pleasant day, Margaret. Let's stroll in Hyde Park before I have to go to the House."

Her pulse picked up speed. She loved the park and being on Harry's arm made it all the more alluring. She placed her book on the table. "That sounds glorious."

Life flowed all around them. The early June flowers and trees in full bloom, squirrels and rabbits happily romping, children laughing and running from their nannies all fed Margaret's soul as she breathed in the air, still crisp from the preceding rain.

She glanced at Harry, catching his eyes sparkling with the same joy.

"Did you have an enjoyable evening at White's, Harry?"

"I did, thank you, Margaret. While there, I chanced upon my boyhood friend, Andrew Weatherby, and I've invited him and his wife to call on us. I'm eager to meet his wife," Harry said, all smiles and enthusiasm. "I have my doubts she even exists."

A thrill of delight traveled up Margaret's spine at the word *us*. The pleasant vision of being by Harry's side as they welcomed their guests resurfaced. *Our guests.* She held Harry's arm a little tighter, and the day grew lovelier.

A group of women stood in the path before them, their heads together in animated conversation. Margaret's joy evaporated as quickly as morning dew on a sunny day. Lady Cartwright's head inclined toward the group, as she presumably relayed a piece of juicy news to Lady Harcourt, Lady Easton, and a young woman Margaret didn't recognize.

Wife of a viscount, Aurelia Cartwright had been Margaret's mother's equal, but they had not been friends. Margaret learned from a young age never to trust the woman. Unfortunately, her distrust failed to protect her later in life.

Aurelia's diminutive height belied the length and sharpness of her tongue. It reached across London, its destruction of reputations legendary.

Margaret had no delusions of avoiding her, but had hoped her first full day back in London would be gossip free.

All heads in the group turned in unison as they approached, each set of eyes locked on Harry.

Harry tipped his hat, and Margaret prayed they could continue their walk in peace.

Prayers often go unanswered.

"Your Grace!" Lady Cartwright called, her tone ingratiating. "Please, won't you stop and chat for a moment?"

Harry darted a glance at Margaret, his expression apologetic, before addressing the group. "Of course, madam. Lady Cartwright, is it not?"

She curtsied deeply. "Oh, dear sir, you remembered!"

The woman's sickening sweet tone turned Margaret's stomach.

Lady Cartwright turned her ample body toward Margaret and bobbed a curtsy so quickly, one would easily miss it. "Your Grace." Her tone chilled the warm, late spring air.

Aurelia's eyes traveled to Margaret's hand where it rested on Harry's arm. Margaret withdrew it as if Harry had suddenly caught fire, then clasped it with her other hand in front of her.

Lady Harcourt sent Margaret a commiserating glance, and Margaret introduced her and Lady Easton to Harry.

Lady Cartwright's focus returned to Harry. "Your Grace, may I present my daughter, Miss Priscilla Pratt?"

Margaret didn't remember Priscilla. She appeared to be about eighteen. She executed a perfect curtsy, her blonde curls peeking out from her bonnet and bobbing in tandem. "Your Grace. It's an honor."

Harry took Priscilla's offered hand and bowed, his lips brushing it in a light kiss. "My pleasure, Miss Pratt."

The girl turned her icy blue eyes on Margaret. "Your Grace." Her mother had taught her well.

"The news of your arrival is most welcome, sir," Aurelia said. "And just in time. I'm hosting a ball two weeks hence and would be honored by your presence. This is Priscilla's second season. With all her beaus, I expect it to be her last as an unmarried lady. I wouldn't want you to miss the opportunity."

Margaret understood the implications of Aurelia's words. She chanced a quick glance and caught a slight twitch of Harry's lips.

"We're grateful for the invitation. Her Grace and I shall consider it."

A lovely tingle spread through Margaret's chest, and she restrained a satisfied smile.

Daggers shot from Aurelia's eyes. "Well, of course, if Her Grace feels so inclined, she is welcome. She *is* still in mourning."

"So everyone reminds me," Harry said. "However, I see no harm, since it's been almost a year."

An uncommon blush covered Aurelia's cheeks as she stammered, "Of course."

The sound of wood cracking and a high-pitched cry echoed nearby, capturing Harry's attention and answering Margaret's prayers for salvation from the uncomfortable encounter.

He sprinted toward the figure of a young boy lying on the grass beneath a tree. Margaret followed, pulling up her skirts as she ran after him.

The boy writhed in pain. Tears streaked his dirty face. Out of place in the posh area of London, his ill-fitting, tattered clothing were several sizes too small. Blood oozed from his forehead, and he grabbed his right arm which lay at an odd angle to his body.

Harry bent down to the child. "What's your name, boy? What happened?"

The lad groaned. "Manny. Fell from the tree."

"His shoulder looks dislocated," Margaret said, well acquainted with that particular injury.

Harry's head jerked up toward her, his eyes full of questions.

Aurelia and Priscilla joined them and gathered around the boy.

"I'm going to swoon," Priscilla announced with dramatic flair, although the color in her face appeared normal.

Harry's focus remained on the boy. "One of you ladies lower Miss Pratt to the ground so she doesn't injure herself when she falls."

Margaret moved to take Priscilla's arm, but Priscilla jerked it away.

"Thank you, but I'm recovered now."

Of course she is, since I'm not Harry.

Margaret kneeled next to the boy's head. She pulled a handkerchief from her reticule, and dabbed blood from the child's wound. "Where are your parents, Manny?"

"I ain't got none."

Margaret exchanged a concerned look with Harry.

"Did you reach for a tree limb trying to break your fall?" Harry asked.

"Yeah, but it broke." The branch, no more than a thin stick, lay a few feet from the fallen boy.

"Manny, use the hand on the arm that hurts. Can you touch your other shoulder?" Harry asked.

Manny lifted his hand toward his uninjured arm, but grimaced in pain. "No, it hurts like bloody hell."

Harry chuckled. "Watch your language, young man, there are ladies present." Harry moved Manny's arm gently, then met Margaret's eyes. "It's definitely dislocated. Brilliant diagnosis. Will you help me, Margaret? Not feeling faint, are you?"

"Not in the least."

"Good. Manny, how old are you?"

"Eight, I think."

"You're very brave for eight," Margaret said.

Harry nodded toward Margaret, indicating he was ready. Margaret held Manny still while he carefully moved the boy's arm away from his body. Grabbing Manny's hand, Harry pulled it toward him, sliding the joint back into position.

Priscilla groaned and feigned a swoon, lowering herself to the ground in slow motion, her hand strategically positioned to fall on Harry's arm.

"Lady Cartwright, I suggest you take your daughter home if the excitement is too much for her," Harry said.

He brushed Priscilla's hand from his arm and pulled Manny to a sitting position. "You'll need a sling."

As Harry untied and yanked off his cravat, Priscilla moaned again.

"Your Grace, for the sake of decency," Aurelia said.

Margaret had stomached enough of the woman's prattle. "For goodness' sake, Aurelia, the child is in pain, it's no time for propriety. I suggest you listen to His Grace and take Priscilla home if she is uncomfortable. The well-being of an injured boy takes precedence over the delicacies of a weak-kneed woman."

Aurelia pulled herself up to her whole four-foot nine-inch height. "Well, I never." Grabbing Priscilla's arm, she huffed off with her daughter in tow.

Harry finished fastening the cravat on Manny as a makeshift sling. "Think we lost our invitation to the ball?" His grin informed her it would be no loss.

"Oh, you'll still be invited. I doubt I ever truly was."

Harry examined Manny's head. "That's a nasty cut, Manny. Looks like it will need stitches."

"Wha? I ain't seeing no doctor. I ain't got no money."

"No money required. I'll tend to it."

"You? A fancy man like you knows how to stitch up a bloke?"

"I do. Will you accompany me to my home? I promise there will be some biscuits for you as a reward for your bravery."

"Got anything to eat asides biscuits? Like some meat?"

Harry grinned at the boy. "I can arrange that. So, what do you say?"

"How's I know you're not some sick bloke that catches boys and sells 'em to work on the ships?"

"I give you my word as a gentleman."

Manny snorted a laugh. "Like you'd say otherwise." He eyed Margaret. "I'll go if she says it's a'righ'."

"You can trust him, Manny."

With that settled, the trio hurried back to the townhouse. Curious eyes gawked at Margaret's gown caked with mud, Harry's muddied trousers and missing cravat, and the urchin of a boy grinning as he strutted between them holding onto Margaret's hand.

⊗⊗

HARRY WOULD ALWAYS REMEMBER THE EXPRESSION ON BURROWS' face as they entered the townhouse. His jaw dropped so far, Harry wondered if he would have to reposition yet another dislocation.

"Careful, Burrows, you might swallow something unpleasant."

Burrows snapped his mouth shut but continued to stare at the dirty boy. Finally composing himself, he said, "I see you've brought a guest, Your Grace."

"This is Manny. Please bring some hot water, soap, and some

towels to the parlor. Have Cook prepare a plate of food and some milk, tell her to make sure to include meat."

Burrows bowed and, with another quick glance at Manny, retreated.

Manny's wide brown eyes stared at Harry. "He called you Your Grace. What are you, a king or somefin?"

"I'm a duke, but don't hold that against me." He glanced over at Margaret who fought a smile. "Margaret, please take Manny into the parlor while I retrieve items for the sutures."

When Harry returned with his medical bag, he leaned against the doorway, mesmerized by the sight before him.

Margaret kneeled before Manny, gently wiping the grime from his face and hands, her voice soothing even as she admonished him. "Manny, if you must climb trees, you should find ones with thicker branches for both your ascent and descent. However, in my opinion, it would be prudent not to climb trees at all."

"But trees is the best place to hide."

"Are the best place," Margaret corrected. "Why were you hiding, or perhaps I should ask from whom were you hiding?"

"Coodibilis."

Harry jerked at the name. *Latin for detestable?*

"But we call him Cood," Manny continued.

"So, you know this Cood? Why were you hiding? Is he another boy?" Margaret asked.

"Nah, 'e's growed. 'E just got 'is gorge up 'cause 'e thunk I didn't give 'im all the money."

"But you said you didn't have any money."

"I don't. I give it all to Cood, but 'e didn't believe me."

Harry coughed and stepped in, interrupting the discourse. "Let's see what we have here, shall we?"

Margaret moved aside, allowing Harry to kneel before Manny. "Good, nice and clean. Thank you, Margaret. Can you hold still for me, Manny? Three stitches should do it."

As Harry prepared to insert the needle for the first suture, Manny jerked.

"Margaret, perhaps stand behind Manny and steady his head. It will hurt a bit, Manny, but I'll try to be as quick and gentle as possible."

Between the two of them, Harry finished suturing Manny's wound just as Burrows announced the plate of food waited in the dining room.

"Burrows, please show our young guest the way. We'll be in shortly, Manny. I need to discuss something with Her Grace."

Once they left, Harry turned toward Margaret. "Coodibilis?"

"You heard? What do you make of it?" The concern on her face matched his own.

"A boy dressed like that in Hyde Park, hiding? Probably pickpocketing."

"He's just a child, Harry. You won't turn him in?"

"No, but I want to find out who Cood is. Manny said, 'we call him Cood.' So Manny's not the only one this Cood is using for his own gain."

A cough alerted them to Burrows at the entrance to the parlor. "Forgive me, Your Grace. Master Manny is eating, but you have visitors." He held out a card. "A Mr. and Mrs. Weatherby."

"Show them in Burrows."

The couple entered the room, smiling warmly, but stopped short.

"Been gardening, Ashton?" Andrew asked.

Harry glanced down at his muddy trousers, only then noticing Margaret's equally mud-caked gown. "Not exactly. We've had an interesting morning, Weatherby, but do come in."

Andrew shook Harry's hand, patting his back affectionately. "May I present my wife, Alice?"

An unassuming woman, Mrs. Weatherby stood half a foot shorter than her husband. A rosy blush covered the cheeks of her somewhat plain, but not unpleasant face, her blonde hair tucked neatly into her bonnet. She curtsied elegantly to Harry. "Your Grace, it's a pleasure to meet you. My husband has fairly bubbled with excitement upon your return."

"Your husband's praise of your beauty didn't do you justice, Mrs. Weatherby. Why you married this reprobate is a mystery."

Alice laughed and squeezed Andrew's arm. Her gaze turned toward Margaret, her smile forced as she executed another perfect curtsy. "Your Grace."

"Ah, yes, forgive my manners," Harry said. "May I present my sister-in-law, Her Grace, the Duchess of Ashton."

"It's a pleasure to see you both again. I apologize for my appearance. If you will excuse me, I shall make myself presentable. No doubt you would prefer to have Ashton to yourself."

Margaret began to leave, but Harry touched her arm, halting her. "Margaret, come back and join us when you've changed."

Andrew's eyebrows raised, but he remained silent.

She flinched, but recovered quickly. "As you wish."

Andrew's head turned as Margaret left the room, then he met Harry's gaze. "Harry?"

Harry's ears burned. *Damn.* "What?"

"You address your brother's widow by her Christian name?"

"Andrew, don't pry," Alice said, her own cheeks coloring.

"It's all right, Mrs. Weatherby. I could never hide anything from Andrew."

"Well, since everyone else is on a first-name basis, please call me Alice."

Harry smiled. Andrew had chosen wisely. "Thank you, Alice, I'm honored. However, if you don't mind, this is a conversation I would prefer to have with Andrew in private. Please come in and have a seat. I'll have Burrows fetch some refreshments."

As they waited for tea, Harry filled in Andrew and Alice about Manny. "Have you heard of anyone by the name of Coodibilis, Andrew?"

"Can't say that I have. That's Latin, isn't it?"

Harry nodded. "I suspect it's code and not the man's real name. Perhaps I should contact the Bow Street Runners to investigate?"

Margaret rejoined the group, her gown replaced with the lavender one Harry had admired previously. His pulse quickened, remembering how it accentuated the deep blue of her eyes.

"I informed Andrew and Alice of our encounter with Manny." He turned toward Andrew. "You should have seen Margaret. When

I removed my cravat to make a sling, Lady Cartwright objected on the grounds of decency. Margaret more or less told her to take a hike."

Andrew's jaw dropped. "She didn't!"

Harry chortled. "Oh, but she did. What did you say, Margaret?"

"I believe my words were 'an injured boy takes precedence over the delicacies of a weak-kneed woman.'"

Andrew let out a hoot of laughter as he slapped his knee. "I would have paid to see that."

Peter, the footman, brought in a tray of tea and biscuits, laying them on a table between Harry and Margaret.

Famished from the morning's excitement, Harry's gaze fell on the plate. He lifted a gigantic biscuit, holding it up in front of him. "These are huge."

As she handed Harry a cup of tea, Margaret said, "I asked Cook to make them larger in honor of your first proposed improvement."

Andrew and Alice exchanged quizzical glances, and Harry chuckled.

"Upon our first meeting, Margaret asked what types of changes I hoped to make, and I answered 'larger biscuits.'" His heart warmed that she remembered.

"Your Grace," Burrows said, drawing Harry's attention to the doorway. He held Manny's hand in his own. "Master Manny has finished his plate."

Harry motioned them to enter. "Thank you for bringing him in, Burrows, but Manny might feel he's too old for hand holding."

"It seemed prudent, sir, as his hand continued to wander into my pocket of its own accord."

Manny seemed to have a sudden fascination with his feet.

"And," Burrows said as he held up a silver spoon, "This appeared to have grown legs and traveled into *his* pocket."

The glint in Burrows' eyes betrayed his stoic expression.

Making his voice as stern as possible, Harry asked, "Manny, what do you have to say for yourself?"

The boy's beseeching brown eyes met his, and he opened his mouth to speak. "Your Grace, I—"

"Your Grace," Margaret interrupted. "I'm certain that Manny, being overwhelmed with the kindness, care, generosity, and hospitality you've shown him, simply wished to repay you by polishing the spoon, and perhaps he was searching Burrows' pockets for a polishing cloth."

All eyes trained on Margaret as she artfully delivered Manny's set-down, whereas Manny broke down in tears.

Margaret continued, "You see, he's so overcome with gratitude he cannot contain himself."

Manny bawled louder.

At a loss for an adequate response, Harry lifted one of the oversized treats. "Biscuit, Manny?"

CHAPTER 14—GOVERNESSES, GOSSIP, AND GOWNS

Much to Margaret's relief, with Manny thoroughly chastised and repentant, the conversation turned to Lady Cartwright's upcoming ball.

"Thank God you'll both be there. It will be a comfort having friends in attendance," Harry said.

Margaret's heart squeezed. "If you no longer require me to attend—"

"Oh, no." Harry chuckled. "You're not getting out of it that easily. Of course I still want you to accompany me. Andrew will be too busy to shield me from marriage-minded young ladies all evening."

"You'll need an army for that, Harry," Andrew said.

Margaret feared Andrew's statement—although stated in jest—contained an element of truth. A knot tightened in her stomach as she imagined the deluge of women vying for Harry's attention.

"Margaret and I shall both require new clothes for the occasion," Harry added. "I'm dreadfully out of touch regarding tailors and modistes. Do either of you have recommendations?"

"I use Abernathy's," Andrew suggested.

"Madam Tredwell has produced some lovely gowns for me," Alice added.

"I remember Madam Tredwell. She does fine work, indeed," Margaret said as excitement vibrated within her at the thought of new gowns, especially in colors other than black. But how could she afford them?

"Then it's settled, we'll visit them both tomorrow. I'll be relieved to be in something other than George's garments."

Harry frowned when the clock chimed noon. "I'm afraid I must excuse myself to change. I doubt members of the House would welcome me with open arms should I present myself to them in such disarray."

They said their goodbyes to Andrew and Alice, promising to visit soon.

Once they were alone, Margaret asked, "Harry, regarding the clothing. I have little to spend."

He took her hands in his. "Allow me. It's the least I can do. Please don't worry about money while you're here with me. If there's anything you need, simply ask."

"Perhaps some new clothes for Manny are in order as well?" She hoped Harry wouldn't turn the boy back onto the streets.

Manny looked up from where he sat stuffing his face with biscuits and gave them an indignant glare. "Wot's wrong wif my clothes?"

Harry laughed. "Beside the fact they're too small, it appears moths have had a feast."

Manny crossed his arms over his chest and plopped his slender body against the cushions of the sofa. "I can't go back wearing no fancy duds. Cood would wear me out wif 'is cane."

Margaret shot Harry an imploring gaze before addressing Manny. "Do you really wish to return? Cood doesn't sound very pleasant."

"Where else would I go? 'E ain't as nice as you, but 'e's all I got."

The tension in Margaret's chest eased as Harry said, "I prefer you stay here with us, Manny, at least until your arm is completely healed and I remove your stitches. It may not be up to your usual standards, but Her Grace and I will do our best to make you comfortable."

Manny stroked his chin with his—now clean—index finger. "Well, I s'pose I could."

"One thing, Manny," Harry added. "No more polishing of silver, understood? That's Burrows' job, and he becomes cross when he's bored."

Harry turned to Margaret. "I'll have Hastings obtain measurements for new garments, and in the meantime, make him take a bath."

Manny bolted up from the sofa in protest, his good arm flailing wildly. "I ain't takin' no bath."

A noticeable grin appeared on Harry's face as he quit the room.

❧

AFTER HARRY DEPARTED FOR THE HOUSE OF LORDS, MARGARET turned to the daunting task of convincing Manny to bathe. With some bribery and strong-armed help from Hastings, Burrows managed to drag Manny upstairs and deposit him in the tub amid howls of indignation. Margaret prayed Harry had made good on his promise to increase Burrows' wages. He deserved every penny.

Meanwhile, Hastings set off to locate a change of clothing for Manny, while Margaret busied herself selecting books for his edification.

Manny, now bathed and dressed in the fresh shirt and breeches Hastings had procured from a neighbor, pulled at his collar as he sat on the sofa in the library.

"This itches somefin' fierce," he grumbled.

"Well, stop tugging at it and concentrate on something else." Margaret laid *Robinson Crusoe, Gulliver's Travels,* and *Ivanhoe* on the table in front of him.

"Wot's that?"

Margaret narrowed her eyes. "Books. Which would you prefer to read first?"

The tips of Manny's ears reddened, and Margaret regretted her assumption. She made a promise to herself to purchase copies of *Lessons for Children*, then lowered herself to eye level with the boy. "Manny, would you like me to read one to you?"

He shrugged and dropped his eyes to the books.

Margaret picked up *Ivanhoe*. "I haven't read this one yet. I hear it's exciting, all about knights, tournaments, and a witch trial. If you're not interested, I think I'll try it. I hope you don't mind if I read aloud." She settled herself on the sofa next to him and began to read. Before long, the story captivated the boy, and he huddled close as Margaret's finger pointed to each word on the page.

A cough from the doorway drew her attention away from the tale.

"Your Grace, Lady Camilla Denby to call," Burrows announced.

"Please show her in, Burrows."

As she rose to greet her friend, Margaret resisted the urge to bounce on her toes. She hadn't seen Camilla since she'd last been to London three years ago.

The moment Camilla appeared, Margaret thrust aside her vow to maintain decorum and pulled her friend into an embrace.

Camilla's warm, brown eyes sparkled, and her throaty laugh assuaged any concerns Margaret may have had regarding their reunion.

"Maggie, you look wonderful. I was thrilled when I received your letter but concerned when I read its contents." Camilla angled her head to peer around Margaret. "Who do we have here?"

In her excitement at receiving Camilla, Margaret had forgotten Manny's presence in the room. "Manny, may I present my dear friend, Lady Denby."

Camilla smiled. "I'm pleased to meet you, Manny. What happened to your arm and forehead?"

"Fell outta a tree. Harry fixed it and sewed me up."

"Oh?" Camilla turned questioning eyes toward Margaret.

"Manny," Margaret said, "why don't you find Burrows or

Hastings and see if either would like to play a game with you? We'll resume reading after Lady Denby's visit."

Manny ran out of the room yelling, "Oi, Burrows!"

"Well, we *do* have a lot to discuss," Camilla said, taking a seat on the sofa where Margaret joined her. "When did you acquire a child?" Camilla's voice lowered. "Is he the duke's son?"

"No, no. Ha . . . Ashton and I discovered him at Hyde Park this morning. As Manny stated, he dislocated his shoulder when he fell out of a tree, and Ashton tended to him."

Camilla's brow furrowed. "I'm confused. The boy said Harry helped him. He calls the duke by his first name?"

"It's a long story. Let me start at the beginning." Margaret spent fifteen minutes recounting Harry's relationship to her deceased husband, George's pitiful bequeathal in his will, and Harry's insistence that she accompany him to London which culminated in the events of the day with Manny.

Camilla, who had rarely been at a loss for words, worried her bottom lip as Margaret finished her explanation. She clasped Margaret's hand in hers. "Oh, Maggie, I heard rumors of a brother who died in the war, but George forbade anyone to speak of him. He said if he discovered I told you, you would suffer. But I had no idea he was George's identical twin! How horrible. How are you managing?"

"It's not like that. He may look like George, but that's were the similarity ends. Harry's been generous and kind to me."

Camilla's delicate brow raised. "So Manny isn't the only one referring to the duke by his first name?"

Margaret's cheeks pinked from her slip. "He insists on it, Cammie. He calls me Margaret."

"And he's a physician?"

"Yes." Warmth filled Margaret's chest, remembering Harry with Mr. Whitcomb and Mr. Turner. "He will be such a great asset to his tenants."

"Your explanation has left me with more questions than when I arrived, but that's neither here nor there at the moment. What's this nonsense about seeking a post as a governess?"

Margaret's back stiffened. "It's not nonsense. As I said, George left me nothing. I will need to support myself.'

Flinching as if burned from Margaret's words, Camilla's drew a hand to her chest, her eyes widening. "But, Maggie, a governess?"

"I might enjoy it. Manny and I were just reading *Ivanhoe*, and the prospect of teaching a child to read seems most rewarding."

"Yes, you always did love children, but do you think you could find a position?" Camilla pressed her lips together before continuing. "May I speak frankly as your friend?"

"Of course."

"If you weren't my friend, and you came to my home seeking such a post, I would send you packing. You're much too attractive for any woman to want as a member of her household."

Margaret's jaw clenched. "Are you implying I would be after someone's husband?"

Cammie's face blanched. "Oh, no, Maggie, please don't misunderstand. However, I do fear that a woman may view you as a temptation for her husband."

"Would you have with Hugh?"

Camilla winced, her shoulders slumping, and she exhaled a sigh. "No, but I trusted in Hugh's love for me and mine for him in the same way I trust you as my friend. But not all marriages are founded on love. You of all people know this."

"Harry thinks I should remarry."

Camilla nodded. "I would agree, but I sense that's not something you would consider."

"I didn't . . . until . . ."

"What? Have you met someone?" Camilla's face brightened.

"I . . . well . . . what I meant is I've begun to question if my experience with marriage is not the norm." Margaret leaned closer. "Cammie, yours and Hugh's was a love match. Did you find the marital bed . . . uncomfortable?" Heat rushed up Margaret's neck to her face, burning her cheeks. She dropped her voice to a whisper. "Is it supposed to be . . . painful?"

Camilla's eyes widened. "Goodness, Maggie. I knew you didn't love him, but did George force you?"

Unable to meet Camilla's gaze, Margaret stared at her hands folded neatly in her lap, and she blinked back the tears welling in her eyes. "He would strike me, and sometimes he would tie me down. When I struggled, it inflamed him even more."

She squeezed her eyes shut, forcing aside the memory of George's hideous laugh as he assaulted her. "Eventually, I stopped fighting back, and he grew tired of me and found other outlets. That was my only blessing."

Camilla gathered Margaret in her arms. "Oh, my dear Maggie. I'm so very sorry. Not all men are like George. Many are tender and eager to please their wives. When passion develops, it's because both husband *and* wife desire it."

Margaret nodded and dabbed the wetness from her eyes. "I apologize for being so indelicate. I've often wondered, as my parents had such a happy marriage." She smiled at her friend. "As did you and Hugh, even though it was brief."

Camilla smiled warmly. "Don't be embarrassed, Maggie. When two people love each other, marital relations are extremely pleasant. Quite honestly, it's why I haven't remarried. I doubt I would ever find anyone I would love as much as I did Hugh."

Camilla's eyes glazed as she stared vacantly into the distance, then she shook herself. "Perhaps you should seek a position as a governess for a widower with no lady of the house to fret over your presence? I shall make it my mission."

"Oh, would you, Cammie? That would be wonderful."

"On one condition," Camilla said. "You keep the option of finding a new husband open. I understand Lady Cartwright has invited you to her ball. Perhaps you'll meet an eligible gentleman there."

"How did you find out about that? It just happened this morning."

Camilla's throaty laugh rang through the library. "My dear, this is London. Word travels fast. I ran into Lady Easton at Gunter's, and she practically drooled over the news of the new duke's arrival. Of course, she couldn't resist mentioning that she saw you on his arm."

Margaret shook her head. "And you allowed me to proceed with my lengthy explanation when you knew very well about Harry."

"Well, of course," Camilla said. "I wanted to hear your side of the story. You know I don't believe half of what those gossips say."

"Which is?"

"Are you certain you want to know?"

"Forewarned is forearmed."

"If you insist. Lady Easton declared Ashton seemed quite taken with Miss Pratt. She predicted Lady Cartwright would be ordering Priscilla's wedding gown any day."

Margaret snorted a laugh, remembering how Harry had brushed the girl's hand off of his arm. "I'm sure Lady Cartwright would like nothing more than for her daughter to ensnare a duke. What else?"

Camilla pressed her lips together. "I suppose you should prepare yourself. A rumor has spread that George's death wasn't an accident. Most men don't give it credence, but I'm afraid the women are another matter. You may want to steel yourself against some icy receptions."

"I expected as much. Even Alice Weatherby seemed initially distant this morning, and she has always been so gregarious. Although, she graciously apologized for believing in idle gossip."

"Your attractiveness aside, those rumors may also impede your search for a position as either governess or companion."

"Or my option to remarry, if I entertained it. I'm sure no man would want a woman who he worried might murder him."

"As I said, men don't seem to give credence to the rumors, but you're right. A mother or sister can poison a man's mind."

"It would seem the odds are not in my favor."

After saying their goodbyes, Margaret pondered her options again. Things did indeed appear bleak.

THE NEXT MORNING, A MIXTURE OF EXCITEMENT AND TREPIDATION swirled in Margaret's chest as she and Harry set out for the modiste and tailor. Stopping at Madam Tredwell's first, Harry informed the modiste to send the bill to him. He motioned Madam Tredwell aside, speaking to her in whispers. She nodded, then turned her head toward Margaret with interest in her eyes.

Once Harry bid goodbye, heading for Abernathy's, Madam Tredwell gave Margaret her full attention. "His Grace instructed me to provide only my finest materials and workmanship for as many gowns as you desire, but he insisted a ball gown should take priority."

"Is that what he discussed with you privately?"

"Now, Your Grace, you know I can't divulge confidences." Madam Tredwell's enigmatic smile gave nothing away. "However, the matter does have a connection to your ball gown."

She busied herself pulling out bolts of cloth. "I've acquired some fine fabrics from the linen-draper. How about this lovely satin?"

More black! "Perhaps another color, a darker shade, of course."

Madam Tredwell opened her mouth, then snapped it shut. They settled on a deep sapphire-blue satin for the undergown and a gossamer net for the overdress. The modiste described the design she envisioned, and a giddiness rose in Margaret she hadn't experienced in years as she imagined the gown flowing gracefully around her as she danced. A brief image of being in Harry's arms flitted in her mind.

The bell on the shop door tinkled, and both women raised their heads as Alice Weatherby entered, beaming a warm smile.

"Madam. Your Grace." Alice nodded at the modiste then curtsied in Margaret's direction. "With the mention yesterday morning of your planned visit here, I'd hope to find you."

"Mrs. Weatherby, it's lovely to see you again," Margaret said, her happiness increasing at encountering a friendly face. "I would love your assistance in choosing some fabric and designs for my gowns."

Alice proved invaluable, providing support in Margaret's insistence for color, albeit subdued. They chose muslins in deep mauve, lavender, and cornflower-blue for morning and walking dresses. Margaret's fingers lingered on a print of rich blue adorned with lily-of-the-valley. It would make a splendid afternoon or dinner dress. Madam Tredwell had stepped away to retrieve her tape measure, and Margaret sighed.

"It's exquisite, Margaret," Alice said, agreeing to Margaret's request to use her Christian name in private. "Why are you hesitating?"

"I fear I would have little occasion to wear it."

Alice's brow furrowed. "I'm afraid I don't understand."

Heat rose up Margaret's neck. "My husband's bequeathal is not sufficient for a livable income. I plan to seek employment."

As Margaret expected, Alice's eyes widened and her jaw fell slack. "But surely Harry will assist you?"

"Harry has been most generous, it's true. But once he marries, I can't expect him to provide for me. How would that look to his bride?"

Alice nodded. "I do see your point."

Madam Tredwell returned, and the ladies turned the conversation to the merits of muslin.

HARRY DECIDED TO WALK TO ABERNATHY'S AND INSTRUCTED HIS carriage driver to wait at Madame Tredwell's for Margaret. He headed down the street with a spring in his step and a satisfied smile on his face regarding his special request to the modiste. *Won't Margaret be surprised!*

As he entered the tailor's, the shopkeeper, an older man with a bent back, greeted him with an exaggerated bow and wariness evident in his gaze.

Harry rushed to reassure him. "Sir, although my brother's appearance and mine are similar, you'll find I'm much easier to please. I'll need an entire wardrobe, but at the moment, let's concentrate on a few select pieces."

"Yes, Your Grace," the man answered, a smile replacing his former grim expression.

They discussed the items of clothing Harry wished to take precedence, and the tailor proceeded in taking measurements. As the man measured his inseam, Harry struggled not to think of Margaret.

The tailor pulled out bolts of material for Harry's consideration, and Harry selected those the tailor recommended.

"Some fabric will be arriving from Madam Tredwell, the modiste, and I should like a waistcoat fashioned from it," Harry said.

If Harry's request bewildered the tailor, he hid it well. He simply nodded and added another note to what he had already written.

Harry pulled out the paper with Manny's measurements Hastings had provided. "I also require some boy's garments made. The child is about eight, so whatever is appropriate, but nothing too formal or stuffy. Something sturdy would be best."

"Ah, do you have a son, sir?" The old man's eyes lit up, Harry imagined from the prospect of providing clothing for a growing heir.

"No. Just a lad less fortunate whom I wish to aid."

"Your Grace is most kind and generous."

Harry chose not to pursue the flattery. Instead he thanked the man, bade him goodbye, then stepped outside to the warm June day to head back and wait for Margaret at Madam Tredwell's.

"Ashton!"

Harry turned and nodded in greeting at Andrew strolling his way. "Are you following me, Weatherby?"

"In a manner of speaking. I hoped to catch you here. We have some unfinished business to discuss."

"I don't recall anything left unsaid." Harry continued walking, and Andrew fell in step beside him.

"Harry," Andrew scoffed. "You yourself said you would speak to me in private regarding Margaret. Do I detect some attraction between you two?"

Blast! "Your meaning?"

"Are you going to answer each of my questions with your own? You're on a first-name basis. What exactly is your relationship?"

"She's my sister-in-law. We've been sharing the same house for the past week. You know I hate all the formality."

Andrew's eyebrows quirked in question. "So there's nothing more going on? You seem especially fond of her."

Harry exhaled an exasperated sigh. "She's dished up, Andrew. George left her virtually penniless. I'm simply concerned about her and trying to be of assistance until she sorts out her future."

"So, the fact she's extraordinarily beautiful has no bearing on things? You don't find her attractive?" A mischievous glint appeared in Andrew's eyes. The man had the nose of a hound on the hunt who'd caught the scent of a fox.

Drat! Harry's skin at the back of his neck itched as if he had suddenly contracted an irritating rash. "Of course I find her beautiful. I'd have to be blind not to notice. But she's more than that. She's kind, intelligent, and strong. My God, what she endured from my brother would have broken anyone, but she's survived."

Andrew grinned. "I see."

Harry halted and spun toward Andrew. "And just *what* do you see?"

"Oh, nothing," Andrew said and continued walking as Harry chased after him.

A troublesome tic developed in Harry's left eye, and he swatted the air in front of him with his cane. "Now look here, Andrew. If you're implying there's something going on between Margaret and me, I'd urge you to dismiss the notion." Harry's voice rose in frustration, and people who passed gawked.

Andrew laughed. "The question is, Harry, do you wish there was something going on?"

Harry's ears burned as he struggled for an acceptable answer. "I . . . I . . . damn it!" He huffed. "When I arrived back home, I expected her to be cut from the same cloth as George. Cruel, arrogant . . . heartless."

"And you discovered she's not."

Harry shook his head. "No, she's not. It all took me by surprise. I'm at sixes and sevens. Perhaps I'm misinterpreting concern for her well-being for something more."

"Well, there's one way to find out."

"And what, great sage, might that be?"

"Get your mind off her. Find another lady on whom to lavish your attentions. There should be no lack of candidates, especially now."

Harry snorted. "They'd just want my title."

"You didn't have a title when we were at university, and—if memory serves—your bed never grew cold."

"Perhaps you're correct." Catching Andrew's widening grin, Harry added, "Not for that, but perhaps I should concentrate on finding a wife."

"Ah, but with the right one, your bed still wouldn't grow cold."

HARRY STARED INTO HIS RAPIDLY COOLING CUP OF TEA, HIS MIND wandering for the tenth time that morning.

"Don't you agree, Your Grace?"

He jerked his head toward the interrupting voice where Priscilla Pratt gazed at him with doe-eyed hunger. He resisted the urge to shudder in horror. "Forgive me, Miss Pratt, my mind must have veered. Would you mind repeating?"

"I said the waltz is the most romantic dance, don't you agree?"

"Yes, I suppose so," he said, hoping that his agreement would allow him to drift back into his thoughts.

Priscilla Pratt continued her soliloquy on the merits of romantic dancing, and Harry's mind returned to its sanctuary.

For the last week and a half, he had called on eligible ladies, hoping one would spark his interest and push Margaret from his malleable mind.

He had escorted Miss Beatrix Marbry for a walk in Hyde Park, only to think of Margaret assisting him with Manny.

Horseback riding with Miss Amelia Newberry along Rotten Row evoked thoughts of Satin and Margaret bowling the ball toward him.

A dinner party with Lord Easton's daughter—he couldn't

remember her name—where they served Brussels sprouts, again led to thoughts of Margaret and their common detest of the vegetable.

Miss Pratt was the eighth such candidate, and he had only agreed when Lord Cartwright had cornered him at White's and begged him to come for tea.

"I'll never hear the end of it from my wife if you don't come, Ashton. Please help a fellow out," Lord Cartwright had pleaded.

So he sat, smiling politely, all the while wondering what Margaret would say or do. Every pair of batting eyes, every light touch on his sleeve, every compliment became Margaret's—and every other woman came up short.

"Please say you will, Your Grace."

Once again, his eyes darted toward Priscilla, who sat fully expecting an answer. He swallowed. "Certainly, Miss Pratt."

The smile spreading across her face sparked an ominous dread in his gut. *What did I just agree to?*

CHAPTER 15—THE BALL

The night of the ball, Harry stood before the mirror as Hastings made the final adjustments to his cravat. The waistcoat had turned out splendidly. Lines of silver stitching decorated the rich sapphire-blue satin, and Harry found it most elegant.

Hastings stepped back, admiring his master. "Old Abernathy outdid himself on your waistcoat, sir. Brummell himself would be proud."

After instructing Burrows to send the carriage around, he waited for Margaret in the foyer of the townhouse. He paced the floor, hoping to relieve the tingling sensation shooting through his body, but it only increased the pounding of his racing heart. He resisted the urge to rake his hand through his hair. Hastings would have his head if he mussed the carefree style. Lord, he was as nervous as a lad.

The rustling of skirts drew his attention to the staircase as Margaret descended, and his breath caught in his throat. Her gown, the same sapphire-blue as his waistcoat, wasn't lined with silver thread but dotted, creating an illusion of stars upon the night sky. The sheer gossamer overdress softened the effect. A wide silver ribbon under her bosom accentuated her breasts and slim figure. Thinner silver ribbons edged the puff sleeves at her arms.

Flora's skills at hairdressing had significantly improved, arranging Margaret's hair with luscious curls interspersed with tiny seed-pearl hairpins. Delicate tendrils dipped seductively around Margaret's ears and nape of her neck. His fingers itched to play with a lock . . . or two . . . or three. His gaze roamed over her, drinking her in to the point of intoxication.

Her smile widened as she approached. "The material of your waistcoat appears familiar."

He grinned. "Yes, I wanted us to match."

Something flickered in her eyes, and he struggled to name it. *Hope?* His gaze drifted to her bare neck, devoid of ornamentation. "No necklace?"

Her cheeks flushed pink as her hand reached to her throat. "My selection is limited. Nothing seemed to complement."

"Wait a moment," he said, momentarily grabbing her hands before rushing up the stairs.

Where is it? Rummaging through his belongings, his fingers landed on the velvet pouch, and he removed the star sapphire pendant that hung on a silver chain.

Back downstairs, he held it before her. "My mother gave me this before her death. She said it had always brought her luck. When I served in the army, I wore it hidden under my shirt during battle to keep me safe. I cherish it as much as the memory of my mother. Would you do me the honor of wearing it this evening?"

A tiny gasp escaped her parted lips. "It's lovely, Harry." Her eyes shimmered when they lifted to his. "Will you put it on me?"

She turned, and he reached around her and fastened the clasp at her neck. His fingers lingered as he brushed her delicate skin, pleased that it pebbled under his touch. The urge to lower his lips to the place his fingers caressed was checked as she spun to face him.

She fingered the pendant. "I'm the one honored to wear this, Harry. It's perfect."

And it was—simple and elegant—as perfect as the woman who wore it.

MERCIFULLY, IT WAS A QUICK RIDE TO LORD AND LADY Cartwright's townhouse. The air seemed in limited supply in the carriage compartment, and Harry struggled to pull it into his lungs with each glance at Margaret.

After a servant announced them, Lady Cartwright whisked Harry away to introduce him to her guests. He glanced back, his chest suddenly constricted and empty as Margaret stood alone. Their eyes met, the connection between them stronger, and he tamped down the desire to yank his arm free from Lady Cartwright's grasp and run to her side.

As he made his way around the room, Harry struggled to remember the names of endless women who begged for his attention and name on their dance cards. He peered over the head of Miss Marbry, searching for Margaret. *There, chatting with a brunette.* Lightness flooded his chest at Margaret's smile. *Thank God she's found a friendly face.*

He scribbled his signature on Miss Marbry's dance card, then edged away from the group, ignoring calls from people he passed as he approached Margaret.

Her smile broadened as she made eye contact with him, and the brunette turned in response.

"Ashton, may I present my dearest friend, Lady Camilla Denby. Lady Denby, His Grace, the Duke of Ashton."

Lady Denby offered her hand, and Harry bowed over it. "A pleasure." A memory surfaced as her name registered. "Denby, you say? Hugh Denby's wife?"

Camilla's brown eyes misted even as they crinkled at the corners. "His widow, yes. Did you know my husband?"

"I did. I had the privilege of serving with him during the Peninsular Wars. Colonel Denby fought valiantly. He spoke of you frequently."

Camilla's face brightened. "Sir, Margaret mentioned you are a physician. Would you perhaps be Captain Radcliffe?"

"I am, although since I've resigned my commission, I'm no

longer a captain." A image of cannon fire flashed through Harry's mind. The light touch of Margaret's hand on his arm brought him back to the present, and he noted her concerned gaze.

"Sir, I cannot begin to tell you how much your letter meant to me. Maggie, Captain Radcliffe wrote to me upon Hugh's death, enclosing a note written in his own hand of Hugh's final words." She turned toward Harry. "I apologize, Your Grace. In my elation at meeting the man who did my husband such a kindness, I've forgotten my manners."

"No apology necessary. I was proud to be of service to such a fine gentleman who clearly adored his wife."

"You were with him when he died?"

Harry fought the memory of his friend dying in his arms and his failure to save him. "I was. His only thoughts were of you."

A bittersweet sadness enveloped the group as an uncomfortable silence settled between them.

"If you will both excuse me. I'm parched, and a glass of ratafia sounds delightful," Margaret said.

Harry's heart lurched at her retreating figure, wishing he had reached for her arm to stop her.

"She feels she's intruding," Camilla said. "She's always had a keen perception regarding people's wishes."

Harry nodded, but his eyes refused to release Margaret as she made her way to the refreshment table. He returned his attention to Camilla when she began to speak.

"One thing puzzles me. Hugh was not an eloquent man, preferring to express his love in other ways. His first letters to me, although I still cherish them, were simple declarations of his affection. As he continued to write, while the handwriting remained his, the words changed, becoming . . . poetic."

"War changes how a man views the world."

"Perhaps, but I noticed a similarity in style with the letter you wrote informing me of his death. Yet his final words, albeit written in your hand, were . . . simple, direct and very much like . . . Hugh."

Her eyes never left Harry's, boring into him for the truth. "I'm not angry, Ashton, I'm grateful. Those letters are dearer to me than life, as I know they're what Hugh had in his heart but was unable to express. So, did you help him write them?"

Harry swallowed down the guilt of betraying a confidence. "As you said, I simply provided the words he struggled to form. The sentiments were entirely his."

Camilla's eyes shone as tears welled. "The lady you choose for your wife will be lucky indeed. I pray you find a love as great as Hugh's and mine."

Harry's gaze darted to Margaret, standing alone by the refreshment table, then returned to Camilla who cast him a knowing glance.

She sighed. "These balls make me miss him even more. Hugh loved to dance. As I said, he was more of a physical person."

"Then will you do me the honor in Hugh's memory?"

They took their places, but the nature of the dance limited their conversation to brief, whispered snippets as they passed each other or promenaded during the steps.

Camilla leaned in during their first pass. "Margaret tells me she's looking for a position as a governess."

"Yes," Harry replied on the next pass.

"I fear she won't find such a post."

"I do as well."

"She should re-marry," Camilla said as they began the promenade.

"She seems quite against it."

"I believe she's reconsidered. I thought perhaps Laurence Townsend, Lord Montgomery, might be a good match. He's in line for the title, and he was one of Maggie's suitors years ago. Perfect, wouldn't you say?"

Harry bit back the growl forming at the idea and struggled to reply politely. "No. I met him when I had dinner with his family. He seems intolerably dull. He would bore Margaret to tears within a month."

Camilla gave a bright laugh. "You do have a point. Perhaps you know of someone better suited?"

They broke apart for the final steps, and a sly smile spread across Camilla's lips. As they bowed and curtsied at the end of the dance, Camilla winked and said, "Don't worry, sir. Your secret is safe with me."

A strange healing flowed through Harry during the dance with Camilla, a melding of his memories of the war with the pristine ballroom. Camilla became a conduit linking past and present that gave him hope for his future. Margaret had chosen her friends wisely.

After ending the dance with Camilla, she returned to join Margaret who sat with the group of widows in a corner of the room, leaving Harry exposed to an onslaught of eager debutantes and the challenge of finding a suitable candidate for a wife among them.

Surely there must be one woman in the crush who would appeal? One after another, they came at him in a steady stream, all chattering away on silly topics—gowns, the weather, the benefits of marriage. He was introduced to, danced with, and bored by countless women. He didn't know there were this many unmarried ladies in all of England, much less London society, and every one of them had her sights set on him. Like a lamb thrown to a den of lions, he yearned for an escape. Camilla Denby proved his salvation.

"Ashton, you look positively green. Perhaps a break from the stifling heat of this ballroom would help."

"You are a godsend, Lady Denby. Where might I find such an oasis?"

"Sneak out and turn right, follow the hall to the library, the third door on your left. My father is there to shield you from any compromising situation that could arise with an overzealous debutante. I shall create a diversion."

"Bless you."

As promised, Camilla's voice boomed over the throng of noise. "Oh, dear, I feel faint." While people gathered around her, Harry grabbed the opportunity to weave his way through the crowd and out into the hall.

The door to the aforementioned room stood ajar, and he poked his head in, checking for stray women.

Lord Harcourt motioned him in. "Close the door, Ashton."

Harry blinked. "You're Lady Denby's father?"

"I am and damn proud of it." He moved to the sideboard and lifted a decanter of whiskey. "Join me? Looks like you need one."

"Oh, God, yes, please."

Harcourt laughed. Tall and lean with salt and pepper hair, Harcourt put Harry at ease.

They settled in two wingback chairs. "Camilla tells me you're having a hell of a night. It reminds me of my youth, although I wasn't in as high demand as you. A barony pales next to a dukedom. Still, I remember the hellish onslaught of women until I found my wife." He chuckled low as he stared into space. "Not something you would imagine a man complaining of, hey?"

"Indeed." Harry instantly liked the man; he and Camilla had much in common. "So, were you acquainted with my brother and his wife?"

Harcourt sipped his drink. "Yes, although I had few dealings with your brother, but I've known Margaret since she was a child."

Harry smiled, remembering Camilla's nickname for Margaret. *Maggie.* He would tease her later, but he loved it.

"Her father and I were close friends. Margaret and Camilla played together as children whenever we visited. Camilla's a few years older, but Margaret always seemed more mature. She had a calming influence on my wild daughter." His smile faded. "Forgive me for saying so, but she deserved better than your brother."

"No need to apologize, I wholeheartedly agree."

Harcourt's eyes narrowed, his finger tapping the side of his glass. "She shouldn't have married him."

For many reasons, Harry wouldn't argue with that. "Yes, it would have been better if she hadn't married my brother."

"You misunderstand, Ashton. It's true it would definitely have been better, but what I mean to say is she didn't choose to marry him, she was forced to."

Harry's back straightened. "By whom?"

"She didn't tell you?"

Harry shook his head.

The baron's head cocked, eyes still narrowed. "I'm an observant man, Ashton. I've been watching you and Margaret this evening. She cares about you, it's clear. What I want to know is what are your feelings toward her?"

"I don't see what concern of yours—"

Harcourt held up his hand. "I'm not trying to pry, but Margaret is like a daughter to me, and I'm concerned. She was attracted to your brother when they met, there's no doubt there. He could be charming when it suited him. Margaret had men flocking around her like hounds on the hunt. She could have chosen any one of them. She didn't choose your brother—he chose her. He asked for her hand, and she turned him down flat. George didn't like to lose."

"I'm well aware of that." Harry traced a finger down the scar on his face.

"It happened at a soiree similar to this one, with a crush of people in attendance. Margaret doesn't particularly like crowds, so she sought respite just as you have tonight. Unfortunately for her, she was instructed to go into a room where your brother lay in wait. I have no proof, but I suspect he had accomplices in his scheme to compromise her. He attacked her, ripped her gown, and at that moment, our hostess for this evening discovered them."

"Lady Cartwright?"

Harcourt nodded. "Of course it would be the biggest gossip in London. Again, I have no proof but . . ."

"You think George planned it?"

"What else could Margaret do when your brother apologized and in front of everyone promised to marry her? She could have refused him, but in her state of disarray, few would have believed she was . . . unspoiled. Edmond, Margaret's father, had two choices, agree to the marriage or call your brother out to defend her honor. She'd just lost her mother, so to Margaret there was no choice. She married your brother within the month."

"Why are you telling me this, Harcourt?"

"As I've said, I've watched her tonight. Even secluded with the gaggle of widows, she's more radiant than I've seen her in six years. Something has changed her. I believe that something is you, and although you haven't admitted it, I suspect your feelings are similar. You forget I was at White's that night you warned Nash about besmirching her reputation. Would you do that for any woman? As a gentleman, possibly, but I saw the look in your eyes, and it wasn't just common decency that spurred you to defend her."

Harry shifted in his chair, the sensation of insects crawling along his neck.

"Camilla told me about your military service, and what you did for Hugh. You're a man of honor, of integrity, and from what I've heard, a man not afraid to buck society when necessary."

A knock sounded, drawing their attention, and Andrew poked his head around the door.

Harcourt stood, downed the rest of his drink, and placed a hand on Harry's shoulder. "Ah, my relief has arrived. I hope I didn't speak out of turn, Ashton." He nodded to Andrew and exited the room, closing the door behind him.

"What was that about?" Andrew asked.

"He told me why Margaret married George." Harry stared into his glass. For too long he had used alcohol to forget, to push things aside. *No more.*

"Oh," Andrew shuffled his feet. "She's not the first woman caught in a compromising position, and she won't be the last. Don't be too hard on her."

"Hard on her?" Harry coughed out a disgusted laugh. "She was innocent, and my brother trapped her into marrying him. Harcourt told me everything. If she hadn't married George, she might still be free."

"Although I doubt that, I sense a hidden meaning in what you say." Andrew strode to the sideboard and poured himself a drink. With his back toward Harry, he asked, "Did you come to a conclusion about your feelings toward Margaret? Did you find any candidates for a wife sufficient to chalk things up to brotherly concern?"

Harry rose and moved to face him. "No."

Andrew smiled. "I suspected as much. And what did you deduce as you danced and flirted with countless women?"

"God help me, I'm lost. Completely, utterly, hopelessly in love with her." Harry raked a shaky hand through his hair. "How did you stand it, Andrew? They niggle at your brain until you can't think of anything but them. It's as if a fever has possessed me. Every time she walks into the room, I can't breathe. When she's out of my sight, it's as if a surgeon has carved into my chest and ripped out my heart. How did you keep from going mad?"

"I married her."

Harry slumped against the wall. "But you see, that's the problem. I can't." He turned desperate eyes toward his friend. "Although it would help her as well. I could provide for her, and she wouldn't have to scrabble for work as a governess or companion . . . or worse. This title is a millstone around my neck, and I can't shake it off."

"It's an obstacle because you're allowing it to be one."

"She's my sister-in-law."

Andrew huffed. "You and your damned integrity, your compulsion to always do the right thing. For once in your life, take a page from your brother's book and put your own happiness first. You're not blood related, no matter what people say. You could get married outside the country where no one knows you."

"But the title, if we have children, when I die . . ."

Andrew patted Harry's back. "Well, I suppose you have to decide what's more important—life with the woman you love, or leaving your children an inheritance." Andrew finished his drink. "Now I believe they're getting ready for the waltz, so I suggest we leave and return to the ballroom to find the ladies of our choice."

DESPITE BEING SURROUNDED BY DOWAGERS AND THE OTHER WIDOWS, isolation pressed in on Margaret throughout the evening. She tuned out the chattering of the women who purposely excluded her as they positioned their chairs away from where she sat.

Invariably, her gaze returned to Harry as he had gracefully maneuvered through the steps of a cotillion with the next in succession of the unending parade of debutantes. As he moved around the dance floor, she momentarily closed her eyes and pretended she was the recipient of his smile and subtle touches.

She sighed inwardly, careful to maintain decorum, as he grasped the lady's hand in the promenade, remembering well how his fingers had felt, the tingle of energy his touch evoked as his thumb pressed against her wrist. Tucking her foot so as not to peek from under her gown, she tapped to the rhythm of the music.

Margaret stared at her dance card which remained woefully blank. Why she had even accepted one seemed foolish. Although coolly respectful, for all intents and purposes, people treated her like a pariah.

She drifted back six years, closed her eyes, and remembered. Her dance card had been filled, not one blank space remaining as eligible gentlemen swarmed around her like bees to honey. How she had flirted and laughed—and danced. Goodness, how she missed dancing.

Voices shattered her blissful thoughts, forcing her to face the bleak reality of how her life had gone horribly wrong.

An excited chatter rose from the seats next to her.

"I wonder whom he'll choose," the Dowager Countess Easton said.

"I have it on good authority that Miss Pratt has her sights set on him," the widow Berkeley replied, the cap on her gray head bobbing.

The dowager countess scoffed. "What unmarried woman doesn't? The question is, who does *he* favor? I surmise the key is in whom he chooses for the waltz."

After an intermission for the orchestra, the only waltz of the evening was next on the program, and Margaret ran her fingers over the blank space that would have held her partner's name. Was the dowager countess correct, and if so, could she bear to witness the woman he chose?

She rose to refill her glass of ratafia, wishing it were brandy. Her mind invariably returned to Harry. No matter what she did, he occupied her thoughts. The way he smiled when she entered a room caused her heart to skip a beat and then race furiously. When his fingers had lingered as he fastened the necklace, a delicious tingling had coursed throughout her whole body. The smell of leather, mingling with something masculine and uniquely Harry, she had found so alluring.

She searched the room for him to no avail. Did he remember to be on guard against entrapments? Immediately, her eyes scanned again for Priscilla, and she breathed a sigh of relief upon seeing her blonde curls bouncing as she flirted with another gentleman.

The orchestra resumed their positions and tuned their instruments. People began filing into the room and locating their partners for the waltz.

Margaret contemplated her strategy. As soon as the dance commenced, she would excuse herself and go out to the balcony. As she turned to plot her route of escape, a familiar voice interrupted her plan.

"Ladies, I hope you're enjoying the entertainment," Harry asked. His smile, so charming, created a flutter of giggles from the matrons. He cast a furtive glance her way, and his smile widened. Her heart tumbled in her chest, giving a thunderous thump at its landing.

"It is most enjoyable," the dowager countess answered. "You and Miss Pratt make a superb couple."

"You're most kind, Countess. I fear I may have smashed her delicate feet in my clumsiness."

What is he talking about? His grace on the dance floor is obvious.

"Although I do enjoy chatting with you lovely ladies, I had a precise purpose in coming over."

Margaret imagined the creak of old bones as each woman straightened in her chair at the prospect of privileged information.

"You see," Harry continued, lowering his voice as if ready to convey a state secret. "I find myself in a bit of a dilemma, and I need your sage advice."

Bodies moved in unison, gravitating toward the man before them.

"I plan to do something rather unorthodox."

Now he had Margaret's attention as well.

"The next dance is a waltz, and I would very much like to ask one of you to be my partner. However, I understand, given the circumstances, it might be frowned upon."

Titters of excitement rose from the women as they cast quick glances at each other, wondering who would be the lucky recipient.

Even the dowager countess' cheeks pinked as she flirtatiously waved her fan. "Dear sir, I assure you, as duke, you may do what you wish, and any one of us would be honored to be your partner."

Margaret almost choked on a laugh when Harry placed his hand on his heart in mock relief. She added his playful side to things she loved about him.

"Your approval is paramount as I desire to remain in your good opinion. You see, the lady in question is officially still in mourning."

To everyone's astonishment, including Margaret's, he turned to face her, then executed a deep bow. "Would you do me the honor, Your Grace?"

The collective intake of breath was audible, each woman bearing the same wide-eyed, open-mouthed look of disbelief, and the rebellious demon in Margaret emitted a silent but wicked laugh.

"The honor would be mine, Your Grace." She fought the smirk threatening to appear. He extended his hand, and she slipped hers in it as he led her to the dance floor.

As they waited for the music to commence, Harry slid his arm around her waist, sending a shiver up her spine.

A mischievous grin appeared on his face. "So, Maggie."

She groaned. "A silly nickname from our childhood. I have the urge to throttle Camilla."

"Don't. I'll be ever in her debt for her slip. I love it."

Love. She latched onto the word and savored it as it rolled from his rich baritone voice.

His eyes bore into hers, then dipped toward her lips before returning to meet her gaze. Did her limbs just go weak? She struggled to pull air into her lungs.

As Harry skillfully led her in the waltz, it was as if she floated like a feather, her slippers barely skimming the floor, with only Harry's arms to ground her to earth.

His eyes never left hers when he whispered, "Do you expect this will appear on the scandal sheets?"

She laughed. "I'm sure they're writing them as we speak."

"So, you're not angry I may have sullied your reputation?"

"Since it was already in tatters, I doubt dancing with a handsome duke will worsen it."

He blinked, his grin widening. "You think I'm handsome?"

"Don't plead false modesty, Harry. I'm sure all your other admirers have told you so this evening."

His eyebrow quirked. "*Other* admirers?"

Heat rushed up her neck to her cheeks. *Oh, dear.* She stumbled on her words. "I meant . . . that is . . . your admirers. The myriad of women vying for your attention."

His eyes probed hers in unflinching interrogation.

She swallowed the Brussels sprout sized lump in her throat. "I do admire your waistcoat."

He broke his penetrating gaze, his eyes crinkling in the corners as he laughed. "My waistcoat?"

"Yes. The color is most becoming."

He laughed again, the sound rolling through her like the sea tides at Ramsgate. "You've given me such a lovely compliment, and I feel remiss that I've failed to tell you how beautiful you look this evening."

The lump she swallowed a few moments ago rose to her throat again. It had been ages since anyone had called her beautiful. She searched his eyes for insincerity and found none. Now she was certain her slippers didn't touch the floor.

As Harry spun her close to the crowd of spectators, her gaze landed on Priscilla staring directly at them, her fists clenched at her sides. *Is it simple jealousy or something more?*

The dance ended too soon for Margaret's liking, and he executed another graceful bow.

"Thank you for asking me to dance."

His smile warmed her like sunshine on a winter day. "My

pleasure. I couldn't bear to see you sitting there in such misery one more moment."

Ice replaced the warmth, and her heart plunged. *He pities me.*

Harry's eyes widened. "Maggie, what is it? What did I say?"

Before she could answer, Priscilla appeared, her eyes narrowed on Margaret, and her mouth set in a harsh, straight line.

"Ahem."

Harry spun on his heel toward her. "Miss Pratt, forgive me, I didn't see you standing there."

"Had you forgotten, Your Grace?"

He blinked several times, and his gaze clouded. If it weren't for the uncomfortable situation, Margaret would have found the bewildered look on his face comical.

Harry's brow furrowed. "I beg pardon? Forgotten what?"

"Our dance. You promised the waltz to me."

Harry's jaw fell slack as his eyes darted between Priscilla and Margaret. "I did?"

"Yes, at tea the other day. We discussed the merits of the waltz, and I asked if you would save it for me. You agreed."

Oh, dear. Poor Harry.

He hung his head, pressed his fingers to his brow, and muttered, "So that's what it was."

"What?" Priscilla asked.

He raised his head and met her gaze. "I apologize, Miss Pratt, I—"

"Please don't blame His Grace, Miss Pratt," Margaret said. "It's my fault. You see, he took pity on me when I asked to partner him for the waltz."

Harry's head jerked toward Margaret as she continued her fabrication.

"He argued, of course, but he's such a gentleman, and I prodded him shamelessly. What could he do? Please forgive him. He much preferred you for his partner."

Priscilla straightened and lifted her chin, tossing her blonde curls in the process. Her lips contorted in a self-satisfied smirk as her eyes roved over Margaret. "Of course, he does." Her smile sweetened as she turned back to Harry, tapping her fan lightly on his forearm. "I shall forgive you on one condition. I'll have Mama request the orchestra play another waltz. Just for us."

Harry bowed low. "I'm in your debt, Miss Pratt."

She rested her closed fan on her heart. "Shall we then?"

"Certainly." He held his arm out to Priscilla and bowed toward Margaret. "Excuse us, madam."

Priscilla threaded her hand through Harry's arm, her smirk returning, and she shot one last look over her shoulder at Margaret as Harry led her away.

Margaret trudged back to the widow's area, her feet no longer skimming the floor, but stuck to it as if warm wax coated the boards. *Does Harry understand the fan signals?* Surely he must.

Murmurs of curious onlookers floated through the ballroom as the orchestra commenced another waltz, and Harry and Priscilla took their place on the dance floor.

The cloying air and the closeness of the room became stifling. Margaret desperately needed distance from the sight of Harry dancing with Priscilla as he smiled charmingly at the girl. She yearned to pull every blonde strand out of the chit's vacuous head.

The solitude of the balcony beckoned to her like a siren's call, and she moved cautiously and slipped outside. She breathed a sigh, not of relief but of despair, as she acknowledged her feelings. How could she have fallen in love with him? But she could no longer deny the truth. Like a thief in the night, Harry had crept into her heart, stealing it completely.

"Well, this is fortuitous."

She spun toward the deep voice behind her. Lord Nash leaned casually against the railing. The orange tip of his lit cigar glowing in the dark.

"Nash, you should have made your presence known."

"I believe I just did."

He straightened, threw his cigar down, crushing it with his boot, and took a step toward her. She instinctively stepped back.

"You look especially lovely tonight, Margaret."

He approached, methodically, like an animal ready to pounce, and she continued to retreat until she found herself trapped against the opposite railing.

"I heard you're seeking employment." Unlike the deliciously pleasant sound of Harry's voice, a sinister component colored Nash's chuckle. "I have an option you may not have considered."

His body now pressed uncomfortably close to hers, his arousal evident. "George said you were cold . . . unwilling, but I think"—his fingers trailed down her cheek and moved to play with a loose tendril of hair—"you simply need the right man."

She tried lifting her arms toward his chest to push him away, but he grasped her forearms and pinned them to her side. "Don't fight it, Margaret. George surely had taught you that. I'm stronger than you. You won't win." The heavy scent of alcohol assaulted her nostrils.

His head bent, and before his lips reached hers, she jerked her face aside, his kiss landing on her cheek. He laughed against her skin then moved to suckle her neck.

She squirmed against him, realizing her mistake as her movements only served to make him grow harder.

"Be my mistress, Margaret. No one will hire you, and even if they did, you're not cut out to be a governess."

She struggled to free herself from his grip. "Take your hands off me! You're drunk."

His arms, still trapping her own against her sides, reached behind her, pulling her even closer.

Nash's height blocked her view of the ballroom, but she prayed someone had heard her cries over the music and laughter within. She screamed again.

He forced his mouth on hers, the stale taste of the cigar gagging her. His tongue thrust into her mouth, and she bit down hard.

He jerked back and bellowed, "You little—"

As he stared at the blood he wiped from his mouth, a hand grabbed his shoulder and pulled him away from her.

"I warned you, Nash."

Harry!

Nash sneered and raised his fists. "Well, let's get to it, then."

While Harry was removing his coat, Nash struck out, delivering a punch to Harry's jaw. Harry fell backward, landing hard against the stone floor.

"Harry!" His name flew from Margaret's mouth without thinking, her only concern his safety. She lifted her skirts, preparing to run to his side.

Nash momentarily spun toward her, grabbing her arm and thwarting her progress, then turned back to Harry. "Oh, this is perfect. Been dipping your wick in your brother's leftovers, Ashton?"

Harry scrambled to his feet and charged. Nash released Margaret's arm and swung again, but Harry ducked and followed with his own swing, landing a direct hit on Nash's face.

Nash doubled over, cursing. "You broke my nose!"

"One advantage of being a physician is the knowledge of anatomy."

With fists raised, Harry remained ready for Nash's retaliation. "Margaret, get inside where it's safe."

The instinct to run warred with her desire to stay by Harry's side, the latter winning the battle. She moved away from Nash and stationed herself behind Harry. "I'm staying here."

"Apologize to Her Grace, Nash."

Nash sneered. "Or what? Are you challenging me, Ashton?"

Margaret touched Harry's forearm and whispered, "Don't, Harry. His marksmanship is renowned."

Harry's eyes never left Nash's face as he flexed his fingers then clenched them at his sides. "Since Her Grace is the injured party, I will respect her wishes, but my warning stands, Nash. If you continue to harass her, I *will* call you out."

Harry ushered Margaret back inside the ballroom, and after saying rushed goodbyes to their hosts, they boarded their carriage for home.

Now in the safety of the carriage, the ordeal with Nash impacted her with full force, and she hugged her arms around her shaking body. Her eyes latched onto Harry as he stared out the window into the dark night.

"I'm so sorry your evening had to end in such an unpleasant manner," she whispered.

He turned toward her and smiled. "Actually, I've always wanted to plant a facer on Nash. It felt damn good." His smile faded. "Forgive me for taking pleasure in what certainly was a horrendous experience. Are you certain you're unharmed?"

"Yes. I refuse to allow it to spoil an otherwise lovely evening."

He nodded. "Good. Although I'm not entirely sure you had an enjoyable time. I'm sorry I deserted you for such a lengthy period."

"Ah, but you so gallantly came to my rescue at precisely the right moment. Thank you again for the dance."

"It was my pleasure. My toes needed a rest from Miss Beatrix Marbry."

Margaret stifled a giggle. "The poor dear. I overheard the Dowager Countess Easton say Beatrix's mother refuses to allow her to wear her spectacles for fear men will think her a bluestocking. If she had, your toes may have been saved."

"Indeed. I never quite understood the belief that men don't find intelligent women attractive."

She couldn't withhold her laughter. "Because most don't." She studied him. "And you, Harry. What traits do you find attractive in a woman?"

"Other than one who doesn't smash my toes?"

How he made her laugh! "Surely there must have been at least one lady who caught your attention this evening?"

He made a great show of pondering her question, his head tilting in a jaunty manner, his eyes studying the ceiling of the carriage, and his finger tapping his lips.

Oh, those lips!

"Well, there was one lady I found very enchanting."

Her heart plummeted. "Oh? And her name?"

The devilish grin he wore sent a thrill through her, traveling all the way to her toes. Would it be too foolish to hope he meant her?

"What sort of gentleman would I be if I told you?"

"What if I guess?"

He simply continued to grin.

"Is she short or tall? Slim or plump?"

"She's the perfect size to fit in my arms comfortably."

"Oh? So you danced with her?"

"I did."

Margaret ran through the list of debutantes who had found themselves in Harry's arms. She started with the obvious. "Miss Pratt?"

"No names. You will have to use your deductive reasoning."

"Is she young, or a bit older?"

"She's the perfect age for me."

Margaret exhaled an exasperated sigh. "You are no help."

He merely laughed.

"Her hair color, eye color?"

"My favorites."

"You are incorrigible! And your favorites are?"

"Those of the lady in question."

"You aren't going to tell me, are you?"

"No. You'll have to guess."

"I can't guess if you don't give me any clues." She struggled to find the perfect question. "How many times did you dance with her?"

"Just once."

He danced with Beatrix and Camilla twice. How many times did he dance with Priscilla—once or twice? Lord, she couldn't remember. There were so many girls!

"But," he continued, "One time was all I needed to become completely enraptured."

Pain threatened to rip her heart apart. The thrill of dancing with Harry and the excitement of Harry's altercation with Nash wherein he defended her honor were now dampened by Harry's admission of attraction to one of the women at the ball. *But who is she?* Margaret's spirits sank, and she chided herself for being a foolish female yet again.

He remained ominously silent as they entered the townhouse. After Burrows welcomed them home and took Harry's hat and cane, Margaret prepared to say goodnight.

"Would you mind joining me in the parlor for a moment?"

Her blood chilled. *This is it. He will ask me to leave.* She nodded and followed him into the room. Her eyes met his in question when he closed the doors.

"It's best this conversation remain private," he said.

She opened her mouth to speak, but no words came. She had never felt so lost and utterly crushed. Her muscles tensed, and her heart increased its intense pounding. She clenched her fists to calm her shaking hands as he strolled to the sideboard and poured a glass of brandy.

After taking one small sip, he laid the glass back down. "I need your assistance, Margaret."

He took two steps toward her. "I'm concerned how to approach the lady in question."

Her heart squeezed, sending a dull ache through her body. "I'm afraid I don't understand, Harry."

"How might I best win her affections?"

The sincerity of his gaze bore through her as if he saw into her very soul. She wished with all her being she could transform herself into the woman of his desires. She pushed down her pain. "If she is susceptible to flattery, you could compliment her beauty."

He continued to close the gap between them with two more slow, deliberate steps, his deep voice captivating her like the purr of a dangerous animal. "So, if I said I ached to run my hands through her raven locks, to gaze deeply into her violet eyes, to touch her velvet skin, to breathe in her intoxicating fragrance, would she allow me to kiss her?"

Dizziness threatened, and her knees buckled as she fought to pull air into her lungs. She grabbed the corner of the settee for support. "I . . . I . . ." His words suddenly registering in her addled brain, she stared, her brow furrowed in confusion. "But Priscilla has blonde hair."

He moved closer, standing directly in front of her, and nodded. "She does."

"But you said raven locks."

"Did I?" His lips curved in a sly smile. "Hmm, so I did."

His hand lifted to brush aside a lock of hair near the base of her neck. His fingers lingered on the sensitive area, sending a shiver of pleasure through her. "And what if I said her dress reminded me of the night sky, the silver threads like stars twinkling brightly, making me wish I was a sailor at sea with those stars to guide me home?"

Margaret swallowed, casting a quick glance at the gown he described so well.

He leaned in closer. "So—theoretically speaking—if the woman were you, would you allow me to kiss you?"

The gap between them remained no more than an inch. A puff of his breath, smelling slightly of the brandy but mixed with something sweet and alluring, brushed gently against her lips.

Her eyes darted to meet his, and her lips parted as they uttered of their own accord, "Yes."

His eyelids dropped to half-mast, shading the smoldering she witnessed beneath. The gap between them disappeared as he pressed his lips firmly to hers.

The strength of his arm wrapped around her waist kept her upright as she collapsed against him, while his other hand cupped her face, tilting her head for better access. Her heart beat a furious tattoo as his lips continued their delicious seduction.

Compared to reality, the kiss they shared in her dream a few short weeks ago paled miserably. This kiss was glorious. Every fiber of her being awakened, alive and tingling with possibility.

Her hands slid up his chest, and she threaded her fingers through his hair, marveling at its softness as it curled around them. When she raked her nails lightly across his scalp, he moaned, and she smiled against his lips, taking pride she affected him as much as he had her.

When they finally pulled apart, her head was spinning. "What about Priscilla?"

"I don't care about Priscilla. The only woman who's on my mind is the same one who has occupied my thoughts for the last few weeks." He pressed his lips to the sensitive area of her neck just below her earlobe, and her skin pebbled with pleasure. "The only woman I want is you, Maggie."

The deep baritone of his voice speaking her childhood nickname transformed it into something curiously sensual, and an ache developed low inside her. Her head dropped back, and her eyelids fluttered closed as all reason left her.

"Marry me, Maggie."

CHAPTER 16—THE HEALING TOUCH OF LOVE

"Marry me, Maggie." The words fell from Harry's lips before he realized what he had said. Yet peace settled over him at the rightness of them.

Margaret pulled back, her face flushed, but her eyes widened. "We can't. It's prohibited."

"We'll find a way." Harry lowered his lips to hers again, pulling her against him and drinking deeply. For the past two weeks, he had imagined kissing her, but his imagination paled in comparison to reality. *God she tastes good, as sweet as honey.*

Heat ignited within him, and he longed to be closer. The pressing need to join with her became not only a carnal desire—although it was undeniably primitive—but something spiritual.

And Harry was not a religious man.

The distant clacking of carriage wheels drifted through the open parlor window, echoing his hammering heart. Billowing curtains fanned in the sweet scent of the late spring wisteria as it wafted on the breeze and mixed with Maggie's distinct fragrance.

His hand inched up her side from her waist. Fingers skimmed her corset through the silky fabric of her gown, coming to rest below her breast. The pounding of her heart beat a rapid tattoo against his palm, its rhythm synchronized with his own.

A candle flickered from a sudden gust of wind. The flame sputtered out, casting them in shadows. Every nerve in him tingled, each sense heightened to a state of euphoria.

He teased the seam of her lips with the tip of his tongue, and they parted, welcoming him. Her response, at first tentative, became bolder, and she met him play for play. A growl of pleasure escaped him as her body molded to his, and he wrapped his other arm tighter around her in support.

Pressed so closely to him, heat emanated from her, and like a moth to that flame his palm found her breast, its softness filling his hand to perfection. Her head fell back, breaking their kiss, and her eyelids fluttered.

Encouraged, he tugged down the sleeve of her gown, exposing the curve of her shoulder, and his mouth traveled down the long column of her neck to the swell of her breast that beckoned him. His mouth lingered on the delicate skin, the thrum of her heart vibrating against his lips. No, Harry wasn't a religious man, but at that moment, he believed in God.

A crash of metal sounded from somewhere in the house, and Margaret jerked away, stumbling against the settee.

"Come back here, you imp!" Burrows bellowed from outside the closed doors.

Manny! "I'll kill that boy," Harry said through gritted teeth as he started for the door.

"Harry, stop."

He spun around. The pink of Margaret's cheeks deepened to crimson.

He glanced down when her gaze dipped to his trousers. "Oh."

"I'll go," she said, pulling up the sleeve of her gown before slipping from the room.

Harry let his body fall in a heap onto the settee, and he stared at his arousal. "Damn." He swiped a hand down his face, trying in vain to decide if the interruption was good or bad. How far would he have gone with Margaret? Would he have taken her right there in the parlor? It hadn't been his intention to seduce her, but blast it if she hadn't made him lose all reason.

The words of his proposal surfaced in the morass of his mind along with the realization she hadn't given him an answer. He rose from the settee and exited the parlor in search of her, following the voices rising from the dining room.

Margaret crouched in front of the boy, demanding his attention. "Manny, you cannot raid the kitchen like that. Cook becomes very upset when someone disrupts her things." Her voice was soothing but serious as she reprimanded him.

Harry crossed his arms and leaned against the doorframe, chuckling at the sight. Manny had a colander on his head and Harry's regimental sword in his hand, the scabbard tied around his skinny hips.

"But I'm Ivanhoe, and I needed a helmet for the tournament," Manny whined.

Harry pulled himself from the doorway and moved into the melee. "I have it on good authority they've postponed the tournament until tomorrow morning. Now, it's bedtime for you, young man."

Burrows jerked to attention from where he slumped in a chair. "I apologize, Your Grace. The lad stole into your room and found the sword, then proceeded to ransack the kitchen."

"It's quite all right. I can't expect you to watch the boy twenty-four hours a day." Harry narrowed his eyes toward Manny. "Especially when he's supposed to be in bed."

Harry extracted the sword from Manny's hand. "This is not a toy. You'll cut yourself and I'll have to stitch you up again. It's been scarcely a week since I removed the ones on your forehead."

Manny's lip protruded out so far Harry was tempted to grab it and lead him upstairs by it. "That may work on Her Grace, but I'm immune to those tactics." He turned Manny around and gave him a gentle swat on his backside with the flat of the sword. "Now, back to bed."

Margaret grasped Manny's hand. "I'll take him and tuck him in."

Harry rolled his eyes but touched her arm before they left the room. "When you're finished, I would like to continue our . . . conversation. I'll be in the library."

The flush of Margaret's cheeks made it clear she understood his message.

Harry's mind cleared enough to observe his butler fully. Caring for Manny had taken a toll on the older gentleman. "Burrows, why don't you go to bed. You look exhausted. I'll lock everything up for the night. And tell Hastings I won't need his assistance this evening."

After checking the front door, Harry waited in the library, hoping Margaret wouldn't dilly dally. Not only did he want an answer to his proposal, but he ached to hold her in his arms and continue their silent communication.

As he paced the floor, thoughts of a future with Maggie filled his mind. All his concerns about his duties as duke, leaving his medical career behind, and marriage to a title-seeking woman evaporated. Excitement of a dream now within reach shot through him, and he perused the available books in the library, deciding to add a few medical tomes to the collection.

The last two weeks' sessions in the House of Lords had convinced Harry the poor desperately needed assistance. He toyed with the idea of starting a free medical clinic in one of the impoverished sections of the bustling city. He would need financial support, but now, as duke, he could shame his fellow peers into healthy contributions. Perhaps power did have advantages.

It would also provide him the opportunity to remain active in medicine. He grinned thinking about Margaret's admission to him of her own desires to help the poor and her denial of completely altruistic motives. No doubt Margaret would approve and support this challenge, and with her by his side, he could accomplish anything.

If she would only arrive and give him her answer.

"Harry?"

The whisper of his name pulled him back to the present, and he gazed at her, relishing the idea of her as his wife.

"Did I interrupt? You look deep in thought."

He held out his hand, beckoning her to him. "I was simply eager for your return. Come join me on the sofa."

She maintained her position at the doorway. *Why is she hesitating?*

His hand fell heavily to his side, mimicking the sensation of his heart. "Maggie?"

Her gaze dropped to the carpet, and she pulled her bottom lip between her teeth. When her eyes met his again, a blush covered her cheeks. "I fear if I come nearer I won't have the courage to speak what I should."

His body plummeted to the sofa. "You're refusing me?"

"You drove every sensible thought from my head, but now that I've had time to . . . collect myself, I won't hold you to your offer. Your thoughts must have been as muddled as mine from our kisses."

Her words hit him as if someone had poured a pitcher of cold water over him. "Your words have cleared my mind well enough. Yet I refuse to retract my proposal."

"Harry, there are so many reasons we shouldn't."

He stretched out his hand. "Come sit and tell them to me, and I'll provide a solution to each."

She smiled weakly, her eyes conveying what he interpreted as hope. After several hesitant steps she sat on the far end of the sofa, her back rigid and her hands folded neatly in her lap.

"Be at ease, Maggie, I promise I won't make any unwelcome advances."

She sighed and her shoulders relaxed. "They're not unwelcome, but when you kiss me, intelligent thought leaves me."

He chuckled low, resisting the urge to do just that and have it be his primary argument against all her reasons. "Very well. We shall both be level headed about this. Your first reason?"

"The obvious, of course. As George's widow, what clergyman would marry us?"

"We'll go out of the country. Germany perhaps? Or I've always thought about honeymooning in Italy."

"You deserve better, someone who will give you an heir. I've never been able to conceive."

"The issue could have been with George. A horse threw him, then kicked him in the groin when we were young. There could have been damage."

He edged closer and took her hand in his, glad when she didn't pull away. "Inability to have children can happen to anyone. There's no guarantee I would have any children, much less a son with any woman I choose as a wife."

"If we do, what about their inheritance? The next in line could contest their legitimacy."

"I'll admit, that poses a problem. But no one will dare contest anything while I'm alive. I'm George's rightful heir, there's no doubt there. Now that I'm in the House, perhaps I can effect some legal changes. And if we don't have natural born children, we can still fill our home with others—Manny and other orphans in need of a loving family. As far as an inheritance, the most our son would lose is the title and the lands. I would stipulate in my will that my children all be provided for monetarily. We would rear them to value more important things than titles and power.

"If you marry me, I'll provide for you. You'd have a home, a comfortable life."

She cringed, and he regretted his bungled words.

"You shouldn't be saddled with me to make amends for George. You deserve to marry a woman you love and who will be able to love you . . . completely."

He smiled as he shook his head. "Don't you see, Maggie? I *do* love you. I've been in love with you since the day we fulfilled our duty to Satin. Hell, probably before that."

The last words of her statement registered, generating a horrible sinking in his gut. "Are you saying you don't . . . can't love me? It's because of my likeness to George, isn't it?"

Her eyes misted. "No, I mean, it's not because of your appearance, although I'll admit at first all I could see was him. Now"—she ran a finger down the scar on his face—"I only see you."

Her fingertips lingered on the thin, pale line, her touch as gentle as a summer breeze, and he resisted the urge to clasp them and bring them to his lips.

"But you don't love me?" He held his breath for her answer.

"I do love you, Harry, more than I believed possible."

A whoosh of air left his lungs, and his heart soared with her declaration. "Then all our problems are solved."

He reached to pull her into his embrace but stopped as the tears that had welled in her eyes trailed down her cheeks. "What else, Maggie? There's something more you're not saying."

"I don't know if I could . . . satisfy you." She blushed scarlet.

Oh. He cupped her face, brushing away her tears with his thumbs. "Are you concerned about the physical aspect?"

She became intensely interested in her lap, then nodded almost imperceptibly. "I so want to please you, but I'm worried I can't."

With a finger, he lifted her chin so her eyes would meet his. "You do please me, Maggie. If our kiss is any indication, I please you as well."

Fear lingered in her gaze, but she blushed nonetheless. "Camilla said it could be enjoyable."

"Yes, very enjoyable."

"Not painful?"

Anger surged in him from what George must have done to her, but he tamped it down. Witnessing rage in his eyes would only substantiate her experience. "I would never hurt you. You have my word. Will you at least consider my proposal?"

Her eyes, so hauntingly beautiful, stared into his, before she gave a short nod. "Yes. I'll consider it."

The pressure in his chest eased, and he clung to the hope she would acquiesce. "May I have one more kiss goodnight?"

Her cheeks pinked, but she held his gaze. "I would like that."

Careful not to push her, he cradled the back of her head with one hand and wrapped the other arm around her waist. Her eyelids fluttered closed, and his own drifted shut when his lips met hers. He savored the kiss but—determined to win her trust—resisted the urge to deepen it further as he had done earlier.

When they broke free, Margaret's eyes were dusky, even more violet-like than usual, and her breath came in short pants.

Satisfaction filled him at her response. He bit back the grin. "Was that enjoyable?"

She gave a girlish giggle and trailed her fingers down his waistcoat front. "You know it was."

He rose from the sofa and pulled her to her feet. "Now, if I'm to remain a gentleman, perhaps we should bid each other goodnight."

When he remained standing by the sofa as she moved toward the door, she asked, "Aren't you coming up?"

"In a while. You go up and get some rest. I'll see you in the morning."

His gaze followed her retreating form then lingered on the empty doorway. He exhaled a heavy sigh and anticipated another sleepless night. Even so, a strange but not unwelcome sensation rose in his chest. If he dared name it, it could only be—hope.

⁂

THE THRILL OF HARRY'S LIPS ON HERS REMAINED EVEN AS Margaret ascended the winding stairway to her bedroom. Soft, yet firm, warm and . . . insistent. Could it be true? She suppressed another giggle, and the lightness of her spirit traveled down to her toes, creating an illusion that her feet barely skimmed the treads of each step. Could a coupling be pleasant and enjoyable?

The curiosity that had plagued Margaret as a child resurfaced, and her mind demanded an answer, refusing to put the question aside.

Her heart ached at Harry's expression when she'd refused him. But he had been resolute, laying out logical arguments for each of her concerns. She couldn't bear to disappoint him again. Before she agreed, she must be certain.

She rang for Flora, and while she waited, she silently prepared the speech she intended to deliver to Harry.

As Flora unpinned and brushed her hair, Margaret stared into the mirror, wondering how to approach him and if she had the courage to follow through. *If I'm to remain a gentleman,* he had said. Clearly he desired more than a kiss, and in her heart she did as well.

Vaguely aware Flora had spoken, she looked at the reflection of the maid staring back at her.

"I'm sorry, Flora. My mind wandered."

"The necklace, Your Grace. I can't unfasten the clasp. It seems to be stuck."

Harry's mother's necklace. She fingered the pendant. His lovely gesture provided the perfect excuse. "I'll remove it later."

Flora assisted Margaret in removing her gown and changing into her night-rail, then bid her goodnight.

As Flora turned to exit, Margaret held up a hand. "Flora, I plan to sleep in tomorrow. Please don't disturb me. I'll ring when I need you."

Flora gave a much improved curtsy and left Margaret alone, closing the door behind her.

After a few minutes had passed, she opened her door a crack and waited, listening for Harry's footsteps. She prayed he wouldn't wait too long before deciding to retire; her nerves would never survive. Her heart beat against her ribs like a wild animal throwing itself against a cage.

The clock in the hall chimed the quarter hour indicating she had been waiting for at least thirty minutes, and with each minute her courage faded.

Movement downstairs drew her attention, and she moved to stand by the door, listening carefully. Soft footfalls rewarded her patience, and she opened the door wider as Harry's figure rose along the stairway.

She took a deep, fortifying breath and called to him as he reached the landing. "Harry?"

His eyes grew wide upon seeing her. "Margaret? Is everything all right?" He stepped toward her.

"The necklace. Flora was unable to unlatch it."

"Oh, yes. I forgot to mention there's a little trick to it. Allow me." His eyes locked on hers as he moved forward, then broke as he stepped behind her.

Gooseflesh formed as his fingers skimmed the back of her neck, and her courage soared. With the ends of the necklace clasped in his fingers, he transferred one end of the chain to join its twin in his other hand. He rested his free hand on her neck and trailed a lazy finger down the curve to her shoulder. Heat pooled low inside her.

"It's a temptation seeing you in your nightdress. I should allow you to return to your room," he whispered as he leaned forward. The puff of his breath brushing against her ear sent delicious shivers up her spine.

"About that." She turned toward him and took his hand, pulling him into her room. After closing the door, she stood with her back pressed against it.

His lips quirked in an amused half smile as he tucked the necklace into his pocket. "Maggie? What are you up to?"

All the words of her rehearsed speech bid a hasty retreat as if they were a part of a forlorn hope, and she fumbled calling them back to action. "I . . . that is . . ."

She closed her eyes, summoning their return with a rallying cry, concentrating on the gentleness of his touch, his promises of pleasure. A few lone soldiers responded, and she prayed they would be enough. She opened her eyes and met his, waiting, curious but patient. "As a physician, you're a man of science."

His eyebrows lifted. "Yes?"

"And from my reading, men of science conduct experiments to test hypotheses, do they not?"

"They do." The amused half smile returned to his lips.

"I should like to test a theory."

"In your nightdress?"

She was bungling this. "Well, not exactly. You see, I want very much to believe that a physical relationship can be pleasant. But before I would agree to marriage again, I would like proof."

His chuckle, although low and sensual, did nothing to relieve her nerves. "Maggie, making love is hardly like conducting a scientific experiment. Science is cold and calculated. Whereas"—he traced an index finger across her lips—"making love is heated and passionate."

Heated proved to be an accurate word as warmth flooded her cheeks. "I only meant to appeal to your logic when presenting my suggestion."

He sighed, heavy and long. "Nothing about my feelings for you has any semblance of logic. Yet, they're strong and true. I have no need of an experiment to prove their validity. The question is, why do you?"

She cringed. "Oh dear, I'm making a muck of this, and it appears you have misunderstood my meaning."

"Maggie, why don't you just tell me instead of using theoretical analogies?"

She reached deep inside to pluck up her remaining courage, but he was right. Furthermore, he deserved the truth. "I fear if I agree to marry you, you will be sorely disappointed on our wedding night. I couldn't bear it if you were shackled to me in misery for the rest of your life. You deserve happiness; it is my utmost desire."

The expression on his face softened, and he opened his mouth to speak, but she lifted her hand to stop him.

"Please, let me continue lest I lose what little bravery I have left." She met his eyes and blurted out the words. "I want us to make love now, then if I disappoint you, I'll understand if you withdraw your proposal."

She waited for him to laugh.

He did not.

Nor did he respond in any way. He simply stared at her. At any moment, she expected him to turn on his heel and bolt from the room.

Silence permeated the air as if some enchantress had cast a spell upon them both.

She jumped when he broke it.

"Maggie," he said, taking a step closer. "I have no fear you will disappoint me, but *your* happiness is paramount to me. So, if you're sure, and if you'll allow me, let me prove to you that I can give you pleasure. In doing so, it will give *me* pleasure and put an end to your doubts."

He threaded his left hand into her hair and pulled her close with his right. Then, tilting her head to the perfect angle, he lowered his mouth to hers, at first, a tentative brush as if tasting a new wine, then deciding it satisfied, he drank deeper.

The steady pressure of his lips weakened her knees, but his arm around her waist steadied her. Kisses trailed from her lips, across her jaw, and down her neck. Coherent thought left her, and her mind became a muddled mess, so much so she barely realized he had spoken, but she had no clue what he had said.

"W-what?" she stammered.

His eyes, dusky and sensual, penetrated hers, and a smile crept across his lips. "Do you trust me?"

God, how she wanted to—needed to. She struggled to force the affirmative answer from her lips.

As if sensing her hesitation, he added, "I would never hurt you, Maggie. If I do anything you don't like, tell me."

"Yes." The word clung to her tongue as she forced it out, but once it had left her mouth, the rightness of it settled in her heart, and she answered again with conviction, "Yes, I trust you."

He reached for the ribbon on her night-rail, giving it a gentle pull. "I want to look at you," he whispered against her ear. The material of her gown spread open at the neckline, and he tugged the shoulder of it free before lowering his lips to the curve of her neck, then the hollow of her throat.

"Your pulse is quickening," he said.

His breath against her hot skin did nothing to slow it. The rightness of everything he did slammed into her heart as surely as her heart slammed into her ribs. He was right, there was no logic in this, only feeling, the emotion so strong she worried it would crush her.

Yet when he slipped the gown off her shoulders and down her body, she froze when he gasped.

She had forgotten about the pale scars that crisscrossed her breasts, stomach, and legs.

Unable to meet his gaze, she turned her head. The words would come easier if she didn't see the aversion in his eyes. "He marked me, saying no one else would ever want to look upon such a sight."

She stooped to lift the night-rail back into position, but he grasped her forearms and pulled her upright.

With gentle fingertips, he tracked the marks, his touch as light as the night air floating in through her window. The action, almost reverent, delivered healing to her soul.

"Oh, Maggie." Pain laced the whisper of her name. "I hate that he did this, but it makes you no less beautiful to me."

What he did next astounded her. He kissed each of the silvery lines on her body. The tenderness of his lips on her flesh both soothed and excited her, and her nipples peaked as he found his way to her breasts. He laved one then the other, nipping at the delicate skin and teasing with his tongue.

A moan echoed through the room, and her muddled brain recognized her own voice.

The light stubble of his beard tickled her skin, heightening the sensation, and she shuddered.

He gave a low chuckle. "Pleasant?"

"Yes." The word came out breathy.

He kissed her lips again, then stepped away, his hands untying and pulling his cravat from his neck. "You asked once about my scars from Waterloo." He shrugged out of his coat and waistcoat, allowing them to pool carelessly onto the floor. After unbuttoning the two buttons of his linen shirt, he pulled it over his head and stood before her.

A jagged, red welt cut across his abdomen from sternum to hip, and a round, puckered scar the size of a shilling dotted his right side under his ribcage.

She reached out, as he had done, and traced the long transverse scar.

"That was from a saber slash as I ran out into battle toward the wounded. I stitched it up myself, none too tidily I'm afraid." He touched the circular scar on his side. "This was from a bullet I received while pulling a soldier from the field. I removed the bullet and cauterized the wound."

She gazed at him through misted eyes. He had never been more handsome. "You're a hero."

He shook his head. "No, the heroes were those who gave their lives."

"Then you are *my* hero." As he had done to her, she bent and kissed his scars, hoping her touch would ease the frightful memories associated to the marks.

He sucked in a breath as her lips touched the slash by his hip. A surge of power swept through her at his reaction.

Without a word, he scooped her into his arms and carried her to the bed, laying her down in the center as if she were a piece of bone china that would break if handled too roughly.

Although she was not so fragile, his caution gave credence to his trustworthiness, and she loved him for it. She should have felt vulnerable and exposed lying naked on the bed, but she didn't. Instead, anticipation built in her, thinking about what was yet to happen.

He pulled off his boots, letting them drop to the floor with a thud, then removed his stockings. He stood at the side of the bed, gazing at her, his eyes intense—passionate yet tender. "You are so beautiful."

The curtains fluttered in the breeze as the soft patter of rain splashed the windowsill, filling the room with the clean fresh scent of early summer. It seemed fitting, as if it washed away all the past, leaving only something new and full of promise.

He climbed onto the bed next to her, still clothed in his trousers. She reached to unbutton the fall, but he stayed her hand.

"Not yet," he whispered as he brushed his lips against the pulsing vein in her neck.

He resumed his kisses, down her neck, across her torso, suckling a delicate nipple, each time coming back to claim her lips with urgency, and each time, his hands replacing where his mouth had been.

"Still pleasant?"

God yes, her mind screamed, but her tongue couldn't form the words, so she merely nodded. Pressure built in her like a tea kettle ready to whistle.

He moved down her body, placing gentle kisses on her thighs, and she clutched the bed linens in her fists.

"Do you trust me?" he asked.

Something unintelligible flew from her mouth; she sounded like a fool, but he didn't laugh.

A flash of lightning lit the room, and the rain beat harder against the window, splattering on the windowsill and floor.

Before she knew it, his mouth found the sensitive area at the juncture of her thighs, and an urgency cascaded through her. Her mind became muddled, even nonsensical.

An answering call of thunder rumbled in the distance.

As he continued, the building pressure within her threatened to explode, and she arched into his ministrations. Moans echoed in the room. Unsure whether they were hers or his, she decided she didn't care. Her hands released their clutch on the sheets and threaded into his hair. Then she came apart, shattering into pieces.

Nothing had ever felt so wonderful.

As the spasms of her climax lessened, Harry replaced his mouth with his hand and moved back up toward her.

"Pleasant?" He grinned at her.

Why she should blush after what they had just done was a mystery, but her cheeks flamed as she said, "I had no idea. Every part of me tingled as if stars exploded inside me."

He trailed a finger across her lips. "One advantage of being a physician is the knowledge of anatomy."

She giggled, the words he had said earlier in the evening to Nash now taking on a new meaning. The sheer masculinity of him took her breath away as she ran her hands along the hard planes of his chest and abdomen.

Her gaze dipped down to where his trousers bulged. His arousal strained against the fabric. "But what about you?"

"Are you certain?" He ran his hand through the dark curls between her legs, then kissed her eyelids.

She had never been more certain of anything in her life. The desire to please him as much as he had pleased her overshadowed her fear. She answered him by reaching for the buttons on his fall, and this time he didn't stop her. Her fingers shook as she slid the first button from its home, but grew bolder with each one until he sprang free.

When she touched the velvety skin at the tip, his head fell back, his eyes shuttering closed, and he moaned, low and guttural. Encouraged by his response, she grasped him, circling her fingers around him, and ran her hand up and down his length. His moans increased until he placed his hand on hers, halting her motion.

"If you don't stop now, I won't last." He pulled off his trousers and threw them over the side of the bed.

To her eyes, he looked like the Greek god Apollo, so perfectly formed, yet battle-scarred like Ares, the juxtaposition oddly fitting.

As he leaned over her, he smelled like rich wood, leather, and— her. When he kissed her again, their tongues dueling in a battle neither wanted to end, he tasted spicy yet sweet.

Another clap of thunder followed a flash of lightning, the storm growing closer, and although the room chilled from the open window, their bodies remained heated and perspiring.

He lowered himself over her, settling his hips between hers, and as he pressed against her, she welcomed him. A curious thought from her youth flashed through her mind but faded as soon as it had appeared. The rightness of their lovemaking, now affirmed, became all encompassing as he moved within her, slowly at first, then with more urgency.

Initially tentative, she grew emboldened from his moans of approval when she matched his movements and explored his body. Muscles in his arms and back flexed from exertion as she ran her hands over them. But she didn't fear the strength they contained. These arms protected her.

The strange, sweet crescendo built inside her once more, and he slid his hand between them, teasing the nub until she shattered again and cried out, "Harry."

"Maggie," he moaned. "I love you." A guttural cry followed the murmured words. With a final thrust, he found his own release.

After the last spasms faded, he slid out of her and settled next to her side, pulling her into his arms and stroking her hair. He whispered words of love and endearments, kissed her forehead, then her nose, before claiming her mouth again, brushing her lips with tenderness. And she had never felt so loved—so cherished.

She stared into his eyes. "Aren't you going to ask me?"

His lopsided grin reminded her of a small boy who knew very well he would avoid punishment for whatever mischief he had wrought.

He touched his fingertip to the end of her nose. "And what might that be?"

"If I found it pleasant."

He threw his head back and laughed, the sound filling the room and washing away the sounds of the past. "I don't have to ask that question." He gazed into her eyes. "But I do another."

"Oh?"

"Now will you marry me?"

CHAPTER 17—AN OMINOUS ENCOUNTER

Nestled in Harry's arms, Margaret sighed contentedly. She hadn't displeased him; Harry still wanted to marry her. Everything fell into place, and the fleeting thought from her youth that had flashed through her mind as they consummated their love resurfaced.

She played with the dusting of golden hair on his chest, reveling in its softness, and breathed in his masculine scent. "My father gave me a wooden puzzle for my tenth birthday. I assembled the majority of it with ease. However, two pieces appeared so similar I would inevitably put them in the wrong place. Although at first they seemed to fit, rough edges protruded, scraping my fingers and causing the puzzle to appear misshapen. But once in their proper places, the effect was quite remarkable, the seams of the pieces somehow vanishing to form an unbroken whole.

"It's as if someone had placed the wrong piece in me for so long, but now, the right one, seated firmly has found its home and made me complete."

His brow creased momentarily then his eyes widened. "Is that your long-winded way of saying you'll marry me?"

She laughed, fully and without restraint, then kissed him on the mouth. "It is."

He tugged her closer and chuckled. "That's a relief." His fingertips traveled up and down her arm in lazy strokes. "I think we should marry quickly as soon as the Season ends. Would you like to go to Italy? We can marry in Germany then travel south."

"What about America?"

He scrunched up his nose, looking perfectly adorable. "It's true it was my home and I loved it there, but I don't know if I can stomach the journey again. But if that's your desire—"

"Germany and Italy it shall be."

He kissed her shoulder. "I made a wise choice asking you to be my wife."

Harry stared at the ceiling, and Margaret studied him, uncertain what he could discern in the dim candlelight.

She ached to discover each little thing about him—his hopes, his goals, his plans. It thrilled her to be part of his life and—she prayed —his dreams. She placed her hand on the hard plane of his chest. "What is it? You look deep in thought."

He returned his gaze to her, soft light from the candle by the bed flickering across his face. "What do you think about the idea of opening a free medical clinic on the East End?"

Clearly she had a lot to learn about the workings of his mind. The question alone brought a smile to her lips, but the fact he desired her opinion delighted her. "What makes you think of that?"

He chuckled. "I sound daft, don't I? Here I am lying in bed with a beautiful woman whom I adore, and I'm talking about medical clinics." He kissed the tip of her nose. "I can't imagine any other woman who would support me in such a venture. But with you"— he tugged her close to his side—"you will be my partner in all things. Perhaps you might help me secure contributions?"

"It sounds ambitious and . . . well, wonderful. One of my first impressions of you when you arrived at Briarfield was the good you could do as a physician. But how would you manage it? You have the estate and your duties in the House."

"That's true. I would have to hire other physicians, but it would at least give me the opportunity to use my training when possible. How do you feel about living at Briarfield? Archer seems to be a capable steward, perhaps we could lengthen our stays in London, only going home to the country for a few months?"

Briarfield held no happy memories, whereas here in London she now found peace. "It would be no hardship to remain here longer. Truthfully, I've always thought Briarfield to be dark and depressing."

He nodded, then sighed. "Yes, I agree." He propped up on an elbow, and she missed his heat as her hand slid off his chest. "We can redecorate. You can choose whatever furnishings and colors you wish. The work could be completed while we're on our wedding trip. If it isn't finished when we arrive home, it will provide an excuse for us to return here."

"That sounds lovely."

The curtains flapped from a strong gust of wind, and she shivered.

"I'll close the window," Harry said, "then I should go. I wouldn't want to shock poor Flora when she comes to wake you in the morning."

He started to rise, but she held his arm, calling him back.

"Close the window, but stay with me. I told Flora I planned to sleep in, and I'd ring when I needed her."

He grinned like a fox who had raided the chickens. "You planned this? Oh, yes, your experiment. In the heat of things I'd forgotten. Would you say it was a success?" He chuckled, low and sensuous, causing desire to flame in her again.

"I understand that with most scientific experiments repetition is recommended," she said, fighting to keep her expression serious.

"On that, I couldn't agree more."

❦

WHEN HARRY WOKE SPOONED AGAINST MARGARET EARLY THE NEXT morning, he ran a finger down her arm and smiled, remembering the passion they had shared. The strength and power of it had overwhelmed him. Although not a novice at lovemaking, the experience of sharing himself with someone he deeply loved had proven so emotional, all reason left him. He yearned to wake like this every morning.

They must marry soon. So lost in his ecstasy, he failed in his intention of pulling out before climax. She might be carrying his child. The idea didn't worry him, in fact, he welcomed it. But what of Maggie? If she conceived before they were wed, would it sully the memory of her experience? He regretted his selfish act. He would be more careful next time.

She stirred as he rose from the bed and gathered his clothing, slipping on his trousers.

"Harry?" she said, her voice still drowsy with slumber.

He placed a kiss on her forehead. "Shush, my darling. It's morning and I must sneak back into my room before Hastings comes to wake me."

Her eyes opened and a slow smile built on her lips. "I wasn't dreaming?"

"Not unless I had the same dream. A most pleasant one, I would say, wouldn't you?"

Her smile widened to a full-fledged grin. "Most pleasant."

"Now I should be off."

He cracked the door and peeked out into the hallway, breathing a sigh of relief that it was free of servants wandering about.

When Hastings arrived to wake him, Harry had already washed and dressed in fresh trousers and shirt. He whistled a merry little tune as his valet finished tying his cravat.

"You're in high spirits today, sir. I expected you to be bleary-eyed this morning," Hastings said as he held out Harry's coat. "Did you enjoy the ball last evening?"

Harry chuckled. In truth, he hadn't slept as soundly in years. "It energized me."

Hastings gave a tight-lipped smile, bowed, and exited.

Harry hurried downstairs, already eager to see Margaret again. *Has it really only been a mere hour since I'd last kissed her?* It seemed like ages.

The jam for his toast had never tasted sweeter, so he helped himself to another serving. He had nearly finished eating when Margaret entered the breakfast room, and he rose to greet her. Her new mauve morning dress brought out the pink in her cheeks. After she served herself, Harry held her chair, and as she took her seat, he leaned in to whisper, "You have a glow about you this morning."

Something fluttered in his chest from her laugh, bright and melodic.

"Flora said precisely the same thing as she dressed my hair."

"Oh?"

"Yes, she suggested I attend balls more often."

"Your answer to that suggestion?" He kept a straight face as he retook his seat.

Her blush deepened, but her gaze remained on her plate. "I agreed that I would very much like to repeat the experience as often as possible."

Harry sat straighter in his chair, warmth expanding his chest until he worried he would pop the buttons on his waistcoat, suspecting he grinned like a fool at her implication. "Let's take a walk in the park or perhaps a trip to Vauxhall Gardens. We'll take Manny with us, although it would make it more difficult for me to whisk you aside for a kiss as we hide among the shrubbery. Then we can go for ices at Gunter's."

She laughed again, the sound something he would never tire of. "You're ambitious this morning." She took a bite of her toast, chewing thoughtfully.

"Is it wrong I want to parade around London with the most beautiful woman on my arm?"

Her cheeks pinked enough to indicate his flattery hit its mark.

"I would love to, Harry, but I promised Camilla I would call on her this morning."

"Oh." His heart sank like a small boy who had been told there was no Father Christmas.

Her smile disappeared. "Are you that disappointed? I could send a message to Cammie and tell her I'll come tomorrow?"

"No, no. Don't change your plans because of me. Perhaps I might accompany you?"

She blushed again. "I was hoping to speak with her alone, but of course, you may."

His face tingled as heat rose up his neck, and his throat tightened with remorse. She should be able to visit with her friends without him hanging on to her like a lovesick pup. He sighed, admitting the truth of that comparison, and struggled to salvage his pride yet provide her the freedom she deserved.

"Let's compromise. I'll escort you to Camilla's then leave you to your visit. Manny and I will content ourselves to be two carefree bachelors."

"As you wish," she answered. But the smile on her lips confirmed she had seen through him.

Peter the footman approached with a silver tray brimming with letters and held it before Harry.

Margaret sipped her tea, eyeing the correspondence. "It appears everyone will be seeking your company now that you've made your first formal appearance as duke."

Somehow that prospect didn't seem as distressing with Margaret at his side. He opened the missives, one after the other—invitations to tea, to a card party, to supper, and requests to meet with him to discuss charitable ventures. He put the last in a pile for follow-up, thinking of his idea for a medical clinic. One particular announcement for a social event piqued his interest.

"What is it?" Margaret asked, apparently observing his fascination with the cream-colored card of invitation.

"A musicale hosted by Lord and Lady Marbry." He met her eyes shining with the same enthusiasm. "I do enjoy music. Would you like to attend?"

"I would love to. I wonder if Cammie will be singing? She has a glorious voice. I shall ask her today. Beatrix Marbry plays the pianoforte exceedingly well. It should be a marvelous program."

"Then it's agreed. I'll send our acceptance at once."

"Are you certain I'm included in the invitation?"

He glanced back at the address. *His Grace, the Duke of Ashton.* No mention of Her Grace on either the outer address or the invitation itself, so he lied. "Yes, of course."

Her eyes narrowed for a moment, but she remained silent.

After laying his napkin on his plate, he rose from the table. "What time does Camilla expect you? I'll send for the curricle. Last night's storm has cleared the air, and it promises to be a lovely day."

Her eyebrows lifted, and she laughed brightly. "My, you truly are ambitious this morning. Do you plan to race some young bucks in Hyde Park?"

He leaned down and, making sure no one watched, kissed her neck. "You've made me feel like a young buck."

When he left her at Camilla's, he regretted having Manny along as it prevented him from stealing a kiss while he helped her descend from the curricle. The moment she entered the house, a dull ache of emptiness invaded his chest, and he stood outside, staring at the closed door.

Manny tugged at his coat. "Oi, Harry. Let's go."

He climbed onto the curricle's seat and picked up the ribbons. "Where to? Hyde Park? Vauxhall Gardens?"

Manny scratched his chin with a forefinger. "Never been to Vauxhall Gardens. Are there lots of rich folks millin' about?"

Harry raised an eyebrow. "There will be no pick-pocketing. Understood?"

Manny crossed his arms over his skinny chest and pulled a disappointed face but nodded. Harry decided to keep a close rein on the boy as he snapped the ribbons, urging the matched set of chestnuts forward.

After dropping the curricle with a groom, they strolled through the gardens. The beautiful day had indeed brought out many rich folks as Manny would have said. Harry tipped his hat so frequently he wished he had not worn one.

Too busy gawking at the structures, fountains, and greenery, Manny seemed to have forgotten about pilfering. He pointed at things and asked a myriad of questions. As much as Harry missed Margaret, especially when they passed an isolated copse of shrubs, he enjoyed educating the boy. Yes, he and Margaret should plan on children as soon as possible.

They had agreed to keep their engagement a secret for the time being, but seeing Manny's excitement compelled him to ask, "Manny, would you like to live with Her Grace and me forever?"

If possible, the boy's eyes widened further. "Yer joking?"

Harry shook his head. "I'm very serious. Of course this means, as a member of our family, you would have to uphold the standards of behavior expected. Can you do that?"

Manny's gaze drifted to his feet, which now shuffled on the path. "Like no pinchin' stuff?"

"Yes, that in particular, but also learning how to read, speak, and behave."

The boy's face turned red. "In that case."

Like a spooked horse, he bolted down the walkway from where they had just come. Harry ran after him, wondering what had driven him away. *Reading, behaving?*

Harry skidded to a stop at a curve on the path. Manny stood in front of a man and woman, gesturing wildly and holding out a watch. *Manny!*

"You must 'ave dropped this, your lordship," he lied.

"Oh, what a sweet boy," the woman cooed as she reached down and pinched his cheeks.

Harry suppressed a groan.

"T'weren't nothin', your ladyship." Manny's eyes met Harry's, the plea of corroboration evident.

Harry tipped his hat to the couple.

"Is this young lad your son, sir?" the man asked.

"He's under my care." Harry gave Manny a stern look.

"You must be exceedingly proud of him," the woman said. "Such a little gentleman."

"Yes, we're working on that, aren't we, Manny?"

The man reached into his pocket. "Please let me give the boy a reward. Will a shilling do?"

"That's not necessary. He's learning to do what is right for the sake of right, not reward. Isn't that so, Manny?"

"Yes, Har . . . err . . . Your Grace."

At the title, the man and woman became flustered, obviously

uncomfortable. "Forgive us, Your Grace. We had no idea," the man apologized.

"Think nothing of it." Harry tipped his hat again, grasped Manny by the shoulder, turned him around, and made his way back up the path away from the embarrassed couple.

"I see you're off to a brilliant start. Are there any other dropped articles in your possession we need to return?"

Manny shook his head and wiped his nose with his sleeve. "Sorry."

Preoccupied with chastising Manny, Harry failed to notice Lady Cartwright and Miss Pratt fast approaching. Too late to make a detour onto one of the side pathways, Harry braced himself, hoping to keep the interaction short.

"Oh, Your Grace!" Lady Cartwright called. "How lovely to see you here. You left so abruptly last evening I didn't have the opportunity to tell you how much we enjoyed your company."

"Thank you, madam. It was a pleasure being there." Harry tipped his hat. "Miss Pratt."

Priscilla stared down her nose at Manny as if he were something vile stuck to her dainty slipper.

"Forgive me," Harry said. "This is Manny. Manny, this is Lady Cartwright and Miss Pratt. Say hello."

"'Ello."

Lady Cartwright and Priscilla each raised an eyebrow. "Is he the boy who fell from the tree, Your Grace?" Priscilla asked.

"He is. He's staying with us." Harry placed a hand on Manny's shoulder and gave it an affectionate squeeze.

The ladies exchanged a glance. "Your Grace," Lady Cartwright said. "It's providential we encountered you today. There is something I wish to speak with you about."

"Can it be brief? Manny and I were heading home."

Manny opened his mouth to protest, but Harry caught his eye and gave a discreet shake of his head.

Lady Cartwright assumed the same look of disdain as she gazed down at the boy. "What I mean to discuss is of a somewhat delicate nature."

The back of Harry's neck itched as if a thousand ants crawled up it. Although they hadn't planned to, returning home seemed preferable to whatever Lady Cartwright had to say.

Harry crouched down to Manny. "Go and wait over by that bench. I'll be there shortly."

Manny raced off, taking Harry's positive outlook with him. He waited for the old gossip to begin.

Covering her mouth with a gloved hand, she gave a feeble cough. "Your Grace, this is most difficult for me, but I feel it's my duty as a dear friend of your mother to inform you."

Dear friend indeed. They'd hardly known each other. Harry braced himself. He doubted her difficulty in relaying what he presumed would be bad news. She seemed to relish it.

"It appears several people have been talking about your relationship with Her Grace. Although I find your kindness and hospitality to her admirable, you must be aware that such . . . closeness . . . could prove detrimental in developing an alliance with a *suitable* young woman. Surely, in your duty as duke, securing a bride is foremost on your mind. I would hate to see the right woman driven away because of your brother's wife. I only say this since your dear mother, God rest her soul, isn't here to tell you herself."

Harry ground his teeth, relieved he didn't bite off his tongue. "I'll remind you, Lady Cartwright, that *you* are not my mother, nor have I any need for someone to act in her stead. If *people* are gossiping, it's because they don't have anything more productive to do. I would suggest you do not listen to them. I won't. Now, if you'll excuse me." He tipped his hat—although he envisioned flinging it in the old bat's face—and stomped off to retrieve Manny.

His hands shook, and had Manny not been along, he would have gone to Jackson's boxing academy to pound something or someone. How dare the old busybody tell him whom he should or shouldn't associate with? He would proudly accompany Margaret everywhere possible and flout every supercilious gossip in London. Let their tongues wag.

By the time he and Manny had reached Camilla's to find Margaret, he had calmed down, but the words of warning stuck in his mind. Perhaps Lady Cartwright had a point, albeit not for the sake of securing a marriage prospect. That feat had been accomplished last night. No, he should be cautious for Margaret's sake. Once they returned from a wedding trip, their marriage alone would shock the ton, but by then it would be a fait accompli. No need to cause undue scandal prior to that.

Margaret blushed under Camilla's interrogation. The information she shared with her friend ended just short of the entire account of her night with Harry. She would keep that to herself.

"I knew it," Cammie said, the expression on her face bordering on smug. "I suspected as much when he spoke about you when we danced, but when he asked you to waltz, well . . ." She flattened her hand against her chest and sighed. "I remember the looks Hugh and I used to share." She pulled Margaret into her embrace. "I'm overjoyed for you, Maggie."

"It's like a dream, Cammie. I'd forgotten what it was like to be so happy."

"Aren't you concerned about the gossip?"

"I'll be so busy I won't have time to worry about what people say. Harry wants to open a free medical clinic here in London. He's asked me to assist in securing contributions and finding a location and staffing it." She kept the fact that she and Harry discussed the matter while wrapped in each other's embrace to herself, but she remembered the excitement that lit his eyes when he spoke of it. That he wanted her to partner with him in the venture thrilled her. Her dream of helping the less fortunate was now within her reach.

"When do you plan to marry?"

"As soon as the Season is over and he's finished in the House."

Cammie's butler appeared in the doorway. "His Grace and Master Manny are here, madam."

"Please show them in, Stratton."

Margaret's heart fluttered in anticipation. She hadn't expected him so soon.

One look at his face, and her stomach dropped. The carefree, excited expression he bore when he'd left her earlier had been replaced, his brow now creased in the center and his mouth formed a taut line—the image of George. What had happened? She inhaled deeply and focused on the scar.

She rose and stepped toward him. "What is it?" She held her breath for his answer.

"It's nothing the sight of you won't cure. Forgive me for looking so dour. Might I interest you ladies in a trip to Gunter's for ices?"

"But the curricle barely seats three and only because Manny's small."

"Hey." Manny placed his hands on his hips. In the two weeks since they'd taken him into their care, he'd filled out considerably, his love of biscuits rivaling Harry's.

"Forgive me, Manny," Margaret said. "I only meant small compared to His Grace and me."

The boy gave a curt nod, but a smile said he'd forgiven her.

"It's not that far, and it's a pleasant day. Let's walk," Harry said.

Mindful of Manny's presence, Margaret turned toward Camilla. "Lady Denby?"

"I don't wish to intrude."

"Nonsense," Harry said. "We'd love to have you join us. Besides, an extra pair of eyes on Manny wouldn't hurt. Perhaps you could help with ideas for my venture. Has Her Grace mentioned it?"

"You can call each other by your names. You don't 'ave to be all formal like cause of me," Manny said matter-of-factly.

Camilla lifted a hand to her mouth, stifling a giggle, whereas Harry had no qualms of propriety and bellowed a laugh.

Margaret shrugged. "He does speak his mind."

The four of them set off to Gunter's, chatting amiably. Margaret couldn't remember the last time she felt so free and happy. Her best friend and the man she loved flanked her sides, and the impish child who made her giggle like a girl strutted like a peacock next to Harry.

Manny adored him, imitating his mannerisms. Harry's firm but gentle mentorship would shape him into a fine young man. Her heart swelled with love and pride.

Without warning, a man rushed across the street and grabbed Manny, pulling him aside. "It is you, boy! Where you been? And where'd you get those fancy duds?"

Greasy dirty blond hair plastered the man's head like a cap, his eyes—beady and dark like a bird of prey—darted back and forth at each of them. Tattered clothes covered his filthy body and dirt caked under his fingernails. The stench coming from him turned Margaret's stomach.

Manny writhed within the man's grasp. "Gerroff me! I ain't yours no more."

"Leave the boy alone." Harry pulled Manny from the man's hold.

"Oi! Such a fancy man. The boy belongs to me, give 'im back."

Coodibilis! Margaret's heart raced, and she struggled to breathe as if her corset was too tight.

Harry pushed Manny behind him, then held out his arm, keeping her and Camilla from moving forward.

"You are not the boy's father."

"Who says I ain't? And what're you doin' wi' 'im. Sumptin wicked, I'd bet."

"He is not!" Manny shouted, poking his head around Harry, only to have Harry push him back. Margaret pulled the boy to her, holding him close to her side.

"Margaret, Camilla, take Manny and find a constable. Hurry."

Harry reached out to restrain the man, but Cood took a wild swing at him, and when Harry ducked, Cood bolted, yelling as he ran, "You ain't seen the last o' me. No one steals from Coodibilis and gets away wi' it."

CHAPTER 18—THE MUSICALE

The week following the encounter with Coodibilis had been busy, and Margaret found little time to worry about the man's threats. They devoted themselves to establishing the clinic, dividing their forces. Harry had contacted several sellers of property in the East End attempting to find a building. While he inspected the properties, narrowing down to three prospective choices, she focused on organizing a charitable foundation to secure donations.

Because of her connections and his preoccupation with securing a location, Harry asked Margaret to make calls to solicit contributions. If necessary, he would become involved. They set a goal of £2,500. Margaret started with Lord Harcourt, Camilla's father, who pledged a generous donation of £100. She then secured a promise of £150 from Lord Saxton.

Armed with those, she called on Lord Easton. His son and heir, Laurence, happened to be at home at the time, which proved a distinct advantage. Before she had married George, Laurence had courted her and according to Camilla, he still held affection for her.

After the customary greetings, she took a seat next to Laurence on the sofa, then she inhaled a deep breath and began her prepared speech. "Lord Easton, perhaps you're aware that my brother-in-law, the Duke of Ashton, is a physician. He proposes to open a clinic on the East End. The people are in dire need of accessible medical care. Ashton's plans are not only admirable, but essential. I have pledges from Lords Harcourt and Saxton; may I count on you as well?"

Easton squirmed a bit in his seat. Harcourt was a baron, Saxon was a viscount, and Easton was an earl. Margaret's strategy of starting at the lower end of the aristocracy and shaming those of a higher rank into contributing appeared to be working.

"How much did Marbry pledge?"

A spike of energy shot up her spine. She had him. "Oh, I really shouldn't divulge that information, sir." She may have batted her eyes as she glanced down into her lap.

"It sounds like a good cause, Father," Laurence said. He moved closer to her on the sofa.

She placed a hand on his sleeve and gave a tiny squeeze. "It is, Laurence."

Easton harrumphed and squirmed a little more. "If you tell me how much each man contributed, I might consider it. I promise it won't go further than this room."

Those were Marbry's exact words, and she restrained her grin as she relayed the information.

She left with a pledge of £250 from Easton and another £100 from Laurence. Of course, she had to agree she would save Laurence a dance at the next event. She hoped Harry would consider it a negotiating expense.

A visit to Lord Stratford, a marquess, garnered £400, and His Grace, the Duke of Burwood, who was as ancient as the seas and hard of hearing, had pinched her cheeks and promised £800.

The joy of being productive for such a worthy cause energized her, and she developed a newfound confidence. As she called on additional earls, marquesses, viscounts, barons and baronets, her talent for persuasive argument blossomed. Soon, they had raised funds in excess of £3,000, and some promised monthly continuing donations of lesser amounts.

Interspersed with the efforts of establishing the clinic, she and

Harry strolled through Vauxhall Gardens, took curricle rides through Hyde Park, and attended a garden party at Lord and Lady Harcourt's. Per Harry's suggestion, Margaret agreed they should maintain decorum in public. They reserved the nights for sharing their affection, although she grew increasingly irritated with every eligible young lady flirting with Harry. Occasionally, Harry would risk a brief touch of her hand to assure her, but she began counting the days until the end of the Season.

Even with their busy schedules, they found time each evening to share news of their accomplishments, his securing a location for the clinic and hers working toward its funding. Her dreams from her childhood appeared in reach, leaving her happy and fulfilled.

With the musicale a few days away, only three weeks remained when they would leave for their wedding trip. She became giddy with excitement and squeezed in a visit to Madam Tredwell's to order a few new gowns for her wedding and honeymoon. If the modiste had any suspicions as to the nature of her client's purchases, she kept them to herself. She hadn't even raised an eyebrow when Margaret requested she allow a bit more room in the skirts.

The morning of the musicale, Margaret woke with the familiar monthly pain in her abdomen. Tears welled in her eyes. *Silly.* She chastised herself. Had she genuinely hoped she would be with child? Logic told her she should be grateful. She forced herself from the bed, washed, and rang for Flora.

As her maid brushed and pinned her hair, the accompanying megrim began. The bright morning light streaming from the windows exacerbated the strange colors and waviness at the perimeter of her vision which signaled the megrim's onset. Next rose the slight nausea. Pain soon followed, dull at first, then throbbing and relentless.

"Please inform His Grace that I'm not feeling well and will remain in my room during breakfast."

After Flora left, Margaret closed the curtains and reclined on the chaise longue in her room. The soft tap on the door sounded more like a bang pounding in her skull, and she cringed.

Harry poked his head around the door. "Flora said you were ill."

The earlier tears returned, this time flowing down her cheeks. She silently cursed the emotion that proved so difficult to contain during these times.

Harry rushed to her side. "What is it?" Ever the physician, he lifted her wrist and took her pulse.

"It's nothing. I'm being silly."

He sat next to the curve above her hip on the longue and brushed the tears from her eyes. "I doubt that. Tell me what's wrong."

She threw herself into his arms and sobbed into his cravat like a small girl who had skinned her knee. "I should be relieved. I don't know why I'm so disappointed."

Harry stroked her back. "About what?"

"Not being with your child."

"Oh." He stilled, his gentle, soothing motions halted, then he sighed. "Maggie, it was wrong of me to put you in that position. Especially as a physician, I should have known better than to allow that possibility, but it doesn't mean we can't have children. Sometimes it takes months for a couple to conceive. However, we should be cautious until we're married."

"You still want me?"

He chuckled, his breath tickling her ear. "Always."

She sniffled and pulled back to look into his eyes. "I love you."

He placed a tiny kiss on her lips. "Perhaps the musicale this evening will lift your low spirits."

"It's not just that. A megrim has started. I wouldn't be able to tolerate the crowds and noise. I'm afraid I must stay home."

"Then I'll send our regrets so I can remain to care for you. I would suggest willow bark tea, but I'm concerned it might worsen your other . . . condition."

"No, don't miss it because of me. I'll be no company here. It's best if I remain in a darkened room and try not to move. Besides, you must hear Cammie sing. Promise me you'll go and enjoy yourself."

"If you insist." He rose, grabbed a pillow for her head and tucked her in with a blanket. "I'll check on you throughout the day and before I leave."

She forced a weak smile. "Wake me when you get home if I'm sleeping."

LIKE EVERY OTHER EVENT THEY HAD ATTENDED, THE MUSICALE WAS A crush. Guests milled about the transformed ballroom of Lord and Lady Marbry's townhome. Rows of chairs lined the dance floor, and a dais for the orchestra and performers sat at the far end. Harry scanned the room for a friendly face and breathed a sigh of relief at the sight of Andrew and Alice chatting with Lord Marbry.

He weaved through the crowd, only to be stopped numerous times as people called in greeting and requested he sit with them. Out of the corner of his eye he noticed Lady Cartwright pointing her fan toward him and pushing rudely past others. The throng of bodies blocked his escape, and he soon found himself face to face with the odious woman.

"Your Grace, what a pleasure." She made a show of glancing around. "I don't see Her Grace this evening."

"She's not feeling well. She sends her apologies as she was looking forward to it."

"Oh?"

Harry envisioned the wheels turning in her head and regretted providing information regarding Margaret's health.

"A megrim. She should make a full recovery in a few days."

An evil grin spread across the woman's face, and the hair on the back of Harry's neck stood on end.

"Well, you must sit by us."

"Thank you for the offer, but I agreed to sit by the Weatherbys this evening." He didn't regret the lie. Without excusing himself, he extricated himself from the woman and headed for safety with Andrew and Alice who now moved toward the seats for the performance.

Andrew smiled in greeting as Harry approached. "Where's Margaret? Did she finally catch on to you?" Andrew gave him a playful slap on the back.

Harry had shared with them the news of his and Margaret's plans to wed as soon as the season ended. "She's not well—a headache. I offered to stay, but she insisted I come to hear Lady Denby sing."

"She has a remarkable voice. Andrew suggested we remain at home, but I pleaded with him to come." Alice placed a hand on her abdomen, and Andrew jerked to attention.

"You must sit, my dear." Taking his wife's arm, Andrew led her to a nearby chair.

Harry followed, intrigued by his friend's behavior. "Alice are you unwell?"

The sheepish grin on Andrew's face answered Harry's question.

"I'm fine. He's making a fuss." Alice's statement and accompanying blush confirmed Harry's suspicion.

He leaned in and grabbed Andrew's arm, pulling him closer as he whispered, "Congratulations."

"It's early. She doesn't want anyone to know."

The orchestra tuned their instruments, and everyone moved to their seats. Harry sat next to Andrew who continued to shoot concerned looks at his wife. A tinge of envy wiggled in Harry's chest, but he pushed it aside and repeated to himself the same words he had spoken to Margaret that morning. *Sometimes it takes months.* He would wait to share Andrew and Alice's news with Margaret until after they married. Perhaps by then they might expect their own arrival.

Laurence Townsend, Lord Montgomery, took the seat on the other side of him. "Good evening, Ashton. I wish you well on your endeavor with the clinic. Her Grace practically bubbled with excitement over it when she visited my father and me. Where is she tonight?"

"She's unwell, a megrim."

"Ah. Well, I hope she recovers quickly. There's one final ball before the end of the season, and she promised me a dance." The man sat straighter in his chair, and Harry resisted the urge to tell him to find a different partner.

Maggie had mentioned the promise to him, and while Harry understood her tactics, it would give him no joy to see her in the arms of another man.

He enjoyed the music, but his mind constantly wandered, inevitably making its way to Margaret. *What would she think of this piece? How is she feeling? Has the pain abated?* Wedged between two men, Andrew on his right and Montgomery on his left, he missed the soft lavender fragrance that enveloped her. He longed to reach his hand down and brush hers discreetly, appreciating the softness of her skin, to glance her way, catching her eyes light up as she experienced the notes of the pianoforte or the sweet strings of the violins.

Harry shifted in his seat and stole a peek at his watch for the tenth time, waiting for two hours to pass so he could leave without too much ado. Thank goodness Camilla was now performing. He wouldn't hear the end of it from Maggie if he left prior to her performance.

Montgomery tapped him on the arm and handed him a piece of paper, then pointed to the aisle where a footman waited. Harry opened the note.

Your Grace, your assistance is needed for a medical emergency.

Quickly folding the paper and stuffing it in his pocket, he followed the servant down the hall to a room with a closed door.

The footman opened the door, and Harry stepped inside a small parlor, freezing in place. Priscilla Pratt grimaced as she clutched the side of a table, supporting herself as she balanced on one foot.

Harry spun around to have the footman send for a matron as chaperone, but the man had vanished, leaving him alone with Miss Pratt.

"Miss Pratt, allow me to fetch another woman to chaperone. I'll be right back."

"Please don't leave me, Your Grace. If I have to stand here one more minute, I worry I shall collapse on the floor," Priscilla howled, her face scrunched up in pain.

Harry took a step closer. "What happened?"

"I'm such a ninny. I mis-stepped and suspect I may have broken my ankle."

The battle played out in his mind, his medical vow winning. Still, he proceeded with caution. "It's unlikely it's broken from a mis-step, but you may have sprained it. Let's move you to the sofa, and once you're settled, I'll find another woman to chaperone while I examine you."

Glad the door remained wide open, he moved next to Priscilla. "Place your hand on my shoulder for support. With your permission, I'll wrap my arm around your waist. Be careful not to place too much weight on the injured foot, use it only for balance. Now, ready?"

She nodded, and after he reached around her waist, she put her arm around his shoulder and released her grasp on the table. Managing only a single step, she yelped in pain and collapsed against him, wrapping her other arm around his waist and forcing him to support her full weight in his arms.

Immediate foreboding churned in his stomach, and bile rose in his throat. His eyes darted toward the open door, relieved no one had arrived to bear witness.

"Oh please, Your Grace. I simply cannot walk."

After a moment's hesitation, he scooped her up and rushed toward the sofa. He placed her down, breathing a sigh of relief he avoided what someone undoubtedly would construe as a compromising situation.

"I'll fetch a chaperone."

She clutched the sleeve of his coat. "Please don't leave me, the pain is unbearable."

Against his better judgment, he bent down and lifted her gown, exposing her foot. It appeared perfectly normal, with no evident swelling, as he palpated her ankle. Chills prickled his skin. Without warning, she sat up, grasped his hand, yanking it forward and holding it to her breast. In an attempt to remove himself, he stumbled, losing his balance, and fell on top of her.

"Oh, Your Grace." This time her cry echoed of passion rather than pain.

The rustling of skirts and murmured voices drew his attention to the doorway. He jerked his hand away and scrambled to his feet. His stomach plummeted as Lady Cartwright, Lady Easton, Lord Montgomery, and Lord Nash entered the room.

He was doomed.

CHAPTER 19—COMPROMISED!

T*rapped.* Harry's blood chilled. He blinked and blinked again, but the sight before him remained, unchanging and condemning. He had unwittingly compromised Priscilla.

Lady Easton covered her mouth to stifle her gasp, and her son, Laurence, grabbed her arm to support her.

Lady Cartwright threw the back of her hand against her forehead as she fell to the floor in a faint.

Priscilla jumped to her—uninjured—feet and ran over to her mother. "Mama." She patted her mother's face.

Lord Nash smirked. "It appears you and your brother are cut from the same cloth after all, Ashton. A dalliance with your sister-in-law not enough, you had to go after more virginal prey?"

Now Lady Easton appeared about to swoon, as she held a ring-encrusted hand to her large bosom. "Lord Nash, remember yourself!"

Laurence wrapped his arm around his mother's waist. "I agree, Nash. Leave Her Grace out of this. I will not have her disparaged."

Nash leered at Laurence. "I forgot you had a tendre for the duchess before George stole her from under your nose."

Harry stood motionless as the scene played out, and a brief

flicker of hope rose in his chest as the two men postured before him. Would an altercation between them divert attention, allowing him to escape unscathed?

He was not so lucky.

Priscilla roused her mother. "I'm sorry, Mama. His Grace and I couldn't deny our feelings any longer."

"That's a lie!" Harry bellowed. "Miss Pratt lured me in here under the guise of a medical emergency. She stated she injured her ankle and demanded my assistance."

With Nash's help, Lady Cartwright regained her footing and glared at Harry. "How dare you put the blame for your actions on my daughter, Your Grace? It's beneath you."

"I have proof. A footman handed me a note." *Which pocket is it in?* He tucked his hand in one and breathed a sigh of relief as his fingers touched the slip of paper. He passed it to Lady Cartwright.

Her lips pressed in a hard line as she read the note, then she turned to her daughter. "Priscilla, I'm ashamed of you."

Thank God!

"Asking a man to meet you for an assignation. I've reared you to be better than this."

Nash looked over Lady Cartwright's shoulder at the note, then met Harry's eyes, the look unsettling Harry to his core. "Sorry, Ashton, but there's nothing about a medical emergency here."

"What?" Harry reached out for the note. His hand shook as he took it from Lady Cartwright.

Meet me in the small parlor. I'll be waiting. Yours P.

"This isn't the note I was given." He slipped his hand in his other pocket and, along with the comforting feel of paper, his fingers touched the necklace Margaret had worn the night of the ball. Suffocating pressure crushed his chest, yet he pulled out and scanned the correct note.

"This is what the footman gave me." He handed it to Lady Cartwright.

A crowd began to form in the doorway as Lady Cartwright, Lady Easton, Lord Montgomery, Lord Nash, and Priscilla all lowered their heads to read the note that had led to Harry's entrapment.

Priscilla shook her head. "I didn't write this. It's clearly not written by my hand."

Lady Easton chimed in. "It's true, Your Grace, if you compare the two notes, the writing on each is different."

"But that's the correct note," he choked out the words, his throat closing in as he pleaded. *Why won't they listen?*

"How do you explain the note from Priscilla you pulled from your pocket?" Lady Cartwright fumed. "This other note may be your way of protecting yourself from scandal."

Lord Cartwright pushed through the crowd of onlookers. "What's going on?"

The feather in Lady Cartwright's hair bobbed. "His Grace has compromised our daughter."

Priscilla dropped her head in artificial contrition.

"Everyone, please leave this to my wife and me to sort out in private." Lord Cartwright ushered the gawkers out of the room, but the damage had been done. It would appear in the morning scandal sheets.

Once the crowd had dispersed, Lord Cartwright closed the door. "Ashton, is it true?"

"No, sir, it is not. A footman gave me a note asking for my medical help. Pris . . . Miss Pratt lied about her ankle and begged for my assistance." How many times would he repeat this nightmare?

"And the note?" Cartwright asked.

His wife handed him both notes. "This was the first he pulled from his pocket"—she pointed to the damning evidence—"then when discovered, he conveniently produced another, supporting his ridiculous claim."

Cartwright had always seemed a reasonable man. In fact, Harry pitied him in his choice of a wife. Yet now, an angered father glared back at him.

"That's not all," Lady Cartwright continued. "She was lying on the sofa, her dress raised indecently high on her limbs, and he was on top of her and had his . . . his hand on her"—she lowered her voice to a whisper—"bosom. Lady Easton, Lord Montgomery, and Lord Nash witnessed it."

Cartwright studied him, his watery blue eyes narrowed to slits, and for the first time in years, Harry prayed.

Lord Cartwright's gaze remained trained on Harry as he addressed his family. "Allow me to have a private word with Ashton."

Priscilla grabbed her father's arm. "I'm so sorry, Papa. He said he loved me."

They exited, leaving Harry to face his fate. Sweat beaded his forehead, and nausea roiled in his stomach at Priscilla's lies, the bitter taste of bile rising to his mouth.

"You've put me in a precarious position, Ashton."

You? Harry prided himself in not being a selfish man, but at that moment, all he cared about was his own position.

"I could use a drink," Cartwright said as he made his way to the table where Priscilla had clung mere minutes ago.

As much as Harry wanted a drink himself, he resisted. He must proceed with caution and a clear head as he pleaded his case.

He stood by helplessly while Cartwright took a languorous sip of the amber liquid, studying the glass as if it held the answers they both sought. Harry wished he'd just spit it out, well aware of the words that the man would say.

"I'll be honest, Ashton," Cartwright began. "In the past, my wife has, shall we say, manipulated things to her benefit. I fear Priscilla has learned well at her mother's knee."

The earlier flicker of hope in Harry's chest sparked to full flame.

"However, if what my wife says is true, and you indeed had my daughter on that sofa and touched her inappropriately, and several people in addition to my wife witnessed this behavior, you give me little choice. Either agree to marry her to salvage her reputation, or I shall be forced to call you out to save face for my family."

The spark of hope sputtered out like a candle in a strong wind; still he pleaded his case. "Sir, I assure you, I was called here under the pretense of providing medical care. I have no idea how that other note appeared in my pocket."

"Yet, it did appear. And Priscilla seems to be in good health, albeit manhandled by you, sir." He sighed heavily and dropped to the sofa. "Do you love my daughter?"

"No, sir, I do not." Harry refrained from telling him what he truly thought of a woman who would stoop so low as to entrap a husband. Logic told him it would only serve to antagonize the man further.

"There are unsavory rumors circulating about you and your brother's widow. I don't relish having my daughter enmeshed in such a scandal."

Harry swiped a shaky hand down his face, emotion threatening his composure. "Your wife made me aware of the rumors, Cartwright, but I love Margaret. We plan to marry."

"And risk having the marriage voided?" Cartwright shook his head. "Then more's the pity for you. Think about it, Ashton. An offer for my daughter would quell tongues on all accounts. I'll expect your decision tomorrow." He rose and exited, taking Harry's dreams with him.

The silence in the room grew oppressive, the heaviness weighing him down until his numb body fell to the sofa. A tap on the half-open door barely registered in his mind.

"Ashton?"

His head felt like lead as he lifted it and turned toward the entrance. Camilla's concerned expression proved more than he could handle, and he dropped his heavy head into his hands, fighting a sob.

Her hand rubbed his back. "What happened? You disappeared during my song and didn't return. Lord and Lady Cartwright appeared distraught and left in haste. People are whispering about a compromise."

He recounted the events from the moment he exited the ballroom, and with each word, his heart shattered a little more. "Nothing happened, I swear, Camilla. She trapped me. How can I tell Maggie?"

"You'll find a way. Don't lose hope, Ashton. You're not at the altar yet."

"Denby told me you were an optimist, but there is no hope left in me."

Like a walking dead man, he bade goodbye to Camilla and then his hosts and headed home. Each click of the horses' hooves as it pulled his carriage along the cobblestone streets was as if a scalpel nicked away another piece of his heart. Soon only a gaping hole inside his chest would remain.

He forced his legs to move up the steps to the townhouse and through the door where Burrows waited.

"You're home early, Your Grace." The butler's brow creased. "Are you ill?"

Harry ignored the man's question. "Is Her Grace in her room?"

"Yes, sir. She took a light supper but has requested you call for her when you returned. Shall I have Flora fetch her?"

Harry shook his head. "That won't be necessary, Burrows. I'll go up to her."

Harry trudged up the staircase, grabbing the banister for support. Each step grew harder, and he feared his legs would stop working altogether before he reached the top.

After a brief hesitation, he raised his hand and tapped lightly on her door.

"Enter," she called, her voice so sweet, so welcoming—so soon to be taken from him.

The room was dark except for a single candle on her dressing table. She reclined on the chaise longue, and he longed to lie beside her one last time.

Instead he remained standing. "How are you feeling?"

"Perhaps a little better." She gave him a weak smile, indicating the pain persisted.

"Maggie." His voice cracked, mimicking his shattered heart. And now he would shatter hers.

She rose to a sitting position. "What's wrong?"

He forced his eyes to meet her beautiful violet-like ones, and without saying a word, in their depths it became clear she knew.

"Who?" she asked.

His body dropped to the chaise longue next to her. "Miss Pratt."

She remained stoic, but in the dim light, her chin trembled.

"You're not going to ask what happened?"

Her fingers trailed down his face. "I don't have to. If only I'd been there, I would have stayed by your side the entire evening."

He grabbed her hands and held them in his, remembering how they'd caressed him. He kissed her fingertips. "This is not your fault. I won't have you blaming yourself. My own stupidity has led to this . . . this debacle."

"Is there any way out?"

He shook his head. "Only if I meet Cartwright's challenge. I'm to give him my answer tomorrow. Either offer for her or he will call me out."

"You can't let it come to that, Harry."

He stood and paced the floor, raking a hand through his hair. "What would you have me do, Maggie?" His voice escalated in frustration, but she didn't flinch.

"What you know in your heart is right."

"I'd fire at the ground, I would never harm him. I took an oath."

"But would he? He's defending the honor of his daughter, Harry. I won't have you jeopardize your life."

Like a nervous animal, he moved back to her. "We could run away. Go to America. I would face that ocean again if it meant we would be together."

"People here depend on you. You have a duty, an obligation to them."

He dropped to his knees in front of her. "I'll build you a little house near Briarfield and buy you a townhouse here in London. We could be together whenever possible."

"As your mistress?"

He didn't respond, but his eyes pleaded.

"And you would be satisfied with that?" she asked.

"No," he whispered, knowing full well she wouldn't either.

Still kneeling before her, he laid his head in her lap. "Speak words of comfort to me, Maggie."

Her fingers brushed through his hair, gentle and loving, and he took care to remember every stroke as if it were to be the last. He breathed deep, pulling in her fragrance as he clung desperately to the moment, burning it in his mind.

"I love you, Harry, but this will be the final time I'll say it. This time all your solutions fall short. You're a good man, and you wouldn't be happy living a lie that would destroy you."

It's exactly what he expected she would say. He raised his head to look into her eyes. "You'd have me marry a woman who entrapped me? After what you yourself went through?"

Even in the dim light, her face blanched. "You know?"

"Harcourt told me what happened. You did what you had to do to protect your father. I understand that. George would have aimed to kill and taken delight in doing so. I'm not George, Maggie. I won't harm Cartwright."

"And if he harms you?"

"Death may be preferable to a life without you."

"Don't say that. I couldn't bear it if anything happened to you."

He forced a smile. It seemed ridiculous in the situation. "Perhaps he'll only wing me. Would you love a one-armed man?"

The answer shone in her eyes, yet she ignored his question and said, "And what of Priscilla? I'm well acquainted with the pressures of the *ton* to secure an advantageous union. I suspect her mother is complicit in this. The girl would still be ruined. What prospects could she expect?"

"I didn't ruin her. Nothing happened." His voice raised more than he anticipated.

"But her reputation would be in tatters nonetheless, Harry. Although I don't care for the girl, I do pity her. You must make it right."

Not sure why, he reached into his pocket and pulled out the necklace. It seemed its lucky properties had vanished.

"I found this in my pocket this evening. I want you to have it, to remember the first time we—"

She placed her fingers on his lips. "Don't say it. I can't bear it."

The necklace fell from his grasp onto her lap. "Squeeze against the sides of the latch. That's the trick."

"Promise me something, Harry."

"Anything."

"Strive to love her and make her happy. Perhaps in doing so, you will find happiness of your own."

With that, he rose. Nothing else remained to be said.

As he closed the door behind him, the sound of weeping pierced through him.

THE MOMENT HE EXITED, MARGARET LOST THE SMALL AMOUNT OF control she fought to maintain in his presence. She threw herself prostrate on the chaise longue, pounding her tightly balled fists into the cushion, and wept in heaving sobs. *So close to happiness, now snatched away like a cruel joke.* She cried until it seemed she exhausted all the waters of the ocean—then she wept some more. The agony surpassed the totality of what George had inflicted. That pain passed with time, but this would last the rest of her life. The gaping hole in her heart would never mend.

She cursed her body, giving anything to have been carrying his child. Foolish and selfish as it was, she wished it nonetheless. A part of him to love would have at least been some consolation. But Priscilla had ripped it all away.

The necklace slipped from the chaise onto the floor, landing with a tiny clinking sound. *Squeeze against the sides of the latch.* She reached down and retrieved the precious gift. *As you've squeezed my heart, Harry?* She lifted the silver chain, and the pendant caught the light of the candle, the starburst of the jewel flickering like a beacon. With a grateful heart, she clutched the treasure to her chest, and kissed the latch where his fingers had once been. *I have this.*

The funereal silence of the house—interrupted only by her hiccupping sobs—weighed heavily on her. She rose from the chaise and moved toward her writing secretary to pen two notes, one to Camilla and the more difficult to Harry.

She wished she had the audacity to run away with him to America. But courage or cowardice, she had no doubt it was selfish on both their parts. Could she live as his mistress, knowing he had a wife to whom he was obligated, with whom he might have children?

Her pen hovered above the piece of parchment as she considered her message to him. Once finished, two notes to Harry sat before her, each containing a different message. In one, she relayed her desires, the other contained the words that broke her heart. She would deliver one.

CHAPTER 20—WHEN HOPE IS LOST

Harry rose early the next morning. Sleep had eluded him. He splashed cold water on his face, and bloodshot eyes stared back from the mirror. A vile, bitter taste coated his tongue. The brandy bottle lay on its side at the foot of a chair, the sweet, fruity aroma of its contents now pungent to his queasy stomach. Hastings tapped on the door—the sound like cannon fire in Harry's pounding head—and entered.

Over the course of the month, Harry had grown fond of the taciturn man who sized up his employer's state of mind quickly and responded accordingly. He dressed Harry in blessed silence.

In no mood for food, Harry still peeked into the breakfast room in search of Margaret to find it empty except for Peter the footman, who placed a platter of toast on the sideboard. His hope soared at movement behind him, then plunged at the sight of Burrows.

"Good morning, Your Grace." Burrows' expression was uncharacteristically somber.

"Has Her Grace risen?"

Burrows' gaze dropped to the carpet. *He knows.* "She's asked for tea in her room." He held out a folded and sealed piece of paper. "She requested I give you this."

A war raged within him. Perhaps she had changed her mind and would agree to go to America, or to be his mistress, or encourage him to accept the challenge of a duel. His finger rubbed the seal, hesitant to read the words his heart feared the letter contained.

Drawing a deep breath, he broke the wax seal and opened the note.

Ashton,

I've written to Camilla, requesting I stay with her until I find suitable housing and employment. I shall be gone before you return today.

As members of the aristocracy, we're often stripped of our freedom to do what our hearts desire, and so you and I must both do what is expected. Your tenants and staff rely on you. Fulfill your duty to them and to the dream of your clinic where you will make a difference in the lives of the poor. I shall always remember your kindness. ~ Maggie

Harry met Burrows' knowing gaze. "I'm so very sorry, sir. Please forgive my impertinence, but may I say, the staff had been so hopeful. It's such a shame. We only wish for your happiness."

"Thank you, Burrows. Would you have a horse brought around? I have an errand, and I'd rather not use the carriage."

Burrows nodded, bowed, then left.

There would be no grand show of wealth and finery as he made his offer for Miss Pratt. If she expected such, it would be her first disappointment in being his wife. Even the garments he chose to wear were not his finest. He admitted it was immature and a bit cruel, but he didn't care. Perhaps he hoped she would refuse him, since all she seemed to want was a title. It was a slim hope, but he clung to it like a drowning man holding onto driftwood.

As he plodded toward the Cartwrights' townhouse, he found himself reining in his mount to slow its pace, no doubt annoying the poor beast who preferred a trot. The sun blinded him, mocking him with its offensive brightness and exacerbating his pounding skull.

He handed his card to the butler, who told him Lord Cartwright expected him and led him to a small study.

Cartwright rose as Harry entered. "Ashton. I'm glad you haven't delayed the inevitable."

"If medicine has taught me anything, it's not to let a wound fester."

Cartwright's face scrunched up at the implication, but he motioned for Harry to take a seat.

"I'll stand as I don't anticipate staying longer than necessary. I'm here to offer for your daughter."

His future father-in-law drummed his fingers against the desktop, studying him. "This situation gives me no pleasure, Ashton."

"No less than I. Shall we get on with it?"

"Very well, follow me. You can wait in the parlor while I fetch Priscilla."

While he waited, Harry stood rigid, remembering his military days. Much like the duty of fighting for his country, he wouldn't relish his proposal. His mind drifted back to the night he proposed to Maggie, taunting him as if George prodded him with a cold finger from the grave. That offer had been impetuous, but heartfelt. It now stabbed at his heart.

A shriek from deep within the house pierced his throbbing head, and he cringed at his future wife's shrill voice. Moments later she waltzed in and smiled as if expecting him to fall to his knees in adoration. His stomach lurched.

"Papa said you wished to see me." She batted her eyes and affected a demure pose.

How can she play the innocent? His throat clogged, creating a barrier to the words he forced himself to say, and he coughed roughly, clearing it. "Miss Pratt, I've come to ask for your hand."

"Oh, Ashton!" She rushed toward him, but he held up his hands.

"Make no mistake, my offer to you is due to our compromising situation of last night. No more. As such, I'm pleading with you to think this through for both our benefits."

Her hand flew to her mouth, resting there only a moment before fisting at her bosom. "But my reputation."

If not for the direness of his predicament, her dramatic attempt at outrage over possible ignominy would be comical. She could have a bright future on the stage.

"We both know the truth of that. If anyone is to blame for sullying your reputation, it is you alone."

She appeared ready to burst into tears, and for a moment he pitied her. "Miss Pratt, I have reason to believe someone coerced you into this plan."

She opened her mouth to protest, but he held up a hand to silence her.

"Let me offer a solution. Accept my proposal, but before the wedding, call it off. Give any explanation you choose. Tell people I'm a cad and a philanderer, whatever is necessary to garner sympathy. I don't care how black you paint me. You're young. If you break it off, within time people will forget and move on to the next scandal, and your prospects will improve."

She wrinkled her nose as if smelling something foul. "I won't take that chance."

"You prefer to be married to a man who doesn't love you? Who, in fact, loves another woman? Think, Miss Pratt. Don't you wish to have a marriage based on love, to have a husband who loves you and cherishes you as you would him?"

"We will grow to love each other. Many people do."

Maggie's words echoed. *Strive to love her and make her happy.* He sighed. *Oh Maggie, you ask too much.* "Then you will not refuse me and secure happiness for us both?"

She stared at him blankly. "But I *am* happy."

"I see. Very well, then. I'll leave the arrangements to you and your family. Advise me of the details. Good day." He moved to depart.

"Ashton, since we're now betrothed, may I call you by your Christian name?"

"You may address me as Ashton or Harrison. But never call me Harry."

"Won't you kiss me, Harrison? I believe it's customary when securing an attachment."

"Since your fabrication has done a fine job at establishing our attachment, I'll leave signs of affection to your imagination as well." With that, he left.

Harry mounted his horse, debating whether he should return to the townhouse or go to White's. The urge to see Maggie proved too powerful, so he snapped the reins of his steed and proceeded toward home at a fast trot. He shortened the time it took for the journey by half, praying he hadn't missed her. He jumped off the horse, tied the reins to a tethering ring, and bounded up the steps to the townhouse.

A harried Burrows greeted him. The man's eyes appeared as red as Harry's had in his reflection that morning.

"Is she still here?"

Burrows gave a slow shake of his head. "No, sir, she left in the carriage a few moments ago. She requested a servant pack her belongings and send them to Lady Denby's. She took only a small trunk."

If I'd only ridden faster to the Cartwrights. "Did she take Flora with her?"

"No, sir. She left alone."

"I should like to speak with Flora. I'll be in Her Grace's room."

Burrows nodded and left to fetch the maid.

Memories of his torturous ascent of the stairs to deliver the news to Margaret invaded his mind, and his feet replayed the experience, trudging upward with each heavy lift of his boots.

His hand rested on the doorknob for a moment, then he entered. Her lavender fragrance lingered in the air, and he inhaled deeply, remembering the scent as he lay next to her. He moved to the bed and ran his fingers across the undisturbed coverings. *Had she slept in it at all, or had the maid already been in?*

A seed pearl hairpin lay on the floor by her dressing table, and he picked it up, running his finger against its surface, imagining her thick black locks trapped in the pin's confinement. She had worn one like it in her hair the night of the ball—the night they made love the first time. He tucked it in his pocket as a secret treasure.

A piece of paper sat crumpled on the grate in the unlit fireplace, and a portion of script peeked from a curled corner. He lifted it, hesitating at first as his conscience accused him of invading her privacy. Yet, he smoothed the note on the desk and read.

My dearest Harry,

My head and heart are at war within me. I know what is right, what we should do, but I cannot bring myself to do it. Regardless of society's expectations, I am unable to relinquish my love for you. I've written to Camilla, requesting I stay with her until you are certain of your course of action. Whatever you decide, whether that be to abandon your duty here as duke and leave for America, or to stay and keep me as your mistress, I'm yours always, however you want me. Forever ~ Maggie.

He raised his head at the soft cough sounding from the doorway. Flora waited, dropping her gaze to the floor, her expression melancholy. It seemed grief had enveloped the whole household.

"Please pack all Her Grace's belongings as well as your own. When you're finished, take them to her at Lady Denby's and remain there to continue your service."

"Yes, sir." The girl held her focus on the carpet, refusing to meet his eyes.

They all blame me. He opened his mouth to plead his defense, but snapped it shut. How could he defend what he himself agreed with? He kept his address professional. "I'll continue to pay your salary and pen a letter to Her Grace explaining."

She bobbed a curtsy and moved from the doorway to retrieve Margaret's clothing from the wardrobe. He took a seat at the desk, wrote the letter, and handed it to her. "Advise the rest of the staff I don't wish to be disturbed for the remainder of the day."

He retreated to his room, leaving Flora to complete her task. At the soft click of the door closing behind him, the finality of his situation settled on him, and in the safety of his bedroom, for the first time since he was a boy, he wept.

AT FIRST LIGHT, MARGARET HAD SENT A FOOTMAN TO DELIVER THE note to Camilla, then she waited until Burrows advised her Harry had left the townhouse. After quickly packing a few items into a small trunk, she requested a carriage to take her to Camilla's.

Not having slept, her body ached from exhaustion, exacerbating the existing malaise she experienced during her courses. The pounding in her skull continued, worsened not only from the lack of sleep but from incessant weeping. She refused to allow Harry to see her in such a state. It was better this way, she convinced herself. One look at his face, and she would lose her resolve and agree to anything he requested.

Now, isolated in her room at Camilla's, her hand clasped the pendant fastened around her neck, and she closed her eyes, attempting to sleep. No longer able to fight the call of slumber, she drifted off into a pleasant oblivion where dreams promised wishes that cannot be fulfilled, and found peace in Harry's arms.

When she woke, although somewhat refreshed, she was forced to face the reality of her situation which now loomed one hundred times worse than when George had died. Then, she hadn't known the sweetness of love only to have it pulled from her fingers. *How will I bear to see Harry and Priscilla together and not have my heart ripped from my chest each time?* Her megrim was fading, and she gave thanks for small mercies. She would need a clear head to decide her future.

Someone tapped lightly at the door, and she rose from the bed. "Come in."

Camilla entered and Flora followed closely behind. "Flora's arrived with the rest of your things, Maggie."

"Thank you. But a footman could have brought them."

The girl gave a shy smile. "No, Your Grace. His Grace instructed me to stay with you. He insisted, telling me there was to be no argument." She held out a note.

Are we doomed to converse in correspondence?

As she read, a deeper meaning to Harry's words teased her mind as if he wished to convey something secret.

Margaret,

I am sending Flora with your things. Please indulge me this small kindness and retain her as your lady's maid. I will continue to pay her wages. It's the least I can do for all you've given me. If anything remains that you need, you have only to ask.

Harry

Margaret exchanged a glance with Camilla, who merely shrugged.

"Very well, I'll send a note of thanks to him." She moved toward the small desk to pen the letter.

"That can wait, Maggie. Please have some tea and something to eat. You've been sleeping for a whole day. You must be famished."

After Flora helped her dress, brushed and arranged her hair in loose curls, Margaret forced herself to eat a light meal, the food tasteless. She then joined Camilla in the parlor.

Her friend eyed her, wariness evident in her gaze. "Maggie, you must know nothing happened. Perhaps Priscilla will come to her senses and call off this farce."

"I love you, Cammie, but even your eternal optimism won't salvage this. It's clear Lady Cartwright decided to secure Harry as a husband for her daughter as soon as he arrived in London. I must accept it and move forward with my life. I'm considering going to America." Perhaps there, she could fulfill her dreams. With the prospect of assisting with the clinic ripped away, a different emptiness vied for the vacuum left in her heart from losing Harry.

The teacup in Camilla's hands dropped with a clink to the saucer beneath it. "America! Oh, no, Maggie, whatever for?"

"Harry spoke fondly of having a purpose there." The memory of their earlier conversation poked at the still fresh wound in her heart. "No one would know me, I could start anew, perhaps find employment as a governess. Goodness, do they even have governesses there? Maybe a teacher."

"Your uncertainty is evidence this is a foolhardy scheme. It would be reckless to run away to a foreign country without any awareness of what awaits."

The heaviness in her limbs returned as if she hadn't slept at all, and her heart beat dully, reminding her it still remained in her chest. "How can I stay here, Cammie? To witness them together at every event?"

"But to leave your own country? Your friends? For something unknown? Promise me you won't act rashly. Consider your other options."

"Such as?"

Camilla stared into her teacup, her mouth pressed in a taut line. "You won't like what I have to say."

"When has that ever stopped you?"

"If you're determined to start fresh, why not here? With some planning, you could avoid Harry whenever possible." She set her cup down and picked up a letter lying on the table, handing it to Margaret.

Margaret broke the seal, then opened the note to read.

My dear Duchess,

Allow me to express my outrage at His Grace's recent behavior and my support at your decision of removing yourself from his household.

It would give me great pleasure to call upon you now that your period of mourning is at an end.

Ever your servant,

Montgomery

Margaret raised her eyes from the letter to meet Camilla's waiting gaze.

"He delivered it himself. Laurence is a good man, Maggie, and he'll inherit. He's not Harry, but he's always held affection for you. Why don't you see him?"

Margaret agreed with Camilla's assessment of Laurence Townsend. Quiet and reserved, albeit bookish, he never attracted scandal or gossip. Marriage to him would be like floating on a calm pond instead of the waves of passion she experienced with Harry. "Very well. I'll pen a response at the same time I write to Harry thanking him for sending Flora."

The next day, Margaret's tears had abated to the point she only cried in the privacy of her room, and she found Camilla's company a useful diversion. Now seated together on the sofa, Cammie chattered away, relating some silly thing she had heard about Beatrix Marbry. Margaret struggled to pay attention.

"The poor dear," Cammie said. "She tripped over her own feet and fell right into the rose bushes. If only her mother allowed her to wear her spectacles in public."

Margaret gave her friend a weak smile as she remembered saying the same thing to Harry as they returned to the townhouse the night of the ball. Tears threatened, but she choked them back.

Stratton appeared at the doorway of the parlor. "His Grace and Master Manny have come to call, madam."

Margaret stood, and in her haste of placing her cup on the table, tea splashed on the wooden surface.

She shot an apologetic glance at Cammie and proceeded to rush from the room. Before she could make her retreat, Harry and Manny appeared in the doorway, and air whooshed from her lungs.

As their eyes met, the moment seemed suspended, and her heart gave a painful thump.

"Forgive the intrusion. Manny missed you," he said, his gaze never leaving hers.

"I've missed him, too." Her eyes remained locked with his, answering his unspoken words.

They both finally remembered the boy of whom they spoke. "Have you been behaving for His Grace? No more stealing colanders from the kitchen or swords from His Grace's bedroom?" Margaret asked, doing her best to smile.

He puffed out his small chest. "I ain't nicked nothin' in a week."

Mixed with the pain of Harry's visit, a sense of lightness filled her at the sight of the boy. How he always made her laugh. Perhaps the doctor in Harry did know the best medicine for her ills. "That's an admirable start. You must do your utmost to break that record."

"Why don't I take Manny to the kitchen for a treat," Camilla said, grasping the boy by the shoulder.

Margaret started to protest. "Oh, no—"

"Thank you, Camilla," Harry said, and before she knew it, they were alone.

"Maggie."

He took a step toward her, but she held out her hands. "Please, don't, Harry. If you come closer, I won't be able to say no to whatever it is you've come to ask."

"In that case." He stepped forward.

"Harry!"

He stopped, but his jaw moved as if he were chewing a particularly tough piece of beef. "As you wish. However, I assure you my intentions are honorable."

"I've never questioned that. It's myself I don't trust." She searched for a safe topic of conversation. "Have you been well?" He appeared haggard, as if he hadn't slept. *Do I look as tired?*

"As well as can be expected. And you?"

"Cammie has kept me occupied."

The exchange was stiff and uncomfortable, much like when they had first met, and she missed the ease with which they had shared their thoughts before this nightmare began.

He tilted his head as if studying her, and his lips curved in a smile. "You're wearing it."

The necklace. Her fingers reached to her throat. "Yes."

"Manny isn't the only one who's missed you. Is there anything you need? Anything at all, you've but to name it."

She shook her head. "No. Thank you for sending Flora, she's been a godsend. I've grown quite fond of her."

The question she dreaded asking pricked at her mind, and like a fool, she couldn't resist. "When is the wedding?"

He blanched and at last broke eye contact with her. "In four weeks, as soon as the banns are read."

Etiquette demanded she wish him joy, but she couldn't bring herself to say the words, so she simply nodded.

He shuffled his feet, opening and closing his mouth several times before speaking, but his eyes flickered with longing. "Maggie, I found another letter in your room. Dare I hope——"

Dizziness threatened, and she struggled to pull enough air into her lungs to form the words. "I wrote that in a moment of weakness and meant to destroy it."

His whole body seemed to close in on itself, compressing his large frame, so it appeared as if a small boy now stood before her. "Of course, forgive me."

A cough drew her attention to the doorway where Laurence Townsend waited behind Stratton.

The butler averted his gaze as he announced, "Lord Montgomery here to see you, Your Grace."

She had forgotten about his promise to call that morning.

Harry raised an eyebrow, and her stomach twisted, churning the tea that now sat heavily within.

"I've obviously come at a bad time," Harry said, then turned to Stratton. "Would you retrieve Manny and tell him we're leaving?"

He gave a curt nod to Laurence, who had stepped into the parlor. "Montgomery." Walking around the man, Harry exited the room.

"Excuse me a moment," Margaret said to Laurence as she raced after Harry.

She caught up with him in the hallway where he waited by the door for Manny. Instinctively she touched him on the sleeve. "Harry, you don't understand."

His eyes flashed, and for an instant George stood before her. Then his face softened, and she breathed easier.

"I do understand, Margaret, and I don't blame you. Montgomery's a good man, I've no right to be jealous, but God help me, I am. You deserve some happiness."

How she longed to wrap herself in his embrace and tell him the truth; she could only be happy with him.

"Oi, Harry!"

She turned at the sound of Manny's call to find Laurence watching them intently.

CHAPTER 21—THE CLINIC

Margaret hugged Manny as he bade her goodbye and complained about the shortness of their visit. She peeked through the door's sidelight, stealing a final glimpse at Harry, then turned to the man who had come to call. If Laurence Townsend suspected her feelings toward Harry, no indication shone in his warm, brown eyes as he stared intently in her direction. He remained ever the gentleman, and for that she was grateful.

"Would you prefer to postpone our walk?" he asked.

She appreciated Laurence's perception and offer, but the hopefulness in his eyes threw salt on her wound of guilt. He deserved better, and agreeing to accompany him for a stroll was the least she could do. Since Harry had driven off in his curricle, there would be little chance of encountering him again, and the fresh air had always lifted her spirits.

"No, I promised, and it is a lovely day."

Laurence beamed, and Margaret marveled at the honesty in his face. She had always felt safe in his presence. No insidious intentions or malicious motives lurked behind his smile.

"Very well." She retrieved her parasol and reticule, and he held out his arm, then led her outside into the warm summer day.

They walked in silence for a while, nodding cordially to people passing by. Laurence squeezed Margaret's hand as it rested on his arm. "I never imagined having this opportunity again."

She cocked her head. "Walking in the park?"

Although his gaze remained fixed ahead, his lips curved. "With you."

Oh, dear. "Laurence—"

"Hear me out. We're friends, are we not?"

"Of course."

"I have no delusions, Margaret, but I hope, with time, affection might grow from our friendship."

"You deserve more than that, Laurence."

His eyes closed briefly as if contemplating her words. "Will you at least consider the possibility, and in the meantime, allow me to escort you while you remain in London? I've grown tired of attending events alone."

"It's not that I don't enjoy your company."

"Ah. You hope to avoid seeing specific people."

"Yes."

His eyes bore into her. "May I speak frankly? I have no desire to cause you discomfort, but I also respect you enough to know that pretending things are not what they are is unfair to both of us."

"I'm not certain I wish to hear what you have to say." She turned to head back, but he grabbed her elbow to stop her.

"Which is all the more reason you should."

Her spine stiffened. He had never spoken so forcefully to her.

"Margaret, about Ashton."

She jerked her arm from his hand. "What about him?"

"I'm not blind, it's clear you have . . . feelings for him. But I fear his . . . predicament has placed the clinic's funding in jeopardy."

She hadn't expected that. "But how?" A chill settled deep within her core. *No! Not the clinic!*

His eyes focused on a spot above her head as if he were afraid to meet her gaze. "There is some gossip that Ashton coerced you into soliciting contributions. Father is debating withdrawing his pledge."

Heat replaced the earlier chill as indignation grew within her. "Coerced me how?"

Color rose to Laurence's cheeks. "I'd hoped to avoid the word seduced, but that is the essence of it."

"That's ludicrous." If anyone had been seduced, it had been Harry, but she refrained from saying so.

Laurence met her gaze, his eyes searching as he appeared to struggle with what he wanted to say. "Of course. However, some have speculated that he duped you as well as Miss Pratt, and the money secured for the clinic will be used for other . . . pursuits."

"Laurence, you don't believe he actually compromised Miss Pratt?"

A flicker of something crossed his face as he lifted his hand and tugged at his cravat, but she was unsure of its meaning.

"I was among those who discovered them, Margaret. I saw it with my own eyes." He reached for her arm, but she pulled away.

She stared at him, unable to form a retort.

"Whatever the truth is regarding the situation with Miss Pratt, I trust you would not support the clinic blindly. Permit me to propose a solution."

"I'm listening." Cautious, she scrutinized his face for any sign of ulterior motive.

He nodded and drew in a breath as if seeking courage. "If it became clear another man held your interest, it would quell the rumors that your endorsement of the clinic was anything but strictly altruistic. Allow me to do this for you, Margaret."

"For *me*? This sounds suspiciously like blackmail."

The color drained from his face, and he stumbled back. "My God! No. I'm merely suggesting we maintain appearances to ensure the success of the clinic. I promise, regardless of your decision regarding our relationship, I'll convince Father to continue his assistance, and I'll strive to make certain the other pledges are secure as well. My opinion of Ashton aside, I support his endeavor to assist the poor. Forgive me if I implied otherwise."

Movement by a group of trees distracted her attention from Laurence, and a chill ran up her spine.

"Margaret, what is it?"

"I had the distinct impression of a person staring at us over by those trees. Someone . . . familiar, yet threatening."

Laurence turned toward where Margaret gazed. "I don't see anyone. It's this talk of keeping up appearances that's sparking your imagination."

She gave her head a slow, thoughtful shake. "I don't think so."

"Would it ease your mind if I go over and check?"

She reluctantly admitted her nerves had been on edge the last few days. "No, I'm sure you're right. Perhaps the sun cast a shadow that appeared to be a person. But I am a bit tired. Might we return?"

He held out his arm. "Of course."

But as they made their way back to Camilla's, Margaret had the unnerving sense that, hidden from view, someone followed.

HARRY HAD STORMED DOWN THE STEPS OF CAMILLA'S TOWNHOUSE and jumped into the seat of the curricle. Had he really expected she would change her mind and agree to run off with him? To become his mistress? And why was Laurence Townsend there? Yet, what right had he to question her choices? None.

"You all ri', Harry?" Manny's small hand squeezed his arm.

"No," he snapped, immediately regretting taking his jealousy out on the boy. "I'm sorry, Manny. Let's go home."

"When I'm feelin' low, I find sumfin' to do like throwin' rocks in the water."

If it were only that simple. He forced a weak smile toward the lad. *Maybe it is.* He needed to occupy his mind with something productive—like the clinic.

He had secured the location the day before, settling on a vacant building wedged between a butcher's shop and a pub. The place required extensive work to ready it before he could accept patients. He ached to lose himself in hard labor, to use his muscles and empty his mind.

Filled with new purpose, he snapped the reins and headed home to change into some practical clothes and recruit a few footmen and maids willing to help.

Upon arriving, he had Burrows gather the staff.

"None of you are under obligation to assist me, but I would like a few of you to accompany me to the clinic building and begin work on renovations and cleaning. Don't be concerned about your regular duties here, this takes precedence. I'll pay you an extra three shillings for each day you work. If you're interested, please step forward."

In unison, the entire staff responded in the affirmative, even Burrows, causing Harry to chuckle. He'd almost forgotten what it was like to laugh.

"Although I appreciate your willingness and exuberance in this endeavor, I do need a few of you to remain here to run the house."

He eyed Burrows, who grinned sheepishly. "Plus I doubt we'd have working room with everyone crammed into the space. I think three men and two women should do it. If you coordinate, perhaps you can trade off duties with another of the staff so everyone can have the opportunity for the additional wages. Discuss among yourselves who will join me today, then for each subsequent day. Once you decide, those who are accompanying me, change out of your livery and uniforms and into old clothes. Gather cleaning supplies, hammers, saws, nails and whatever else we might need. Burrows, have two carriages brought around while I change."

Manny tugged on his sleeve. "What about me?"

He crouched in front of the boy and tousled his hair. "You will be my second in command."

Upon arriving, Harry prioritized the necessary tasks for the renovation. Peter the footman had some experience in building, having helped his parents repair their home after a fire. Harry explained his ideas and consulted with him in what needed to be done, then purchased the lumber and other supplies necessary.

The women swept the floors and scrubbed all the surfaces, with Manny pointing out when they missed a spot. Harry worked shoulder to shoulder with the men, constructing the frame for a wall to separate the soon-to-be waiting area from the treatment rooms.

With his shirtsleeves rolled to the elbows and hands on his hips, Harry admired their work.

Peter patted him on the back. "Well done, Your Grace."

Harry mopped his perspiring brow, relieved that he hadn't thought of Margaret for the last five hours. She crept into his mind then, bittersweet. *What would you think, Maggie? Would you be proud of me?* He knew the answer.

A woman he didn't recognize stood at the entrance, eyes wide as she gazed around at the activity. "Wot's goin' on 'ere?"

Hastings, who seemed quite out of his element in his worn trousers and shirt hanging open without a cravat, addressed her. "We're preparing a medical clinic."

"A clinic? Like doctorin'?"

"Exactly."

"When's the doctor goin' to be here?"

Harry stepped forward, using his handkerchief to wipe away the sweat that now trickled down his neck. "I'm the doctor."

"Somethin's wrong with my little girl. I was off to fetch the midwife. Figured she might know wot's wrong."

He grabbed his medical bag he had brought along in case there was an injury while they worked. "Take me to the child."

"I ain't got no money."

"No money is necessary. This will be a free clinic."

Her eyebrows drew together to form a V as her eyes narrowed. "How's I know I can trust you?"

"Dorrie," he called one of the maids who had been washing surfaces. "Please accompany us. Manny, you come, too. If I need anything, you can run back for it." He returned his gaze to the woman, who nodded.

"That your boy?" she asked.

"Yes."

"He looks familiar-like. You from around here?"

Manny turned away, suddenly interested in the opposite direction from where the woman walked beside Harry.

"No." Harry made a mental note to inquire about Manny's former residency. "Tell me about the child. What are the symptoms?"

"She started whining two days ago, more 'un usual, mind you. Won't nothin' stop her. Been making funny noises, too."

"Any rash, fever?"

The woman shook her head. "No rash, not sure about fever."

"What's your name?"

"Molly. Molly Hawkins."

"I'm Dr. Radcliffe, Molly," he said, careful to leave his title out of the matter.

Molly led them to a run-down building three streets from the clinic. A mangy dog lay in front of the doorway, and she shooed it away. A man shouted from one of the open windows above them. "Hey, stop yellin' at my dog."

Molly bellowed an expletive back at him.

They ascended a rickety stairway to the second floor, the treads creaking precariously under their feet. Stained wallpaper, its original color now unrecognizable, was peeling from the sides. Musty smells of stale body odor and decay of something organic rotting assaulted Harry's nostrils, and he fought back the gag reflex. The place was ripe for the spread of disease.

As they entered the small but clean apartment, a boy of about seven shot to attention from his position by a cradle where a baby howled. "Mum." The relief on the boy's face tugged at Harry's heart. A toddler with a mass of brown curls sat on the floor next to the cradle.

Harry pointed between the toddler and the infant. "Who is the patient?"

Molly indicated the girl on the floor, who gazed up at Harry with soulful blue eyes. "Her, o' course."

"Hello, young lady, what's your name?" He laid down his medical bag and lifted the child in his arms.

"Annie," the girl answered, the tone nasal.

"Your mother says you've been making some noises. Can you make them for me?"

"Like she's blowin' her nose," Molly said.

Harry retrieved his handkerchief from his pocket, positioning it. "Blow."

The child gave a snort, the sound more of a wheeze, then she whined.

"Hold her." Harry transferred Annie into her mother's arms. "Move over to the window and lay her back."

He pulled the curtains aside to allow more sunlight as he examined her. "Ah, there's the culprit." From his bag, he retrieved his long nosed forceps used for removing bullets, then he reached into the child's nose and extracted a bean.

"Wot? How'd that get in there?" Molly asked, her eyes wide.

"Annie, beans are for eating, not for stuffing up your nose," Harry admonished, trying his best to appear stern.

The child reached for the bean, still clasped in the tongs of the forceps.

"Not this one." Harry chuckled, pulling it away. "She's lucky we removed it now before it swelled further. The pressure caused her discomfort."

"And I don't owe you no money?"

"None."

"Thank you, doctor. When d'ya expect the clinic to be ready? I know lots of folks who'd be wantin' to pay you a visit."

"We've just started, but I'm hoping within a month. I'll have Manny here pass out flyers when we open." Harry patted Manny on the shoulder, but the boy scooted behind him.

After bidding goodbye, they headed back to the clinic.

"What were you so shy about?" Harry asked Manny.

"Nuffin'."

Harry chuckled then frowned. "I don't believe it. Did you steal from that woman?"

"No, I swear. I never pinch from poor folks."

"Well, no more stealing from rich folks, either, remember?"

Manny nodded.

Harry beamed as they made their way back to the clinic. His first patient, and they hadn't even opened the doors yet. He remembered Margaret's words, and his joy became bittersweet. *You could make such a difference in the lives of the poor.*

By the end of the day, the shell of a clinic began taking shape. He ached from exhaustion and called for everyone to finish their current tasks so they could head home.

Cobwebs clung to his hair, and dirt covered his linen shirt, damp with perspiration. The physical labor had left him in a state of disarray. No wonder Burrows' eyes widened as he greeted Harry when he entered the townhouse.

"Your Grace, you have visitors."

In his frame of mind, Harry didn't relish the idea of company. He longed for a hot bath, a hearty meal, then his bed where he hoped he would sleep peacefully. "Who is it?"

"Lady Cartwright and Miss Pratt. They've been here for several hours. I told them I didn't expect you back soon, but they insisted on waiting."

"Of course they did," Harry muttered.

"Considering the circumstances, I thought it wise not to force them out."

"It's fine, Burrows. You did your best. Where are they?"

"In the small parlor, sir."

Harry took a deep breath and headed into the quagmire awaiting him. Hopefully he would deal with whatever they wanted swiftly, and he could send them on their way.

He threw open the doors and glared at his future wife and her mother. "Ladies." His stomach soured and a foul taste rose in his mouth.

Priscilla's jaw dropped so far Harry could have examined her tonsils had he been standing closer. Her mother's head jerked back as if someone had slapped her, which gave him a wicked satisfaction.

"Your Grace?" Lady Cartwright said, her voice rising in pitch. "Has there been an . . . accident with your carriage? Are you injured?"

"No, I'm perfectly fine. I've been at the clinic making repairs and preparing it to receive patients."

"Lady Easton mentioned that, but the idea seemed so preposterous I was convinced she was mistaken."

"Preposterous? To provide medical care for the poor?"

"Ashton, I only say this out of the utmost concern for your reputation as your future mother-in-law. A duke shouldn't be sullying his hands in such matters. It's not dignified."

"You weren't all that concerned about my reputation when you entrapped me into a betrothal to your daughter. I'll take my chances. At least my *dirty hands* from working at the clinic will produce something worthwhile."

Priscilla gasped, color draining from her face.

Lady Cartwright's mouth snapped shut with an audible click of teeth.

He moved to the sideboard to pour himself a brandy. "Now, what is it you wanted that required waiting for hours on end?"

He turned toward them, catching Lady Cartwright nudge Priscilla with an elbow.

Priscilla's blonde curls bobbed in the direction of her mother, then her eyes met his. "About the boy . . . Manny, I believe."

"What about him?"

Priscilla cast a sideways glance at her mother, who nodded. "Is it your intention to rear him?"

Muscles in his neck and jaw tightened, and he suspected the sensation was not entirely due to physical exertion. "Yes."

"I see. Well . . . Mama . . . that is . . . I believe he would be best served at a boarding school."

Harry slammed his glass down on a nearby table, the brandy sloshing over the side. "You want to send him away?"

Priscilla flushed, her gaze focused on her folded hands in her lap. "Yes. As a newly married couple, having a child underfoot might interfere with our . . . relationship."

Movement at the doorway to the parlor drew Harry's attention. Manny stood with a plate of biscuits in his hands, his wide eyes darting between Harry and Priscilla. He lifted the plate higher. "Burrows asked me to bring these."

Harry motioned the boy forward. "Thank you, Manny. That was kind of you to deliver them."

After taking the plate, he placed a hand on Manny's shoulder, squeezing gently. "Why don't you get cleaned up for supper. Our guests will be leaving soon."

Manny craned his neck around toward Priscilla as he exited the room, and Harry expected him to stick out his tongue at the girl.

After ensuring the boy had proceeded toward the stairway, Harry closed the doors to the parlor, then lowered his voice. "When and if Manny *ever* attends a boarding school, it will be my decision alone. That boy has had more hardship in his young life than you or I could ever imagine, and I will expect you, as his surrogate mother, to treat him with kindness, do you understand?"

Lady Cartwright's lips formed a taut line, and Harry envisioned her biting her tongue. Priscilla simply nodded.

"Now is there anything else? As you can see, I've had a busy day."

"Yes," Priscilla said. "I wanted to thank you for asking the former duchess to leave your home."

Heat rose up Harry's neck at the mention of Margaret, and an overwhelming need to defend her pressed in on him. "Lady Cartwright, may I have a word with Priscilla alone?"

Priscilla's mother bristled, no doubt ready to protest indignantly.

Harry held up his hand to stop her. "Are you truly worried about propriety? As we all know, nothing untoward happened between your daughter and me, and the fact that we are to marry protects her from any more unsavory gossip."

"Very well," she said. "But I shall be right outside should you need me, Priscilla."

No doubt listening with your ear pressed to the door.

A perplexed expression covered Priscilla's face. With the mask of haughtiness removed, the girl actually appeared rather pretty. He took a seat across from her.

"Priscilla. Indulge me a moment, if you will. If you insist on proceeding with this farce of a marriage, there are things you must understand. I didn't ask Margaret to leave my home; she chose to do so of her own free will because of her integrity. If it were up to me, she'd still be here, and I would provide for her for the rest of her life."

Priscilla blanched. "As your mistress?"

"If you must know, yes. But I'm sorry to say she wouldn't accept my suggestion because she has the decency to worry about how that would affect you and"—he swallowed, preparing to force the next words out—"any children you and I might have."

Priscilla shifted in her seat.

"Your mother seems to think the clinic is a whim and—because I'm part of the aristocracy—is beneath me. But you might have heard that Margaret worked to secure pledges to fund it. She supported me in the endeavor, understanding its importance in making me feel productive and satisfied with my life. I've no doubt she would have even worked side-by-side with me if I had asked her. Such things weren't *beneath* her, and I love her for it as much as I love her for her beauty and strength, because compatibility and common purposes don't fade with time."

He studied her face for any signs of weakening. A dusting of pink covered her cheeks, which were previously drained of color, and her eyes shifted to focus on her lap.

"I love Margaret, Priscilla, and she loves me. Her life with my brother was anything but comfortable. She endured much at his hand, and she deserves better than what is being delivered to her. She's my heart, and your rash and dishonest actions have ripped it away from me."

Priscilla's eyes darted up to his, the pink on her cheeks darkening to a deeper rose.

"Say the word to end this, and I will be forever grateful."

"But my mother expects . . ." Her gaze jerked away, and his hopes plunged again.

"I understand more than most about promises made to mothers. But I've also come to understand that mothers desire happiness for their children. At least caring mothers do. If any promise or expectation interferes with her child's happiness, surely she wouldn't hold her child to it." He left it at that, hoping she would digest his words.

She rose and wiped her hands on her dress. "I should go."

"As you wish." He escorted her out of the room to join her mother, slamming the door behind them. Then he poured himself another brandy.

THE FOLLOWING WEEKS, HARRY BUSIED HIMSELF RENOVATING THE clinic. The work exhausted him physically, but he looked forward to opening its doors with eagerness. It provided a perfect excuse to avoid a honeymoon, and he planned to spend many hours working within its walls. Priscilla could occupy herself with her friends and relatives for all he cared.

A week before the wedding, the clinic officially opened for business. Patients trickled in at first, but once Molly had spread the word, the small area used for a waiting room soon became overcrowded. He began the search for additional physicians in earnest. As Manny had suggested, it had indeed occupied his mind, and Margaret only entered his thoughts late at night. However, even productive work could not prevent the inevitable.

The evening before his wedding, Harry pored over a medical book in the library in an effort to distract his mind. The attempt failed miserably. He drew a hand over his face and rose to stretch his legs. Perhaps a brisk walk would help clear his head. He strode toward the entrance of the townhouse when scuffling coming from his right captured his attention.

"Manny, what are you doing?" he asked the boy who was peering out the window.

"I'm waitin' for Margaret."

His heart dropped. He crouched before the boy, who stared with hopeful eyes toward the deserted streets. "Manny," he said with a voice as gentle as he could muster. "Margaret's not coming back. Tomorrow Miss Pratt will come to live with us. You must treat her with respect and kindness, as you always did with Margaret."

Manny scrunched up his nose as if he smelled something foul. "I don't like her."

He could hardly argue the point with the boy.

"Besides, Margaret *is* comin'. I asked her to."

Harry's eyes widened. "When did you ask?"

"I sent a letter while you was eatin' supper."

A mixture of anger and gratitude mingled oddly in his chest. *Will she come? Will I have a chance for a final goodbye before I'm a married man?* "You should have spoken to me first, Manny."

"Weren't no time," he answered, still staring out the window.

"Who delivered it?"

"Some friend of Cook's."

"A friend of Cook's? Where did you meet this person?"

"In the kitchen, o' course." He gave Harry a look that implied his surrogate father should have known as much. "She's the one said to write to Margaret, said she'd take it to 'er at Lady Denby's."

"Come away from the window; if and when she comes, Burrows will let us know."

The remainder of the evening, Harry lifted his head with each sound in the house, waiting for Margaret to come.

※

MARGARET STRUGGLED TO CONCENTRATE ON THE EMBROIDERY IN her lap. She had already pulled out several misplaced stitches. *Who am I fooling?* After placing the needlework aside, she rose and moved toward the sideboard where the decanter of brandy beckoned. Perhaps if she drank enough, she would sleep through the entire next day, and once she awoke, it would be over. Harry would be married.

A footman entered carrying a silver tray. "This arrived for you, Your Grace."

Scrawled in an uneven hand on the outside of the letter, it was addressed to Hur Grase.

"Who brought it?"

"A woman, Your Grace, perhaps a maid. I believe she said from the duke."

A messy splotch of wax sealed the back, but no crested stamp had left an imprint. She opened it to read.

Deer Margrit

> *Pleez kum home. Harees mizerbul. I seen him cry when he didnt no I wuz lookin. Dont let him maree that gurl. She hates me an says shes gonna put me in a bordin skool.*

> *Luv*

> *Manny*

> *PS I ben praktisin mi ritin can u tell?*

Carefully deciphering his atrocious spelling and grammar, she pictured him, his tongue poking out at the side of his mouth and his brow furrowed in concentration. She missed him horribly. *A boarding school.* She expected Priscilla wouldn't be pleased being a mother to Manny—not when she would expect to have her own children soon —but Manny was in no way ready for the rigors of boarding school. He needed a gentle hand to guide him and teach him the basics before sending him to such a structured environment. The other boys would taunt him, initiating a fight and his subsequent expulsion before the first week had passed.

Her mind whirled for a solution. If she married Laurence, she could bring Manny to live with them, and she would continue his instruction. She would make it a condition of her acceptance of Laurence's proposal. She had little doubt he would agree, although she hated the manipulative ultimatum.

One other solution niggled at the corner of her mind. She could accept Harry's offer to become his mistress and request Manny stay with her for company.

With Harry's wedding scheduled for the next day, she had to decide and act immediately. She peeked out the front window of Camilla's townhouse; daylight waned and twilight approached. Camilla had taken her carriage to visit her father, so Margaret decided to walk, rejecting the idea of waiting for a hackney coach.

If she hurried, she'd make it to Harry's before dark, then ride home in his carriage.

Although the late July heat would lessen with the setting sun, the nights remained too warm for a pelisse. So slipping on her spencer, she sneaked out the front door unnoticed. She proceeded down the deserted street toward Harry's. Now that the season had ended, many had left London, returning to their country estates.

As she passed a small gap between two townhomes, footsteps sounded behind her, and she increased her pace. Not having thought things through, she worried whoever followed would see her enter Harry's home.

She turned at a corner as a diversion tactic, hoping the person would continue past, then she could backtrack and resume her journey. A shiver of panic snaked up her spine as the footsteps followed, but before she had time to react, a hand covered her mouth. She gagged as the fetid stench of the person's skin made its way to her nostrils.

"Don't scream and I won't hurt you, understand?" The man's sinister voice hissed in her ear.

She nodded, praying he was truthful.

CHAPTER 22—KIDNAPPED

Margaret's consciousness threatened to withdraw to the secret place it had retreated during George's punishments, finding the sanctuary necessary to endure. But she resisted, fighting back the urge. The situation required a clear head and her wits about her. It was no time for cowardice. *Should I kick him and attempt to run? Should I play along then wait for another opportunity to escape?* The questions mingled with others in her mind. *Who is he? What does he want?* The latter were answered first.

"I told that nob the boy belonged to me. Now I've got something of his." Standing behind her, he tightened his grip.

Coodibilis.

With his left hand still covering her mouth, he scraped a knife across her throat with his right. The point pricked into her delicate skin, and following a sting of pain, a drop of blood, warm and wet, trickled down her neck.

"I'll slit your throat if you so much as make a peep."

She bit back the cry rising in her throat. Panic shivered up her spine like a serpent ready to strike.

He pushed her through a narrow passageway, then into a waiting hackney carriage. Once seated, he removed the knife from her throat long enough to beat on the carriage door, alerting the driver to move.

"How did you find me? What do you want?" she demanded, doing her best to sound forceful.

In the dim light of the coach, the grin on Cood's face assumed a macabre appearance, reminding Margaret of the theatrical mask of Mephistopheles in the play *Faust*. She had seen it as a child, and the image had appeared in her nightmares for months.

"Been watching you for weeks. You're nigh on impossible to get alone. Took a bit of doin', it did. The boy helped."

She remembered the summons to Harry's. "Manny would never agree to this."

He laughed, spittle spraying from his lips and dotting her face. "Not on purpose, no. But we knew he'd take the bait quick enough." He rubbed his chin with his grimy hand, the scratching sound from the coarse stubble of his beard sent gooseflesh up her arms. "A bit tricky, we had to time it just right, we did." She sucked in a breath when he drew a line down her cheek with the point of the blade. "But it worked out fine."

"You said we. Who else is involved?"

"Shut your mouth! You ask too many questions." The tip of the knife pricked her cheek, and another trickle of blood dripped down her face. "Your fancy man will pay handsomely to get you back, but less if you're marked. It's up to you."

Her stomach lurched and a bitter taste coated her tongue. She choked it down, reeling from the nausea.

As the carriage traveled through the streets, Margaret concentrated on each turn, struggling to decipher their destination. The carriage jerked to a halt, and Cood pulled her out.

He pressed the knife to her ribs as he moved her to a dilapidated building. Something about the area seemed familiar. A mangy dog barked as they passed.

A woman stared from an open window and Margaret sent an imploring gaze her way, but twilight had faded and moonlight was now at her back, leaving only the outline of her form in the darkening night.

"Make a noise, and I'll ruin this pretty frock of yours." He laughed low and menacing, his breath hot against her neck. She stumbled, her legs shaky beneath her, as he pushed her into the entrance of the building where a small boy crouched on the floor. Cood kicked the child out of his way, and the boy howled.

"Leave him alone." Margaret struggled to free herself from Cood's hold.

He released her arm but grabbed a handful of her hair, giving it a hard yank. Several locks fell loose against her neck as hairpins clinked against the dirty floor. A sharp prick in her ribs followed the sound of fabric ripping. She fought the urge to cry out. *Stay calm. Stay alive.*

"Now that's a shame, but I did warn you."

The boy stared with wide eyes as Cood hauled her up the flight of stairs and into a small windowless room. "Get me some rope," he bellowed, and moments later the boy entered with a filthy piece of hemp rope. Cood tied her wrists and feet, then shoved a dirty rag into her mouth, securing it at the back of her head. The stench and taste of the cloth made her stomach lurch, and she fought the urge to vomit.

After restraining her, Cood threw her to the floor. Pain ripped through her as he kicked her in the ribs for good measure. Darkness edged her vision, and she struggled not to scream. Her heart pounded and for a fleeting moment, she feared he might kill her to silence even the smallest of sound she produced. She squeezed her eyes tight to hold back the tears and fight the hopelessness of her situation. With his wedding tomorrow, Harry wouldn't have time for rescuing former lovers. A booted foot connected with her head and, mercifully, she lost consciousness.

THE DRIZZLE OF RAIN MATCHED HARRY'S SPIRITS THE MORNING OF the wedding. He stood before the mirror as Hastings searched through the assortment of waistcoats. "Anything will do, man. Just choose something and let's be done with it."

"But sir, you should be resplendent on your wedding day." The valet held out the sapphire waistcoat with the lines of silver thread —the one Harry had worn the night of the ball that matched Margaret's gown. "What about this one, sir?"

Harry shook his head. "No. Anything but that one."

Hastings lifted a gold one with lily-of-the-valley embroidered on the collar points for inspection, and again Harry shook his head. Must each one remind him of Margaret?

Why didn't she come last night?

His valet sighed deeply. "You said anything. I do believe you're stalling, sir."

"Fine, then. That one will do." Harry raised his arms and Hastings slipped the waistcoat on and fastened it against his chest.

Once dressed to Hastings' satisfaction, Harry trudged down the steps. The house was bustling with activity as Burrows ordered the staff around in preparation for their new mistress. After the ceremony, the bride, groom, and guests would arrive for the wedding breakfast. The thought turned Harry's stomach.

He sat alone in his carriage as it bounced along the streets to St. George's on Hanover Square. Andrew had offered to accompany him, but Harry declined, stating he was in no mood for his friend's usual jocularity. Instead, he would meet him at the church. Even Manny insisted on staying home, refusing to leave his room.

Why hadn't Margaret come?

Harry entered the church as if he were attending his own funeral. Lavishly decorated with roses and baby's breath, a heady scent filled the nave and transept. An arrangement containing late-blooming wisteria caught his attention, and he remembered their fragrance drifting in through the windows the night he and Maggie . . .

Why didn't you come, Maggie?

A cough from behind pulled him back to the present.

Andrew studied him with compassionate eyes. "All right, Harry?"

"No. But I suppose that doesn't matter."

People trickled in, filling the pews on the bride's side. Lord Nash smirked from his seat behind Lady Cartwright, and Harry's stomach roiled again.

The groom's side remained sparse, with only Alice and, surprisingly, Lord Montgomery in attendance. *Why is Montgomery here? To gloat?* Harry cast a quick glance in the man's direction, but Montgomery merely nodded.

Harry waited, the scene more like a nightmare than a dream, but nonetheless chimerical. Minutes passed unevenly, at times so slowly he swore he could see a mote of dust suspended in front of him, and other times so quickly he had little time to think.

He tucked his hand into the pocket of his coat, and his fingers stroked the seed pearl hairpin like a talisman.

Why hadn't Margaret come?

Before he knew it, Priscilla stood next to him, dressed in a pink gown edged in delicate lace. His bride. Had she been Maggie, joy would have swelled within his heart. Instead, only apathy remained in the gaping hole of his chest.

The priest droned on, much like an annoying insect buzzing in his ear. The man's mouth was moving, but Harry was hard pressed to understand the words.

Priscilla shifted on her feet, and Harry glanced over at her. She seemed ready to cry, but not the tears of happiness one often sees in brides. She appeared utterly miserable as her eyes darted over to her mother.

Promises to mothers. He remembered his plea to his bride. *A mother would want her child to be happy.* Not only her mother, but his own. He recalled the necklace his mother had given out of love. *Perhaps you will give it to your bride, Harry.* He had placed it around Margaret's neck, given in love.

Harry realized the priest watched him intently. *Is he waiting for something?* "I'm sorry," Harry said lamely.

"Do you take this woman—"

"Oi, Harry! Stop!"

Harry spun around at the desperate sound of Manny's voice. The boy was running up the aisle toward him, with Burrows trying valiantly to keep up from behind.

"'E's got 'er, Harry. You've got to save 'er!"

"Manny, what are you talking about?"

"Cood, 'e's got 'er." Manny held out a dirty piece of paper.

Burrows had finally reached them, bent over and gasping for breath. "Sir . . . it's true," he said, his words coming in short pants. "This note . . . arrived . . . right after . . . you left. Peter said . . . a small boy . . . delivered it."

Harry's hand shook as he opened the filthy scrap of foolscap.

Your loftiness,

I have your woman. If you want her back in one piece, either bring that brat, Manny, or £1,000. Manny knows where to find me.

Coodibilis

"You're certain it's not a trick?"

"Yes, sir. We called at Lady Denby's. She's been worried about Her Grace. When she returned home from her father's last evening, Lady Denby thought Her Grace had already gone to bed. But her room was empty this morning."

Harry's heart pounded as terrifying thoughts raced through his mind. *What if Cood hurts her? Rapes her? Kills her? How can I live without her?*

A strange clarity replaced the fog of chaos that had occupied his mind for the past month. *Nothing else matters.*

He turned toward Priscilla. "I'm sorry, I can't do this." A gasp sounded behind him, and he spun toward Lord Cartwright, who propped up his swooning wife. "If you insist, I'll meet your challenge, but first I have something to do."

"Trade me, Harry," Manny said.

"Absolutely not. We'll get her back, I promise."

Lord Montgomery shot up from his seat in the pew. "Take me with you, Ashton."

"He's dangerous, Montgomery."

"I don't care about that. Another man might prove helpful."

"I'll go, too," Andrew said.

Harry placed a hand on his friend's arm. "No, Andrew. You need to stay here, for Alice," he lowered his voice to a whisper, "and for your child. Montgomery will assist me."

Lady Cartwright had sufficiently recovered from her swoon and glared at him. "You can't leave, we're in the middle of a wedding."

"For once in your life, be quiet, Mama." Priscilla grabbed his arm. He prepared to curse and shake her off, but his eyes widened when she said, "Find her, Harrison, and bring her home."

"I will. Thank you, Priscilla." For the first time, he graced her with a genuine smile. "And call me Harry."

Finally breathing normally, Burrows asked, "What can I do to assist, Your Grace?"

Harry's gaze jerked toward Manny. "Where will we find him?"

"East End, three streets from the clinic."

Harry turned back to Burrows. "Locate a constable or Bow Street Runners and meet us there, but be cautious. I don't know what he'll do if he sees anyone but me. Manny, come with us. Sit by the driver and give him directions."

They raced out of the church where onlookers had gathered, expecting the happy couple to emerge. Harry barely registered the hushed murmurs and dropped jaws as the two men jumped into the waiting coach.

Inside the carriage, the tension weighed heavily on Harry, his gut squeezing as if wrapped in a tourniquet. Montgomery stared out the window at the passing streets.

"Why were you there, Montgomery?"

Montgomery startled, jerking toward Harry. "Pardon?"

"At the wedding. On my side. We're hardly friends."

The man stared at his knees and brushed at an invisible speck of dust. "A precaution."

An urge flared to reach across the small space of the carriage and grab Montgomery by the throat, but he restrained the desire. "Against what? Are you involved in this?"

Montgomery blanched and fell back in his seat. "No! How could you think such a thing? I would never put her in harm's way."

"You're not answering my question."

"This isn't the time. Shouldn't our priority be finding Margaret?"

As Harry opened his mouth to protest, the carriage slowed and bounced to a stop. Perhaps Montgomery was right, but Harry made a mental note to resume his questioning once Margaret was safely back home. He bolted from the vehicle, Montgomery on his heels.

The coach had stopped in front of the clinic. "Manny, I thought you said it was three streets from here."

Manny thrust his hands on his skinny hips. "You don't wanna 'ave Cood see you comin', do you?" The boy's eyes traveled up and down Harry's person. "Comes to think on it, you stick out anyways."

During the weeks of work preparing the clinic, Harry had dressed in older clothes and, for the most part, blended in with the people of the area. Now it was obvious he didn't belong. He stripped out of his bottle-green superfine tailcoat—handing it to Manny to hold—and yanked off his waistcoat and cravat, motioning for Montgomery to join him. They threw their discarded garments inside the carriage.

Manny nodded his approval. "Follow me."

They wove down several streets and into an alleyway. "There's a back entrance 'ere," Manny said. "Stay 'ere whilst I check to see if there's a lookout."

Harry and Montgomery pressed themselves against the brick wall of the building while Manny crept to the edge to peek around. He waved his hand, indicating they should remain where they were, then disappeared around the corner.

"I still want an explanation, Montgomery," Harry whispered.

"You shall have it, Ashton, but let's rescue Margaret first."

Manny reappeared and motioned them forward.

They moved toward the back of the building where another boy waited by a set of steps leading to a door.

Younger than Manny, the boy appraised them with thoughtful eyes. "G'wan then, hit me," he said, steeling his small body for the attack.

Harry's gaze darted toward Montgomery, the man's horrified expression surely matching his own. "I'm not going to strike a child," Harry said.

"You got to, Harry," Manny said. "It's got to look like you knocked 'im out. Otherwise there'll be a beatin' waitin' for 'im."

Harry folded his arms across his chest. "No, absolutely not."

Manny rolled his eyes and huffed. "When a man needs somfin' done . . ." He drew back his arm and landed a solid punch on the boy's chin, knocking him over. "Sorry, Pockets."

Pockets rubbed his jaw. "That was a good 'un, Manny." Then he lay on the ground as if unconscious.

Harry glanced back at the prostrate boy, then exchanged a horrified look with Montgomery as they started up the steps and through the door of the building.

"Interesting company you keep, Ashton," Montgomery muttered.

Harry placed his finger to his lips, and they continued following Manny up the narrow staircase. They progressed slowly, careful to avoid placing their heavy boots where Manny indicated a creaky board waited. As they approached the landing, their diminutive guide held out a hand to stop them.

Voices rose from somewhere ahead.

". . . told you. You'll get your money. That's if the fancy nob actually comes for the bitch. I sent my boy with the note this morning."

"And if he doesn't?" The woman's voice was strangely familiar, and even in the late July heat, Harry shivered as if hit with a cold blast of air. "I did my part making her available; I want compensation."

A pop of flesh against flesh rang through the building.

"How dare you strike me!" the woman hissed.

"I'll kill you as quick as I will her if you don't shut your trap and stop your nagging. If he doesn't come, there's a ship headed to the colonies. I'll sell her. She'd fetch a pretty penny, I'd wager."

Harry's muscles tensed, preparing to spring from his hiding spot and beat Cood to a pulp. Montgomery grabbed his arm, holding him in place, then shook his head, no doubt stopping Harry from ruining everything.

With his emotions somewhat in check, Harry crept closer to the top of the stairwell, then peeked around the corner. He fought back a gasp as Jane pushed past Coodibilis and headed further down the hallway.

He stooped to Manny, keeping his voice as low as possible. "The woman, Cook's friend who said she'd deliver your note. Was that her?"

Manny nodded, his eyes wide.

"You know her?" Montgomery whispered.

"Margaret's former lady's maid. Margaret dismissed her."

He straightened himself and stole another glance. Cood moved to one of the doorways in the hall and tested the lock. Seemingly satisfied, he pulled up a chair and positioned himself in front of it.

"That must be where he has Margaret," Harry whispered. "We need a distraction to draw him away."

"I have an idea. Can he recognize you?" Montgomery asked.

"He's seen me once that I know of."

Laurence was shorter and leaner than Harry, his hair chestnut brown instead of Harry's blond. "If I redress with my coat and cravat, and wear my hat, perhaps he will mistake me for you from a distance. I shall lead him away."

Harry nodded. "Be careful, he's dangerous."

He patted Harry on the shoulder. "Fear not, Ashton."

"Under the circumstances, call me Harry."

"And I'm Laurence." He held out his hand, which Harry grasped. "Wish me luck."

With surprising stealth, Laurence crept back down the steps and out of the building.

The heat in the enclosed stairwell grew oppressive. Sweat trickled down Harry's forehead into his eyes, and the linen shirt clung to his body as time moved at a crawl. Manny had lowered himself to a sitting position on the stairs, but Harry remained alert, watching for any signs of movement from Cood.

Quick footsteps of someone running up a flight of stairs had Manny bounding to his feet and looking behind him, but the sound came from the other direction.

"Oi, Cood," a boy's voice called. "There's some fancy nob wandering about out here."

Cood jerked upright from his slouched position on the chair.

Get up and go look. With every ounce of strength in him, Harry willed the man to vacate his post.

"Bring him here," Cood ordered.

"I tried; 'e says 'e'll only talk to you."

Cood muttered an obscenity, then rose from his seat and headed down the hall, presumably to the front staircase. Heavy footsteps confirmed his descent.

Harry and Manny sprang into action, reaching the locked door in seconds. Harry grasped the doorknob and, in vain, twisted. He slammed his shoulder into the wood, but it didn't budge. A soft moan came from within the room beyond, increasing his urgency.

His hands splayed against the wood, he pressed his face close, fearing he'd draw Cood back if he spoke too loudly. "Margaret, it's Harry." He slammed into the door again, cringing from the pain radiating from the point of contact down through his arm.

He raked a hand through his hair. "We need the key, or something to pick the lock." His hands ran down his torso only to be reminded he had removed his tailcoat. "Damnation!"

"What 'bout this?" Manny held up the seed pearl hairpin Harry had kept in his possession since the day Margaret had left.

Harry stared in wonder. "We shall discuss this later." He snatched the pin from the boy's hand and proceeded to insert it into the lock.

Frustration rose and valuable time ticked by until Manny tapped him on the arm and held out his hand. "Allow me." The boy cracked his fingers theatrically, took the hairpin, and after a few moments of jiggling it in the lock, a glorious click rewarded his efforts.

Harry bolted into the darkened, windowless room, his eyes adjusting to the dim light as he raced toward the figure lying on the floor.

His heart sputtered as he turned Margaret over and pulled the gag from her mouth. Dried blood caked on her cheek, and beads of it dotted her throat like a gruesome necklace. Sticky blood coated his hand as he wrapped it around her waist, discovering her ripped dress. "Maggie." He patted her face tenderly, then placed his index and forefinger against her throat, praying he would find a pulse.

Strong and steady. Thank God. "Maggie." He grasped her shoulders and gave a gentle shake. Her eyelids fluttered then opened, and she stared at him, reminding him of when they'd first met. He drew her against him and covered her face with light kisses. "I'm here, my darling."

"H-Harry? Am I dead or dreaming?"

"Neither. But you are injured."

"Oi, Harry, 'urry up," Manny urged from the doorway.

Harry tugged at the knots in the thick rope that secured her wrists, cursing the fact he didn't have a knife. His fingers scraped at the rough hemp, finally loosening it enough to free her hands. He reached under her knees. "Wrap your arms around my neck."

"If you untie my feet, I can walk."

"There's no time." He lifted her, and she grabbed onto him for balance.

"I'd say you were out of time," the sinister voice hissed.

CHAPTER 23—HOPE RESTORED

H arry spun around with Margaret in his arms. Cood held Manny against him, a grimy hand over the boy's mouth and a knife to his throat.

"A clever trick, sending your friend to lure me away. Too bad it didn't work."

"Where is he? What have you done to him?" Harry's eyes darted to the blade that gleamed red.

Cood sneered. "He won't bother nobody no more."

Margaret's grip tightened around his neck.

"I think I'll be keeping the boy *and* taking your money. There's a ship leaving the port that's needing another passenger. By the time they discover your bodies, I'll be long gone."

Manny squirmed against Cood's grasp, his eyes focusing on Harry's.

Harry's gut clenched at the terrified expression on the boy's face.

"Put her down." Cood pressed the tip of the knife into Manny's throat, and he emitted a muffled cry.

Harry leaned close to Margaret as he lowered her to the floor. "Don't worry." His whispered reassurance did little to assuage his own fear.

She mouthed *I love you*, and he gave her a weak smile.

A shadow trailed across the floor in the hallway. Too large to be the small boy they had encountered on their way inside, it moved slowly in their direction. Harry forced his gaze away and met Cood's stare.

Behind Cood, a booted foot inched into view at the doorway. His movements slow, Laurence appeared, blood staining his white waistcoat. He raised a finger to his lips as his eyes connected with Harry's.

Harry assessed the situation and formulated a plan of action. Relieved that Manny had worn his new boots with the hard heels, Harry gauged their position between Cood's feet as the man held the boy before him. The material of Cood's shoes appeared worn and thin.

"Coodibilis," Harry said. "Let the boy go. Let's discuss this like gentlemen."

Cood's mouth curved in a sneer. "I ain't no fancy nob."

Harry stared into Manny's eyes, willing him to understand. "The boy's not high in the *instep*. He's no use to you." Harry chanced a quick glance toward Laurence. "Use your *head*, man."

Laurence nodded, and Harry took a tentative step forward.

Cood waved the knife in front of him. "Stay back."

"Now!" Harry shouted.

Manny stomped on Cood's foot. The man howled and flailed his arms, releasing the child.

Harry motioned for Manny to get behind him. Manny scurried out of the way, racing toward Margaret.

Laurence grabbed Cood's hand that held the weapon, turned him around, and head-butted him. Both men stumbled backward, and Cood howled in pain. "Bloody hell," he yelled, wind milling his arms to regain his balance.

The blade dropped from Cood's grasp, sliding across the wooden floor.

Harry spun around, searching for the knife. Manny had retrieved it and was furiously sawing at the rope binding Margaret's feet.

Grunts sounded behind him, and Harry pivoted back. Laurence's face grew pale as he restrained Cood in a chokehold. His grasp weakened, and Cood delivered a sharp elbow to Laurence's injury. Laurence doubled over and fell to the floor. He screamed in pain as Cood dispensed a direct kick to his wound.

"Manny!" Harry shouted, motioning for the boy to throw him the weapon. The moment his fingers curled around the handle, Cood pounced on him. They wrestled for possession of the knife. Cood landed a solid blow to Harry's jaw. The coppery taste of blood pooled in Harry's mouth.

Cood pinned Harry to the floor. His fetid breath inches from Harry's face. Pain seared Harry's wrist as Cood twisted, pointing the blade at Harry's chest. The man was stronger than Harry had imagined, and he fought to regain control as the blade inched closer to his heart. A growl erupted from Harry's throat. He would not allow this man to harm those he loved.

Movement behind Cood drew Harry's attention as a rope looped over Cood's neck. *Margaret!* Cood released his grasp on Harry's wrist, and he clawed at the ligature around his throat. Harry seized the opportunity, landing a blow on Cood's face and knocking him further backward. Margaret toppled to the floor and scrambled away from the despicable man. Cood lay on the floor, gasping for breath as his hands still clutched his throat.

Heavy footsteps pounded on the stairs, growing louder, coming toward them.

Harry glanced up, the tension in his muscles easing, as three Bow Street Runners entered.

"What's going on here? A man named Burrows reported a kidnapping." He reached for Cood, and another runner grabbed Harry by the arms.

Well done, Burrows.

"Release him. He's the Duke of Ashton," Margaret said, her voice forceful. She pointed toward Cood, who stumbled as the runner lifted him to his feet. "This is the man who abducted me."

Cood shouted a few choice expletives as the runner bound his hands with the same rope used on Margaret.

"Shut up, you, if you know what's good for you," the runner said.

"She's a liar," Cood bellowed.

"I'm the Duchess of Ashton. I do not lie."

Locks of her hair hung in odd arrangements around her head. Blood caked her face and soaked her torn dress. Rope burns marred her delicate wrists. And she'd never looked more beautiful. She struggled to stand and turned toward Laurence, who lay motionless on the floor. As she took a step, color drained from her face, and she staggered.

Harry yanked free of the runner's hold and rushed forward, grabbing her arm. "Maggie, sit back down."

Her violet eyes implored him. "Laurence is injured."

"I'm a doctor," he said to the runner who had restrained him.

"Go on then," the runner said.

He nodded and made his way to examine the man who had risked his life for them. "Laurence, can you hear me?"

Brown eyes opened to meet his. "Is Margaret safe?"

Harry smiled. He would grow to like this fellow. "Yes, she is. Weak, but she'll be fine. I'm concerned about you."

"A minor scratch. I fear I was careless."

"Nonsense. You saved us all. Now, allow me to examine your injuries." Harry pulled aside Laurence's coat and lifted his blood stained waistcoat and linen shirt, noting the laceration on his abdomen. More of a slash than a stab, the bleeding from the wound itself had slowed. "You'll need stitches, but you should make a complete recovery."

Another Bow Street Runner entered the crowded room, pulling Pockets by his collar. "Found this one lurking about outside."

Manny jumped into action. "Leave 'im be."

"He's a thieving scoundrel," the runner said, then eyed Manny. "Maybe you're one, too."

"As the boy said, leave him be. I'm responsible for them," Harry said.

The runner's brows lifted. "There's a gang of them, Your Grace. Would you be taking responsibility for all of them?"

"If necessary, yes. In the meantime, I have a medical facility not far from here. If your men would be so kind to help me get Lord Montgomery there so I can attend to him and Her Grace, I'd appreciate it." Harry turned toward Manny. "Run back to my carriage and have the driver pull up here."

Two runners dragged Cood out of the room, still struggling and proclaiming his innocence. Manny stuck out his tongue at his former "employer" before leaving to follow Harry's instructions. Two more runners helped Laurence to his feet, assisting him out of the building.

Alone in the desolate room, Harry lifted Margaret in his arms. "I thought I'd lost you, and I've never been so terrified in my life."

"I've been such a fool, Harry."

He searched her eyes. "How? You couldn't have known Cood was going to kidnap you."

"Well, that, yes, but about us. I was on my way to tell you I don't care about propriety. All that matters is you. If you still want me, I'll be your mistress." A faint blush rose to her cheeks, coloring her pale face.

"No, that won't be necessary." He kissed her forehead. "There was no wedding. I left her at the altar."

Margaret nestled her head in the crook of his neck and whispered. "It's wicked to admit, but I'm glad."

"Once I tend to you and Laurence, I'm taking you home. No arguments."

And she gave none.

Margaret lowered the book she'd been trying to read. It became a near impossible task as she stretched out on the sofa in the large parlor. Manny and Harry fussed over her, asking every few minutes if she needed anything.

For the hundredth time, Harry fluffed the pillow behind her head. With all the pampering she'd received since she arrived back at Harry's townhouse, it had been hard to imagine it had only been twenty-four hours since her ordeal with Cood.

"Honestly, Harry, I'm fine. Stop fussing." She grinned at him. "Why don't you go to the clinic and help someone who truly needs it?"

He answered by kissing her soundly on the lips. "Tomorrow, if you're better."

"Your Grace," Burrows said from the open doorway, "Lord Cartwright, Miss Pratt, and Lord Montgomery wish to speak with you."

Margaret exchanged a look with Harry, then straightened to a sitting position on the sofa and prepared to have the brief respite of calm upset. "Why would Laurence be with them?"

Harry shook his head, then rose as the trio entered.

Each bore a serious, if not grim, expression, and Margaret's heart stuttered at the possibility Lord Cartwright had arrived to confront Harry. Priscilla's eyes locked onto the floor, and she wrung her clasped hands as if she were washing them raw.

"Are you here to challenge me, Cartwright?" Harry asked, his voice steady and authoritative.

How can he be so calm?

Lord Cartwright turned toward Laurence. "Perhaps you should start?"

"I suppose I should." Laurence's eyes flicked toward her but didn't hold her gaze. He pressed his hand to his injured side, grimacing. His shoulders hunched as if bearing a heavy weight. "The night of the musicale, I glanced over at the note you received. I apologize, Ashton."

Harry stood in profile to her, his face turned ashen. "Wait, are you saying you saw the contents of the original note?"

Laurence hung his head. "I'm afraid so."

Harry strode toward Laurence, and Margaret tensed.

Laurence held up his hands. "Please allow me to explain. You wondered why I was at the wedding. The precaution I mentioned was to ensure it did not take place. I'll admit I should have spoken up regarding the note when we discovered you with Miss Pratt, but my own selfish motives overshadowed my judgment."

"You wanted Margaret for yourself," Harry said matter-of-factly.

Laurence shuffled his feet and tugged at his cravat. "Yes. I hoped if you were out of the way I would finally have a chance of winning her. I'm so sorry, Margaret."

"It's Ashton who deserves your apology," Margaret said.

"Of course. Forgive me, Ashton."

Harry simply stared.

Laurence coughed, clearing his throat, and continued. "After spending time with Margaret, I realized the futility of my efforts. Although with persistence I might have won her hand, I would never have her heart . . . not fully. Perhaps it's also selfish, but I hope to find that type of love for myself someday and a woman who would love me so deeply.

"I approached Miss Pratt and begged her to reconsider, imploring her to wait for her own happiness rather than steal from someone else." His gaze darted toward Priscilla, who blanched and continued wringing her hands.

"Without an admission of complicity, I needed proof. The other note and who was embroiled in the scheme puzzled me. Unfortunately, my mother adores gossip, so it's no surprise she and Lady Cartwright are close friends."

Lord Cartwright groaned.

"But my mother isn't malicious, Ashton, truly. I questioned her and she mentioned that Lady Cartwright had implied Lord Nash was instrumental in securing the match between her daughter and you, Ashton."

Color flooded Laurence's cheeks. "I don't mean to brag, but I have a rather uncanny ability that allows me to visualize things from memory. It occurred to me there was a particular curve to the letter s in the original note that is quite unique. My memory also serves me well at the card table, and I hold Nash's vowels, so I examined his signature and found the s to be a match. Of course, I approached Nash who denied it as expected, but it was proof enough for me. I offered to dismiss his debt if he would admit to his part in the deception.

"My presence was to ensure someone stopped that wedding, and if neither Miss Pratt nor Lord Nash rose to the occasion, I was prepared to state my evidence."

Margaret's head spun with the knowledge of the depths to which the parties had sunk to ensnare Harry. No wonder Harry had been reluctant to be embroiled in the toxicity of the upper class.

"Perhaps I should thank you, but you should have spoken up sooner," Harry said.

"I'll not deny that, and I'm dreadfully sorry."

"And you, Priscilla, are you sorry?" Harry asked.

Her father nudged her with his elbow. "I am, Your Grace. I don't expect you to forgive me. What I've done is despicable. Your words when we spoke here ate away at me. Like Lord Montgomery, I wish to have someone love me the way you love Her Grace, but I fear my actions have doomed me to failure. It shall be my penance." Tears flowed down her face and Margaret's heart softened toward the girl.

"Please don't blame my daughter entirely, Ashton. Her mother put her up to this, and she also is paying the price. I have moved out of our household. The question remains whether Priscilla wishes to reside with me or her mother."

Margaret rose, and Harry grasped her arm in support. She patted his hand. "I'm fine." He released her, and she proceeded toward Priscilla.

The girl trembled in front of her as Margaret raised her hand. Everyone seemed to hold a collective breath, then Margaret brushed away the girl's tears and pulled her into an embrace. "I would suggest you stay with your father as he has your best interest at heart. With time, Priscilla, people do forget as other scandals capture their fascination. The right man will see past your mistakes."

Priscilla gave an audible sigh. "May I ask you something, Your Grace?"

"Well, that depends," Margaret said.

A blush covered Priscilla's cheeks. "Is having someone love you so deeply as wonderful as it sounds?"

"Yes, and even more wonderful if you love them in return."

"So there is to be no challenge?" Harry asked Lord Cartwright.

"My daughter's sullied reputation is her own doing and her mother's, not yours. There is nothing to challenge."

Harry offered his hand to the man who might have been his father-in-law. "Then let us make amends."

Lord Cartwright grasped Harry's outstretched hand. "Thank you, Ashton. Now, we should bid you good day and leave you in peace." He grasped Priscilla's arm and led her from the room.

"Laurence, may I have a word?" Margaret asked, touching him on the arm.

He glanced at Harry as if seeking his permission, then nodded.

She took his hand in hers. "Thank you for risking your life to help me. Give Harry time, he's a reasonable man." She turned and smiled at the man she loved, then kissed Laurence softly on the cheek. "Be happy and have faith."

With their visitors gone, Harry moved to her side and wrapped an arm around her waist. "Manny, why don't you see if Cook has any biscuits in the kitchen?"

Manny grinned. "You just want me to leave so you can smash your faces together."

Harry laughed, the low rumble vibrating up Margaret's arm from her hand pressed against Harry's chest. "Biscuits, Manny, now!"

Manny dashed off, leaving them alone, and Harry's hazel eyes glinted with mischief as he drew her closer.

She plucked at the button of his waistcoat. "Did you really want biscuits?"

"Always. But I want this more." He lowered his lips to hers, teasing at first, then capturing her mouth fully.

They had shared many kisses since her return from the ordeal with Cood, but this touch of lips seemed particularly wonderful. His tongue teased at the seam of her mouth, and she opened without hesitation. Every fiber of her being trusted him with her very life.

When she threaded her fingers through his hair, he growled, the sound primitive and exciting. His tongue danced with hers in the rhythmic motion their bodies had duplicated, and he pulled her tight against him.

She sighed as they separated and laid her head against his chest. "Is it really over? No wedding, no challenge?"

He stroked her back. "Oh, there will be a wedding—ours."

A cacophony of voices boomed from the hall.

"Damnation!" Harry blew out a breath. "Can't a man have a moment's peace in his own home?"

Manny burst into the room. "She's 'ere, Burrows's got 'er."

Margaret jerked from Harry's arms, straightening her dress and hair.

Held between Burrows and Peter, Jane tugged furiously, attempting to free herself. "Let me go. I don't know what you're talking about. I simply came to speak with Cook."

"Manny saw her in the kitchen, Your Grace, and alerted me straightaway." Burrows glared at the odious woman. "I've sent Hastings to fetch the closest constable or runner."

Margaret had learned of Jane's involvement in her abduction, although Harry wasn't sure of her connection to Coodibilis.

"There's been a mistake, Your Grace," Jane pleaded. "I don't know what the boy is talking about."

"Liar!" Manny shouted. "You was the one who tol' me to write the note, and we seen you with Cood."

Jane's eyes darted around the room like a rat cornered. "I was just trying to help."

"Help yourself, you mean?" Harry said, his face reddening and his fists clenched at his side.

Margaret reached over and took his hand in hers to calm him. "What I want to know is why? Was revenge your only motive? Are you that petty, Jane, to do something so contemptible?"

Jane sagged, her body crumpling. Had it not been for Peter and Burrows holding her arms, she'd have fallen to the floor. "He made me do it. He said he'd tell if I didn't help. I had a good job with Lady Smythe-White. He was going to ruin it all."

"Coodibilis?" Margaret asked.

"I hate that name. He gave it to himself. I only know him as Bertie. Bertie Darrow."

Burrows sucked in a breath, and Margaret's gaze shot to Harry. *Jane's last name is Darrow.*

"Is he your relation?" Harry asked.

"My brother. He said he'd go to Lady Smythe-White and tell her about my background. I worked hard to pull myself up from the gutter. I'll be damned if I let him tear that away."

"And yet, here you are," Harry said. "You should have come to me."

Jane sniffled and refused to look at them, her head hung low. "Have mercy, Your Grace."

"If you cooperate and testify against him, perhaps the court will show mercy. It's out of my hands." Harry turned to Margaret. "Do you have anything you want to add before she's removed?"

Margaret stared at the broken woman before her. The rage that had flowed through her when Jane first appeared now dissipated, and only numbness remained. "No, please take her out of my sight."

Peter and Burrows dragged Jane from the room to wait for the constable or a runner to take her away.

"I'm afraid to ask if it's really over," Margaret said as she fell into Harry's arms.

"I can't imagine what else is lying in wait for us, but if there is something, we'll face it together." He pulled her close for a deep kiss, promising exactly that.

Two days later, the waiting area in the clinic bustled with activity. Although still recovering from her ordeal, Margaret had healed sufficiently and volunteered to assist Harry until he hired at least one additional physician. She currently assessed one such candidate before her.

Well dressed, his haughty air permeated the room. Several waiting patients grumbled, and a few rose to leave.

Margaret took a deep breath, doing her best to remain calm. "Have you had experience working with the less fortunate?"

A vein in the man's temple pulsed, and his face reddened. "This is ludicrous. I demand to speak with the doctor, not some woman. My time is valuable."

Harry emerged from the treatment area, his brow furrowed. "What's going on here? I'm trying to treat a patient."

"Thank goodness," the obnoxious fellow said.

Harry darted a quick glance at Margaret, concern etching his face before he turned toward the man. "May I help you?"

"Are you Dr. Radcliffe?"

"I am."

"I'm Dr. Benson. I've come about the position, and this woman" —he pointed at Margaret—"wasted my time with useless questions."

Harry's eyebrows arched toward his scalp. "I see. Well, I'm sorry to have wasted your time."

The man harrumphed his agreement. He waved his arm around the area. "I must say this wasn't what I expected. It's a bit primitive."

"You've misunderstood, sir. When I apologized for wasting your time, I didn't mean by discussing the position with my future *wife*. I meant we have no need for your services. Good day."

"But . . . but." Dr. Benson's confusion-filled eyes jumped from Harry to Margaret.

"Anyone with no respect for women, has no place in my clinic. Good luck to you. Now if you'll excuse me, I have a patient to attend to." Harry returned to the treatment area.

Dr. Benson huffed, closed his gaping mouth, and headed out the door, bumping into a man entering. He did not apologize.

The new arrival smiled as he approached. "I say, that chap could use a large dose of jolly." Young, perhaps Harry's age, the man's handsome looks had probably turned many a lady's head.

Thick dark hair, although a bit unruly, fell in waves, half covering his ears. His bright blue eyes sparkled as he winked at her.

Margaret couldn't help but smile back. "May I help you?"

"I was hoping to help you. I saw a posting seeking a physician. If the job entails working daily with you, I'll reduce my fee." He winked again.

She laughed at his outrageous flirting. "I'm afraid I'm simply helping out temporarily. I hope this doesn't dissuade you from applying for the position."

He melodramatically lifted his hand to his forehead. "I suppose I shall have to forge onward." Like Dr. Benson, he looked around the area. Unlike Dr. Benson, his eyes lit in interest. "I say, this looks splendid. What a capital idea."

"I'm glad you approve. I have a few questions, if you don't mind?"

"For you, good lady, anything."

"Well, first your name."

"Oli—" The man's jaw fell slack as Harry followed a patient into the waiting area.

"Keep the burn loosely covered and the wrappings clean. Change them if necessary. Remember the instructions for the willow bark tea, Mr. Brown. It should ease the pain. Come back if the area starts oozing." Harry's face broke into a wide grin when he glanced over in Margaret's direction. "Dr. Somersby? Is it really you?"

Margaret suppressed a laugh at the two grown men staring at each other. The pleasure evident on Harry's face of seeing Dr. Somersby confirmed her initial impression of the man. It appeared they had just found another physician for the clinic.

"It is. But, Your Grace, are you practicing medicine?"

Heads popped up from the people in the waiting area, and they exchanged quizzical glances.

Harry leaned in to Dr. Somersby and whispered, "Here I'm simply Dr. Radcliffe, and to you, Harry."

"Please call me Oliver, sir. I'll admit, I'm surprised to see you again. When we last met, you expressed concern over your inheritance. I presume the situation turned out better than you expected."

Harry clapped Oliver on the back. "Indeed it did. Forgive my manners, I see you've met my fiancée."

"How do you two know each other?" she asked.

"I met Dr. Somersby on my journey home. He was the ship's surgeon."

Oliver darted an embarrassed look at Margaret. "I beg your forgiveness, dear lady. I had no idea." He turned toward Harry, his cheeks flushed. "She's been most kind, although I don't know her name as yet."

Harry raised an eyebrow, then grinned at Margaret. Carefully keeping his voice low, he said, "Margaret Radcliffe, Duchess of Ashton."

"But you said fiancée, so I presumed you've not yet married?"

"You presumed correctly. It's a rather lengthy story, and one I hope to share with you over supper tonight at my home. Margaret, should I hire this man so we can go on our wedding trip?"

"I believe that would be a very wise decision," she said.

"It's settled then. If Margaret approves, how can I go wrong? It doesn't pay much, the hours are long, but the satisfaction of helping the less fortunate is priceless. Will you accept those terms?"

"With pleasure."

"Good. Now let's put you to work. Margaret, who's next?"

With Oliver's help, they managed to treat all the patients by six pm. Harry locked the door and turned toward Margaret, threading her arm through his. He gave a contented sigh as he stared at the building. "It should have a name."

"Radcliffe Clinic?" she suggested.

He scrunched his nose and shook his head. "It's not about me, it's about what it offers."

She closed her eyes, understanding dawning. "Hope," she said.

Warmth spread through her at his broad smile.

"Perfect. Let's commission a sign from young Tom Morrison. We'll hang it in the front window."

"Goodnight, Hope Clinic," she said.

HARRY STRETCHED OUT HIS LONG LEGS AND TOOK A SMALL SIP OF HIS brandy. After an enjoyable supper, with entertaining conversation thanks to Oliver, he and Margaret remained alone to discuss renovations on Briarfield and their wedding plans. His mind wandered as she chattered about her ideas to make the estate a less foreboding place. Her soothing voice lulled him into an euphoric peace.

What did I agree to? Something about murals? An astonished expression appeared on her face, and an unpleasant tingling skittered across the back of his neck. Change in topic to their wedding trip recaptured his interest.

"Perhaps we should marry in the Netherlands rather than Germany," she suggested. "It will be a shorter route to Italy."

He tilted his head back, allowing his eyelids to drift closed, content in the moment. A grin crept across his lips. "I *will* be anxious to begin the honeymoon."

A needlepoint pillow hit him in the face. One eye popped open, and he checked for more flying objects.

"Be serious," she said, although the sparkle in her eyes implied her mind traveled down the same path.

He reached for her, pulling her close. "I've never been more serious. Let me prove it." And he kissed her, deep and passionate. *Definitely anxious for the honeymoon. In fact . . .*

EPILOGUE

KENT, ENGLAND, DECEMBER 1823

Margaret boarded the carriage, waving goodbye to the Morrisons. After their wedding in the Netherlands and a three month long honeymoon in Italy, renovations on Briarfield neared completion, so she and Harry had headed home.

Pastels and brightly colored murals replaced the dark wallpaper. Gas lighting adorned with lovely etched glass shades supplanted the heavily gilded sconces. A few fixtures, such as the ones in their bedchamber, had colored shades, evoking a sensual atmosphere.

Harry had bristled a bit at the pastels and murals, but insisted whatever made Margaret happy pleased him as well. He had taken care—sparing no expense—to ensure the safety of the new invention of gas lighting.

Briarfield now welcomed her, and she had gained a sense of contentment within its walls. She found fulfillment in London as emissary for Harry's medical practice and on the estate ensuring the tenants' needs were met. She still cringed at the sobriquet "the Angel," but experienced great joy being able to provide for them without fear of discovery or reprisal.

Light snow crunched under the carriage wheels as it moved along the road near the cemetery. Margaret tapped on the door, requesting the driver to stop.

Pulling up the hood of her cloak, she descended from the carriage and made her way down the small path. Flowers were in short supply on the cold December day, but she had brought a small offering of Christmas roses and English primrose from the greenhouse.

A snowy blanket covered the new grave of Mr. Turner, who now lay next to his beloved wife, Kate. His death had occurred shortly after their return from Italy, and both she and Harry had been at his bedside to ease his departure from this life.

His raspy words still rang in her ears. "If you so much as raise an eyebrow at our Angel, I'll haunt you from the grave, Your Grace. And don't be thinking I won't just because you're a duke."

She brushed a tear from her eye and placed the bouquet of primroses between the two graves. "Take care of your Katie girl, Mr. Turner." If she and Harry had a portion of the love Mr. and Mrs. Turner had shared, they would indeed be blessed. So far, the odds appeared in their favor.

Owen and Lily McDougall now occupied what had been Mr. Turner's farm, their new home completed a mere month before Mr. Turner's death. During her visit with them, Lily had blushed and placed a hand on her abdomen, saying it was a good thing as they would need the space.

Cold wind snapped against Margaret's face, but she had one more stop before heading home. As she wove her way up the path to the mausoleum, she reflected on how much her life had changed since her last visit.

She threaded the Christmas roses through the handles of the door. "For you, Emmeline. I'm sorry they're not lily-of-the-valley. I promise I'll bring some next year."

The Christmas roses had no scent, but a sweet fragrance swirled in the surrounding air. She paused, inhaling deeply, the sweet, fresh and uplifting smell reminding her of the bell-like flowers she promised to bring in spring.

After saying a silent prayer for the sister-in-law she would never know, footsteps crunching against the snow drew her attention. She turned, expecting to find the coachman encouraging her to return to the carriage. The snow had picked up. Heavy flakes now drifted from the sky, obscuring her vision, and she blinked, unsure of the figure that moved on the path. Her breath caught in her throat at what appeared to be a young girl strolling away from her, a small black bundle of fur hopping alongside her. When Margaret blinked again, they had vanished.

She spun back toward the mausoleum doors, still chained and locked.

She added a final sentence to her prayer, this time spoken aloud. "Thank you, Emmeline, for giving me my freedom."

HARRY SAT IN THE LIBRARY STUDYING THE LATEST MEDICAL TOME. Although they had renovated much of Briarfield, the library remained—for the most part—untouched. Both he and Margaret agreed that, as the first place they met and most likely had fallen in love, they should leave the memory of it undisturbed.

He searched the contents as he struggled to find an answer to a particular problem. Oliver had written, seeking Harry's consultation regarding a baffling case at the clinic. So far, his efforts proved fruitless. He stretched back in his chair, picking up the letter again and re-reading the symptoms. His eyes strayed to a subsequent paragraph.

Although Oliver had kept things professional, Harry had to chuckle at a portion of the letter regarding the fairer sex. "Why is it," Oliver had written, "that women of the aristocracy appear to peer down at you even when you stand several inches taller?" Harry wondered what *ton* beauty had captured his attention. There is none so smitten as he who protests so much, a fact Harry was well acquainted with.

As if reading his mind, Margaret knocked at the library door. He raised his head and smiled at her approach. "What have you been up to? Burrows was downright secretive when I asked him where you were."

He pulled her onto his lap for a quick kiss. "Your nose is cold as ice. What on earth were you doing outside? A blizzard is brewing." He rubbed her frigid hands between his own.

"I stopped at the cemetery to lay some flowers for the Turners and Emmeline." She chewed on her bottom lip and fidgeted, playing with his hair.

"What is it? Something's troubling you."

"I can't hide anything from you." She curled against his chest.

He'd never tire of having her in his arms, and he stroked her back. "You should never have to."

She nodded, her head nestled against him. "Harry, was Emmeline's kitten black?"

His hand stopped mid-stroke. *What an odd question.* "Yes." With his index finger, he lifted her chin to look in her eyes. "Did you see something that upset you?"

"No, nothing upsetting." She blew out a breath. "I'm sure it's my imagination. The snow is blinding. If anything, a sense of peace settled around me."

He stared into those incredible eyes for more than a few moments until he was satisfied she truly was fine. "What's this?" He reached down to the small object lying on her lap.

Before he could take it, she snatched it away, teasing him. "It's a surprise. I also visited the Morrisons. I commissioned a gift for you from Tom."

"Oh? Another carving?"

She nodded, her eyes sparkling with excitement. "I planned to give it to you for Christmas, but you might be able to persuade me to give it to you sooner."

He chuckled at her exuberance. "I'll do my best." He kissed her again, this time he lingered, drinking in the sweetness of her lips. "However, no gift is better than this."

"Should I take it back?" she asked, running a hand up his arm then sliding it around his neck.

He growled in pleasure. *God, she drives me mad with desire.*

273

"Considering Manny already has stolen a peek at his gifts, I should be allowed to open one early, don't you think?"

Her laugh, bright and airy, filled him with joy. "If you insist." She bit her lip as she gave him the gift. "I hope you like it."

His eyes grew wide when he removed the velvet cloth surrounding the small object. A perfectly carved replica of a fawn lay in his hand.

"A new addition to our family. It should look lovely next to your stag, my doe, and Manny's young buck, don't you agree?" she asked, her voice a whisper, soft and reverent.

"Margaret . . . are you saying?"

She nodded again, this time the tears shimmering in her eyes fell freely. "Yes, I believe so, but perhaps a doctor should examine me to be sure."

A broad grin spread across his face as he gazed at her in wonder. "That can be arranged."

He held her tightly and whispered in her ear, "This is the best news I've ever received."

When the letter arrived in Boston summoning him home a year ago, he had thought all his dreams had ended. Who would have believed by becoming duke, they would all come true?

⚜

He thinks she's a bossy shrew. She thinks he's rude beyond measure. It's hate at first sight.

A Doctor for Lady Denby

SCAN THE CODE TO CONTINUE THE JOURNEY OF *THE HOPE CLINIC* series with *A Doctor for Lady Denby* now and watch the sparks fly!

CURIOUS ABOUT ANDREW AND ALICE? READ THEIR STORY IN THE prequel novella *No Ordinary Love.*

No Ordinary Love

WANT A PEEK ELEVEN YEARS INTO THE FUTURE FOR HARRY AND Margaret?

Sign up to my newsletter! Scan this QR code and receive a complimentary extended epilogue exclusively for readers of *The Reluctant Duke's Dilemma.*

The Reluctant Duke's Dilemma Extended Epilogue

IF YOU ENJOYED *THE RELUCTANT DUKE'S DILEMMA*, WHY NOT LET other readers know by leaving an honest review on Amazon. Scan the code below to take your there! And don't forget to spread the word. Easy peasy.

Review The Reluctant Duke's Dilemma

Turn the page for an excerpt of *A Doctor For Lady Denby*.

EXCERPT: A DOCTOR FOR
LADY DENBY

The hair on the back of Camilla's neck rose to attention as a tall, dark-haired man approached. His blue half-mask only added to the excitement. He moved like a sleek animal as he crossed the room—strong, powerful, determined. The only thing tentative about him was his slight, half smile. Impeccably dressed, his clothes hugged his body perfectly, and her breath hitched in her throat. *Marvelous.*

"Would you care to dance?" he asked, the purr of his voice adding to the animalistic illusion.

"I'd love to." She made her retreat from Laurence. "Please excuse me."

A thrill she hadn't experienced in years shot up her spine when she placed her hand on the handsome stranger's arm as he led her to the dance floor. The steps of the country dance didn't allow much contact between them, but each time their hands did touch, the energy passing between them was undeniable. What she had interpreted as a tentative smile she now recognized as the perfect mixture of confidence and arrogance. Remarkable eyes as blue as the mask he wore peered at her. The way his lips quirked at one corner sent waves of desire coursing through her.

During one of the longer periods of the dance in which they faced each other he said, "Please tell me that wasn't your husband?"

She would not show all her cards yet. Her own lips curved in a sly smile. She had missed the game and enjoyed playing again. "No. He wasn't my husband."

His deliciously low chuckle sent more shivers up her spine. "Perhaps I should rephrase and be more direct. Are you married?"

"Would it matter to you?"

He stopped in the middle of the dance, perplexing the other couples around them at the disruption to the line's formation. "I don't play games. Yes, it would matter very much. Are you married?"

His boldness reminded her of Hugh at their first meeting. Direct and no nonsense, Hugh had simply said he found her attractive and would like to keep company with her. A bittersweet sense of familiarity flashed in her mind. "No. I am not. Are you?" she asked, knowing the answer, but curious to see if he would be honest.

He flashed her a smile, and her heart sputtered. There, in his left cheek, the most glorious dimple formed. *Oh, my!* The room began to sway, and she reached out, grasping his arm.

The dimple disappeared. "Are you all right?" he asked, concern lacing his voice.

"My apologies. I feel a bit flushed. Perhaps some air?"

"It's February, too cold to step outside. Perhaps a less crowded room?"

She nodded and took his arm, allowing him to lead her from the ballroom. "There's a secluded parlor tucked down the hall." The scandalous nature of her suggestion added to the excitement, and she wondered what he thought about her utter lack of concern for propriety. Yet, he didn't object.

Thankfully, other than a few servants, no one wandered the hallway, and they were able to slip into the room unobserved. Only a few candles on a sideboard provided light, casting the majority of the room in shadow. After depositing her on the settee, he moved to light another candle.

"Don't," she said, and he turned toward her. "It might attract attention."

His mouth quirked up and even in the darkness of the room, the dimple announced its presence.

"Perhaps some brandy?" He motioned to the decanter next to the candles.

"Yes, that would be lovely."

Music sifted in, providing enough atmosphere without being intrusive. It couldn't have been more perfect if she had planned it.

He poured two snifters and moved to sit next to her. "May I?"

"Of course."

As he settled next to her, an almost palpable power emanated from him. This was a man used to getting what he wanted, and a trill of danger crawled up her neck.

WANT MORE? SCAN THE CODE BELOW TO CONTINUE THE JOURNEY:

A Doctor for Lady Denby

AUTHOR NOTE

When this story popped into my head, the idea of a woman coming out of an abusive marriage to fall in love with her husband's identical twin brother seemed to present the perfect conflict. How would a woman reconcile her attraction to a man whose face is the same as the man who abused her? Add to that the possibility she may have murdered her husband, and the story developed another layer of conflict.

Little did I realize that seemingly "great" idea would present its own conflicts. Here's what I discovered during my research.

Historical fact: Prior to August of 1835, marriage between a man and his deceased wife's sister, or a woman and her deceased husband's brother, although not explicitly prohibited, was considered "voidable" and was generally considered taboo. Some couples did marry if they were not known to the clergy, and others traveled abroad. Jane Austen's brother, Charles married his deceased wife's sister. For most, this was a moot point, but for someone with a title and wealth, this could spell disaster, as a relative in line for the title could sue and have the marriage voided and the children declared illegitimate. It's an interesting bit of history that actually took until the early 1900s to resolve completely.

ALSO BY TRISHA MESSMER

The Hope Clinic Series

No Ordinary Love (Prequel Novella)

The Reluctant Duke's Dilemma

A Doctor For Lady Denby

Healing The Viscount's Heart

Saving Miss Pratt

The Hope Clinic

Different World Series (Contemporary Romance):

The Bottom Line

The Eyre Liszt

Look With Your Heart

Different Worlds

ABOUT THE AUTHOR

Trisha Messmer had a million stories rattling around in her brain. (Well, maybe a million is an exaggeration but there were a lot). Always loving the written word, she enjoyed any chance she had to compose something, whether it be for a college paper or just a plain old email. One day as she was speaking with her daughter about the latest adventure going on in her mind, her daughter said, "Mom, why don't you write them down." And so it began. Several stories later, she finally allowed someone, other than her daughter, to read them.

After that brave (and very scary) step, she decided not to keep them to herself any longer, so here we are.

She hopes you enjoy her musings as much as she enjoyed writing them. If they make you smile, sigh, hope, and chuckle or even cry at times, it was worth it.

Born in St. Louis, Missouri, Trisha graduated from the University of Missouri – St. Louis with a degree in Psychology. Trisha's day job as a product instructor for a software company allowed her to travel all over the country meeting interesting people and seeing interesting places, some of which inspired ideas for her stories. A hopeless (or hopeful) romantic, Trisha currently resides in the great Northwest.

Printed in Great Britain
by Amazon

14170365R00169